D0032979

A Good Death

A Good Death

Elizabeth Ironside

FELONY & MAYHEM PRESS • NEW YORK

All the characters and events portrayed in this work are fictitious.

A GOOD DEATH

A Felony & Mayhem mystery

PRINTING HISTORY
First UK edition (Hodder & Stoughton): 2000
Felony & Mayhem edition: 2008

Copyright © 2000 by Elizabeth Ironside
All rights reserved

ISBN 978-1-934609-19-4

Manufactured in the United States of America

Library of Congress Cataloging-in-Publication Data

Ironside, Elizabeth.
  A good death / Elizabeth Ironside. -- Felony & Mayhem ed.
    p. cm.
  "A Felony & Mayhem mystery"--T.p. verso.
  ISBN-13: 978-1-934609-19-4 (hardcover)
  ISBN-10: 1-934609-19-6 (hardcover)
    1. France--History--German occupation, 1940-1945--Fiction. 2.
World War, 1939-1945--France--Fiction. 3. France combattante--Fic-
tion. 4. Germans--France--Fiction. 5. Collaborationists--Fiction. 6.
Married people--Fiction. I. Title.
  PR6059.R6G66 2008
  823'.914--dc22
                        2008034542

To
Joan and John

The icon above says you're holding a copy of a book in the Felony & Mayhem "Foreign" category. These books may be offered in translation or may originally have been written in English, but always they will feature an intricately observed, richly atmospheric setting in a part of the world that is neither England nor the U.S.A. If you enjoy this book, you may well like other "Foreign" titles from Felony & Mayhem Press, including:

PAUL ADAM
The Rainaldi Quartet

KARIN ALVTEGEN
Missing

ANNA BLUNDY
The Bad News Bible

ROBERT CULLEN
Soviet Sources
Cover Story
Dispatch from a Cold Country

NICOLAS FREELING
Love in Amsterdam
Because of the Cats
Gun Before Butter

TIMOTHY HOLME
The Neapolitan Streak

STUART KAMINSKY
Death of a Dissident
Black Knight in Red Square

PAUL MANN
Season of the Monsoon
The Ganja Coast

CLAIRE TASCHDJIAN
The Peking Man Is Missing

BARBARA NADEL
Belshazzar's Daughter
The Ottoman Cage

L.R.WRIGHT
The Suspect

For more about these books, and other Felony & Mayhem titles, or to place an order, please visit our website at

www.FelonyAndMayhem.com

or contact us at

Felony and Mayhem Press
156 Waverly Place
New York, NY 10014

A Good Death

PROLOGUE

THE INVADERS HAD left. The sun, barely above the horizon, striped the field where they had camped with long black shadows. Only a bleached light reached inside to reveal the disorder of life abruptly abandoned.

In the early morning silence the children reoccupied the house. They walked through the open front door and found a leather suitcase standing upright in the hall, still waiting for its former owner to leave. They skirted the case and in unspoken agreement went straight up the stairs. Here were more signs of an interrupted life. In their old bedroom a sweat-stained shirt hung over the back of a chair beside the bed. The drawers of the chest between the windows were pulled out. The wardrobe door swung open revealing one black jacket, hanging hollow. Up here they touched nothing, simply sniffing the air for the scent of those who had gone. They looked at the bed, its pillows and covers dented by the shape of a body, of someone who had flung himself down on them for a moment's rest. That mark of absence seemed to fill the house.

Below, in the library, burned papers lay in the hearth and more lay beside the fireplace. A cigarette, half-smoked, had been ground out in an ashtray, buckling under the pressure.

Beside it was the packet out of which it had been taken, nine cigarettes untouched. One of them reached out and took the cigarette butt, fitting her own lips to the faint red rim. This broke through their reluctance to touch things. As she spat out the smoked cigarette, she seized the packet and began to tear the contents to pieces so that a storm of tobacco fell to the ground. Next they found on the desk a pile of letters tied into a bundle. They picked them up and shook them onto the floor, tearing the paper as they did so. Writing paper, ink, a pen, all lay ready for the reply that would never be written. They unscrewed the inkpot and dribbled it carefully over the scattered papers. They now opened drawers and cupboards, frenziedly pulling the contents out and strewing them on the floor. After a while the fury that had affected them both abated and they paused, looking idly at certain objects, not searching for anything in particular. Odd things attracted their attention for a moment, soon to be abandoned in favour of something else.

They found treasure in a cupboard: a flat brown paper parcel, still addressed to Major Udo Knecht. It had been unwrapped once, that was clear, then bundled back into its coverings, an unwanted present.

They studied the writing, the unfamiliar gothic letters and German stamps, for a time before folding back the paper to discover a box with, on its lid, a picture of a knight in armour, riding on his charger, trampling a fallen enemy beneath its feet. They carried the box across the hall into the dining room and emptied the contents onto the table. Absorbed in what they had found, they ignored the overturned chair, the unstoppered brandy bottle, the pool of alcohol. Without speaking they sorted the wooden shapes, turning them the right way up, selecting those with straight edges, tentatively placing one against another to link them together.

The sun had risen fully now and half the courtyard was out of shadow. If they had looked through the window, they would have seen the group of women gathered around the body of the man who lay naked, face down: the last one, who would never leave. But enthralled with what they had found they were oblivious to the cries and movement outside.

They were still at work on the jigsaw when the police arrived.

Part One

BONNEMORT
7 September 1944

1

THE CAR DROVE fast along the narrow lanes. The light was failing and the beam of the headlamps merged with the dusk, which still lacked the clarity of darkness. The driver gripped the wheel, leaning forward. Since their journey began they had met roadblocks and blown-up bridges, tank-trap trenches and shot-up trucks, the debris of war left deliberately or involuntarily on the road. The passenger beside him gave directions, never doubting his route.

They did not talk. While the driver concentrated on the blurred road in the decaying light, the other gazed at the countryside with a passionate intensity of focus, devouring the scene with his eyes. For four years he had been starved of his homeland, and now he was back. He was filled with a joy composed of recognition, reunion and a triumphant sense of vindication. He had been right; he was returning victorious, resurrected. The opposite of the prodigal, he was the justified son.

He had felt this ever since he landed in the country, three months ago. In the north, people had welcomed them, shouting and waving as they passed through the towns. Here, they had seen no one in the last few hours. The landscape was secretive, yet to him deeply familiar. It was hilly, gouged by valleys, covered with forest. The chestnut trees absorbed the evening light, breaking the horizontal rays of the sun into bewildering patterns. The car ran through tunnels of oaks whose branches closed out the sky, their meagre trunks wrapped in vivid moss. Then, suddenly, they would emerge into a high meadow and, just before the road plunged once again into the trees, they would glimpse a panorama of layered hills, the thick pelt of the forest cut away here and there on the uplands into clearings round a farmstead.

About an hour later, night having fallen, they halted at their first roadblock. Rounding a corner, they were forced to an abrupt halt. The light from their headlamps struck two chestnut poles blocking the road which had been narrowed by a lorry parked on one side. Three figures stepped into the light. They wore berets, belts and armbands, but there all regularity of dress ceased. All were armed, two with Brens, the inefficient sub-machine gun air dropped by the thousand to the Resistance, the youngest with a Mauser rifle.

The driver revved the engine and pulled the gearstick into reverse. The passenger took his pistol from its holster and laid it on the ledge in front of him.

'Wait,' he said. He did not attempt to get out of the car, but lowered his window so that they could make out his uniform. He had his papers ready to show them.

'Cazalle, Colonel, on a mission from General de Gaulle to the Regional Commissioner of the Republic. My driver, Corporal Dorchin.'

The youngest of the guerrillas took the papers, bending to examine them in the headlamps. While he waited, the colonel studied their insignia. These people were annoying but necessary. For four years their reluctance to join the struggle, their undisciplined enterprises, their divisions and animosities had been the stuff of his days. He could see that the lorry carried the emblem of the United Resistance, the V sign with the cross of Lorraine superimposed, and their armbands were marked FFI, Forces Françaises de l'Intérieur. However, they did not look like farm boys, more like artisans from the nearest town, and he guessed that these men belonged to the communist underground.

The young man, still holding the documents, gestured to the colonel to get out of the car. He led the way behind the lorry. The colonel hesitated, reholstered his pistol and opened the door.

'Keep the engine running,' he said to the driver, then nodded to the two remaining partisans to precede him. Only a few yards into the wood stood a car, one of the wood-burning vehicles in use everywhere in these days of fuel shortages. Beside it, a fire had been lit and a folding table erected. Seated there was a man in a beret and a loose, belted shirt, reading by the light of a hurricane lamp. For all the world like one of Napoleon's field marshals on campaign, the colonel thought, or a Russian commissar. The young partisan saluted and presented the documents. His commander read them carefully.

'You're well out of your way here, Colonel,' he said. 'Have you lost your road?' Although he acknowledged Cazalle's rank, the tone was republican, undeferential.

'No, I've already seen the commissioner. I'm on my way to visit my home for one night before returning to Paris. I come from here.'

'Oh, yes? Where's that?'

The colonel could read the subtle wish to make him an invader, without rights on the ground. He resorted to formality. 'You are...?' he said.

'This is Gilles of Group Noix. These are his colleagues, Marius and Cyrano.' The commissar did not introduce himself.

'I'm from Bonnemort in the commune of Lepech Perd-rissou.'

'Ah.' Recognition of a kind, not necessarily approving. 'And you're on your way to Bonnemort now?'

'I am. A detour of a hundred kilometres was worth it. It's been four years.'

He should have read the warning then, in Gilles' smile, the glance between Marius and Cyrano.

'There's a lot been going on at Lepech in recent days,' the commissar remarked.

'Oh, yes?' The colonel was anxious to end the civilities and get on with his journey.

'You haven't heard?'

'How could I? I've come from Paris. There isn't even a phone line.' Then he asked, because it seemed expected, 'What sort of things?'

'A German officer murdered. They only just escaped the most terrible reprisals.'

Cazalle was not prepared to pay attention to local dramas. One dead German did not sound much in a world at war.

Gilles added, 'His throat was cut.'

The commissar waited, as if for a sign of greater curiosity. The colonel did not gratify him, so he shrugged and let him go.

'Not far now,' the colonel said, speaking to himself rather than to the driver, as they got back into the car and set off once more.

'I'm from here,' he had said to the *maquisards*, claiming his rights as a native-born. His decision to go into exile at the time of the defeat had been immediate and visceral. He had never had any doubt, even at the most painful moment: leaving his home and his wife. Bonnemort was so remote that he had succeeded in imagining it untouched by the war, waiting for him to return to open the gates of the time-arrested castle and release its occupants to new life.

'Slowly now,' he said. 'It's on the left.'

With exaggerated care the driver turned the car onto a stone track, rutted with the run-off from years of rain. A bird flew down, as if strafing the car; the driver ducked involuntarily. It flew ahead of them, its greyish wings undulating like a white flag in a breeze. At the bend ahead he saw a large dog.

'Lascar,' he exclaimed aloud. The driver's pressure on the accelerator eased and the dog was gone. The verges were wider here and before they swung to the left, the headlights touched the form of an upturned vehicle in the ditch. Another two kilometres and they were climbing steeply. Dorchin made his first unprompted remark of the journey. 'Bloody hell, it's the end of the world,' he said.

They were over the crest now and descending sharply towards the house. He regretted arriving so late in the day. As a child he had liked to stop the pony and trap that used to collect him from the station and look down at the roofs and the smoke rising through the trees. He now recalled that vivid second when his heart seemed to loosen with relief that the place was really still there. He always feared that it might have disappeared, or never have been there at all, existing only in his imagination. This time he had no confirmation of its existence until the car drew up in front of the entrance, the headlamps shining through the wrought-iron gates, which were emphatically closed. He had never seen the gates shut, even during the Great War. In the courtyard a dog was barking.

'Lascar,' he called again, but it ignored him, joined now by a pack of rough-haired terriers, showing their sharp lower teeth and jumping on legs stiff with fury.

He could not open the gates, for a padlock and chain secured them. There was no bell. He looked at his watch. It was only ten past ten. They must be asleep. He rattled the gates noisily, shouting, 'Henri, are you there, Henri?' He turned back to the driver. 'Sound your horn, will you.'

Closed gates and barking dogs that refused to recognise their master; this was not as it should have been. He was annoyed that he had not started earlier, travelled faster, announced his coming. The eye of a torch wavered towards them. It stopped short of the lights and he heard the voice of Micheline, Henri's wife.

'Who is it?' She, too, was shouting, her tone resentful and afraid.

'Micheline, open up. It's Theo.'

She advanced slowly, sceptically, the beam of her torch absorbed into the car's lights. She wore a blue button-through pinafore and below it the hem of her black skirt drooped to her wooden-soled clogs.

'Mr Theo?' She was searching in her pinafore pocket and took out the key. They pushed open one gate each and the car slid into the courtyard, stopped; its lights died away.

Micheline and her torch vanished, the dogs trotted back into the farmyard, and he and Dorchin were alone again. He looked up at the house, its grey shutters closed; it was deserted. Had his wife left? He led the way towards the arch into the farmyard and the house where Henri and Micheline lived.

They met Micheline, coming from the tower that filled the corner between the main house and the farmyard.

'Mr Theo, Mr Theo,' she said, opening her arms to him. They kissed three times.

'How are you, Micheline? How's Henri, the family? It's been a long time.'

'A long time, a long time.' She was agitated; tears stood in her eyes. For a moment she seemed bewildered, as if she did not know what to do. 'And now you're back.'

'Just for one night, Micheline. I was at Toulouse and I had to come when I was so close.'

'Let me find you something to eat. You must be starved.'

The peasant answer to every situation: food. She was leading him across the yard towards her own door. An oil lamp stood on the kitchen table, its soft light revealing the ribs and whorls that were etched into its whitened surface. The eyes of both men were drawn to the light and fixed on a chipped white platter, heaped with figs. For years neither of them had seen such an abundance of fruit. Theo looked at the sweet, slackening skins, green, black, purple, and thought of the presents he had brought with him, the American chocolate bars. Who would want American chocolate when they had figs from their own trees? He was jolted out of the timetable of war into the rhythm of the country year. Vine-peaches, pears, apples, quinces would all be ready now. Walnuts, cobnuts, chestnuts soon. He saw Dorchin swallow, his eyes fixed on the fruit.

Taking pity on him, Theo said, 'Do you mind if we take a fig?'

Micheline did not spare them a glance; she was busy at the stove. 'Go ahead, take them. They're yours in any case. But you need soup. The bread's not fresh, but the soup is good.'

She spread a cloth at one end of the table and put down two plates, placing large bowls on top of them. Dorchin was already sitting down. Theo realised that he was hungry. He had eaten at midday with the commissioner, but since then had had nothing. Micheline ladled out the soup.

'And Henri,' Theo said again. 'Where's Henri?'

Micheline replaced the saucepan on the stove. 'Henri's dead.'

Theo's oldest ties were to Henri with whom he had baled hay, harvested maize, shot pheasants and gathered chestnuts in his childhood. It was impossible for Henri to be dead. Henri had always been at Bonnemort; he had been like an older brother to him. He was not old, only in his late fifties. He had never had a day's illness in his life. But Micheline, always a robust woman, now confirmed the passage of time. Her cheeks had sunk and her wavy brown hair was dulled with grey.

Behind him the door opened; Micheline looked over his head. 'You remember Florence.'

He did indeed remember Florence. She was wearing black, too, and her mourning cast grey reflections on her face, the shadows of misery. The girl he had known, too well, had been so full of energy that he used to say he could hear her hair growing. It was now cut to shoulder length and looked as exhausted as she did. He rose, shook hands, kissed her on both cheeks.

'What happened? When? Micheline, I am so sorry...'

She didn't wait for his condolences. 'He was shot three weeks ago, three weeks to the day.' She was at that stage when it was necessary to be precise about small things, accuracy about dates, meal times, routine duties. If she let them go, the world would fall to pieces.

Dorchin had stopped eating his soup, his respect for the dead triumphing over his hunger. A huge rearrangement was taking place in Theo's mind, the ivory tower of his home was falling.

'Three weeks ago,' he repeated slowly. 'Only three weeks ago.'

'They were still here three weeks ago, the Germans. The SS were billeted here for weeks, since the beginning of June. There was an ambush and Henri was caught with Pierre Rouget, you know, the son of the Rougets at Cavialle, the younger one, and Philippe Boysse was shot too, and...'

'Begin at the beginning. Tell me exactly.'

She pulled out a chair. Her speech fumbled for a moment; she could not really tell him. With four years to account for, she did not know what was significant any more. Clinging to exactitude, she said, 'It was Wednesday afternoon. They were coming back, the Germans, back to Bonnemort and they were attacked on the track just the other side of the hill. Several Germans were killed. And then they escaped, our people, I mean. But Henri was wounded, so they got him and Pierre Rouget too and some others, and they took them down to the village.' Her voice was emotionless. 'They banged on the doors and forced everyone out of their houses. The German officer was mad with rage, they say. They tied Henri up and shot him in front of everyone. Then they strung up the rest of them from the tree. There were seven executed altogether that day. The mayor agreed that they would bury the dead German soldiers in the cemetery. And they all went there and had to dig, everyone, even the baker's father, eighty-five years old. Then they were allowed to go back to their houses. And the next day they were gone, Germans, Milice, everyone.'

Dorchin could wait no longer. He dipped his spoon once again into the thick mess in his bowl. Theo did not move. The spareness of the story increased its horror. Only three weeks ago.

He thought of his meeting with the partisans, only an hour or so ago. *There's a lot been going on at Lepech...*

Florence said, 'Someone got the German officer.'

Micheline carried on, with no sign of vengeful pleasure, her reply as flat as the rest of her account, 'They cut his throat and left him here.'

'Here?'

'Yes. Naked as a pig in front of the house. We got up in the morning and there he was. But we didn't know what had happened to Henri then, until Petignat came up from the Gendarmerie to tell us, so we didn't understand why they killed him.'

'Micheline,' he began. He should have been here three weeks ago. He should never have left. 'And the rest of the family?' He remained standing, prepared for the worst. Micheline pushed aside those troubles as old ones, reduced to nothing by her present grief.

'Georges was deported to Germany. We haven't had any news from him. Roger and Claude are in the Maquis. Claude is Florence's intended. They were to be married last year, but...' She couldn't be bothered to explain the events that had produced this minor family tragedy.

Florence was holding the door open. 'Madame is in her sitting room. I went to tell her.'

'She's here? I thought she must have left.'

'No, she's here. The children are asleep, of course. I didn't wake them. The ladies are always up at this hour, but I haven't told them yet. I thought you'd want to see Madame first.'

She walked with him across the courtyard, solicitously shining her torch for his footsteps, as if he did not know the way.

'We haven't used the house since the Germans came.' She was gabbling now, as if the words flowed while her mind was absorbed elsewhere. 'The family all moved into the tower and spent their days in Madame's sitting room.'

She was opening the tower door and leading him up the stone steps. He had a strong feeling of unease. Why had Ariane not come down to meet him as soon as she heard he had arrived? He had the sense he was being ushered in to visit a prisoner.

Answering his unspoken thought, Florence said, 'Madame was already in bed. She wanted to prepare herself.'

A glow in the fireplace, where someone had thrust some wood into the embers and the flames were reviving. No other light. His wife standing by the chimneypiece, posed to meet him. He could see her tension in the firelight that framed her silhouette. She was a tall woman, athletically built with strong shoulders, large hands and feet. She had never been beautiful, still less pretty, although she had always had the money to achieve elegance and the status of *jolie laide*. He saw, and his heart was touched, that she must have been hastily dressing up for him. She was wearing a peacock-blue dress, tightly belted at the waist, one he had always liked. Round her head she had wrapped a silk scarf, blue, yellow and red.

'Ariane,' he said and moved quickly forward. 'Ariane.'

He smelled her scent, the same as before. He could never remember what it was called when he went to buy it. He embraced her and felt her thin torso, less substantial than four years ago. He put his hand to her neck and felt a faint clinging of perspiration beneath his fingertips.

Her arms hung at her sides and her face was pressed against his neck. He leaned back to look at her, putting his hand to her head. Hers followed, but it was too late; the silk scarf slid to the floor. A metamorphosis was taking place in front of his eyes and he was holding a stranger in his arms. Her familiar face became unrecognisable, a mask fixed to a skull that was covered with black stubble, white skin flecked with black like a plucked fowl's, repellent to the touch.

Part Two

PARIS AND BONNEMORT
10 September 1944–
28 January 1945

2

SWORDS AND SHIELDS, flags like silk scarves, blue, yellow, and red, hung on the walls of the dining room of the Hôtel de Brionne. This was the Ministry of War where the general had taken up his function as a minister on 7 June 1940, just ten days before leaving for London and exile. Now he was back, sitting down to lunch as if there had been no interruption. The smell of the meal rose agreeably to the nostrils of the four men as they took their places. Even with the current difficulties of procurement, the Ministry's food was good, which was nice for the guests. Nothing else about the meal would be designed for their enjoyment. In the last four years Theo de Cazalle had eaten many meals with the general, so he knew what to expect. His fellow guests, two eminent members of the Resistance from the National Committee of Liberation and the National Front, were not accustomed to the tension, so bad for the digestion, that was often a feature of dining with the general, at least when he had lessons to impart, as he had today.

They drank their soup in a silence that exaggerated the sounds of swallowed liquid. Theo watched the great jaws masticating bread and waited for the metaphorical chewing up that was to come. He avoided the eye of Palewski, opposite him, who was looking preternaturally grave, and concentrated instead on the armour-covered walls. Four years of close association with the Big Man had produced familiarity, but not intimacy. He was always courteous to his staff, but difficult to handle on any subject where the facts did not fit his wishes. The general recognised Theo's skill at mediating between him and the Resistance, who had rarely fallen in with his line, but he did not admire him for it.

Theo, like his leader, was a career army officer, the son of an officer. His family came originally from the Touraine, but during the course of the nineteenth century a combination of obstinate monarchism and financial incompetence had left them with just one decaying château on the banks of the Loire. Theo's father had been forced to sell even this remnant and the only property that remained was the farm of Bonnemort. It had been kept because it was the home of the aunts, his grandfather's sister and sister-in-law, who had both been widowed young and pensioned off in this obscure house.

Here his mother had fled from the heat of Algerian summers and the deadening routine of the cantonment. Here Theo had come every holiday of his childhood in the golden age before the Great War. His father was killed at Ypres before Christmas 1914; the aunts had lost their five sons by 1918 when Theo himself entered cadet school, aged just eighteen. The women's fervent prayers on his behalf caused the war to end just in time to ensure his survival. The luck that had saved him from the carnage of the western front continued to shine on him in peace. He enjoyed his profession and was proud to be an officer in the best army in the world. He managed his career with some success so that he did not have to spend years in a barrack yard in the desert. After a suitable time, when he was promoted to captain, he married, Louise, a distant cousin; a daughter, Sabine, was born; his wife died.

The general was speaking now. Wiping his lips firmly with his napkin, he began the urgent subject of the moment, the cleansing of France. The question of what was to be done with the supporters of the previous regime was not new, but it had become urgent. The courts martial that had been planned must be set up, region by region, to deal with the crimes of Vichy. It had to be done as rapidly as possible in order to contain the popular fury which, since the landings in Normandy, had erupted in summary justice all over France. For the men of London, and above all for the general, it was necessary to seize control and to reforge national unity. For the Resistance leaders in France it was another matter. They wanted revenge for the deaths of their comrades, for the tortures, deportations, requisitions they had undergone.

'France requires us to forget, to concentrate on the re-establishment of the authority of the Republic,' the general was saying now.

'But some examples must be made...'

'Of course, the guilty must be punished, the leaders, but it would be a disaster to rummage through the injustices of four years to try to right every wrong. France must be strong and united to take her rightful place among the Allies at the peace conference. We must put the past behind us.'

The two guests glanced at one another. They had stayed and suffered and now the exiles came back to tell them to forgive their enemies. They did not want to give up one of the sweetest fruits of victory.

'We must examine what went on in the local administration,' said one of them. 'And in the police, the town halls... It was there that Vichy weighed on the people.'

'It is these areas, in particular, that have to be controlled,' the general contradicted him. 'They are precisely where individual resentments and personal enmities are exercised. We want no revolutionary justice. The state must take over as soon as possible. Some terrible scenes have been enacted, shaving of women's heads, beating of men, even here in Paris.'

Theo shuddered as an image of Ariane's skull, darkly shadowed, the black quills just growing through the skin, superimposed itself on his memory. What had she done to deserve such treatment? What can lead a woman to betray husband, country, herself? Fear? Pain? Greed? Love?

He forced himself to concentrate on what the general was saying.

'Justice, true justice is an element of sovereignty. It is impersonal, detached. The Republic, with calm and authority, must take it over from the people. No justice is done in passion.' Even in private the Big Man's sonorous tones sounded with a portentousness equal to a national broadcast.

Had there been a mock trial of Ariane with testimony of her guilt. Or a spontaneous outbreak of rage in the local community at the sight of a woman, his wife, who had...done what?

The murdered German officer had been her lover. His mind had made that leap at once, while he was driving through the night away from Bonnemort back to Paris. That was why his killers had left his body in front of her house. It was obvious. Micheline had implied that the murder had something to do with Henri's death, but he dismissed this connexion. The outline was clear to him, but, like Micheline, he groped for detail to anchor himself.

'Swift and limited.' De Gaulle had eaten enough. He was crumpling his napkin with finality. 'No, no.' He waved away the unspoken protests of his guests. 'Some people will get away with their ill deeds, but we need them. And loyalty is due to France herself, not to the inadequate individuals who represent her from time to time.'

That night Theo had not acted with the philosophic generosity that his leader advocated; he had turned on his heel immediately and left. Such was his rage at the time that he did not even speak to Micheline or Florence to say goodbye. Seating himself at the wheel, he had shouted to Dorchin from the yard.

The previous time he had left home, in the midst of disarray and defeat, he had been a happier man. The Germans had crossed the frontier on 10 May in 1940 and six weeks later France had collapsed. Theo had been wounded in the neck and taken to a field hospital from which the doctors had already fled. The wounded were evacuated to Bordeaux where, feverish and hallucinating, amid scenes of desperate overcrowding, he was unaware of the nightmarish reality taking place beyond his sickness. When, after three weeks, it was all over and he had more or less cured himself, he found that it was, indeed, all over.

He had always been a man with friends and even in the hospital a friend discovered him. Dr Maniotte, a pulmonary specialist who had a country home at Lepech Perdrissou, was still at work as a doctor of all trades, sewing up wounds, delivering babies, setting broken limbs. Somehow, he recognised his former tennis partner in the unshaven face and bandaged torso lying unconscious in a corridor. From him, Theo heard the news of the Armistice, the castration of the army, the occupation of the north. The country was now divided into two zones and there was no communication between them. Lying in fever, he had not heard de Gaulle's appeal from London, broadcast by the BBC on 19 and 20 June. Later, as he lay semi-conscious, he heard diatribes against the Anglo-Saxons and the traitors who had joined them, and he understood that the British hadn't yet been defeated. He decided at once to join the fight wherever it was, even if it had to be in the gloomy greyness of London.

He had been under no illusions about his legal position. He was about to become a deserter from the army, which had been ordered to lay down its weapons. As de Gaulle had already been sentenced to death *in absentia* by a military court, Theo could not expect more lenient treatment. He decided to save his family from the confiscation of his property by disappearing from the records in the neatest possible way: he would fake his own death. Maniotte, who obtained the appropriate papers and saw to their countersigning, said to him, 'This is the first time in my medical career I have ever committed a fraud. I'm now a criminal.'

'You'll do it many more times before we're through,' was Theo's robust reply.

Before the Armistice in June 1940, Maniotte had sent his family to his house in the free zone, very close to Bonnemort. Theo persuaded him to join him in crossing the Line of Demarcation, still officially closed. Only Ariane had seen him on that brief visit to his home. He had told her of what he intended with a clarity which showed that no other plan was possible. He warned her to expect notification of his death, a fiction she should maintain with all the other members of the family. He promised to send messages when he could, but she would have to accept that there would be no way of knowing if the pretence had become reality until the war was over. She had not argued with him. He was not sure now whether she had approved of his actions, or was simply too shocked to attempt to dissuade him. He had left early the next day, shedding his name, his country and his past.

If some abstract idea of nation and people had determined him to resist when defeat came, the more personal vision of his home and his wife had made him endure the years of exile. Now, with that ideal shattered, he was overtaken by a profound sense of pointlessness. Corruption was everywhere; nowhere was safe if it had penetrated to the remoteness of Bonnemort.

His encounter with his wife, about which he had told no one, pressed on his vision and he began to realise that it entailed larger consequences than personal grief. Having a 'collabo' as a wife was not just emotionally painful, it did not look good. The communists, who declared themselves the party of the martyrs of the Resistance, would certainly make use of it, not just against him, but against the Big Man, too. Even within his own camp, there were those who would like such information for the damage it could do him. So one course of action open to him was to embrace the general's policy of not enquiring too deeply. He had suppressed a smile during that lofty discourse. The general himself was slow to forget a wrong. In Theo's experience, his long-burning resentment never faltered.

Theo felt, like Othello, that he would have found life sweet if he had not known. But he did know, and, he wanted to know more. He wanted every detail. Who had shaved her head, who had watched, with eyes full of guilty pleasure? He was astonished at the power of his imagination. Sitting at his desk in the Ministry of War, he would be roused by the sound of the telephone, or the entrance of an assistant, and realise he had been thinking of his wife for the last fifteen minutes. If only he could discover what had really happened, perhaps he could rid himself of his most persistent and disgusting obsession: picturing Ariane with the unknown officer, his enemy, the occupying German, dining with him, drinking with him, fucking him. He had become a perverse voyeur, creating images he did not want to see and shuffling through them, like a vendor of pornographic postcards. No forgetting would be possible before he knew what he had to forget. Fantasy was unforgettable; it recurred, with embellishments. Only the truth could be forgotten.

3

THEO WAS WALKING across the Concorde Bridge late at night, his head sunk forward between his shoulders, his eyes on the rhythmical reappearance of his toecaps. He stopped in mid-crossing to look upriver. The surface of the water, puckered by the light rain, was just visible, a greyer, liquid variant of the ambient darkness. He had made no progress in the two months since his visit to Bonnemort. The obvious course was to confront Ariane. Time and again he unscrewed his pen to begin a letter to her and found that no words would flow with the ink. Rage, disgust, indignation, injury still dominated his thoughts. They would have to meet; at the very least, justice demanded that Ariane be allowed a hearing. But not yet, not yet.

In the meantime, he had written long letters of condolence to Micheline and Florence, but had had no reply, nor had he expected any. It occurred to him that he should announce his return, his resurrection, to his daughter, and so he wrote to explain his disappearance four years ago, his eagerness to see her again, 'when the war is over, as it soon must be.' He wrote to his great-aunts; when time permitted, he would give himself the pleasure of visiting them at Bonnemort. From them he received letters of joy at his return from death and exile, with no reference to Ariane. No sign of any kind had come from his wife.

It was one of the commonest situations in the world, he told himself: the husband away at the wars, the wife finding solace for loneliness and hardship. It happened all the time, on every side, in every war, in all ages. But its being usual did not make it forgivable. This was the result of marrying someone he hardly knew, from an alien background. It could only lead to disaster, as his family and friends had warned him at the time. She was everything he was not: urban, Protestant and rich. He would have said, until he met her, that she was everything he disliked in a woman.

When he left for London in July 1940, they had been married for a year, and had not lived together since the start of the war in September '39. The war that had separated them had originally brought them together. They had met in '38, just after Munich, in that odd period when, for an instant, those holding opposing political views were united in shame. He had been prepared for war, at last, and was infuriated at having it torn away from him, with a dishonourable peace offered as a triumphant alternative. His reaction cut him off from many of his friends, whose passionate relief he could not share.

'Life's so simple for you, Theo,' they said, forgetting, as he often did himself, his daughter's existence. 'You have no family, no responsibilities. You're just a soldier.'

One evening that autumn at a dinner of anti-Munich sentiment, he joined a group of people who would never normally have met around a table, to lament and foretell disaster. There he had met Ariane Wolff.

His world had not included unmarried women like her, whose wealth gave her enough power to count, almost, as a man. Certainly she was deferred to, not with gallantry, but with respect, and not only for her money. He was used to women who were smiling and complaisant, who did not discuss politics or contradict men. No woman that he knew would have telephoned a man to arrange a lunch, as she did the following day, with the excuse of introducing him to a friend, a certain Socialist, anti-Munich member of the National Assembly, who wanted a military light thrown on the situation. After that, things moved with such speed that they were married within seven months. He had never been so happy.

He turned from the view of the oily water and his shoes rang on the cobbles, slicked with the mild rain. He felt he could not wait until he returned to Bonnemort; he must do something even at a distance; he would speak to his father-in-law.

Although they could not have been more different in their characters or backgrounds, Theo had always found Ariane's father a sympathetic figure. When they had announced their marriage, his own family had been horrified. Pascal Wolff, on the other hand, had made no protest, even though, on material grounds, he had every reason to question the choice of his only child. He was an immensely rich industrialist, inhabiting a huge villa in the XVI arrondissement, amid hideous and valuable collections of Compagnie des Indes porcelain and baroque bronzes. What had become of them, of him, Theo wondered.

He telephoned one evening. A maid answered. He was put through and heard the dry familiar tones, 'Pascal Wolff.'

Theo spoke formally, as to a stranger. 'Theo de Cazalle speaking.'

A pause before the old man said, 'Welcome back to France and welcome back to life, which is more or less the same. It must have been deathly, I imagine, living for four years in London.'

Theo laughed. 'We were in Algiers for some of the time.'

'A different climate, not much better.'

'No.'

'It's been a long time.'

'Yes.'

'We'd better meet, eh?'

'Whenever you're free.'

'We can meet tomorrow for lunch. One has to eat, after all.'

They met at a café near the Ministry and sat down at one of the small tables in the room behind the bar. Around them clerks from neighbouring offices were eating the *plat du jour*.

'What is it today?' Pascal Wolff asked the waiter. Then, turning to Theo, 'You know already the condition we have sunk to here, but perhaps you have access to all sorts of good things, to make up for our deficiencies.'

Theo denied any privileges. 'It was just as bad in England,' he said. 'And there they couldn't make good food even when they had everything.'

'The misfortunes of others are always a comfort,' Wolff said. 'To know that someone is worse off has kept many of us warm in cold weather.' They handed over their ration coupons for the meal.

His father-in-law had aged by more than the four years that had passed. His face was grooved rather than wrinkled, and these crevasses had deepened; the faintly pigmented skin around his eyes had darkened in contrast with his pale cheeks. The silver hair smoothed back from his high forehead was sparser, but his detached, observant humour remained.

Neither of them knew how to broach the subject of Ariane.

'Wonderful news about Strasbourg,' Pascal Wolff said. Alsace had been liberated by General Leclerc two days earlier.

'Yes, we should drive them out of France completely in the next month or so.'

The waiter slapped down in front of them two plates: a stew of beans and cabbage. Pascal Wolff picked up his fork and spoke quickly, as if to get it over. 'You want to know about Ariane.'

'Yes.'

'She won't see you.'

'Oh.' This did not surprise him.

'I didn't tell her I was meeting you today.'

'She's here, in Paris?'

'For the last two months. Didn't you know? She's living with me.'

'No. I had no way of knowing.'

Silence. Finally Wolff spoke. 'I don't know what happened down there. I don't ask. She certainly won't tell me. I don't know what happened between the two of you. All I can say is she is my daughter. I have to support her.'

'How is she?'

'Not well. She doesn't eat and she doesn't sleep. She doesn't talk. I've tried to send her somewhere out of the war, where she can have a complete rest and recover her equilibrium. She won't go. I've called the doctor. She won't see him. I've called a psychologist. She won't see him either. Good thing. He would say it was all my fault.'

Perhaps it was all his fault. He had made Ariane his companion and friend since she was five years old, when her mother died. Wolff had little need for the company of women. His sense of self-esteem needed no reinforcement from their admiration and he was too busy to require their skills of making time pass pleasantly. He had married the daughter of a Protestant banking family and handed over to her the care of running their houses and organising their domestic life. When she died, he rapidly discovered that these tasks could be as well fulfilled by good staff and there was really no need for a wife. A year or so after her death, he began a discreet liaison, and continued it for many years, with the widow of an old friend who had no wish to remarry because of the terms of her husband's will. The relationship, paradoxically intermittent and passionate, suited them both. Nothing about his chilly personality or in his rationally ordered life suggested that he would be a doting father, yet Ariane became more and more necessary to him as she grew older.

He loved her all the more because, unlike her mother, she was not beautiful. She was dark, like him, with heavy eyebrows, a prominent nose, a purposeful chin. Large, both in height and strong build, she was full of energy. She rode and shot and skied and sailed, without fatigue. She was clever, too, and just as with all sports she had a passion to win, so at school she had a drive to excel. She was always among the first in the class and after her *baccalauréat*, instead of doing what the daughters of all his friends did: tea parties, good works, balls and marriage, all within the tight circle of the Protestant *haute bourgeoisie*, she entered the Ecole Normale Supérieure.

He should have made a stand then. After that, what followed was inevitable, as he was warned by the grim smiles of the older women who knew about these things. She was not going to marry suitably, they predicted; she would choose for herself and the man would be an outsider. Marriage was not in question for a long time. She completed her degree, then her *agrégation*, coming second in her year, worked for a time in a school in Lille, discovered she was a hopeless disciplinarian with no gift for teaching, resigned, and returned to Paris, to write and to study.

With this background, how had she managed to meet and fall in love with a widowed, aristocratic, Catholic, conservative army officer, ten years her senior, with a seven-year-old daughter and no money? The psychologist might have made imaginative hypotheses about guilt and self-worth and father-fixations. In the furious reaction of the two families to the wedding in May 1939, her father had thought that she must have chosen Theo in order to cause the maximum uproar. The real reason for the marriage was obvious: passion. This was probably why both sets of relatives were so furious. All the proper considerations for the foundation of a family on which they were united, Protestant and Catholic alike: compatibility of fortune, status, religion and milieu, were being ignored in favour of overwhelming sexual attraction. The fuss was compounded by the haste of the marriage, driven by the sense of impending disaster. Wolff had made no objection and indeed he found his son-in-law an agreeable, well-read, amusing companion, although he seemed neither sufficiently intellectual nor sufficiently worldly for Ariane, to counterbalance his other qualities, or defects. They had had a civil ceremony only and Wolff had taken good care, in the light of all that militated against the success of the marriage, that Ariane's property was well protected. What else could he do to save her in her happiness, he had thought with a parent's helpless anguish, looking at her radiantly ugly face.

Where had it gone wrong? Perhaps all the disapproving cousins were correct; sexual passion was a bad basis for a marriage. At all events, a husband who pretends to die and disappears for four years can hardly expect to find his wife unchanged at the end of that time.

'It's certainly not your fault,' Theo said.

'Yes, let's leave blame aside, shall we?'

'Yes. It would be wisest, certainly.'

'You want to see her?'

Theo surprised himself by saying, 'I want to hear...'

'It won't be soon. She hardly talks, even to me. She only concentrates on the child.'

'The child? Sabine?'

'Sabine? Oh, your daughter. No. She's still at Bonnemort with your aunts, didn't you know?'

Theo's relationship with his daughter was evidently not what Wolff's had been with Ariane, if he did not know where she was living. 'No, the other one, Suzie they called her.'

'Who is Suzie?'

'Don't you know about her? No, how could you? So much happens in four years.'

'I've never heard of her before now.' But he recalled Florence's words, *The children are asleep, of course. I didn't wake them.*

'She's the daughter, or rather the granddaughter, of a friend of mine. Her grandfather was one of our suppliers for years; he was in metallurgy in Düsseldorf. His son became a prof at the university, and in thirty-three or thirty-four, right at the beginning of Hitler, he was sacked. He left Germany altogether, came to Paris and worked as a journalist. So when the Germans arrived here, he sent his wife and child to the free zone, where he thought they would be safer, to Clermont Ferrand, for some reason. In forty-two he came to see me, to ask if I knew anyone in the Auvergne who could help his wife who was sick. There were money problems, too. He was desperate, but he didn't want to bring her back to Paris. The only person I could suggest was Ariane. She went there and brought the child back to Bonnemort.'

Theo's mind had not engaged with this story and he could not understand why his father-in-law was telling it in such detail. Then he grasped that this child was a witness, had been at Bonnemort, had seen everything.

'And she's living with you here?' he asked.

'Yes, we put her into the *lycée* around the corner. I found out that she hadn't been at school the whole time she was down in the country. God knows why, Ariane taught her and Sabine herself.'

Theo imagined questioning the child, then realised that there were some things he could not do. Wolff was standing up.

'It's been good to see you, Theo. My advice about Ariane, for what it's worth, is to leave her alone for a while. As the President says, we have to learn to forget.'

He shrugged on his old Burberry and stepped out of the restaurant, bidding his son-in-law goodbye with a wave of his folded newspaper.

Theo made his way back to the rue St Dominique. The important information that he had gained from this encounter was that he was free to return to Bonnemort. Ariane was not there; he could go home without having to confront her.

4

THIS TIME HE arrived at Bonnemort before dusk and saw the golden stone of the walls glowing in the winter sunshine. January had come before he could leave Paris. His prediction to Pascal Wolff that the Germans would have been driven out of France before the end of the year had been proved wrong, and Strasbourg itself had come under renewed threat in December. He had spent Christmas with the Big Man in Alsace and only well into the new year could he obtain a few days' leave of absence.

His home had been built in the eighteenth century as a hunting lodge, on the site of some minor medieval fortification. The fortress had disappeared, leaving only its little Romanesque chapel abutting the newer dwelling. At the other end of its regular façade rose a large square tower and from it sprang an archway leading into the farmyard. In front of the house the land spread out as far as the cliff's edge, at the foot of which lay a lake reached by a steep and rocky path. Below the water the land fell again, less abruptly, to the valley of walnut orchards. In the field he could see Ariane's two horses grazing with the aunts' apricot-coloured donkeys.

In the summer of '39 they had spent their honeymoon here. They had ridden for miles over the hilltop pastures, through the chestnut and oak woods, while he persuaded her that this would be the place for her to come if, or when, war broke out. He never expected her to obey orders like a good army wife; she was too used to her independence. She would live at Bonnemort, or not, as she pleased. And it must have pleased her, for although she went there reluctantly in September '39, she had stayed. During the phoney war she had sent for her horses and with her car, driver and maid she had established a life of *urbs in rure*. Her chauffeur was soon called up, and the maid, terrified by the filth and savagery of country life, left within weeks. Yet Ariane had remained.

He had taken the precaution of phoning Micheline to warn her of his arrival. The aunts, with Sabine in attendance, waited to greet him beside the fire in the library. As he embraced them, he saw how much they had changed. A thousand years old when he was a small boy, they had, if anything, grown younger as he grew up. Now he realised that Madame Veyrines, Aunt Odette, must be over eighty, and her sister-in-law, Madame de Cazalle, Aunt Marguerite, in her mid-seventies. Although he always thought of them as a pair, 'the aunts', they were in truth very different both physically and in character.

Aunt Odette, his grandfather's sister, was a gentle, accommodating woman with white hair ingeniously constructed into a roll around her head. She had the figure of a feather pillow, sagging and downy; the skin of her cheek as he kissed it had the texture of cashmere, infinitely soft and faintly furred. Aunt Marguerite, Madame de Cazalle, widow of his grandfather's brother, Geoffroi, was thin and fragile with cropped iron-grey hair and a gentle face, which belied her energetic and managing disposition.

And Sabine was unrecognisable. He had last seen her at Easter 1940, when he had visited her at her convent. She had been a withdrawn and unattractive child, rejecting his inexperienced attempts at arousing her interest. Now she was tall, already developing and obviously uncomfortable with her new body, lumpily crouching by the fire.

His family had always dealt with facts that they did not like by ignoring them. As he had expected, they made no mention of his delay in coming to visit them, nor of the absence of his wife. *What happened here? Tell me about my wife,* he wanted to say. He could ask the question and knew that they would not be able to reply. The reticence of good manners was as difficult to break through as the deliberate refusal to speak of the political prisoner. He imagined their skulls cracked open to his view, like a walnut shell, to reveal the intricate whorls of the nut inside. But to see inside the shell would not reveal what the brain knew. That was secreted in another form, like the taste of the nut, which could not be sensed by the eye.

He was the centre of their attention, recounting his adventures, his flight, London and Algiers, life with the Big Man.

'We suspected that you might be in London,' remarked Aunt Odette, 'although Ariane never told us. But we didn't know until the Germans left.'

'She wasn't sad enough. She tried but she's not an actress. Henri knew something. He was even worse at acting than Ariane.'

'They were not so bad at hiding some things.'

What things? Her lover?

'We used to listen to *Ici Londres*. The general speaks very well, better than Mr Churchill, we think.'

They had had enough of his four years of exile. He was back and life would go on.

'Tell me about your war,' he said. 'I've told you mine.' *Tell me about Ariane and the German officer.*

'What's war to two old women in the depths of the countryside? We followed everything on the wireless.'

'We had our atlas.' Aunt Marguerite rose to fetch the large volume kept on the table behind the sofa. It opened where a magnifying glass was wedged into the map of Eastern Europe, marked from Danzig to Galicia, from Leningrad to the Crimea, with lines crossing the continent.

'What with the Balkans and North Africa and Hawaii and Singapore, world war has been good for our geography, hasn't it, Sabine?'

'It's shocking to say it, but it didn't make so much difference to us. We could see life getting harder for Henri and Micheline and Ariane. To run the farm without men or fuel or seeds or fertiliser, wasn't easy. But for us...'

'Marguerite's donkeys became useful for the first time in their lives. That was one change.'

'Yes. We go to mass in the donkey cart.'

'But we'd never even seen a German until June when they moved in here.'

'How many of them were there?' Theo asked.

'About fifty, I think Ariane said. There seemed to be so many of them.'

'The officers took over the house and used the reception rooms as offices; the men used the storerooms down in the field.'

'They were perfectly correct, you know,' Aunt Odette continued. 'Look at the house. You wouldn't believe they had been here, would you? Really no damage at all.'

'So strange that they behaved so well here, when you think how they acted elsewhere. They would kill innocent people in reprisals. Sometimes if they were out hunting the *maquisards*, they would just shoot a farmer in the fields in passing, for no reason at all. And women too.'

'There was a reason, Odette. If you make violence indiscriminate, no one can ever feel safe. It helped us a lot that Ariane spoke German,' Marguerite went on.

He hadn't known she spoke German. More proof.

'Yes, they didn't speak French at all, even the officers.'

'She means they weren't people you'd expect to be officers.'

'But here they behaved correctly,' Odette repeated.

Marguerite de Cazalle was reflecting that feelings are forgotten so quickly. Now that it was over, she could hardly recall the fear of those weeks when the Germans were with them, like living with an ill-trained dog whose reactions could not be predicted. Now they could give them credit for one thing, being correct.

At the moment of their arrival, when the motorcycles had roared into the courtyard, she had had only one thought: that the house would be set on fire and the family summarily shot. She and Odette could not flee, so they remained in their room. Odette even continued with her gros point, but she, Marguerite, moved from window to window, watching what was going on in the courtyard. She studied the Germans' uniforms as they strode purposefully about. The officers wore black, the jackets buttoned up to the neck, belted, decorated with a number of mysterious insignia, of which she only recognised the swastika and the double lightning bolts: the SS. One had a cross at his neck and four gold studs on either side of his collar. On their caps, she could just make out the blank eyes of the death's head. The men were wearing the pudding basin helmets that made them so sinister: featureless and inhuman. Their movements were swift and businesslike. They had never been to Bonnemort before, yet they occupied the space immediately.

'Marguerite, come and sit down. It's undignified to be peering out of the window.'

'I'm not concerned with dignity at the moment. I want to know what they're doing.'

'They'll do it whether you're watching or not.'

'I want to be conscious of what is happening to me.'

'Well, what do you see?'

The men, who had scattered on their arrival to search the outbuildings, were returning. A non-commissioned officer was shouting new orders, pointing. The trucks reversed through the gates and lumbered into the field; the men unloaded their packs. The midsummer sun beat down from a radiantly blue sky. The air in the valley trembled. Marguerite could hear through the open window a high-pitched mewing above the bass notes of the machines, and looking up, she saw a buzzard, circling on the air currents, hanging on its outstretched wings.

Ariane had gone out to meet them. She was wearing the breeches and boots that were her everyday clothes. The aunts both felt it was unsuitable to dress in this way, but had to admit that it was practical. Now she looked feminine to the point of caricature alongside the soldiers' uniforms. She was calling the dogs to her.

'Oh, oh, he's killed her. He's hit her.'

At that even Odette's composure broke. 'Ariane?' she cried.

'No, no, the dog. Oh, the brute.'

One of the terriers, more persistent than the rest, had continued to yap at the heels of the soldiers. An officer with a peaked cap had turned on it. A casual stamping blow with a rifle butt caught it behind the ears and broke its neck.

'Ariane's speaking to one of them, now. Or rather, he's speaking to her. The one that killed the dog. He looks as if he is giving her orders. She's looking at the ground. She's shaking her head. Now she's pointing at the farmyard.' She suddenly drew back behind the curtains. 'She's pointing at the house. What can she be saying?'

'We'll find out soon enough.'

'Now they've been joined by another officer. He's wearing a black patch over his eye.'

The fear that filled her stomach as she picked up her book was not for herself. When you reached her age, you did not expect to live for ever any more. It was fear of the alien and the unknown: the impossibility of understanding those foreign voices, their indifferent faces, the logic of their actions so far removed from the life of Bonnemort. And fear for the others, for Ariane, of whom she had become truly fond, for the children, for Micheline and Henri who had looked after the family for decades. She noticed with admiration that Odette really was passing the needle through the canvas, leaving a trail of completed stitches behind it as evidence of her concentration. For herself, she had self-control enough not to go downstairs to ask Ariane what was happening, to hold her book in her hand, but she could not make her action real and read the words she was looking at.

When Ariane opened the door, Marguerite rose at once.

'My dear, what do they want? What are they going to do?'

'Sit down, Marguerite, allow Ariane to speak.'

'This is a security unit,' Ariane explained. 'They're here to deal with gangs and they'll stay indefinitely.'

'Here?'

'Yes, they are going to occupy Bonnemort.'

'What do they mean by "gangs"?'

'The Resistance,' Ariane said briefly. 'They call them gangs of terrorists. I've explained to them who lives here. They'll check our papers, and I hope we won't have any problems.' She drew a hand over her forehead, as if to calm herself. 'They're taking over the house. We'll all move into the tower. The girls will sleep in the dressing room. I thought you wouldn't mind taking the second floor. The stairs will be a problem for you, Aunt Odette, I know.'

Marguerite had noticed that as she became accustomed to their presence her fear died and it was harder to maintain her dislike. When they were wearing their soft caps, she could distinguish their features and begin to tell one from another. They were so young.

'They were so young,' she said aloud. 'Only a few years older than Suzie and Sabine. They had skin like babies, or those terrible spots on their necks. Just children, yet they were killing people.'

'Or old. There were the older men, who used to stay to keep guard.'

'Even the officers were young. The major was about thirty, and the lieutenant, the one with the eyepatch, the same.'

'That poor young man who was killed...'

Theo felt as if he was stalking a butterfly, or a tiger. He had suddenly glimpsed his prey and did not know whether to freeze or to fire. *Tell me about my wife's lover. Who was he?*

'Who was he?' he asked when it was clear that neither of them was going to elaborate.

'Sabine, would you like to wash your hands before dinner.' The child rose meekly and left the room.

'He was in command of the unit.' Aunt Marguerite liked clearly defined questions. 'He was called Major Udo Knecht.'

'Was it ever established what had happened?'

Their voices fell over one another in their eagerness to talk.

'We never knew.'

'We could never find out.'

'It was such a terrible time. Henri was killed, so the death of the German, well, no one cared about it.'

'And whom could we ask? Normally Micheline or Florence or Ariane would tell us the news, but they were so distressed by Henri's death...'

'It was not something we could ask the children about. It was shocking enough that they saw him.'

'We all saw him. He lay there, completely naked.'

'There was a lot of activity in the night. The engines of cars, headlights. We didn't go out or even open the shutters. We prayed.'

'The Resistance must have caught him.'

'How? Where?'

'We'll never know.'

'Whoever killed him left him there as a warning to his comrades.'

'But fortunately for us, the Germans had left, because if they had still been here, and they had found the body rather than Micheline...'

'I imagine we would have all been shot.'

'I can't think that killing individual Germans was a sensible tactic. It led to such terrible repercussions: three for one, or ten for one.'

'That was the communists. They didn't care about reprisals. They thought it would incite the population to revolt.'

'When he broadcast from London, the general forbade attacks until the liberation.'

'Yes, but Maurice Schumann said on the wireless that the time for the settlement of accounts would come.'

Aunt Odette struggled out of her chair and found her cane. 'Theo, you have had a long journey, so we must give you a moment to prepare for dinner. And afterwards we must allow you some time with Sabine.'

5

THEO WENT TO his room to unpack. He found his wardrobe full of his old clothes and took out a tweed jacket, thick woollen trousers. As he put them on, he felt he was assuming his old life, before Ariane. Sabine was his first responsibility, he told himself. When he was in exile he had had half-formed ideas about the future, when the war was over, of living in Paris with Ariane and Sabine and other possible children, making a new family with a normal life of school holidays and family festivals. Those visions were dead before birth. So Sabine would have to go back to the convent. He wanted her to be like her mother, gentle, domestic, with no conversation or interests outside the family. He had had enough of modern women; he had no wish for her to be highly educated, as Ariane was. The convent would do very well.

Dinner was served in Micheline's house, at the table where he and Dorchin had sat that evening at the beginning of September, and they all ate together, the aunts, Sabine, Micheline and Florence. Aunt Odette felt the oddity of dining in the servants' quarters and said in explanation, as Theo escorted her across the farmyard, 'Ariane suggested we eat over here, because it made things easier for Micheline.'

The meal was like a memory of childhood, food that he had dreamed of in Blitz-darkened London. In the centre of the table, covered with a coarse linen cloth, was an ancient tureen, the porcelain scattered with flowers. Micheline lifted its chipped lid and said ceremoniously, *'Le tourain.'*

The smell of garlic and goose fat that was released as she ladled the soup into their bowls almost brought tears to Theo's eyes. He and Henri used to have it in the early morning before they left to go shooting, or in the evening on their return from the fields. Micheline and Florence bent low over their bowls. Aunt Odette was eating with aristocratic slowness; Aunt Marguerite pursed her mouth, critically.

'It lacks salt,' she remarked.

'It would,' Micheline replied without taking offence. 'Not enough bacon, so I added salt to compensate. But you're right. Not enough.'

Sabine was playing with her soup, lifting a spoonful to her mouth and returning it untouched to the bowl. She rose quickly to help Micheline, removing her own bowl and surreptitiously tipping the contents into the pig's pot. The next course, produced to acclamation, was a round of foie gras with a black truffle as its hub.

'Micheline, you're a creator of miracles. I never thought I would see foie gras again,' Theo said.

Micheline looked pleased. 'I made these foie gras in the autumn of either thirty-eight or thirty-nine, I forget which. You said you must always face war with a full cellar and a full store. So I made foie gras and *confits*. I bottled vegetables and fruit. I made jam. And I hid a few for when the war was over.'

'You've eaten all the rest? You must have had a good war here.'

The instant the words were spoken, he wished he could have caught them in the air, shot them down and destroyed them. A good war: Henri dead, Georges a forced labourer in Germany, Roger and Claude volunteers in the Alsace-Lorraine brigade, now fighting with the First Army. Fortunately, Micheline's mind was a literal one; she only thought of her food reserves.

'I lost a whole lot at once. We didn't realise that the Requisition would take everything. They marked every beast, they counted every chicken. And last summer almost finished us off. We had the Maquis to feed and young men don't live on nothing, I can tell you. Not that I gave them my foie grass *truffé*.'

She was handing round a white platter, on which a pile of bottled green beans was surrounded by the legs of preserved duck in their crusted skins. Sabine took a few beans. Micheline seized her fork and transferred a piece of duck to the child's plate. Sabine made an expression of distaste, but said nothing.

After dinner the family walked back to the library, leaving Micheline and Florence in their own kitchen. They sat together and listened to the news, which was a sacred part of the aunts' day.

'Now it is time for you to talk to Sabine.' Aunt Odette was searching for her cane. Sabine had been sitting on a stool, huddled close to the fire. She had pulled forward a lock of her hair, running it through her fingers abstractedly as she listened to the wireless. It was hard to tell if she had paid any attention.

'Oh no, Aunts, please stay.'

'There's no need to go.' Theo was as reluctant as Sabine to be left, for he could think of nothing to say to his daughter. Between his experience and hers was a gulf he had not the imagination to bridge.

'You've grown so much,' he said. 'I hardly recognise you.'

'Yes.'

'What… What…' He was about to say, *What have you been doing*, but could see that this had too wide a scope. 'What are you studying now?'

There was no reply.

Aunt Marguerite said, 'Theo, you always reach the heart of a problem with uncanny understanding.'

'Is there a problem?'

'I am studying English,' Sabine said. 'I listen to the BBC and I read Dickens with Aunt Odette.'

'Schooling is a problem, Theo,' Aunt Marguerite answered him. 'And we were awaiting your arrival to settle the question of what to do for Sabine's education now.'

'When she first came here in 1940 she went to the village school, which was very difficult in the winters.'

'When Suzie came to us in forty-two, Ariane removed Sabine from the school, saying that she did not think the teacher, Mr Vernhes, was satisfactory. I think she was right.'

'So what did you do for their education?'

'Ariane taught the girls herself. She has a doctorate, after all.'

'And you did too, Aunts,' Sabine insisted.

'Yes, even Odette and I took part, if Ariane was busy.'

'You could do everything, Aunts. We really didn't need her.'

'Very flattering of you to say so, my dear, but not truthful.'

'And since Ariane's return to Paris,' he referred to her absence without hesitation, 'you have continued with her studies?'

'We do mathematics, French, literature, history, geography, Latin, English, philosophy…' Sabine recited.

'An impressive programme.'

'Less impressive than it sounds, I assure you, and not adequate for Sabine's needs.'

'The convent…' Theo began.

'No,' Sabine shouted, leaping up from her stool. 'I won't go back to the convent. I won't. I'll run away.' She suited her actions to her words by covering her face with one hand and rushing out of the room, knocking over a small table on the way.

'You look shocked, Theo,' Aunt Odette said drily. 'Marguerite and I have learned about the upbringing of young girls in the last few years.'

'Much more vexatious than boys.'

'The convent?' Theo repeated.

He had found the convent boarding school for Sabine when his wife died. He could not care for a child of six himself, so the nuns were the obvious answer.

'You could insist. She may come round to the idea.'

'She misses Suzie and Ariane. She needs companions. She should go back to the sisters.'

'It's so odd. When she arrived, she was furious at having to leave them.'

'And at the time she did not seem so very fond of her stepmother.'

'It has been particularly hard since Ariane left...'

'We didn't mean to bring this up as soon as you arrived, but since it has arisen...'

'She doesn't eat...'

'She goes for long walks, or rides alone. It's not suitable.'

'It's not safe.'

'She behaves abominably. She answers back and is rude to Micheline.'

'We can do nothing with her.'

'Next it'll be boys.'

'We need a man's authority.'

Theo was aghast. This was not what he had come home for. The door opened and Sabine came back in and sat down again by the fire. 'I'm sorry, Papa,' she said.

'Sabine,' said her father, 'I don't want to force you to go anywhere you would be unhappy. If necessary, I shall find another school. Did you not like the convent?'

Sabine did not reply.

'You liked it once,' Aunt Marguerite said, encouragingly.

'I hated it. I won't go back.'

It was a world impossible to describe to anyone who had not lived there. They had lived within an invisible barbed wire fence, so that they could see the outside world, but were never part of it, held captive by the discipline of self-denial and spiritual exaltation. She had been so young when she was sent there that she had thought this was the world outside home, how it had to be. This is what the sisters taught. Others might live otherwise, which would only lead to their damnation, but within the wire, contained by their strict routine, they were leading the good life: obedience to God, to the Reverend Mother and the sisters, to priests, to men, to older people. Since she had left, she had cancelled as much as she could from her memory, and all that was left was sensation:

Cold: no heating in the dormitories; a single pipe in the classrooms running, against all scientific principles of the conduction of heat, along the ceiling. Throughout the winter they all had running noses, raw upper lips, chilblains swelling their fingers and toes, cracking and suppurating.

Fear: the rules were tyrannical in their senseless detail and precision. The least infraction (walking on the wrong side of the corridor, inattention during the twice-daily services) was punished by deprivation of food and public humiliation, standing in a reserved spot during mealtimes while the rest ate.

Hunger: the food was horrible, inedible. She could visualise the dry, gristly slice of grey meat that appeared on their plates twice a week, which she would chew and chew and could never swallow. She used to hide it in her handkerchief, tucked into her sleeve. On Fridays and fast days the glutinous gratin of fish with its seasoning of fine bones made her stomach heave.

Pain: for the most heinous offences beating was prescribed, and at first, failing to understand the system of deceit for self-protection, she was often caught in some dereliction and beaten on her bare legs.

At the beginning she could only weep. Her tears, an appeal for help as well as an expression of misery, only aroused impatience in the teachers and mockery from the pupils. Sympathy between the children was suppressed by competition for rare favours; a harsh self-sufficiency was the norm. Anyone who betrayed weakness was derided and ostracised. The admired ones were strong, those who never showed emotion, who were ostentatiously dutiful in their religious observance and their demeanour to the sisters. They ruled their classes as miniature tyrannies, in imitation of the authority above them, taxing their companions for admiration, hair ribbons, or bread saved from their meals.

Sabine was a victim from the moment they saw her. Every instinctive gesture she made, seeking friends, exposing her weakness, was wrong. In the secret life of the long, vaulted dormitory where twenty girls slept in order of age and status, she was the runt. When the lights were out, they took it in turns to run silently to her bed and tweak her hair, to seize the pillow she had pulled over her head, to take one of her shoes and throw it to the other end of the room, to lift the covers and pour water onto her sheets.

Over time the tortures evolved, becoming more creative once they were taken in hand by Antoinette, one of the older girls who had been absent for some months, as the result of having had appendicitis. When she returned from hospital and convalescence, all things medical had become her obsession and Sabine was her patient. The sisters esteemed modesty highly and the girls took their weekly baths clad in their voluminous nightgowns. So the fascination for the whole dormitory of Antoinette's operations was greater than simple defiance of the rules of the night. Over and over again she scored in chalk on Sabine's skinny abdomen the line of her own scar, while two others, designated as nurses, held the patient's nightgown over her head as a visual anaesthetic. From this the surgeon progressed to further examinations. Sabine was turned on her face for the administration of injections with needles from the sewing baskets; pencils were inserted into her anus for a length of time carefully monitored by Antoinette, before being removed and read as a thermometer. Sabine's childish body made the modelling of ribs and spine, the muscles of buttocks and thighs a lesson in anatomy and reaction to pain. The experimentation took a new form in the summer when Antoinette acquired a knife from the dining room to make her work as surgeon more real. Unfortunately, it was not sharp and its effect was little different from that of the chalk, so Antoinette was able to carve and butcher her patient for some weeks, until by sawing too hard, in a cut that was to slice Sabine from the slit between her legs to the breastbone, blood was drawn. The surgical team and its audience fled, expecting to awake to a corpse in Sabine's bed. However, the patient survived and did not even complain, for she could think of no one among the sisters that she could speak to on such a subject, as the body was an area of the strictest taboo.

It was perhaps in examining herself for damage after these operations, soothing her own pain, that she discovered the comfort of the lonely in physical pleasure and her nighttime tortures were relieved in orgasmic fantasies of revenge. When her enemies had been torn apart in some episode of biblical violence, she would at last fall shudderingly asleep.

She found protection at last in a new sister, recently arrived from the order's work in Algeria. Sister Barbe was young, with a low, intense voice and so powerful a personality that her classes, French language and orthography, were among the most dreaded. Whether for faults of behaviour, restlessness or whispering, or of performance, a blot on the page, an ill-spelled word, punishment, in the form of sarcasm and beating, was swift. Sabine, however, felt safer in this regime of terror, which lay on all of them impartially. To Sister Barbe she made her only attempt to tell an adult of her suffering. The response was curious.

'Denunciation,' she told Sabine, 'is despicable. Each person must assess her own sins, confess them, make retribution for them. We are not placed on this earth to take the speck from our brother's eye, but to remove the mote from our own. You will make your confession on Saturday as usual. In the meantime, I must punish you myself.'

The beating was brief but severe. The surgical experiments ceased. Sabine never discovered how Sister Barbe curbed Antoinette's medical obsessions, for she saw no sign of sanctions placed on her or on the others. It was enough that she was saved and she was deeply grateful for the protection she had won from the nightly torture. It was worth the price. Sister Barbe's beatings, although harsh, were infrequent. She willingly bartered the gift of her pain for a sort of safety. She knew Sister Barbe watched over her, was interested in her studies and her devotions. For the first time since her mother's death she was special to someone, even in a perverse fashion.

When her stepmother removed her from the convent, without warning, in September 1940 and brought her to Bonnemort, she missed the protection and the pain. She had hated Ariane for it. It was a long time until she found a substitute for what she had lost.

6

THE FARMYARD WAS shimmering with frost when Theo left the tower next morning. He could see by the dark footprints in the rime that Micheline and Florence were already at work. In her kitchen Micheline made him a bowl of ersatz coffee with milk and cut him a slice of bread. He took his breakfast to a chair by the fire, its whitened ashes rekindled and burning with fresh wood. He dunked the bread into the coffee, to soften one and disguise the taste of the other.

'I should go to see Dr Maniotte this morning,' he remarked. 'I'll take one of the horses. They could do with exercising, I imagine.'

'No need. He's dead, too.' Micheline was stirring the pigswill in a battered cauldron. When Theo said nothing, she went on, 'His wife is still at La Grande Pénétie with the younger children.'

'What happened to the doctor?'

'He was arrested a long time ago, September forty-three it would have been. She'll tell you. She's found it hard alone.'

'I'll ride over this morning.'

His route led him through the forest. On the opposite ridge Lepech Perdrissou sat on its hilltop around its grassy square, gardens and orchards descending the slopes, cut up by neat stone walls, woodsmoke wavering upwards in the silver air of the early morning. It looked like an illustration from Perrault's *Fairy Tales*.

After ringing and knocking and receiving no reply, he walked around the house, to the back door which was opened by a middle-aged woman wearing socks rolled at her ankles, a shapeless cardigan and an apron. In his instant of non-recognition, Theo almost made the unforgivable error, but somewhere in the collapsed face a spark of the appealing Madame Maniotte of five years ago remained and he did not ask for her mistress. He greeted her correctly.

She was flustered, ashamed of her dress, her house. 'Oh, Colonel, I didn't know...' She blocked his way, hanging onto the door.

In London they had had no time for pretension under the bombs. *Don't you know there's a war on?* those sarcastic English voices used to demand. He was impatient of the demands of gentility now. 'I came to offer my condolences, Madame.'

Her mouth twitched, but she was long past tears.

'May I come in?' he insisted.

She submitted. 'You'll have to come in here, it's too cold anywhere else.'

They sat in the kitchen, amid an intimate domesticity, the children's shirts hanging on a clothes horse in front of the stove where the iron was heating, the smell of laundry in their nostrils.

'It all began with you, really. He helped you leave for England, and then he just carried on, helping others do the same. There was always someone who needed him, even in 1940 before anyone else was a resistant.' Her tone told him what she thought of such activity. 'I never liked it.'

The truth was she'd never liked Colonel de Cazalle, either. She'd been happy enough to have him join their tennis parties on summer weekends. In the segregated worlds of the French provinces, the gentry did not often mix with the doctor and the lawyer and the dentist, the notables of the local towns. But the social achievement was the only advantage of his presence, as far as she was concerned. He had a dry humour, made odd remarks. He was like a rebel within the citadel. Not that he ever discussed politics or religion with her, but she was certain that his views were not what they should be. When he remarried it was even worse. His new wife was rich, arrogant, far grander than he ever was, with her cars and her clothes and her furs. And who was she after all? Just the daughter of a businessman, who was a Protestant, or even a Jew, and probably a freemason into the bargain.

She might have known it would be Theo de Cazalle who would lead her husband into danger. At that stage Lucien still confided in her, and so she knew all about Cazalle's supposed death, although she never let on to that b— at Bonnemort. She couldn't formulate the epithet even in her thoughts, but she meant it all the same. And Cazalle turned him against the Marshal. As far as she was concerned, Marshal Pétain was right in every respect. The country had been ruined since 1936 by socialists and radicals, and defeat was the result. The marshal was putting the country back on its feet. She felt safe when she looked at posters of that benevolent face.

Lucien knew how she felt and although he stopped telling her what he was doing, he could not conceal his odd hours, his comings and goings which had nothing to do with his practice now that he had set up as a general practitioner in Montféfoul. At least he didn't bring his runaways to the house. These people were wanted by the police. For her, that meant they must be criminals. The Marshal was against communists from the start. Anyone known to have been a party member was rounded up. Jews, foreign ones, immigrants, were put in camps; and Republicans from the war in Spain. All these people were dangerous and needed to be sent back where they belonged, which seemed perfectly reasonable to her.

But not to Lucien, apparently. He hid them and moved them on to Spain. He worked with the printer, Monsieur Sarrazin in Montféfoul, and forged identity documents, ration cards, demobilisation papers. When she discovered this she almost died of fright. The bundle of food tickets that she had found in one of his suits was, for a joyful moment, like winning the lottery, too good to be true. Then she realised it was indeed not true: they must be false. The shock of his involvement in illegal activity on such a scale was terrible.

She remonstrated with him, angrily reproaching him with risking his family's safety. He had sat with his back to her, hunched on the edge of their bed with its wooden headboard carved with true lovers' knots. He had made no reply, for he knew he was in the wrong. So she tried a new tack. Who else was in it with him? Why couldn't he just leave it to them? She had wept and pleaded and he had comforted her, while saying, 'I have to do it. I can't go back now.'

So she guessed. It wasn't difficult. Recently he'd often had ham or butter from Henri Menesplier, whom they'd never really known before. Then she had a flash of real understanding.

'She's in it too, isn't she? Madame de Cazalle? That's why you're doing it?'

'Léonie, please don't make a jealous scene.'

She knew that she had guessed correctly. 'You should leave it to *her*. We're not like that. We're respectable, we obey the law, we don't take risks.'

'Léonie, it'll be all right, I promise you. It'll all come right.'

Once she had started to weep, they had both known how it would end. He came round to her side of the bed, to hold her and let her cry and then make love to her. He'd never admitted anything, but she knew, just as if he'd spoken.

And now here was Theo de Cazalle sitting in her kitchen with an assumed face of sorrow listening to her story. Things had come all right for him, as they always did for people like that. She would make good and sure that any glory due to Lucien wasn't shared with his b— of a wife. She would make Cazalle see that Lucien got his posthumous medals and she got her pension. She would be the widow of an acknowledged Resistance hero. She would play the part and exalt his memory. It was ironic that, if only the Marshal had not been misled by his ministers, like that nasty Laval, then Lucien would still have been the disgraced figure he had been during the year before the liberation.

He'd certainly been betrayed. In September 1943 they'd been waiting for him in a village thirty kilometres away. A few days later, Henri Menesplier had been picked up too. The French took them, but that didn't mean anything since the Germans had occupied the southern zone. The police had come to search their house. She was terrified of what they might find, but knew no more than they did where to look in order to destroy whatever it was. Nothing was discovered, thank God. Lucien had at least had that much care for her, keeping nothing incriminating at home. She went to the Prefecture to ask for news. She was told that he would probably have been taken to

Paris, or sent to a camp at Fresnes, or Compiègne, or if he had been handed over to the SD, the Sicherheitsdienst, he might be sent to a camp in Germany. If he wasn't shot, of course.

After the liberation she heard from a fellow prisoner that he had got no further than Bordeaux. Lucien had been flung into his cell there in the early hours of the morning in December '43, three months after his arrest. His ribs had been crushed and one had pierced a lung; his fingernails had been pulled out; his body was covered in burns. The following night he was taken away for another session and returned a few hours later, his spine smashed, his legs paralysed. He died there a few hours later.

He hadn't talked, the man told her, as if she cared, in spite of the degree of pressure applied.

Theo watched her tell her tale, sitting opposite him, her hands balled in her lap, pressed between her thighs. He listened to what she said in her bare recital, and what she didn't say, in the tone of her voice and the turn of her head. She had still not forgiven Lucien. For her he was not a hero of his country, but a traitor to her and her children. He knew, too, that she must hold him responsible, and that he had only added to her resentment by arriving unexpectedly, catching her unprepared. He could see no means to put any of it right. He had never bothered to charm Lucien's boring little wife in the past, and it was too late now.

'You mentioned Henri Menesplier...'

'Yes, well, you know all about it from them in any case. Henri was arrested about the same time, but he was released, I don't know how. Maybe your wife had something to do with it. She used to dine with the German officers, drink coffee with the *chef de brigade* of the Gendarmerie in Racinès. She had influence.'

The blow went home. She saw it had and felt the easing of pain transferred to another.

'You were there when Henri was shot?'

'Yes. And we all thought we would be next. Especially when we had to dig graves. You want to know about Henri?' For a moment her corroding bitterness ceased its work. 'I don't think *he* betrayed Lucien. I never thought that. He was a good man, Henri.'

In the late afternoon of 17 August 1944, everyone remembered that date now, it was etched in the town's memory, a whole rowdy lot of the Maquis had come into town. She had refused to go out to see them, so she didn't know what they were up to. They were thugs and hooligans, everyone knew that, the roughest youngsters, the least responsible men, probably foreigners, like that drunken Russian, Mr Nikola from Pechagrier. Then the shooting had started. The Germans or the Milice, the French paramilitaries who served alongside them, must have arrived. All she felt was irritation that there was no one to whom she could say, *I told you so*. She and the children were safe in the house and after a while things went quiet again. And that was the end of the danger for the day, or so she thought.

Later that evening, she had been making the children's supper, when she heard the Germans coming back, the roar of their lorries, the shouting through a loud hailer, '*Raus, raus.*' She ignored it, just as she had ignored the Maquis' arrival earlier in the day, but a soldier came knocking at the door, waving his machine gun at her, grabbing one of the boys and pulling him out with him into the street. She had had no alternative but to take the other children and follow him and all the others who were being herded into the square.

Here her indignation evaporated, burned away by fear. For when they had been sorted with shouts and blows, men on one side by the Mairie, women on the other by the school, she saw that there were seven men, she could see their faces, tied up under guard in front of the oak tree. A soldier had taken a ladder and propped it against the huge trunk. He was almost hidden in the foliage, but his purpose was suddenly made apparent when a noose snaked down from the branch on which he was perched. That tumbling rope struck terror in them all and in silence they watched him secure five more ropes to different branches.

They were addressed by the major from Bonnemort. He spoke in German and he had a soldier translating who repeated what he said in very bad French. Five German soldiers had died that day, he said, because of the action of terrorists. Seven of the criminals had been captured and would pay with their lives. Their deaths were to be witnessed by the whole town, so that everyone would understand that the Germans still controlled France and would severely punish any disorder.

She thought: well, they had it coming to them. The so-called Resistance never thought of ordinary people and how they had to pay the price for their criminal activities. This time at least it was the Maquis who were going to suffer. As long as it stopped there. A chill went through her when she thought of those other towns, Tulle, Terrasson, Oradour, where the populace had been assembled by the German army to learn some lessons.

Then she saw them leading them up. Pierre Rouget of Cavialle, who couldn't have been more than nineteen was first. He was as pale as death already, but he wasn't crying out or weeping. They stopped and she saw Henri Menesplier at the end of the line. The major was pointing to the six nooses, the seven men. A soldier ran off to look for more rope, but the officer was impatient. He looked at the row of Resistance fighters, walked up and down in front of them, prolonging the decision. He was enjoying that drawn-out moment of choice. She had been caught up in it, waiting to see what he would do. Finally he pointed to one of them. Henri Menesplier was led forward.

He had been good to her, Henri, after Lucien had been taken, in quiet ways, leaving food, calling in to see if she needed a hand, at a time when other people were steering well clear of her. *She* must have trapped him into working for her, just as *she*'d got Lucien involved. *She* was death to anyone who came into contact with her. Tears came into her eyes as the firing squad was formed. Tears for Henri, tears for Lucien.

She had never seen anyone die before, let alone shot. They hadn't put a bandage around his eyes and she wondered how they could do it, the firing squad, look him in the eye as they took aim. Henri had a broad face with wide brown eyes. You could see everything in his expression in the endless seconds while he was tied up, before the order was given: his wife, his children, the grandchildren he would never see. Everything was there. She had cried out when they fired. It was so quick. Henri crumpled to the ground and a stain spread through his shirt. Then the hangings started.

The memory of her fear brought tears to her eyes.

'And why was Henri caught, they're asking,' she said. 'The Germans were ready for them. The Germans had divided themselves into two and their second party came up in the rear, once the attack started. That's what they say. Henri and his men must have been betrayed. Who would have denounced them, that late in the day? That's what people ask. Who would have bothered to try to save the Germans, when they were bound to leave anyway? Everyone knew they were on the run. It wasn't someone who hoped for a reward. Oh, no. It would have to be someone committed to them, who wanted to save the Germans' skins at all costs.'

'You're saying that there were dedicated Nazis in this region?'

She looked sly. Then she burst out, as if she couldn't hold it back, 'Committed Nazis, no, they weren't so common round here. We knew nothing of the Germans before they came to Bonnemort in June last year. Someone in love with a Nazi, more like.'

He rose and kissed her hand, as if they were at a dinner. She had had her revenge, he thought, scattering her rancour as widely as she could. A wife betraying and a friend betrayed: if her object was to sow suspicion, she was successful. Her own suffering was repaid with his. Ariane was accused and convicted on both counts, of resistance and collaboration.

'Your husband was one of the bravest men who served France in this war,' he said. 'It was my honour to have been his friend.'

Her twisted smile accepted his statement and denied his sincerity. 'I've talked too long about the trivial incidents of the war here to someone who has been a witness of great events.'

'I needed to know what happened here at home. Village war is not less significant than world war. In fact, village war is world war.'

She saw him out and watched him ride off, before turning back to her washing. She'd tried to have her revenge once before, on that b— at Bonnemort, but her letter, written anonymously, had produced no result. This had been more profoundly satisfying. Telling the story had comforted her. He had understood what she had said, and what she hadn't said. She'd settled a lot of scores that morning.

7

'LET ME TAKE that.' Theo put out his hand for Micheline's basket, filled with vegetable debris, cabbage stalks, carrot scrapings, leek tops.

'Don't be daft.'

He followed her into the yard where the rabbit hutches were stacked neatly in a double row. Flickering whiskers, quivering nostrils pressed against the netting at the sound of Micheline's voice. She began at the top left-hand cage, opening the door, pulling out the occupant by its ears and slipping it into the cage below while she cleaned out its soiled straw.

'Madame Maniotte told me about her husband's arrest.'

Micheline was already talking. 'Sabine usually does the rabbits. She and Suzie liked to gather leaves in the paddock and feed them every afternoon. They cleaned them out and gave them all names. Now I can't get her to do anything.'

'She'll have to stay here a bit longer,' Theo said shortly. 'Paris is no place for a child at the moment. Madame Maniotte... Can we send her something, a rabbit, a chicken?'

Micheline shrugged. 'If you want. It won't make her like you any better.'

She had finished the second cage and the rabbit hung from her hand in a long rope of fur. She put her other hand beneath its scut to insert it into the cage and it bunched itself into a ball. Theo took some leaves from the basket and fed them to the freshly cleaned rabbits.

'She said that Henri was in the same network as her husband.'

'That's right.'

'Micheline, please tell me about what you did in the Resistance.'

She was working her way back along the lower row, bending to peer inside the hutches. 'Look out for that one, it's the buck. He has a nasty kick. It wasn't every day, you know. We had the farm to run.'

'How did Henri get involved?' That seemed to him now almost the most interesting question.

'I suppose Madame persuaded him.'

'Madame?'

'Madame your wife. Our first guest was a friend of hers, a communist, and she turned to the doctor for help.'

They'd got into it without realising, or at least she had. Henri perhaps knew better what he was doing. He used to have long talks with Madame about the war and the Armistice and what it all meant. But for Micheline, looking after the communist was no different from looking after the old ladies, or Madame, or Sabine, or her sons and the farm workers. The communist, Gauthier he was called, stayed the longest, at least a month before they'd worked out a way for him to leave. He'd turned up just before Christmas in 1940 and they'd hidden him on the top floor of the house. He had seemed happy enough up there, with his papers and all the books Madame Ariane gave him. He'd been a professor, Madame Ariane told her, who'd been sacked from his job by the Marshal for being a communist. He used to chat when she brought him his food and he'd been a pleasant enough fellow, though he sometimes made remarks about Madame Ariane being so rich, as if he thought she, Micheline, ought to agree with him. She hadn't liked that. He was supposed to be a friend of Madame's, after all. Of course it wasn't just a question of hiding them, the runaways. They had to be moved on; they had to have papers. She knew that Henri helped to organise all that with the doctor. There was even an arms drop early on. Henri was very excited about it. He disappeared for two days and when he came back, riding in on a lorry by night, he brought guns with him. She had seen them, maybe a hundred or so English Bren guns, when she'd helped him and Madame store them down in the natural caves which were hollowed out of the rocky face of the cliff below the house. For centuries these had been used as barns and had been equipped with heavy wooden doors to keep out the weather. They'd carried them all through the night and hidden them in the storerooms where the Germans had lived last summer. But the guns had gone by then. That was the big event of the first two years of the war. There was no one else doing it then, at least round here. That's where the trouble began, when the other groups formed up. But that was later.

They started to get more Jews, after '42. Before that it had been mostly communists, Spaniards, foreigners. But for some reason, from '42 onwards more and more Jews came through, all trying to get to Spain or to the Italian zone. She used to feel really sorry for them. They'd lived quiet and peaceable till the present, why start persecuting them now? Once they'd had a Jewish lady from Poland, an awfully nice woman, who'd lost her husband, taken off somewhere. It was really sad. And the kids so sweet. They never ran or shouted, just crouched inside the house, like pheasants in the grass. None of them had any money; they'd been forced out of their businesses and homes. It wasn't right.

Looking after them, the Jews or the others, was nothing compared with what happened in '43 when the Nazis started taking workers to Germany. It was compulsory for young men, like the call-up for military service. At first it didn't matter to her personally. Georges was exempt as an agricultural worker, and Roger and Claude, too. The young men who came to them then were from the towns, and couldn't get exemptions, and said they weren't going to go to Germany, whatever anyone said about good wages and how it would be doing our prisoners of war a good turn, since one of them could come home for every three workers that went over there. That was a bad bargain, as any peasant could tell you. Why couldn't the prisoners work in Germany, if it was so great, and they were over there already?

Then things got worse and the government withdrew the exemptions for farmers. Georges' call-up came and he said, 'No way.' There was a group of lads already living in the forests the other side of Montféfoul and he wanted to go with them. They'd kept the boys well out of all Henri's business with the doctor. They'd thought it better, safer for them, if they knew nothing. But later, she wished she'd let Henri use them. Georges might have learned that you can't be too careful. One day he was picked up by the police in the market place with half a dozen others. Fortunately, they didn't deal with him as a terrorist. They just sent him straight to Germany. They must have been short on their quota of workers and he and his mates fitted the bill. She didn't know if it was a good thing or not. If he'd been held in prison he would have been nearer home, but who knows what might have been the outcome. But Germany was a long way off and it couldn't be too good there now with the bombing and all. She worried about him a lot. More than about Roger and Claude. They'd taken to the Maquis the moment Georges was arrested. They didn't waste a minute.

Food was what concerned her. Young people eat twice what an older person does, especially when they're living in the open. Bread was a problem. There wasn't so much of it, even on the ration. Potatoes too, unobtainable. Sometimes they stole things from the Milice, the French paramilitaries. Henri kept his boys on a strict regime and there was a rota of supply from all the neighbouring farms. Some Resistance groups would terrorise the peasants into giving them stuff from their farms, but Henri was against that. He said it just led to denunciations, so there was no point. She was glad when the liberation came, because they had eaten her out of house and home.

'You look as though you still have something left,' Theo said. A flock of guinea fowl ran towards them, gabbling in their hope of grain.

'They make new ones of their own accord, thank God. It's natural.'

'Are any of Henri's group around?' he asked as they walked back.

'What do you mean?'

'Anybody who was with him during that last attack?'

She shrugged. 'Many of the young ones have now joined up, like Roger and Claude. They're not here any more, they're in the army.' She paused. 'You could talk to the Russian, I suppose, Mr Nikola at Pechagrier. I don't take to him myself, but he helped Henri with the boys, drilling them and all that. He was like Henri's lieutenant. He might have been there.' She took back the basket that he been permitted to carry to the kitchen door. 'Florence went out with the dog,' she said. 'If she had luck, we'll have an omelette with truffles tonight.'

He walked from the farmyard to the front of the house, then took the path down to the lake. There he stood watching the water reflecting the late afternoon light in its mirror-smooth surface. He took out a cigarette, a precious Camel from a packet given to him by an American colleague. Between Madame Maniotte's Ariane, trading favours with the Germans, and Micheline's, starting an escapeline for persecuted communists and Jews in the earliest days of the Occupation, there was a world of difference. Incredibly, when he tested them against his memory of her, he could believe both of them.

Soon after he had first met her, Ariane had invited him to Normandy where her father had an estate. In accepting he had assumed it was a shooting party. The house was enormous; there was room for dozens, but no other guests appeared; even her father was absent. They went out together with their guns, and she proved to be a good companion, a tireless walker and an excellent shot. She concentrated so intently on the day's sport, was so lacking in coquetry, that her manner contradicted the evidence that she had arranged everything to be alone with him. All along the initiative was hers: the lunch with the Socialist member of Parliament, now this day's shooting. However, he came to understand that her concentration was characteristic; in the evening the focus of her attention swung back to him. After dinner they sat together in the vast hall, lit only the log fire, and talked easily, as if they had been friends for years. From one moment to the next he intended to act, but the camaraderie between them held him back.

When the last log rolled forward on the bed of glowing ash, she was still taking the lead. She rose and pushed the log back into position with her shoe, remained standing looking down at the dying fire. In the silence the wood cracked and she said, 'Kiss me.' She walked into his arms and when he kissed her gently, feeling the softness of her upper lip between his, she reached up to take his head in both her hands. Very slowly her tongue ran along the edge of his lower lip where it was rimmed with a day's growth of beard. It was impossible to forget the astonishing erotic power of her eagerness and her kisses. When they drew apart, she took his hand and said, 'Let's make love now.'

He did not move. 'Do you do this often?' he asked. She understood at once the importance of the question.

'Never,' she said. He had believed her, then.

That Ariane, so erotic, so determined, seemed equally to fit the possibilities of the woman described by Madame Maniotte, and by Micheline.

He looked at his watch. The dusk was drawing in; school would be finishing and it would be a good moment to visit the school master. He must make some arrangement for Sabine before he left, for a few months until he could find a new boarding school. He would stop at Pechagrier on his way home. He took Florence's bicycle and set off once more for Lepech Perdrissou.

8

IN THE CENTRE of Lepech Perdrissou was the Place de la République. It was a very rural spot, simply a grassy space with a huge oak tree in the centre, supposedly planted for the birth of Louis XIV in 1638. Around its perimeter stood the principal buildings of the commune: the Mairie, the school, the church, the baker's, the grocer's, intermingled with cottages, their glass-paned doors opening directly onto the dusty road. The playground was empty and Theo could see no lights in the school itself. He rang the bell of the schoolmaster's apartment above the classrooms. No reply. He walked into the square and, seeing a passer-by, asked where the teacher was.

'He'll be in his office in the Mairie,' was the reply. So he was the replacement for the old mayor, whom he'd known in the old days. He tried the door of the town hall; it was unlocked and he went in. He rapped on the counter and said, 'Is anyone there?'

From the office behind came a man Theo thought he recognised. He was of medium height, thin and wiry, with short curly grey hair. The face was younger, narrow and foxy, with grey eyes, as clear and cold as water.

'Mr Vernhes?'

'Yes.' He looked surprised, not welcoming.

'I'm Colonel de Cazalle from Bonnemort.'

'Yes?'

'I've come to see you in your capacity as schoolmaster, rather than mayor.'

Vernhes' expression was not noticeably friendlier.

'I'm only here for a very brief visit, which is why I'm calling without an appointment. I hope it isn't an inconvenient moment.'

Four years of dealing with the petty officials of powerful interest groups had taught Theo that an excess of politeness, oiling the raw vanity of such people, which cost him nothing except a slight self-disgust at how easily he did it, was always worth it.

'Very well. Come into my office. Colonel, you say. The Armistice Army?' The military of Vichy were despised by the Resistance, as were the mothballed officers who had emerged from retirement in June '44.

'Free French,' Theo said briefly. His provenance would not necessarily make Vernhes more sympathetic. The Resistance bore a grudge against the Gaullists for not supplying them with enough arms, not permitting action until the invasion and for generally not valuing their efforts.

'And you, you were active around here?'

'I founded a group of FTP and then I worked in the regional HQ.'

The Franc-Tireurs et Partisans were the communist Resistance. The communists had been driven underground in 1940 by Vichy's hostility, but orders from Stalin had forbidden them to attack the Germans. However, their experience of organising networks of self-protection had meant that when Hitler had launched Operation Barbarossa, his attack on Russia in June 1941, they were ready to act against

the Nazis. They had always been the Resistance group-
ing least susceptible to pressure from the Free French, least
influenced by reprisals by the Germans or hostility by the
local population.

The moment of recognition was simultaneous. Theo
suddenly recalled the three guerrillas who had stopped him
in September 1944 on the road to Bonnemort, the commissar
behind his table, who did not give his name. And he could
see that the other had just recalled the colonel who had then
been so impervious to hints about what had been going on
at his home. So now they knew where they were. Or thought
they did.

So this was Ariane's husband. Vernhes had been curious from
the start about the man who had brought such an exotic creature to the country. He remembered his astonishment when
he first realised what she was, like discovering a zebra in a
field of donkeys. It is shaped like a donkey, it eats and moves
like a donkey, but its stripes show clearly that it is not a donkey and does not have a donkey's nature. When he had
believed, like everyone else, that Colonel de Cazalle was dead,
he had imagined him to have been an army officer in the
classic mode, rigid and dashing, who had won her in the
drama of the war and whose attraction would have faded rapidly even if he hadn't got himself killed. After the liberation
he had heard that her husband wasn't dead after all, had
resurfaced fighting with the Free French, which had put a different perspective on him, and on his wife. All resistants were
exceptions to the norm, he thought complacently, had something that pushed them beyond acceptance of the given situation. What was it in this man? Not much that was visible. He

was older than she was; tall, but not as extravagantly so as his leader the president; with smooth, grey-black hair, a long oval face and small mouth. Even in his country clothes, he looked as if he was wearing a uniform.

Was Ariane with him in Paris? He assumed that was where she had gone to hide herself. What, he wondered maliciously, had the brave colonel thought of her shaven head? He could imagine that this man would not enquire too deeply, perfectly content not to see what he did not want to, as long as no public shame was brought on the family.

Theo was putting Vernhes into context. Micheline had said the first runaway they had sheltered at Bonnemort had been a communist.

'Was Henri Menesplier one of yours?' he asked.

'Henri? No. His group, Rainbow it was called, was part of the Secret Army. It was set up by Lucien Maniotte, whom I'm sure you knew. We worked with Henri at the end, when all the Resistance groups were united under the National Committee, but... Well, he wasn't the most competent soldier, Henri, and it was too late for him to learn. What did they call it in the trenches in the last war, gun-shy? He didn't like a shooting war, would do anything to avoid it, which may explain what happened to him. Not that he didn't do a good job with his escape routes in the early days.'

Theo took note of these comments. 'I didn't come to see you about Henri, I came about your courses at the school. I wondered whether for a few months, until the summer holidays at the latest, you would be able to teach my daughter Sabine?'

Vernhes raised his eyebrows in surprise. He moistened his lower lip. 'How old is Sabine now?'

'Ah...' Theo was calculating, for he had not the least idea. 'She must be...'

'She is approaching her fourteenth birthday,' the schoolmaster told him.

'Yes.'

'And does she want to remain here to study?'

'Yes. That is, I haven't proposed this particular plan to her, but I have no doubt that it would work for a few months, before she goes to her next school. She might have to spend the summer on some special courses to catch up. Or repeat a year. I'm concerned not to lose too much of her education because of the war.'

'Well, if you wish it and she agrees, I see no difficulty whatsoever. I have no other students at her level, but I shall have pleasure in preparing the course she should be following.'

Theo rose and shook hands. 'I'll get her to come in and agree with you when she should start. Next week, as soon as possible. Goodbye.'

'How is Madame de Cazalle?' Vernhes remained standing behind his desk.

'She is well, thank you.'

'She has recovered from her shocking experiences?' He could tell by the sudden arrest of Cazalle's movements that he had understood. 'The liberation of the region and so on, I mean.' He expected a curt reply, a swift departure. Such a man would never reveal anything more than he had just, involuntarily, shown.

Cazalle turned back and sat down again. 'You saw what happened?' he asked.

Vernhes reseated himself. He had stirred up more than he had anticipated, but he was stimulated by hostility and had always been a skilled tactician in meetings. He could cope.

'Oh yes, I was there. It didn't happen here; it was in Mont-féfoul on the Saturday after the town was liberated.'

The sense of arousal that had surged through him when the colonel took up his challenge increased as he recalled that Bacchanalian scene in the forest. He did not drink, so he was sober among the drunken crowds of men, between seventy and a hundred of them, who had liberated the cellars of Montféfoul. She was sober, too. She had been picked up when they were making arrests in the town, gathering in the collabos at the same time as seizing the wine, emptying the grocer's and the butcher's and taking anything they could lay their hands on. He couldn't pretend that he liked what had happened that day. It's never comfortable for a commander to feel that his men are out of his control, but sometimes it is better to let them have their heads, as if you were allowing it, when in reality you have no power to stop it.

He didn't approve of random sweeps for criminals. He preferred to make lists of suspects and to send his men for them very early in the morning when they would know where to find them, still in their beds. The wine he could forgive. An army has to live off the land and they had had lean times. Who was he to grudge the men a day of drinking and pleasure to celebrate their liberation of the region? Montféfoul deserved what was coming to it. Its mayor, Chenu, had been an ardent Pétainist to the end, who hadn't even had the sense to resign and let the Resistance get on with the job. He had tried to keep the French Milice in the town even after the Germans withdrew, but they knew what would happen and retreated with their masters.

They began with the mayor. Vernhes had tried to retain some semblance of order; in any case he liked the trial to take as long as possible, that was the pleasure. He called for the indictment, but accusations were shouted from all sides and no examination was possible, as cries for the sentence took over at once: 'Death. Death. Death.' The mayor was taken for execution immediately, although it took a number of bullets to kill him. He was followed in quick succession by three more: the grocer, a captured paramilitary from the Milice and a peasant accused of black marketeering who had refused supplies to the Maquis.

They lost interest in the male prisoners after that, since someone pointed out that they needed to keep some of them to dig the graves. Vernhes was glad. He wanted to make a proper court, to conduct it in a proper revolutionary manner, to watch his victims suffer. So they turned their attentions to the women.

Ariane was the first. When he saw her being dragged across the clearing, he felt real shock and regret; he would have liked it done in a different manner, lingeringly, not hastily, thoughtlessly. She was wearing a cotton dress and sandals, her legs bare and her hair hanging down to her shoulders. She looked afraid, as well she might. Whatever they wanted these men were going to get, in the mood they were in. Nothing could stop them, and both he and she knew that a beating, a gang-rape, a noose or all three could be her fate in the next hour.

He had given the lead, to try to protect her, taking a handful of her hair, forcing her to her knees.

'This is what they do with the women, lads. Anyone with scissors, a knife? They cut their hair off, shear them like the sheep they are.'

Someone thrust an aged hunting knife with a honed blade into his hand; he sawed at her thick, dark hair. The idea took off: someone produced a pair of scissors, a cut-throat razor. Three men were working at her now. One was pulling her head back while the other two with drunken concentration rasped the blades across her scalp. They wielded the knives with a clumsy skill that might at any moment have veered into an accidental slashing of cheek or ear, or into something more. With her head thrown back her throat was exposed from jawbone to clavicle: a single stroke and she would have been dead. The three barbers went on with their scraping, Ariane's hair falling in thick clumps onto the grass.

They were all watching, the whole band, swigging wine from bottles passed from hand to hand, focusing on the scene with the quiet at its centre. For no one spoke and she did not cry out. For all of them the chief interest was to inflict shame on an aristo. As long as it went on she was safe, but he could not guess what would come after the humiliation was over. In the event, she was saved by the next victim, the girlfriend of a paramilitary, who offered better sport. She shattered the silence with her shrieks. Her ripped clothes revealed spilling breasts, which she nursed in her folded arms. Taunts and laughter broke out again.

Vernhes hustled Ariane away. Her skirt was torn to the waist and the bodice hung down in tatters from the belt. She made no attempt to hold up a shred over her nakedness. He was grasping her by the upper arm as if she was under arrest, but when they had passed the first thicket he released her.

'Go,' he hissed. 'Just get going, now.'

'Not a nice story,' he said.

Even sharply censored for Cazalle's ears, it wasn't pleasant. But he didn't mean it to be. No mention of the shootings, of course, or of the rapes. Cazalle's head was bent. His face bore no expression.

'I did my best for her. I don't know whether you've ever seen men in that state, but it's not easy to deal with them. It's the mob.'

Cazalle was getting up once again.

'I'm sorry,' Vernhes said. He wasn't, of course. He had enjoyed it.

'No. I wanted to hear it. Thank you for telling me.'

It was dark outside and Theo cycled cautiously out of the village in the direction of the little farm called Pechagrier to visit the Russian. Vernhes had given no indication of why his men should have seized Ariane. He implied that he had tried to protect her. Because he had thought her innocent, or because he thought her guilty but did not want to say so to her husband?

At the turning for Pechagrier he dismounted and searched the hillside for a light. The house was dark and lifeless. The Russian was his best hope of discovering what had happened to Henri. He had, perhaps, been with him on the last day and would be able to give a first-hand account of his capture. Although all the shutters were closed, he refused to give up, pushing his bike up to the door to knock loudly. Finally, the silence of the house convinced him there was no one there to answer his questions. He turned away and continued his journey back to Bonnemort.

9

'DID FLORENCE HAVE any luck?' Theo asked as they sat down at the table that evening.

'Wait and see. Everything in its time.' Micheline was putting the tureen on the table, while the aunts were already breaking their bread into their bowls. Micheline spooned thick brown soup on top of it.

'Chestnut soup. What haven't I done with chestnuts these last years—bread, soup, cakes. Sabine gathered the chestnuts at Toussaint, didn't you, Sabine?

The child made no reply, pretending to sip from an empty spoon.

'I went to see the schoolmaster this afternoon,' Theo told them. He savoured the curiously dry texture of the chestnuts and allowed Micheline to give him another helping. All his riding of horses and bicycles had sharpened his appetite. The reaction to his remark was more emphatic than he had expected. Micheline underlined it by dropping the ladle in the sink. Florence jumped up to help her mother. Both the aunts put down their spoons. Only Sabine continued her pretence of eating.

'Mr Vernhes?' said Aunt Odette.

'For what purpose?' asked Aunt Marguerite, a step ahead of her sister-in-law.

'To arrange for him to teach Sabine, of course.' Theo looked around in surprise.

'Ah.' The aunts took up their spoons again simultaneously.

'I thought I explained to you yesterday,' Aunt Marguerite said reproachfully, 'that Ariane did not think him suitable for Sabine. That's why she took her away.'

Theo was used to controlling his irritation at human inconsistency. 'You said yesterday that something had to be done about Sabine's schooling. She doesn't want to go back to the convent. You don't want to go on teaching her at home. The only reasonable answer is the village school until I can arrange an alternative.'

Aunt Odette's lips were set. 'We're talking about a few months, I presume. Marguerite and I can continue for that period.'

'Why are you opposed to Mr Vernhes?'

'Ariane would not approve of this solution,' Aunt Marguerite said firmly, as if that settled the matter. Micheline and Florence were busy at the stove, taking no part.

'It wouldn't be suitable.' Aunt Odette's reply was equally definite. 'He is after all a communist.'

'I can't imagine that Ariane held that against him. She has plenty of friends who are communists.' He found it galling to have Ariane cited as an authority.

'It wasn't that,' Aunt Marguerite said. 'It was much worse.'

'Yes?'

'He beats the children.'

When Marguerite de Cazalle was growing up, it was an axiom that whoever loves, chastises. So when Ariane had announced one evening that she was removing Sabine from the school because the schoolmaster had given the child a beating, she had said, 'Are you sure you're not overreacting, my dear? I don't know what misdeed Sabine is supposed to have committed, but punishment is *sometimes* necessary. Don't you agree, Odette?'

'Certainly.'

'I'm afraid I'm not going to change my mind. I don't approve of hitting children in any circumstances...'

'You are a utopian, my dear Ariane. I am sure you don't approve of the death penalty or war or anything else which, although violent and disagreeable, happens to be necessary.'

'I don't, but I wouldn't object if it were just a question of the odd rap on the back of the hand, but this is out of all proportion. I'll show you.'

When Sabine was summoned, Marguerite de Cazalle had to admit that it was not a pretty sight. The child submitted while her stepmother lifted her skirt to show the backs of her thighs, striped with blows. The switch used had been sharp and flexible enough to break the skin, so the whole extent of her upper legs was not just bruised but marked in blood.

As Ariane dropped Sabine's skirt Aunt Odette said doubtfully, 'Should we write and protest? He wouldn't dare do it again.'

'No,' Ariane said forcefully. 'She's leaving. That's that.'

The conversation broke up in a flurry of activity. Sabine was removing the bowls and spoons; Florence was laying out the plates. Micheline put the omelette, filled with black shavings of truffle, in the centre of the table and the erotic scent of the fungus, faint yet pervasive, filled the air.

'Florence, where did you find it?'

'Up the hill.' She was cutting the omelette into six.

'You have to have lived in Paris or London to appreciate this.'

'We don't get this every day.'

Micheline relaxed, became more like her old self when her food was praised.

'I'll let you take something back to Paris, Monsieur Theo, if you're really so badly off there.'

'We feed like animals; we have to eat swedes.'

'Swedes?' said Micheline doubtfully suspecting a joke. 'How can anyone eat swedes? Eating chestnuts is bad enough. It's what they used to eat here in the famine years. But even then they never ate swedes. How are they served?'

'They're cut into delicate slices, fried in a mixture of oil and butter, only the best unsalted butter, and served with a spoonful of caviar as a garnish.'

'Well, now I know you're joking.'

'I'm not, I assure you. They're pureed like potatoes.'

'Do you remember all that food Madame Ariane took to give to the police chief in Racinès?' Sabine said suddenly. She had picked all the black shreds out of her omelette and was dividing her food into two piles, egg and truffle.

Theo put down his fork. Florence was laughing.

'She wore her best suit and it didn't fit. We had to work very hard at her décolleté.' She saw Theo's face and stopped.

'Even if we eat badly, the Germans are eating worse.'

'How do you know that, Sabine?'

'Madame Ariane told us. She learned it from the officers when they ate dinner together.'

'She used to dine with the German officers?' Theo asked. There was a silence, as if they had not intended him to have this piece of information.

'The stories from the eastern front were unbelievable, according to what she heard,' Madame de Cazalle said, not answering him directly. 'One couldn't understand how they could endure such hardships.'

'Well, that's good to hear,' said Theo. The women looked startled, as if sympathy was due to anyone, whatever their nationality, who was forced to eat badly.

'Ariane heard a lot, as she sat there,' Aunt Odette remarked. 'But she refused to eat with them.'

After dinner, Theo once again sat with the aunts in the library. Sabine came in to receive a goodnight kiss from each of them.

'So Sabine.' Theo would not normally have thought of letting the child decide her own future, especially after her outburst yesterday, but he could see no other way out of the impasse. 'What do you think of going to study with Mr Vernhes?'

She didn't look at him. 'Whatever you think is best, Papa.'

Theo frowned. It had begun to dawn on him that his daughter was clever, subtle, manipulative.

Aunt Marguerite, less devious, said, 'Don't do it, Theo. She can stay with us.'

He sighed. 'I'll think about it. I wanted to relieve you of the burden of teaching.'

Wrapping themselves in their shawls against the cold of the corridors, the aunts set off to their rooms. Theo poured himself a brandy and wandered round peering at the book shelves. He had learned some facts today: about how Henri died, how Ariane's head was shaved, but beyond this outline nothing was clear. Each account contradicted the previous one. Was Henri betrayed, afraid, or incompetent? Ariane, resistant or collaborator? And the SS major, her putative lover, and his murder were as indistinct as ever.

Suddenly he recognised a box wedged onto one of the bookshelves, one of the family treasures. He took it down and the casket revealed a parcel swathed in worn blue velvet. Unwrapping it, he was ten years old again, standing in that same room with his father, on leave from Algeria. His father's brown fingers with dark silky hair on the back of his hands were sliding back the clasp and opening wide the pages.

'It's a Book of Hours,' he was explaining. 'The calendar of prayers is illustrated. Look.'

Theo was already searching for the atlas where the aunts kept the magnifying glass that his father had handed to him. He placed the glass in position under the lamp; the tiny pictures sprang out as they had done for him as a child.

In winter a little town with its church and castle on a hill lay under light snow. Smoke rose into the cerulean blue. Hunters' footsteps marked their track and birds flew up from the bare trees. It was Lepech Perdrissou. In autumn peasants and pigs rootled under the golden trees. From a tower a lady was setting out on horseback, dogs running behind. It was Bonnemort. The detail and realism were extraordinary. The courtly elegance of the painting, depicting an ideal world, contrasted with the factual illustration of the pigs' hairy backs, the dog scratching its ear.

This, he realised, was what he had carried around in his mind for four years of exile. His pleasure at the memory of his father, at the beauty of the object, was also the moment of recognition of his own folly. He had carried Bonnemort wrapped in his imagination, believing it to be sealed away, like the book in its velvet-lined box.

He turned a page. The anonymous painter was a more ruthless realist than he was. He remembered his father's finger pointing to the troop of armed men marching out of the castle in the spring. He was indicating the minutely exact weapons: lances, halberds, crossbows. An injured soldier lying on the brilliant grass was trying to contain a writhing snakes' nest of intestines spilling from his belly. And the chatelaine, if he turned another page, would she be welcoming the enemy into the surrendered castle? It was easy to transpose the excitement of his and Ariane's time together before the war to his nightmares of her passion for the German officer.

One memory came back so intensely that he groaned as he imagined the scene replayed here at Bonnemort, his own role taken by the invader.

He could no longer recall where the original drama had taken place, because the central incident was so vivid. Whether at her father's house, at the opera, at a dinner, it was somewhere public, dangerous. He had just returned to Paris from his unit. In some small antechamber or corridor they had embraced passionately. Through the layers of his evening clothes, he had felt her hands pressing on the small of his back, then, with dexterity, manoeuvring between them, opening his buttons. He gasped as he felt her cool fingers on his flesh, pulling him out. When she dropped to the floor, he reached down to her.

'Ariane, this is madness, Ariane...'

The thought of what would happen in a Paris salon in the aftermath of being discovered being fellated by a woman whose long silk skirts were spread in a pool around his feet occurred to him only briefly before he reached the point of no return. It must have been at a dinner, rather a grand one. He recalled that later in the evening he had met her eye across the table, an exchange of glances full of complicity and amusement. A feeling he had never before experienced overcame him then, compounded of desire, admiration, attachment; he did not know what to call it. At that moment he thought that her strong face, with its heavily marked eyebrows, was the most beautiful he had ever known.

He folded the Book of Hours back into its velvet-lined box. He might one day take it out to show to Sabine.

10

THE NEXT DAY, his last, began with a visit to the Gendarmerie in Lepech Perdrissou. He was looking for Officer Paul Petignat, who had been sent up to Bonnemort to break the news of Henri's death. He turned out to be a young man, in his late twenties, with a strong country accent. He must have been recruited before the war, a local boy who achieved the peasant dream of a government job. He was wary, but eager to please when Theo explained who he was. He was obviously glad that the questioning turned not on his own actions during the Occupation, but on the murdered German at Bonnemort. He was still defensive, thinking he had to answer the charge that proper procedures had not been followed.

No, he said, there had been no enquiry, no examining magistrate had opened a file. He had simply written his report and that had been that. There had been too much going on at the time to worry about a dead German. Usually they looked after their own dead, but this time no Germans were left. And it was a war death, a Resistance killing, so all that was required was a note of the name and number of the victim, time and place; nothing more could be done in the circumstances.

Nothing, Theo agreed. The question was, was it really a Resistance killing? The victim's throat had been cut, he had been stripped of his clothes. Was that the sort of thing they did, the Resistance?

Petignat looked uneasy. His eyes were fixed on his boots, although he darted frequent, nervous glances at Theo.

'Strange things happened then. I don't want to say anything against the Resistance, of course, but… Well, it was war. Not like your war, maybe, but it was still war. And once the Germans had gone, it was time for settling scores. There were Resistance tribunals that shot people or tortured them, raped the women, cut their hair off, terrible things. Thank God, it's calmed down now, but if you were in the Gendarmerie or the Police, you were at risk. If anyone denounced you… It wasn't as if we were the Milice. Here in Lepech we came to an understanding with the Resistance early on, in spite of the mayor who had no time for the Maquis at all. Henri Menesplier was a good bloke. He didn't want confrontation, so he used to let us know what was happening and in return we closed an eye, let him have a few litres of petrol when he needed it. But a mate of mine was taken to a château near Racinès and tortured, beaten, by fellow Frenchmen from the Resistance, just because he transferred into the Milice to see some action. He still can't walk, both legs broken.' He stopped, breathing rapidly. Theo could see a dew of sweat on his forehead.

Such stories were not new. Theo did not want to go into them now. 'The German officer…' he said gently. 'How does all this fit in with what happened to him?'

'What I'm trying to say is that there were all sorts in the Resistance. There were stories of captured Germans with their balls cut off and stuffed in their mouths, or their tongues cut out. It's my theory the major was caught by a Resistance group who had suffered under him. Maybe Group Rainbow. After all, that guy had shot Henri and hanged six others that evening. Mr Nikola, the

Russian at Pechagrier, was Henri's lieutenant. If he was willing, he might be able to tell you a thing or two about what went on.'

'Was he there?'

'When Henri was taken prisoner? I couldn't say. He was in Lepech in the afternoon when the Germans attacked. His voice is unmistakable; I heard him shouting to his men in the streets.'

'And had the German been tortured?'

'No,' Petignat said. 'I didn't mean that. I meant that such terrible things did happen that this wasn't such a big deal. So they cut his throat. Perhaps they'd run out of ammunition, who knows? They'd hit him a blow.

'They'd hit on his forehead, plumb in the middle. You wonder how they got him like that, why he didn't see it coming. His ankles had been strapped together to drag him along. There were score marks all down his back.'

'And why was he left where he was, do you think? Had they been disturbed and abandoned him?'

'Oh, no. It was deliberate. He was…arranged.'

'So, why there?'

'It was defiance, I think. You know, that place was the German HQ. They were saying, nowhere's safe for you.'

'But the Germans had gone.'

'But no one knew that until that morning.'

'And what would have happened if the Germans had still been there?'

'Oh, God, reprisals. It would have been a bloodbath.'

'Talking of bloodbaths, where was he killed? There would have been a hell of a lot of blood after a throat-cutting.'

'I don't know. It could have been anywhere in the forests. They must have caught him on the road and killed him. Then they could have taken him there in a lorry. Who knows?'

'You didn't search the house and grounds to find the place of death?'

Petignat looked surprised. 'No, I didn't. I thought that if they had found a sea of blood somewhere, they would have told me, Micheline and Madame de Cazalle. That's why I thought it must have been done elsewhere and that he was taken there.'

It was hard to describe what it was like to someone who wasn't there. And the colonel hadn't been in France during the Occupation, he couldn't understand anything. The first thing to realise was how what was right and wrong changed. In 1940 there was no question; to follow the Marshal was the right thing to do, no one doubted it, so a gendarme's job was clear. But bit by bit, in ways you didn't notice at the time, things went downhill so that by '44 the Germans were demanding things that a good Frenchman couldn't support, like sending the forced labourers to Germany, for example. People started acting against the government, until at the final stage in June, July, it was outright anarchy, and what was a loyal man to do? The only thing was to try to keep order.

That night, the one the colonel wanted to talk about, 17 August, it was. It was impossible to describe what they'd all been through in the village. In the afternoon the Resistance had entered Lepech. Henri had told the gendarmes what to expect and they had been lying low, pretending not to see or hear what was going on. So when the Germans turned up unexpectedly, they'd treated the gendarmes as enemies, like the rest of the town. He'd often thanked God since then that the Germans hadn't called on them, the gendarmes, to help. That had saved them the next day, the Saturday, when the Germans had gone and the Maquis took over and went mad in Montféfoul. They'd left Lepech alone, even though Gargaud, the mayor, was Pétainist, because of the terrible things that had happened there.

At first light the next morning they had crept out of their houses to find the Germans gone and the corpses of the seven dead Resistance fighters to be dealt with. Henri was lying in the square where he had been shot; Pierre and the others, their feet dangling only half a metre from the ground, hanging from the oak tree. The villagers had left them there the night before when they had finished burying the German dead in the cemetery, thankfully accepting a curfew as the worst that was to happen for the time being. Many of them, wakeful in their beds, had heard the sounds of vehicles moving in the darkness and when day came their hopes were confirmed. The German troops and the French Milice had gone.

In the square the mayor was busy with the removal of the bodies to the church. In the Gendarmerie, when the phone rang and Petignat heard the voice of Henri's daughter, it came to him that, out there at Bonnemort, they didn't know what had happened. So he didn't wait to discover what she wanted, half-hysterical as she sounded. He rushed out to find the mayor to tell him he had to go up there and break the news. But Gargaud rubbed his neck and said in that tentative way which meant that his mind was completely made up, 'You know, we've never got on, them and me. Why don't you go and see what's up. You can tell them about Henri while you're about it.'

Even before he arrived at Bonnemort he'd found seven men dead, lying bizarrely neatly arranged beside the track. They were men from Henri's group, he reckoned, and this must have been where the firefight took place, where the five Germans had been killed, which had made the SS major so mad with rage that he'd executed his prisoners. Who had laid the bodies out like that, he wondered. Their companions from Group Rainbow who had escaped and then returned to the scene of battle? The major had probably turned straight round with Henri and his other captives, taking them back to Lepech Perdrissou to hang them in front of the whole population as a warning.

A little further on he came across a German staff car, all shot up, and recognised Philippe Boysse from St Saud lying dead, handcuffed to the steering wheel. The SS must have taken him prisoner in Lepech during the afternoon clash and had been bringing him back to Bonnemort to question him. Perhaps Henri was making a rescue attempt when he himself was captured. This made sense, but why was Philippe driving the German car? He couldn't make that out.

He counted up the deaths: five resistants had been killed in the afternoon in the village, then seven from Group Rainbow here and Boysse too, then Henri and six others executed in the square last night, not to mention the five German soldiers that they'd had to bury. What more was to come?

He found that out soon enough when he reached Bonnemort.

First there was this guy, naked as the day he was born, lying face down on the flagstones of the courtyard. Then women everywhere, Micheline and Florence, weeping in terror, Madame de Cazalle, with a face as calm as stone, two kids, the two old ladies, one on sticks, standing in a doorway inside the house. They were terrified. Understandable; so was he, after what had happened last night.

Micheline kept repeating hysterically, 'They'll come to shoot us, they'll line us up and shoot us.'

Florence said, 'We wanted to hide it, but we didn't... We couldn't... You must protect us. Where can we go?'

'When did you find him?' They were all standing well back from the body, as if it might be mined.

'Just now, this morning, two hours ago, when we got up.'

'Who is it?'

He began to move forward and he could feel Micheline and Florence following immediately behind him. When he bent down and turned the body over, he understood their terror.

The cutting of the throat had drained a huge quantity of blood out of the carcass, which was glacially white. The face was a darker colour, tanned by the weather, and was no longer in normal relation to the body. It flipped back like a lid on a hinge, exposing the severed carotid artery, out of which life had flowed. The cut, although long, had not been deep; the trachea was only partially severed. He had been hit on the forehead, which must have stunned him. The cropped dark hair was stiff with congealed blood. None of this could disguise the victim's identity. Petignat had watched him the previous afternoon pinning a white piece of cloth to Henri Menesplier's chest, as if awarding him a medal, and then stepping back to say so quietly that it was barely audible, 'Fire.'

He looked carefully at the body. A fine man. The skin which had always been hidden by his uniform had a silky sheen. His chest was hairless, muscular, and a scar, puckered and cartilaginous, ploughed across his abdomen on the right side. His left hand was missing and the stump was reddish, gathered inward like pursed lips. Black body hair like a diamond-shaped shield covered his lower torso from genitals to navel. He was uncircumcised. Petignat took in all these details and then, with the toe of his boot, tipped him back on his face. For decency's sake, with so many women about.

Micheline and Florence were standing immediately behind him; their sobbing had ceased. They had been inventorying the dead man with him. He turned and walked them away from the body.

'And the rest of them?' he asked.

'They left during the night. They didn't sleep here.' This was Madame de Cazalle speaking. 'They seem to have gone definitively. They've taken everything.'

'It's the same down below, in the village. The Milice have gone too. They're on the run.'

'No reprisals,' said Florence. 'They've gone for good.'

'Ah, let's hope so,' said Petignat. He looked round help-lessly. He was feeling distinctly ill. He'd had nothing to eat yet and he had seen enough death to make you heave.

'You need a drink,' Madame de Cazalle said. 'Let us give you something, a glass of brandy.'

They'd walked through to the farmyard, leaving the body where it was. He noticed that the linen boiler was already lit, and steam was seeping out at the edge of the lid. They must have been up early to do the laundry and then found that thing in the courtyard.

So he had to do it. Dealing with the body was nothing, it was no more than a pig's carcass to be carted away. But telling the women about Henri, telling Micheline that her husband had been shot by this very guy, that was worse than anything he'd ever had to do.

They'd sat in Micheline's kitchen, and it was as if the social order was inverted. Micheline and Florence sat down. Madame de Cazalle poured him some brandy. The old girls had disappeared. He told them, straight out, what had happened yesterday. They wouldn't believe him at first. They made him repeat it, begin at the beginning, but where was that? The beginning for him was when the Germans burst into the Gendarmerie and he was herded into the square with the rest of the men. That's when he'd seen Henri, but it wasn't the beginning for him, it was the end.

'He was already wounded,' he said, as if that might com-fort them. 'I don't know how, but they only got him because he was wounded.'

Micheline was sobbing, racking her chest. Florence's tears flowed down her cheeks, her mouth turned down like a clown's. Madame de Cazalle was the worst. She turned to the sink and retched. Nothing came. She probably hadn't eaten that morning either, what with the body and all. But she continued to try to throw her heart up until at last she spat out a gob of greenish phlegm.

Petignat had had it by then. He threw back the dregs of the brandy and left. He lugged the body away by himself, because he couldn't leave it there and he couldn't ask for help. What more could he do? That's the way it was. And he still had the eight bodies on the road to deal with.

Theo rode on to Pechagrier. It was all the more important now, he thought, to identify someone from Group Rainbow who could tell him about the events of that night from the viewpoint of the Maquis. How did their movements fit in with those of the Germans? Who were the attackers, who the attacked? He had caught glimpses of Henri's Group Rainbow in Lepech in the afternoon of 17 August, in the battle at Bonnemort in the early evening, then at their final tragic appearance in the square when Henri was shot and six others hanged. But what was the rationale behind these actions? What had they been trying to achieve? The Russian who might tell him was not to be found. A thread of smoke emerged from the chimney of his cottage and a dog barked furiously from within, but he could raise no other response to his knocks and calls. With regret, he once again abandoned his attempt and rode back to Bonnemort.

11

AFTER LUNCH, THEO took the mallet, wedge and saw and set to work on a pile of logs. Sabine obediently performed some chores for Micheline and then, pushing the wheelbarrow, she climbed up the hill to join her father.

'I'll take them down and stack them,' she volunteered.

Theo paused to wipe his brow with his forearm. 'Can you manage?'

'I carried heavier loads than this when we had the pig-killing,' said Sabine. She stacked the first load and trundled down the path with it.

'You didn't like the village school,' Theo remarked when she returned. 'How long were you there?'

'Two years, until Suzie came. I didn't mind it. I mean, it wasn't like the convent, but it was all right.'

Theo found these unemphatic opinions hard to interpret.

'He was a tough teacher, was he, Mr Vernhes? Was he any good?'

'Yes, he was good. He made us all learn. Even the boys. Everyone was frightened of him'

'He used to thrash them, did he?'

For Sabine her father was an unknown quantity. Even before his wartime absence, when she was at the convent, she had rarely seen him. She had idealised both her parents when she had thought they were dead; now that her father had been resurrected, he did not live up to her imagination's construction. Madame Ariane, as much as she detested her, understood what was said to her. In fact, it was a fault in her that she was so quick that little escaped her eye. Papa, she now realised, for all that he was so important according to the aunts, understood nothing. He had obviously interpreted Aunt Marguerite's remarks about Vernhes' beating the children as meaning that he beat the other children. It had simply never entered his head that the schoolmaster had beaten her. It was inconceivable to him. So what could one say to someone who understood nothing at all?

It was true that the village school had been all right. She had found it alarming at the beginning, especially the presence of boys. The big ones now stayed until they were fourteen. This improvement had been brought in by the Popular Front, she had been told, although the boys themselves, eager to get a man's job, or needed on the farms, complained of the waste of their time. In the playground, as a newcomer, she was subject to some rough treatment at first. But she was so submissive that interest in tormenting her soon ceased. As she put on no airs and made no claims for herself, she was soon left alone. She had no friends.

Vernhes was another matter. He concentrated on the top class and she did not immediately encounter him. But she heard of his fearsome reputation, which kept the tyrants of the playground unmoving in their seats while he lectured them.

They even liked him for it. He was 'a good one', she heard. He stood for no cheek and belted anyone who sauced him. When they at last came face to face they recognised one another at once. A bully, as her experiences with Antoinette and Sister Barbe had taught her, always knows a victim. And she felt the same trembling pleasure of being selected which she used to feel when Sister Barbe's eyes rested on her in a thoughtful way.

Vernhes had been taking two classes at once, for history, for which subject he would dictate the topic for the week and check their exercise books for spelling errors. This was his republican method of dealing with the Vichy curriculum, her stepmother had commented, not unsympathetically, when Sabine had complained of the boredom of it. Sabine wrote swiftly and then watched him as he repeated the phrase and waited for the slower pupils, their tongues projecting from between their lips, their pens grasped tightly in their fists, to finish. He read on, but she did not hear. He stood above them very upright, as still as a hovering buzzard, his eyes grey behind his steel-rimmed spectacles. He caught her eye and held her gaze.

'What was the last phrase, Sabine?' he asked gently. She jumped, looking hastily at her copy.

'…led to defeat, full stop,' she read from the bottom of the page.

He moved forward menacingly. 'What have you been doing that you have been so left behind? Marie-José, please repeat, so that Sabine can catch up with us. Sabine, wait behind at the end of the afternoon for your punishment.'

'Do you miss your friend?' Theo asked. He searched for the child's name. 'Suzie. It must have been nice having a companion.'

'No,' said Sabine, decidedly. 'I liked it when she was here, but she taught me bad things.' She was looking away from him, at the rooftops below them. 'I'm glad she's gone.'

Theo raised the mallet and struck the wedge, driving it deeper into the circle of wood. 'I'm surprised. I thought you were supposed to be good friends.'

'We were. But things happen to change your mind. Anyway, she's Jewish.'

The cylinder of tree trunk that he was working on suddenly sprang apart, and the metal wedge flew out. 'Watch it. Stand back.'

'She was Jewish, was she?' he said, half to himself. He wondered why he had not guessed at once when he heard Pascal Wolff's story.

Sabine bent to gather up the split logs.

'Did you know she was Jewish?' her father asked her. 'She was in hiding, was she?'

Sabine hesitated. 'We all knew, in the end, after the Germans had gone. Your wife told us.'

He ignored the rudeness of her reference to Ariane. She kicked the log pile, stubbing her boot against it repeatedly. 'The sisters used to say that the Jews were the killers of Christ and we must pray for their conversion. And Sister Barbe once told me...'

Theo tapped the wedge into the next log, gently at first. He supposed that his marriage to Ariane must have affected his views more than he realised. He was surprised how shocked he was to hear what his daughter was saying. Yet it was no more than he had been accustomed to accepting, articulated less childishly, in remarks made by fellow officers. He remembered at their second meeting, at the lunch for her friend the Socialist member of Parliament, Ariane had been lighting a cigarette, jutting her chin forward to meet the proffered light and saying, 'We Dreyfusards...' And he recognised then that he had deserted his own kind, who could never admit that Dreyfus was other than a traitor simply because he was a Jew.

'What difference did it make, that she's Jewish?' he asked. 'She was a nice little girl. You liked her. She was your friend.'

'No, she wasn't. She didn't like Lou Moussou.'

'Lou?'

'The pig, the pig, Papa. There must have been Lou Moussou when you were a little boy. There's always Lou Moussou here. Lou Moussou was a secret pig, hidden from the Requisition, and when we had to kill him, she was pleased. I cried and cried. Jews don't like pigs.'

Theo did not know how to reason with this sort of thing. 'You must remember that not everyone is as besotted about animals as you are,' he said impatiently.

It had begun to rain as they loaded the last split logs onto the barrow and retreated to the house. In the library with the aunts, Sabine brought out a large board supporting a skeleton jigsaw. She dumped the aunts' atlas on the floor and placed it on the table.

'Will you help me?' she asked her father. Theo would rather have sat watching the flames, doing nothing, but he was playing his paternal role today, so he sat down beside her. The border was complete and a section on the right had been built to show a pattern of leaves and tendrils.

'What is it?' he asked. 'Isn't there a picture?'

'There is.' Sabine was already bending over the board, moving pieces with the tips of her fingers. 'But you're not allowed to look.'

'Hmh. I always use a picture. I can't even guess what this is.'

'It makes it more interesting.'

That night after dinner Theo stayed by the fire to drink his brandy when the women had gone to bed. A tap on the door interrupted his thoughts. Florence entered.

'I came to see if you needed more logs.'

'No, you didn't. Come here.'

She stood in front of the fire; he took her hand. 'So you are to be married. Who is this Claude?'

'His parents have a farm in Quercy; it's called Les Lunes Hautes.'

'And how did you meet?'

'He came here to the Maquis.'

'Running from the compulsory labour service?'

'No, he's older than that. He'd got into a fight with the Milice, so he just left home.'

'Sit down. Tell me, you knew what your father was doing?'

She sat opposite him, leaning forward, her elbows on her knees, her face highlighted by the fire. 'Not at first. Not until two years ago when Georges was arrested and Roger went into the Maquis.'

'He was enormously brave, your father. Your mother, too.'

'Mum never thought of the risks. She just did whatever was necessary for Dad. And she can't help helping people. When the Germans were here, she'd dress a cut or a blister for them, just as if they were the Resistance.'

'Tell me about Henri's group.'

'It was called Group Rainbow, that was Madame Ariane's name for them. Last year there were about forty young ones escaping from compulsory labour service and then another dozen or so older men who had gone underground for one reason or another. Mr Nikola, the Russian, gave them training with guns. He'd been a soldier fighting against the Bolsheviks. Not that we could practise, because we had hardly any ammunition, but at least we could handle them.'

'You too?'

'Yes, even me. I can dismantle a Bren with the best of them.'

'But you were legal, not in hiding. What were you doing?'

'Messages, mostly, by bike. Things got very bad here once the Germans came. It was very risky. I used to ride miles, me one night and Madame the next. There was a curfew, but in the darkness you could always hear them coming. And the little roads were in our hands. They didn't dare use them.'

He hoped she would go on. He couldn't bring himself to ask her directly about Ariane, he could only hope that she would say something more. Instead, she rose and said, 'So, goodnight.'

He saw his last chance and stood up too, putting his arms around her shoulders. 'What happened here?' he asked urgently. 'I need you to tell me. No one else will.'

She turned away. 'You mean Madame?' she asked evasively. 'No one will ever say. You can ask anyone you like and no one will tell you. I don't know, I wasn't there. I didn't see; I didn't ask. But I think I know why.'

'Yes?' he prompted her, drawing her down again beside the fire.

They'd been out together one afternoon in late June, she and Madame Ariane, a few weeks after the Germans had arrived, and were returning home. It had been a hot day; they still had a long way to go, at least fifteen kilometres, when the chain of her bicycle slipped off. She put her bike in the grass and the two of them were working on it when they heard the sound of vehicles, big ones. They looked at one another and Madame had closed her eyes and sighed. Florence knew how she felt. She was tired and couldn't be bothered to take the bikes into the forest to wait for them to pass. They had nothing to hide on them, so they'd take no notice.

Two German vehicles, one a car and the other a truck with soldiers in the back, passed them and stopped. As soon as they saw the car, they knew who it was. The major had commandeered Madame Ariane's own car, the Hispano-Suiza that she had arrived in at the beginning of the war, and he drove around the countryside in it. That didn't do Madame any good.

The lieutenant, the one with the eyepatch, jumped down from the truck and came towards them, speaking in German, smiling, friendly. He was gesturing towards the lorry and she could guess that he was offering them a lift home. Madame did not smile. She stood up and replied in German, shaking her head, bowing a little. He was insisting; she was refusing. He shouted to the soldiers in the truck and two young lads climbed down, seized the bikes and loaded them into the back.

Madame was furious. She walked away along the road. Florence ran after her. The vehicles came slowly behind them, stopped again and more or less forced them in, her into the cab of the truck, Madame into the car, also in the front, between the driver and the officer. Florence wasn't fussed; she was glad of the lift home. Then she saw the way they were going. They didn't take the little road that cuts directly to the crossroads by the Bonnemort track, they were going round through the village.

She said to the driver, with gestures, 'Turn there, it's quicker.'

He had shrugged and pointed to the car leading the way. When they came to the village, she knew what to do. She put her head down between her knees, so that no one could see her. In the truck they just laughed and the sergeant put his elbow on her back, as if she were an armrest. She could see how, if you let yourself talk to them, you could quite soon be laughing and joking with them, like with any group of lads.

In the car in front Madame hadn't flinched. She just sat upright, seen by everyone, riding in her own car with the German officer. When they arrived home, she didn't speak to the major, but she was angry with the lieutenant. Florence didn't understand what she was saying, of course, but she could see that he wasn't annoyed. He replied to her and all the soldiers laughed, as they unloaded their bikes.

'So I'm sure it wasn't what you think.'

'What do you think I think?'

'You think what all men think, what the men who did that terrible thing to her thought. They jumped to wrong conclusions.'

'And your father?' he asked, stroking her hair. 'What happened to him?'

She had relaxed against him. Now he felt her shoulders become rigid beneath his arm and the muscles in her thigh lying alongside his tensed. She got up again, smoothing her hair.

'There was a gun battle on the track. And he was shot in the village square, as Mum told you. But there's more to it than that. It was an ambush. But who ambushed whom? Was it the Resistance ambushing the Germans or the Germans the Resistance? I've asked, but no one will ever tell you. He was betrayed, I'm sure.' He could see the runnel of a tear slide down her cheek. 'I'd like to know who did it. We got the German, but not the French, the ones who betrayed him.'

She turned away. 'Goodnight.'

When she had gone, Theo leaned back in his chair and closed his eyes with an enormous sense of release. He observed the irony of receiving reassurance from an old lover about the fidelity of his wife. Florence's word carried weight. She was devoted to Ariane; the whole household was, except, of course, his daughter. Surely the aunts, Micheline, Florence would not have remained so loyal to her if she really had been the lover of the SS officer, something that could not have been hidden inside the household. And, another irony: Sabine, who detested her stepmother, had added to the evidence to vindicate her, by revealing that Suzie, the child they had sheltered, was Jewish. This was the explanation he had been waiting for.

12

THE CASE AGAINST Ariane was closed. Theo had now convinced himself of her innocence and was determined to see her as soon as possible. The fact that she was reluctant to meet him filled him with urgency, afraid it would soon be too late to put right what had gone so hideously wrong. The unreality of exile had distorted his expectations. After seven months back in France he had come to understand something of the strange life of the Occupation. Ariane's conduct in that grey world had been beyond reproach, he saw that now. The head-shaving had been an act of drunken violence in the aftermath of liberation by men who had known nothing of her Resistance activities. Their suspicion of someone, especially an outsider, who had quartered the SS for two months, had combined with peasant resentment to produce an unjust act. He had compounded the injustice by his instinctive recoil.

His obsession with Ariane's guilt had distracted him from the question of Henri. Were the hints of betrayal, which he had heard from Florence, from Madame Maniotte, justified? He regretted that he had not been able to contact the Russian, Mr Nikola, who had escaped from the ambush, to learn from him more of what had happened. He would ask

Ariane; she would know. This was his task now, to meet Ariane, to be reconciled.

After so long a silence, he found it difficult to approach his wife and he debated for several days how best to reach her. Finally, he took one of his visiting cards and wrote on the back, *Would you agree to meet me? Thursday at seven in the Napoléon.* On the day before the time set, she replied with equal terseness. One of her visiting cards was delivered to the Ministry, with the single word, *Agreed*, scribbled on it.

He went to the meeting with guilt and unease. He had a high concept of honourable behaviour and was aware that his instinctive reaction that evening in September last year did not live up to what his better judgement called for; yet he did not know how to be humble, if that was what was necessary. He arrived early and sat watching the entrance. Parisian women still went to extraordinary lengths to achieve elegance in spite of the shortages, the rationing and all the physical difficulties of maintaining a high level of self-decoration. In London women had seemed to heave a sigh of relief that, amid all the other problems of war, they could not be expected to worry about being smart.

In spite of his concentration, he missed her entrance and only saw her when she stood before him, drawing off her gloves. They shook hands and, in their common awkwardness, hesitated, then kissed one another coldly on the cheek. She looked pale and gaunt and older. He realised that he had expected her to remain as she had been, fixed at the moment of his departure in 1940.

She had been making her own assessment. 'You've changed a lot, Theo,' she said, speaking his thought. 'You're much greyer. I suppose it's not surprising after what you've been through. And it's not unattractive.' He began at once with his prepared apology, but she cut him short. 'Don't let's mention it. I wasn't ready to see you or anyone. So really I must thank you for giving me time. And your arriving like that, unannounced, meant I never had to ask myself whether or not to tell you.'

The bar was unheated and she kept her coat on. Under her hat, an absurd turban of twisted red velvet with a cockade in front, her hair just appeared. He noticed that she had a habit of tipping her head and pulling gently at a lock on her neck, as if to encourage it to grow. If he had not made that impulsive, unannounced journey, he would never have known. Better not to have known.

'Are you going to tell me?'

'Some things I don't know and others are so horrible it's better for one's sanity to forget them. What do you want to know?'

'I want to know everything, of course. I want to know about your Resistance work. I want to know what happened to Lucien Maniotte and to Henri.'

She had been so calm until then that he was astonished when, at his mention of Henri, her eyes filled with tears.

'I want to know what happened to Henri, too.' She set her mouth and the tears did not fall. 'What did they tell you at Bonnemort?'

'Micheline said he had been executed by the Germans. Then Florence told me there was more to it than that and that I would never find out. Someone else suggested that he had been betrayed.' He did not mention Vernhes' suggestions of cowardice and incompetence.

'Ah, dear Florence is very clever.' She stretched out her arms, as if pushing something away. 'We lived in a world of half-knowledge, or false knowledge, propaganda which everyone accepted at first. And not knowing was a principle of safety. The less you knew, the less harm you could do if you were caught. I was only a very minor cog. Lucien and Henri were the important ones.'

'How did you begin?'

How had it begun? Theo's departure, without debate, to London, had been so shocking that it had called everything into question. Left to herself, she might have taken longer to reject the Marshal and the policies of Vichy. Theo had crystallised matters for her.

Settling at Bonnemort in 1939 during the phoney war had not been easy. Although the aunts had behaved with immaculate politeness to her, there had been no one with whom she had anything in common. She spent hours every day, whatever the weather, riding around the countryside, sometimes in Henri's company. He showed her the cross-country routes, the landmarks of pigeon towers, hilltops, stands of trees on the skyline, teaching her to recognise them from every direction. The knowledge had served her well later on. When they passed through remote hamlets with poetic names, where chained dogs barked savagely, men would regard them balefully, not responding to their greetings. She would shudder at the hostility she felt, age-old, its roots beyond the Revolution, in the Jacqueries of the medieval past. He had found her an ancient pair of field glasses, which weighed heavily on her chest when she slung them around her neck. They gave her endless pleasure in watching the bird life from the windows of her tower, or from the terrace in the garden.

For the first week or so after Theo left for England in 1940 she had passionately hoped she was pregnant. If she had a child, she would have a purpose however long the war lasted and a permanent link with him. When that hope bled from her, she was lost for a time. Theo had instructed her during his nocturnal visit to bring his daughter from the convent in Touraine in the occupied zone, home to Bonnemort. Although her meeting with Sabine at the wedding had not been warm, she decided that Theo's child would have to be a replacement for her own and that living together would be a new beginning for them both. Illusory hope. Sabine was implacably hostile and no effort to please or interest her met with a return of friendship. Sabine gave her the final impulse towards resistance.

They were in the salon one afternoon that autumn of 1940, looking at the view over the valley. Micheline and Florence were walking towards the house, carrying up baskets filled with walnuts that had just been harvested.

'Florence is very beautiful,' Sabine remarked.

Ariane looked out at Florence, then at Sabine, with curiosity. Nothing Sabine said to her was without motive.

'Yes,' she said, in surprise. 'You're right. She is beautiful.'

'My father always thought so, too. I saw him once kiss her neck.'

Why she should accept this story, instantly, as truth, when it was patently told only to wound, she did not know. Nor why it should matter. She had never thought that Theo had lived without women in the years since his wife had died. So why was this information important? Because she suddenly realised that she had no ties. She could resist because she was free.

A week later the letter from Bertrand Gauthier, her Marxist teacher of philosophy, arrived. In cautious language, because of the censorship, he asked for her help in arranging a quiet place where he could recuperate from a recent 'attack'. He had been dismissed from his post in the first months of the Marshal's rule, she discovered later. She wrote back at once inviting him to stay for as long as was necessary.

Theo, watching her, listening to her, felt the strength and clarity of her personality, as he had the evening they first met, when she had expounded the evils of Munich. Talking about the war, she had relaxed. He wanted to say, *Let's forget all this; let's talk about ourselves.* Instead he asked, 'What about Vernhes? Was he involved then?'

'Vernhes? You know Vernhes?' She looked alarmed.

'I've met him, yes. I was at Bonnemort last month, you know. He's the mayor of Lepech Perdrissou now.'

'Do you have a cigarette?' she asked.

He offered her one and lit it for her.

She inhaled deeply. 'Thanks. I don't smoke much now, because men resent seeing a woman consuming something that they feel they have first call on. But I need it just now.' Smoke misted his view of her face, blurring her features. 'Vernhes wasn't active then. This was in the winter of forty to forty-one and he was a good communist. He wouldn't do anything without the blessing of the Party.'

She had already met Vernhes, even before Gauthier's arrival, when she had taken a mutely furious Sabine to register for the new school year at Lepech Perdrissou. Although he kept his party membership a secret, she had recognised him even then as a class antagonist. He had categorised her before she had opened her mouth: a rich bourgeoise, a Catholic, a devotee of the Marshal. The assumptions were implicit in the way he had spoken to her. She had made no attempt to correct him and only hoped he would not be so prejudiced against Sabine as to treat her unkindly. For her own part she had felt, then, an uneasy, distasteful fascination for him. She guessed that he came from a relatively unprivileged background, where a mother had lavished hopes for the fulfilment of her own ambitions on the upbringing of her only son, who was immensely clever, without social graces and with only one sensitivity towards others: the power to recognise a victim.

Right at the beginning, when Gauthier arrived, she had had to confide in Henri and Micheline, for without them she was helpless. She told them of Gauthier's political affiliations with some trepidation, for Henri was socialist, she knew, and there was little love lost between socialists and communists. She had talked to them sitting at Micheline's kitchen table. Henri had folded his worn, brown hands in front of him on the oilcloth. Micheline sat with her hands in her pinafore pocket, looking at Henri for his reaction.

'You can't persecute someone for his opinion,' Henri said. 'Thought is free.'

Theo laughed. 'Ironic that poor Henri should decide to resist in order to fight for freedom of opinion for a communist who would have shot him down without remorse for that very belief.'

Silence fell. They remembered simultaneously how Henri had been shot down and taken prisoner, and the shadow of treachery that hung over his death. She was buttoning her coat up to her neck, preparing to leave. He wanted to hold her back, but nothing would keep her.

13

THEO WAS LEFT dissatisfied with this interview. Although he had not known what to expect, he now knew what he wanted: to be allowed to apologise and to be forgiven; to be told what had happened so that he could understand; to put the whole episode behind them and start again. However, it was clear that his wife was not yet ready for this. He telephoned her to suggest lunch or dinner. She refused both suggestions, but agreed to a walk in the Tuileries Gardens. They met at the main gates between the Jeu de Paume and the Orangerie on a grey and bitterly cold afternoon. Ariane was hunched inside her coat, her hands deep in her pockets; they fell into step and walked towards the pond.

'Tell me what happened to you, Theo,' she said quickly. 'Did you have a good war?'

'Good? I don't know. The only thing I can say is that I'm glad I left for England when I did. I have no regrets there.'

'I wish I could say I had no regrets.'

'What do you regret?'

'Everything, everything. The whole thing has been horrible, a nightmare.' She spoke angrily. 'Suzie, the child who was at Bonnemort, for example. I'm trying to find her family, but I am so afraid it is going to end badly.'

'Can I help?' He knew he couldn't, but he seized the opportunity to offer to do something for her.

'Could you?'

'I can try. I could make some enquiries. I have to warn you there are some bad rumours about what has been happening to the Jews. How did the child survive with the SS living with you last summer?' Theo asked. 'Did you have to keep her in a cupboard?'

'Oh no, thank God. She was legal, with false papers. And when you see her, you'll know why she was safe. She has blue eyes and a fair complexion, so that she looks more Aryan than most French children.' She laughed. 'In fact, I had more problems on that score than she did.'

'What do you mean?'

'Sometime in the summer of forty-two, I was called upon to prove my Aryan credentials. It was after Suzie had come to us, but before the Germans occupied the free zone. I can laugh about it now. They were grotesque, these Vichy people, but it wasn't funny then.'

The letter from the Prefecture appeared at first glance to be no more than irritating. Just another of the interminable checks on the documents that permitted them to exist. She had left it on her desk without any sense of urgency. Only later when she came to read it carefully did she see, with a lurch of her heart, that it was signed by a Monsieur Cayre of the General Commission for Jewish Questions. Instantly, her imagination created a scene of Suzie wrenched from her, screaming with loneliness, to be deported to the East, while she was imprisoned for her crime of harbouring the racially impure.

During the journey to Racinès, by bike, by bus, by train, she rehearsed how she would meet the unknown threat. Suzie's papers would withstand examination, so she would deny that the child was Jewish, but she must do it without arousing antagonism. She must suppress the personal authority that she had always assumed from her birth, her wealth, her education. None of those advantages counted now, least of all with this sinister and irrational offshoot of the bureaucracy. To protect Suzie she would be humble, ingratiating, feminine, flattering, servile, whatever was needed.

The figure behind the desk was almost hidden by the barrier of card index boxes which he had erected between him and the public whom he summoned for interview. He wore round, horn-rimmed glasses and a bow tie.

'Madame de Cazalle, I called you here today…' He avoided her eyes, studying a paper, as if reading a text. 'Because the law of 2 June 1941 requires every person of the Jewish race in France, in the non-occupied as well as the occupied zone, to register his or her name and place of abode at the Prefecture, in the Jewish index. And you have not done so.'

'*I* have not done so?' She could not prevent herself from stressing the personal pronoun. She had been thinking of Suzie. 'Why should *I* do so?'

He took off his spectacles, and revealed his prominent, pale blue eyes. 'Because, as I understand it, you are Jewish.'

She was impassive, in spite of the rage that welled up within her at being trapped in a position where she could only behave badly. To deny with indignation that she was Jewish implied that she was rejecting a calumny, accepting the idea that to be Jewish was a crime. To ask for the evidence against her seemed to acknowledge the truth of the accusation. To refuse to answer would deny the authority of the horrible little man whom she had to placate.

'I am not Jewish,' she said flatly,

'Ah, many people say that to me at first, but I often find that it is a little matter that they have—somehow—forgotten.'

'I can't see how one can forget. I am not of the Jewish faith.'

'And some people find they are of the Jewish race, without ever having known it, even if they are not of the Jewish faith. It comes as quite a shock to them, I can tell you. The laws of 3 October 1940 and 2 June 1941, drawing on the juridical experience of the Nuremberg Laws, state clearly who is of the Jewish race. You are a Jew if you adhere to the Jewish faith, evidently. But even if you are a Christian, and your parents were Christian, you are a Jew if, for example, you have three Jewish grandparents. You are a Jew, even if you are a Christian, if you have two Jewish grandparents and you are married to a Jew or a half-Jew. Moreover, a half-Jew is a Jew, even if he is a second-generation Christian, if he is married to a half-Jew, even if she is Christian.' His face with suffused with triumph. 'Can you now say that you know you're not Jewish?

'I am not Jewish, and I still don't understand what it means to be of the Jewish race.'

He frowned at her stubbornness. 'If you persist in your denial, I shall delay your registration and hand your case over to the Office of Personal Status.' He flipped her papers into a tray, to indicate he had done all he could for her. 'You will have time to produce a proper attestation of your ancestry, so that your case can be judged accurately.'

'One moment.' She forced an ingratiating tone into her voice. 'Can I ask, how is it that you decided to ask for my Aryan credentials? I can't believe that everyone in the region is being subjected to such meticulous scrutiny.'

A sly smile came over his features and he glanced down. 'Oh, no, you couldn't expect me to reveal the contents of confidential files to you.'

A denunciation. Who could it have been? Someone with whom she was familiar, whom she met every day, every week in Lepech or Montféfoul?

'But on what grounds? You can at least tell me the basis of your demand.'

'Let me be frank. According to my information, you arrived in the region at the time of the invasion; you have a Jewish maiden name, Wolff, I believe, and,' here he played his trump card, 'you don't attend mass.'

Ariane could no longer contain herself and spoke with open irritation. 'I came here in 1939 when I had just married someone from this region. My name is Strasbourgeois. My family comes from Alsace-Lorraine and I am Protestant. Is that sufficient to explain your strange accusations?'

He looked as full of distaste as if she had admitted his original accusation that she was Jewish. 'You will have to provide a file of attestations, as I said. Your parents' marriage certificate, the religious one, of course; their baptismal certificates and those of your grandparents are the usual documents required.'

'How can I?' She was genuinely pleading now, regretting her display of annoyance. 'My father lives in the occupied zone, in Paris; my grandparents are all dead; they came from Strasbourg, which, as you know, has been incorporated into the Reich. How can I possibly get this documentation?'

'That is your business. I shall ask you to return in six weeks to see my colleague. An alternative, or supplementary, procedure is to submit yourself to examination by an agreed medical expert who will make a physical assessment of your racial type.' He allowed his gaze to move slowly over her features: the straight dark brown hair, hazel eyes, Roman nose. 'But you might not find that route to your advantage.'

On the train back to Bonnemort she shuddered with humiliation. It was a Frenchman, a representative of the

French state, carrying out French law, who was demanding this. She did not even have the satisfaction of feeling that she was compelled by the Nazis. However, she had already accepted that, whatever the difficulties, she had to submit to proving what she wasn't. She would write to her father at once. Her baptismal certificate, which she had never before had to present to anyone, being an item of no interest to a secular state, must be somewhere in his house. He must have his own baptismal and marriage papers, too. But her grandparents'... If it were not so serious, it would be laughable. But she must prevent them from looking any closer at her household and asking questions more difficult to answer.

Theo listened to her account with sadness. In truth, he had no idea at all of the difficulties that she had faced all the years of his absence. Later, he questioned his father-in-law about this curious episode. Pascal Wolff had had the choice of appealing to the German authorities for the documents he needed about the marriage of his wife's parents, or paying for false ones. After a lifetime of correct behaviour, he had deliberately chosen the course of illegality, procuring false papers to prove the truth of his parents-in-law's marriage ceremony at the Protestant temple of Strasbourg in 1864. The enormous sum demanded for the forgery indicated the importance of such documents, for lack of them meant banishment from France and a one-way ticket to the East. If her father had not arranged matters, Ariane and Suzie too would have been on one of the trains from Drancy.

'Do you have any idea who might have denounced you?'

'Oh, I thought of everybody. The mayor, Gargaud, was a great supporter of Vichy and was always suspicious of us;

Madame Maniotte, who detested me, because of my friendship with Lucien; even Vernhes.'

'Vernhes? Why would he do such a thing?'

'He and Henri didn't get on. Henri was socialist, you remember, and there were often tensions. It was probably none of these. But you lived with fear and suspicion all the time, even of the people closest to you. What do you think you could do for Suzie?'

'There won't be any news of deportees until Germany is defeated.' He couldn't bear to tell her of the stories that were circulating, about a work camp in southern Poland. Half the time he did not believe such tales himself. He thought, desperate people exaggerate to gain help, not realising that when horrors go beyond the bounds of credibility, their power to move is lost. 'But perhaps I should see the child, take some details of her family. Would that be possible?'

'Of course. After school perhaps. The day after tomorrow, at Papa's house.'

She sat up at the table, on the edge of her chair, and took her cup in both hands to transfer it carefully to her lips. She seemed very young for her age, which was thirteen, the same as Sabine's, but whereas Sabine was tall, Suzie's small stature and unformed body seemed to belong to a child two or three years younger. She had an odd little face, almost triangular, narrowing from a wide forehead to a small chin, trimmed to a point by a sharp, upturned nose. Her fair hair and blue eyes gave her an almost Germanic appearance.

'The colonel is here to ask you a few questions about your family,' Ariane explained. 'He is going to help us to trace them, so that we can find them as soon as the war ends.'

Suzie looked at him so blankly that Theo felt that there was something retarded in her understanding.

'There was Papa and Maman,' she said slowly.

Theo waited. 'Did you have any aunts and uncles and cousins?' he prompted. The interrogation proceeded painfully. Relatives she had, but she only knew them by their first name or family nicknames. Where they had lived was equally unclear. Uncle Iza and Aunt Lola had had a big house near Omi and Opa, but she thought they went away a long time ago. She had once met cousins Lena and Ari in Paris. They had a son called Shmuel and a baby who was very sweet.

The only question that elicited more than the scantiest response was, 'Were there any relatives abroad, in America, for example?'

A long time ago... Before... She used to write cards to Cousin Avery who sent her toys. He sent her a beautiful doll with long golden hair. 'We called her Rahel, too. But terrible things happened to her. Policemen came to take her away. One day the children chased her and she lost her purse.'

Theo was bemused. Did she mean that these things happened to her? When he had finished his questioning and Suzie was sent away, Ariane said apologetically, 'She's very shy.'

'We haven't much to go on.'

'Her father was caught here in Paris in forty-two, not the Vél d'Hiver, when they took thousands in one day but another round-up, a month later. Papa went to Drancy to try to rescue him, but since he was German there was no hope for him. He was sent to a camp. Suzie and her mother were at Clermont Ferrand where I found them and took Suzie away. Her mother must have been expelled on 5 September 1942, when all Jews were ordered to leave the city. She was sent to Drancy on 9 October, then on to a camp. These camps seem to be in a Jewish enclave in Poland. Do you think the Russians have reached them yet?'

Theo closed his notebook. 'When the war is over, and it can't be long now, a few months at most, we'll find them for her.' He put his palm to her cheek. 'Ariane, our flat, come and see it again. Meet me there tomorrow.'

She shook her head, turning away from him.

He walked to the métro at the Etoile to return to his office, feeling a slight irritation. He had gone through the drama of finding her shaven-headed on his return; he had come to an understanding of what had happened; he had apologised. What more was there to do? He could not comprehend why their reconciliation could not be real, immediate. Her behaviour was unreasonable, unlike the old Ariane. And as for the children: he had not known Suzie before the war, so it was impossible to judge whether she had always been a little simple, or whether it was the effect of her experiences. All he could say was that she was now simply odd, as if she were refusing to grow up. Sabine, too, could not be said to be behaving like a normal child. They were, all of them, traumatised creatures.

He mentally listed what they had been through: Suzie had been separated from her parents for almost three years now, and had lived with strangers under a false name. Sabine, too, had thought she had lost her father. But both of them had been safe and well cared for, had never lacked materially. Ariane had undertaken great risks for others, communists, Jews, forced labourers, at considerable danger to herself, but she had survived. None of this was unusual in these times. Many other people had endured worse. He simply could not see what the fuss was about.

14

THEO AND ARIANE had lived together for only four
months in 1939. Their apartment was the home of an aborted
marriage, Theo thought, as he stood in the centre of the salon
in darkness. The concierge was shuffling about opening the
shutters, leaning on the grille to pin them back to the wall.

It was bitterly cold. He could see his breath, his words
steaming gently in front of him. Coal was impossible to obtain.
Most people cooked on wood-burning stoves, although wood
was not easily available either. Madame Brugiotti was wearing all her clothes: ankle socks, a sagging black dress, a cardigan, a coat, a shawl. She flapped through the rooms, pulling
her wrappings around her full bosom.

'Are you thinking of moving in?'

'I'm not sure.' He looked round helplessly.

'It won't be easy, that's certain. People who've been here
all through the war, they've got their System D all worked out.
They know how to cope. But to begin now, when it's as bad as
it's ever been...'

'It'll have to be cleaned,' he said to Madame Brugiotti.
'Can you organise that for me?'

He had concluded that only by making a start on the

flat himself could he persuade her to come back to him. Now, faced with the difficulties of setting up home in the chaos of liberated Paris, he saw the flat more as an intermediary between them than as a place to live.

It was an achievement to gain Ariane's agreement to meet him there one Sunday morning. She shivered as he unlocked the door, and moved with palpable reluctance into the hall. In the salon were signs that Madame Brugiotti had begun work: the floor had been swept, the windows and panelling washed.

Ariane went at once to the window and looked out at the bare trees in the avenue, only then turning to assess the room. She lifted the corner of a dust cover to see what was hidden underneath. He opened the next set of double doors into their bedroom. To his surprise the bed had been prepared, the square pillows in starched white cases lay on the coverlet. Behind him he heard her footsteps as she followed him into the room. She halted at the sight of the bed.

'Ariane.'

They stood, apart, looking around the room. His eyes came to rest on the bed, voyeur of their former selves making love, impelled by the threat of war. He glanced at his wife. Her face was set, with no sign of the past understanding, passionate and instinctive, that they used to share. He put his arms around her.

'Kiss me,' he said. She shifted her gaze to his face, leaned forward and kissed his cheek, affectionate, absent.

He was trying to evoke the memory of that night in Normandy, the erotic intensity of which had grown in the nostalgia of exile. He took her head in his hands to tilt it up to him. There was no response as his tongue separated her lips. He had been more than willing, that first time in Normandy that she was refusing to remember, when she had led the way. He persevered in his attempt to resuscitate the past.

'Ariane, forget the Occupation. Write it off. Make love to me now.'

He pulled off her hat, flinging it into a corner of the room, releasing the short curls that now covered her head. He began to unbutton her coat, but halted when he looked from the work of his fingers to her face.

'Theo, I'm sorry... It's been horrible. It's my fault, I should have told you...'

'No, no. It was my fault. Anyway it doesn't matter now. That's the past. Now, kiss me.'

This time she did, throwing off, with an effort, whatever it was that had oppressed her. 'Yes, yes, yes.'

He was pushing her coat off her shoulders and embracing her at the same time. She pulled at his tie and wrenched at the stud that held his collar in order to open his shirt. The removal of their clothes was a clumsy operation, as if they had never made love before and were unfamiliar and uncertain. Once in bed he yelped at the touch of her icy hands, kissing her to generate heat under the covers that made a tent over the ridgepole of his back as he moved over her, to warm her and remind her of their past.

It still worked. They still worked together, whatever else they could not yet settle, and, when Theo pushed off the weight of the blankets, now too hot, and allowed the cold air to chill the sweat on his back, he felt a profound satisfaction of at last achieving the place that he had wanted to be ever since he left. He fell briefly asleep. When he awoke Ariane's eyes were open and she was watching him. Sleepily he put out a hand to stroke the soft olive skin of her breast and turned to lodge himself the length of her body. His mind reached into the future, occupying and peopling it with Ariane, Sabine, a new family.

'When shall we move in?'

'When the war ends,' she said.

'No, much sooner than that.'

'I long for it to be over, for everything to be over. I feel as if this is time out, waiting for victory, rather like the phoney war at the beginning when we were waiting for defeat.'

'It won't be any different, Ariane. Don't expect things suddenly to improve: food in the shops, divisions healed. It'll take a long time.'

He was fully awake now and climbed out of bed to find his cigarettes. Ariane lifted the covers to welcome his return, shrunken and shivering.

'I know,' she said. 'I don't expect it. It's a goal. When we're there, I may feel that everything else was worth it after all, and not just a terrible waste and sadness.'

'It can never be worth it, but the purpose will be vindicated.' He remembered his feeling of self-satisfaction on his drive to Bonnemort in September, the justified son, before he knew that Henri was dead.

'You don't understand. You were so clear about what you had to do and you did it. There are people who still think that resistance was wrong.'

'Yes,' he said. 'I went to see Madame Maniotte.'

'You see what Lucien had to live with. He had to hide what he was doing from her. And nothing that has happened since his death has changed her mind.'

'She said Henri was arrested at the same time as Lucien in forty-three…'

'No, it was a bit later.'

'…and you got him out.'

'I expect she can't forgive me for that. I can't blame her. Two are taken and one is saved. It was so random, unjust. Not that Henri reached the end, either.'

'She was very bitter. She implied that you were somehow able to have Henri released.'

Ariane detached herself from him. 'She knew, or at least she guessed, what we were doing, she blames me for involving Lucien and at the same time accuses me of collaboration.'

'There are some who did both,' said Theo, as if to explain Madame Maniotte's inconsistency. 'Tell me, how did you get Henri out?'

'I collaborated. I paid.' Ariane was shouting. 'I would have done almost anything for Henri to be free. If I'd had to sleep with the head of the Gendarmerie in Racinès, I'd have done it.'

The risks were always with them. The young men fleeing from compulsory labour service would turn up without credentials. It was impossible to tell if they were genuine or agents provocateurs paid by the police, or worse, the Germans. Henri was cautious. At that stage, he only took boys from the locality who came with a recommendation. He moved his group between several sites, would not let them develop a routine, making it harder for the Germans to find them, and distributed the burden of feeding them between the villages. He found Mr Nikola, the Russian, to train the men and keep them busy.

The infiltrators, who were evidently in the pay of the Sicherheitsdienst, didn't enter Group Rainbow, but an allied one, based about thirty kilometres away, called Afrique, which formed part of the regional organisation run by Lucien Maniotte. This they had managed to work out later. At the time the first they knew of the danger they were in was an attack by the Germans on Afrique's camp in the forests. Two boys had been killed, at least twenty arrested and a mere half dozen had succeeded in stumbling away into the woods to hide until the Germans withdrew. To make matters worse, the camp had been a central training point and papers listing other Maquis groups in the region had been seized. They never knew if the papers alone were enough to betray the organisation and its leader, or whether any of the prisoners talked. Henri always said they could not be blamed if they did. Everyone knew torture worked and why. All you could hope for was time to take cover.

A week later he came into the schoolroom at Bonnemort where she was teaching the girls, and led her down to the garden.

'The doctor was arrested yesterday at the clinic. The SD came for him.'

'Oh, God.' However much you prepare yourself, however well you know the risk, you can only go on by thinking it won't happen. And when it does, it's as bad as if it came as a total surprise. 'Where have they taken him?'

'No news.'

'Henri, be careful. Go away to the Corrèze or the Tarn for a month or two.'

'No need for that. The farm… The harvest… Micheline…'

A week later he was arrested in the café of Lepech Perdrissou with a dozen other men. The news was telephoned through to them at Bonnemort by the wife of the proprietor, whose husband had also been taken.

The first questions: Who took them? Where did they go? The answers, the gendarmes, to Racinès, were a relief. Ariane was cheered that Henri had not been sought by name, but simply seized as part of a general round-up. Micheline saw nothing to reassure her. She did not weep; her stoicism was a rehearsal of her reaction a year later when Henri was killed. She went about her work with a dull endurance, doing twice as much as before.

Ariane went into Racinès to make enquiries. She discovered that the supervision of the town had recently become stricter with the arrival of a new boss at the Kommandatur and a new *chef* at the Gendarmerie. The latter, she was told, who was French, was almost as bad as the former, who was German. He was from Alsace, a gross figure; he spoke German and had been especially chosen for his toughness in this difficult region. When she explained her plan to Micheline and Florence, the former was sceptical, even hostile.

'You'll just get yourself arrested,' she said. 'Then where'll we be?'

Florence, however, supported her, killing a chicken, plucking it and wrapping it in a napkin. She descended to the cellar and brought up a tin of Micheline's foie gras and a string of dried mushrooms.

'Have we any ham? As an *alsacien*, he would do anything for a ham.'

'No,' said Micheline, sharply. 'There's no ham.'

'Micheline, it's for Henri.'

'I'd give my soul for Henri,' said Micheline, 'and it'd do more good than that lot. It's wrong to do business with these types and it's stupid, too. You'll see. He'll take everything and keep Henri. I'll give you a dried sausage.'

'It's worth trying,' Ariane insisted. And it wasn't just food she was trying.

She took out a suit that she had not worn for a year, at least since she went to Clermont to find Suzie, and tried it on. Florence looked at it doubtfully.

'You've lost weight,' she said. 'We'll have to do something about that.' She folded up two handkerchiefs and handed them to Ariane. 'Stuff those in your bust. Let's hope he never gets close enough to discover the trick. I'll take the hem up too, to make it look more up to date.'

Wilder was a small man, smaller than she, and obese. His face was swollen with fat, so that his eyes receded into slits. Short, sandy hair contrasted unpleasantly with his unnaturally dark red complexion. In spite of his gross belly, he rose nimbly as she entered. She listened to his accent as he greeted her and did her best to imitate the slight twang to his French. Yes, she too was from Alsace, at least her family was, and she intended to make the connexion work, along with any other that seemed promising.

Afterwards she found she had enjoyed the interview. She played her part with verve, flirting with him, emphasising every feminine gesture, every expression of eye and mouth.

She was distraught, she told him. She was a war widow, living on her property, alone and helpless, and her farm manager had been picked up in the village bar by his gendarmes. He was, of course, totally innocent. A solid family man in his fifties, who had lived in the country all his life. How could he be a terrorist or a communist?

He responded instinctively, like a dog circling a bitch on heat, prolonging the meeting with questions about the farm, to which she answered charmingly. She watched him dispassionately, and asked herself, if it came to sleeping with him, could she do it? She realised, with a shock, that what would stop her was not the significance of the act, but the fact that he was physically repulsive. She tried to imagine him naked, grotesquely white, patched with reddish hair, genitals hanging heavily, pink, tripe-like tubes escaping from his gut, and was revolted. But she knew that her objections, aesthetic not moral, were meaningless. She would if she had to.

She stayed until he reluctantly gave the signal that he

must attend to more important matters. She recalled him timidly to the purpose of her visit, 'My farm manager... You're going to give him back to me?' She might have been asking for a chocolate, or a kiss.

'As to that,' he replied, his smile fading, 'I can't give you a decision at once. I shall have to study the file.'

Micheline had been right in her cynicism. However, since Ariane had lugged the suitcase full of food all the way there, she wouldn't take it back again. She was afraid of being too blatant in her offer of a bribe and left the case by her chair without opening it. In this she was wrong, she discovered later. He was used to goods placed naked on the desk. A glance at the chicken breast would have had more impact than ogling her.

'And plumper too,' she said to Florence and Micheline later, 'even with the handkerchiefs in my bodice.'

Her rendering of the breathy, fluttering creature that she had played made Florence laugh and the two of them became almost hysterical. Micheline was mending the girls' cotton stockings that they wore to mass. They were a patchwork of darns held together by a web of the original mesh. Frowning over her spectacles, she looked particularly severe.

'It's just as I said. He took everything. It doesn't matter what you do. You could sleep with him and it'd make no difference.'

'I decided against sleeping with him,' Ariane said, still laughing. 'And with that great belly, how could he manage? His cock wouldn't emerge from under it.'

Micheline looked yet more disapproving.

'I'm going back in two days' time to try again,' Ariane continued. 'We'll need a duck this time and butter.'

When she was admitted to Wilder's office, she found him in a jovial mood. 'Another little bag of evidence,' he said genially.

She simpered. She had never understood before how

it was done. Now she found that she did it naturally: a suppressed giggle, the chin pulled in, the eyes cast down.

'I hope I shall soon have my farm manager back or I shall have no more evidence to offer.'

He evaded this, tapping his sausage-fingers on the blotter. 'It's such a beautiful day, I suggest a cup of coffee in the square.'

It was mid-afternoon and they sat at a café table in the sunshine to drink the ersatz coffee. This is part of the price, to be seen with him, she told herself, as she smiled and smiled and hoped that no one she knew would pass.

Wilder was talking about food. He missed some of the delicacies of their own area. The foie gras here was not as refined as that of Alsace. And they had nothing like the range of pork products they had in Strasbourg. Eventually he hauled his gross body out of his seat and shook her hand. 'I'll say goodbye to you here. Very nice to have made the acquaintance of a lady from Alsace. I hope you'll find your farm manager comes back to you soon.'

Her persistence was rewarded. The following day Henri returned to the farm.

Ariane took his cigarette from Theo. 'So that's one part of my collaboration.'

'Ariane, I didn't really think…'

'Yes, you did.'

'I'm sorry. I'm sorry.'

'No, you were right to think what you did. I had to make accommodations. We all did.'

'Ariane, this flat. I want us to move back in here, to start again.'

She made no reply.

'And there's Sabine. I can't leave her with the aunts indefinitely.'

'I can see that, yes.' She slipped away from him, out from under the covers, stooping over her discarded clothes.

'I feel it is unfair to send her back to the convent, and it seems wrong for Suzie to be in Paris and not Sabine. If we move here we could have both of them with us.'

She was leaning one foot on the end of the bed, rolling up a thick woollen stocking, fastening it to her suspenders. 'But I don't know when we can move in here. And I don't think Sabine and Suzie should be together.'

'Why not? Don't they get on? I thought they used to be devoted to one another.'

'They were.' It was impossible to explain to him what had happened. 'But at the end, when the Germans were with us, they were... I can't explain. It was a sort of *folie à deux* of two pre-adolescent girls.' She was fully dressed now, powdering her cheeks in front of the huge mirror over the fireplace, about to leave. 'I'm not ready for this, Theo.'

Part Three

BONNEMORT
6 June–18 August 1944

15

THE GERMANS ARRIVED at Bonnemort on 6 June 1944, just before lunch. Micheline was in the kitchen, stoking the range; Florence was in the garden to pull up some leeks; the aunts were in their room with the wireless on; Madame Ariane and the children were in the schoolroom for a lesson in Latin. They were studying *The Conquest of Gaul*. Everyone had been expecting an invasion for days, French and Germans alike. Marshal Pétain had already warned them that morning of what was happening.

Frenchmen, the German and Anglo-Saxon armies are engaged on our soil. France has thus become a battleground.

'At long last.'

'After four years.' The old women were in the habit of talking as much to the wireless as to one another.

The circumstances of battle could lead the German army to take special dispositions in the zones of combat. Accept this necessity. I make this recommendation to you in the interests of your safety.

'Listen.' Sabine cocked her head like a dog.

Out of the open window they could hear the tolling of a bell carrying over the hills from the village. The curé had heard the news too. Pealing or tolling, a celebration or a tocsin, you could take it as you pleased. They returned to their routine, in spite of Sabine's pleading for a holiday. Madame Ariane had chosen the chapter, 'The Fight on the Atlantic Coast'.

'*With the completion of these operations,*' Sabine was translating, holding a ruler under the words, '*Caesar had every reason to think that Gaul was pacified...*'

Had Madame Ariane known, Suzie wondered, that it was going to be today?

Florence, in the garden, was the first to be afraid. She heard engines, which could only mean one thing—no one but Germans had petrol and drove on the roads in the middle of the day. She was already running across the farmyard to alert Madame Ariane, when the dog Lascar, whom they had trained to watch the drive, came bounding through the gates, barking. The terriers joined in for the sake of it, not yet knowing why they were giving the alarm.

They roared in like thunder, the noise of the engines reverberating from the walls, a land-borne blitzkrieg. First came the motorcycles, bouncing ahead of the convoy, swooping into the courtyard in front of the big house, followed by a staff car and, more ponderously, the armoured trucks.

Micheline stepped out of the kitchen, wiping her hands on the skirt of her pinafore, saw the domed helmets above the handlebars and gave a wail of horror. Madame Ariane and the children were already at the door of the tower. She seized the two girls by their shoulders, pushing them ahead of her as she ran, and thrust them, stumbling, onto the path that led up the hill among the trees.

'Run. Get away as far as you can.' She stepped back and waved Micheline and Florence past her.

Florence, taking a last look from the curve in the path, saw Madame Ariane standing under the arch to face the invaders. The roaring of the motors had reached a crescendo, men shouting, dogs barking in descant. She ran after the others, following her mother's back into the underwater green of the forest. The noise died away as they distanced themselves from home. Sabine and Suzie ran fast at first, fleeing up the slope ahead of Micheline and Florence. They halted when their sprint left them breathless and waited, panting, for the other two to catch them up.

'Where are we going?'

'A bit further yet.' Florence took the lead and walked purposefully. The undergrowth swished back from her thighs, slapping against Suzie who was following closely on her heels. After about twenty minutes she left the path, bending low through the bracken. After ascending a slope she opened a space between two bushes and said, 'In you go.'

They crept into the hole and crouched inside, listening to the beating of their hearts in their ears, a drumming that gradually dropped away to leave the busy silence of the woods.

Suzie examined the low, semi-circular chamber, stroking the rock walls with the palm of her hand, wiping the stone dust and cobwebs onto her pinafore.

'Where are we?' she asked.

'About a kilometre from the road to Les Landes.'

'No, what is this place?'

'They built these hides centuries ago, they say, to conceal food from the soldiers who came to steal from the peasants. Now it's just a woodman's shelter. They won't find us here.'

The children were enchanted with their hiding place. They began to play houses, planning to live there for ever, gathering up the leaves and pulling down the cobwebs that hung from the tree roots in the roof.

Micheline commented drily, 'I've never seen you so keen to help with the housework at home.'

She and Florence were crouched on their haunches by the entrance. She said to her daughter, 'You'd better go on to Lepech and tell them there. Try to get a message to your father.'

'I'll come back here then?'

Micheline pondered. 'In a while I'll go back to see what's happened. We'll meet here and decide where to go for the night.'

Florence crawled out.

'We want to stay here,' Sabine said, whining. 'We like it here.'

'You may prefer a softer bed after you've tried lying on these stones for a bit.'

'They're no harder than my bed in the convent.'

'Nonsense. You don't know when you're well off, miss. Now, you're to stay here and not go wandering around the woods. I'll be back within an hour, I hope.' She, too, clambered out, more ungainly than her daughter. The girls listened to the sound of her departure until the bouncing of displaced stones ceased.

They seated themselves on either side of the cave entrance to watch her go, in identical posture, their knees drawn up, like a pair of matching statues. They could hardly have been more different in their appearance. Sabine, the taller and larger, had a broad, white face with rudimentary features dominated by brown eyes, as hard as toffees. Her fine, dark curly hair, held back fiercely by grips and bands, had released itself in their rush through the woods and sprang forward in coils around her neck. Opposite her, Suzie rested her chin on her knee. Her blonde hair, cut in a pudding-basin style around her pointed, anxious face, made her look much younger than Sabine, although they were about the same age, thirteen.

'We could eat our lunch,' she suggested. She could judge a piece of bread to its last gram, and the hunk that Micheline had brought with her was bigger than the slice usually scrupulously doled out for lunch. She spread her legs to catch any crumbs in her skirt and began to nibble her bread.

'We should really find something from the forest to eat with it,' Sabine said. 'Gather some berries, or trap an animal.'

'No berries now,' Suzie said practically. 'No mushrooms, no nuts, no blackberries, not until September. A long wait.'

The bread disappeared quickly, even though it needed plenty of mastication to wash it down without water. Sabine licked a fingertip and pressed it into the grains in her lap, transferring them to her mouth.

'Let's play.'

She crawled forward, taking Suzie's shoulders in her grip, leaning her forehead against hers. 'I'll stare you out. Whoever looks away gets a Chinese burn.'

A moment later she angrily slapped Suzie's cheek. 'You're not playing. You're not even trying.'

She took Suzie's wrist tightly in both hands, twisting them in opposite directions. Suzie did not cry out, but she grimaced and tears appeared in the corners of her eyes.

'Don't, Sabine, please don't. I keep thinking, wondering what's happening at home.'

The Brehmer Division had patrolled the region three months ago to clear the area of terrorists, leaving a pall of fear to dissuade people from helping the partisans. Stories had circulated of the Germans' violence: ten people executed at Lartigue after a Maquis raid; twenty-five hostages shot, a village razed, a round-up of Jews in Racinès, old people who hadn't been able to hide or run away, taken by bus to the river bank and shot. But all these things had happened a long way away; it was more than thirty kilometres to Racinès.

'I heard a story,' Sabine was whispering, her voice a harsh sibilant. 'Henri was telling Micheline last week. I was in the scullery, and I knew he'd stop if I came out, so I hid behind the door.'

Outside in the sunshine crickets were singing. Suzie tried to concentrate on their rhythmical, mindless music, but Sabine's voice was compelling.

'They took the boy from La Tuilière last week. He was in the field with the sheep when a bus full of Milice stopped on the road and forced him to get in. They said the partisans had passed that way and he must know them. They took him to Racinès to the Hôtel du Parc and they *tortured* him.'

'Sabine...'

'Do you know what they did? They hit him in the face. They kicked him in the shins. Again and again.'

Suzie glanced at Sabine who was making boxing gestures with her rolled fists. She looked down at the stones on the threshold where a party of ants was crossing into their lair in a disciplined column.

'Then they stripped him naked and tied him to a table, face down, with his hands in handcuffs underneath. This was in the bar, at a café table. Imagine sitting there, at that table to take a cup of coffee where someone has been beaten. They beat him with a cosh with a lead ball on the end, which ripped his flesh, or with a leather belt with a buckle. They took turns to join in the fun. When one was tired, the others took over.

'During the night he was tied standing up in the cellar with some other captives. That's how Henri knew what had happened to him.'

A lizard lay in the sunshine in a crack between two stones. Suzie could see its neck swelling, falling, swelling.

'In the morning they brought him back to the bar and hung him upside down by his feet. They shouted, Where are they? Where are the partisans? Who helps them? Who gives them food? They beat him and beat him until his kidneys burst and he died. Then they took his body out on one of their trips in the bus and threw it in the ditch. He never said a word.'

Suzie had put her hands over her ears. Sabine reached out and pulled at her wrists. 'And that was just the Milice,' she said with relish. 'Down there it's the Germans.'

'I don't know why you're so pleased about it. You won't like it if they set fire to your house.'

Sabine stretched out her legs. 'War is so exciting. I enjoy it so much more than peace. Today has been really good. Now the Allies have landed, there will be real fighting here. Battles in France instead of somewhere else. You wonder what they've been doing all this time, in Africa and places like that. Why didn't they attack here where the Germans are living?'

'Well, they've done it now,' Suzie said placatingly.

'Perhaps the Germans have killed Madame Ariane by now.'

'Listen.' Suzie held down the branches. They peered out and saw a deer bounding down the hill, the white underside of its tail flashing. 'Perhaps Micheline is coming back with news.'

If she had hoped that this distraction might divert Sabine from her train of thought, she was disappointed.

'We might go back and find her body lying in the courtyard,' Sabine spoke slowly to spin out the pleasure of the fantasy. She slipped her hand under the hem of her dress, tucking it inside the elastic of her knickers. Suzie averted her eyes, hoping that the visit of the Germans was not going to trigger a new bout of murderous imagination in Sabine. The idea of killing her stepmother kept recurring to Sabine and, once her interest in a project was roused, she was obsessive.

'Perhaps they have tied her up and raped her. Perhaps they have hung her upside down, like the boy from La Tuilière and have beaten her with sticks. Or with razors, slash, slash, a thousand cuts.' Sabine rocked herself lovingly.

'Don't, don't.' Suzie's voice rose in pain.

Sabine's was rising too. 'All right, a single bullet, like shooting a deer. Bang and it falls, still running. A little burned hole in her chest, that's all. There's not much blood when you shoot a deer. He might draw out his pistol, the German, and shoot her at close range. Or they could set up a machine gun and dr-dr-dr, stud her with bullets.'

'She'd be a hero.'

Sabine released a long breath. 'Who cares? She'd be dead.'

16

SABINE FELL SILENT, absorbed in her fantasy of pain; Suzie lapsed into her own dream world, which she visited each night before she went to sleep, the make-believe family of Papa, Maman and Rahel. Rahel was a beautiful American doll, her namesake. She always began by remembering the games she used to play with her, but this time, as often happened, inexorable reality broke into the pliable texture of the dream.

She had left Rahel with Maman the day she was taken away. Rahel the doll always stayed with Maman, when she, Rahel as she was in those days, went to school, keeping her company in the damp basement lodging when they lived in Clermont Ferrand. She did not always go to school, although she might set off as though that were her destination. Her mother was too sick to stand in line and had lost the ingenuity necessary to cope, day by day, with new, unforeseen difficulties. She lay in the semi-darkness, coughing, coughing, while the cockroaches walked boldly across the floor. Rahel could not master the offices that Maman used to visit, but she knew how to obtain their food coupons every month and how to queue at the *boulangerie*. Money was becoming more and more of a problem; the last of the funds that had reached them from Papa in Paris was almost at an end.

One day a lady came from the Committee of the General Union of French Jews and, seeing the state Maman was in, said she must be moved to hospital. That time Maman refused. But a month or so later, she returned from school to find another lady sitting beside Maman's bed.

'Rahel, this is Madame de Cazalle.' Rahel curtseyed. 'She is a friend of Omi and Opa, and Papa has asked her to come and see us.'

Rahel shook hands with the newcomer and made a quick assessment of her clothes and manner, a skill she was perfecting in her dealings with the outside world. The woman was tall, dressed in a beautiful tweed suit that dated from long before coupons. She had light brown eyes, like liquid honey in a jar, and thick dark brown hair, smooth and shining, falling to her shoulders under her hat. She was uneasy, her mouth tight, as if her conversation with Maman had distressed her. Rahel bent over Maman for her kiss.

'Rahel,' her mother said, 'you remember when the lady from the Committee come, she want me to go to hospital?'

Rahel nodded. Maman always made mistakes when she spoke French. She spoke fluently, with a large vocabulary, but she made elementary errors, which caused Rahel, with her purist French education, to flinch. She knew that Maman's speech made people think her stupid or ill-educated, and they regarded her with contempt. Long ago they spoke German together, she and Papa and Maman, but then Papa had forbidden it and they only spoke French. Rahel and Maman tried to obey, even in Clermont without Papa. For her it was easy, for she spoke French in school. But Mama could never give up German; it was her language. So sometimes they spoke it together and Maman was happy.

'Yes.'

'I now decide that it is a good time to go and get well. And while I am away Madame de Cazalle will look after you.'

Rahel stared at her new guardian. As far as she could see no one looked after her; it was she who looked after Maman. 'She'll come and live here?' she asked dubiously.

Maman laughed and then coughed. 'No, you will live with her.'

'That will not be necessary, thank you.' Rahel addressed Madame de Cazalle directly.

But she was powerless in this, as in everything else, and it was all arranged. Madame Meyer from the Committee came again and they talked about Rahel's new papers and her food coupons (Category J3). The two women sat on the bed and the chair, leaving her standing beside Maman. The false papers would say that she was born in St Sever in Pas-de-Calais, because the Mairie had burned down there in the thirties and it was impossible for the authorities to check her identity with the records. Madame de Cazalle, equipped with blank cards and a rubber stamp was an expert in making new papers.

'And what were you called? We'd better start afresh; *not* Rahel, I think.'

'No,' Maman said.

'Rahel, what would you like to be called?'

'I like Rahel. I am Rahel.'

'Suzie,' Madame de Cazalle said firmly. 'It's a Jewish name and a French name. Do you like Suzanne?'

Silence.

Maman said, 'I like Suzie very much.'

So she became Suzie and Rahel was left with Maman. Madame de Cazalle explained that life was becoming more and more difficult for Jews in France, especially if they did not have French nationality. The German authorities had just announced that in the occupied zone they had to wear a yellow star...

Rahel listened with boredom. Why was it that adults told you things that you knew perfectly well, as if they were breaking terrible news? Life was always becoming more and more difficult for the Jews. Papa and Maman used to talk about it long ago in Paris, and since they left Paris and came to Clermont it was worse.

Maman opened her eyes and made an effort. 'Rahel, you will live with Madame de Cazalle until the war is over. You won't tell anyone at all that you are Jewish. And when the war is over, Papa come and find us both and we are all together again. So you are Suzie Ollivier now and you do whatever Madame de Cazalle says. If she says you are to go to mass, you go to mass. You do just what her little girl does. Do you understand?'

'Yes, Maman.' Rahel caressed her hand.

'Promise you will never tell anyone who you are.'

'I promise, Maman.'

It pleased her mother to speak to her as if she was very young and very stupid. She played this game too, hiding what she knew and what she guessed, because if they did not speak it, it might not be true. But this was spoken and it was about to be true.

She met Sabine for the first time late in the afternoon in the tower room, always known as Madame Ariane's salon, to distinguish it from the big salon, the little salon, the blue salon, all the other rooms in the enormous house. From the outside its façade seemed to go on for ever; inside there were doors, corridors, rooms without end.

The journey had been long. She had said goodbye to Maman in the early hours of the morning and left without shedding a tear. They took the bus to the station and waited. They sat in the train for three hours. They got out at a country station and waited. They took another train, a stopping one with only two carriages. Suzie hardly paid attention to the changing scenery or their fellow travellers. All the time she thought of Maman alone, with no one to care for her.

At one point Madame de Cazalle said, 'You will call me Madame Ariane, because there is another Madame de Cazalle where we are going. And Madame Veyrines, her sister-in-law. And you're going to meet another little girl, just a bit older than you. She's called Sabine. You mustn't tell her about Maman and Papa. We're going to say that Maman is a friend of mine, which indeed she is. My father has known your grandfather for many, many years, so we must be friends. And you must say that Maman is not well, so you are coming to live with us. And remember, you are called Suzanne Ollivier. The olive tree is the sign of peace, so your new name is looking forward to when peace will come.'

Suzie was not interested in the symbols that were so important to Madame de Cazalle. 'Who is Sabine?' she asked.

'Sabine is…' Madame de Cazalle sighed. 'Sabine is a strange person. I hope you will like her. Here's our train.'

The strange person looked ordinary enough. She had a cloud of curly dark hair and a round pale face too large for her features, round, brown eyes, a button nose, a tight little mouth, like marbles on a board.

When they had been introduced Madame de Cazalle said, 'Sabine, would you take Suzie to Micheline for your tea. She's very tired and she'll need something before dinner.'

The idea that one could eat 'something' that wasn't counted as dinner seemed staggering to Suzie. But it was not important to Sabine, because, instead of leading her to the promised food, she ran ahead into the farmyard, into a green enclosure dotted with fruit trees under which a scattering of hens were pecking. Suzie marvelled at them. It was such an extraordinary place that even the hens were unusual: dull gold, or shining black with a green glaze, or white with shaggy feathers like fur. She stood still, looking round her. Below them was a lake, sky and clouds reflected in its perfect upside-down world, over which black swans, ducks and moorhens sailed, as if the water was the air.

'Come on, come on.'

'Where are we going?'

'I'm going to introduce you to someone. There's someone you must meet. Come in here.' Sabine wrenched open the wooden door of a little house barely high enough to admit her, shutting it firmly behind Suzie.

After the glare of the sunshine on the emerald grass, the interior darkness cut off Suzie's vision with the abruptness of a hand over her eyes. She could only hear a soft snorting, and smell straw and ammonia, a sour vegetable tang. There was a presence, large and solid, moving in the straw, barging questingly against her knees.

'What is it?'

'It's Lou Moussou, Lou Moussou.'

Sabine spoke crooningly. She was slapping it, scratching it. Suzie could hear flesh on flesh, rasping. The creature was naked, huge, mottled, pinkish, with sparse hair sprouting from its body. It grunted in ecstasy. She could make out its snout swinging towards her, its pink eyelids rimming its pinhole eyes, which looked straight at her. Its ears twitched intelligently, listening to Sabine's voice.

'He's my friend, my friend.' She had an odd habit of repeating her phrases. 'And now you're here, he can be your friend too. Look, scratch him here. He likes it.'

Rahel extended her hand gingerly to touch the firm rind with her fingertips.

'He's called Lou?'

'No,' said Sabine. 'It's not his name, it's who he is. It's a respectful way of speaking about him. It means the man, the master, the gentleman in the patois. He's always called Lou Moussou, the pig. Now he knows you.'

She was already on her way out, fastening the latch with swift skill. 'I'll show you something else too.'

She was running back through the paddock, diffracting the jewelled fowl like sunlight through a prism. Gasping for breath, Suzie followed her into the house by the tower door. They raced through an enfilade of rooms. She caught glimpses of gilt frames and misted mirrors, chairs arranged in ghostly groups, their former occupants now ranged on the walls in portraits. Sabine's footsteps rapped on the roads of parquet, the sound muffled out when she crossed the glowing lakes of oriental rugs. She halted at a hidden, silk-covered door, cut into the wall without a frame, and whisked it open.

'This is my secret place. No one comes here, no one.'

They were in a stairwell of bare stone. Another door opened and this time Suzie closed her eyes against the sudden brilliance that confounded them. The late afternoon sun was flowing in a stream of dancing atoms through a window above their heads and striking the white-washed walls with dazzling effect. The room was a hall, double height, although it was lower at the far end where the wall was rounded, like the inside of a beehive. A few rush-seated chairs, oddly low, with high backs, were arranged in a row towards the front of the hall. In front of them was a table covered with a white cloth, with two candlesticks on it, as if it were Shabbat and someone was about to say the Friday night prayer. Sabine seated herself on one of the chairs, with her back to the light.

'Come and sit, sit here.' She pulled another chair in front of her. Suzie squatted on the low seat, the sunlight falling full in her face.

'You've come here to live?' Sabine asked. 'For ever?'

Suzie screwed up her eyes. She could only see her inter-rogator as a silhouette with a dark nimbus of fine curls. 'Well, until my mother's better.'

'Why did *she* bring you here?'

'My mother's sick. She can't look after me.'

'Do you like *her*?'

'Who? Your mother?'

'She's not my mother. She's not my mother.'

'I thought you were Sabine de Cazalle.'

'Yes, we have the same name, but she's my stepmother.' Sabine was leaning forward in the intensity of her feeling. 'I hate her. I hate her.'

'But why?'

'My father's dead. My mother's dead. *She* took me away from the sisters and brought me here. I'm in her power. It's the same for you. She's taken you from your parents and brought you here. You're in her power too.'

Suzie was overmastered by Sabine. Both parents dead; she could not imagine anything worse. At least she had the hope of seeing Maman and Papa again one day, when the war was over.

'So you'll be on my side?' Sabine asked.

How could one not be on the same side as someone who had lost her parents definitively? Suzie's own tribulations seemed minor. 'Of course.'

'Swear.'

'Yes.'

'No, swear by all the saints.'

'I swear by all the saints.'

Sabine rose briskly, taking Suzie's hand to drag her up too.

'Where are we?'

'This is the chapel. I use it as a hiding place. The reason that it's safe is because *she* never comes here. She's not Catholic. Now, I'll take you to Micheline. You'd better sleep in my room.'

From that first day Suzie had been under Sabine's rule. Sabine had wanted to be her friend. For a long time she had had no friends, so Sabine's eagerness for her companionship was at first a solace. But it came at a price. Sabine wanted her alliance in her war with her stepmother and watched Suzie carefully for any sign of defection. Suzie had at first tried to retain the friendship of both, because she needed them both. She could see no harm in Madame Ariane; indeed, she seemed full of good will, refusing to notice Sabine's rudeness to her. But Sabine would not permit any intermediate position. Suzie had to take sides: if she wasn't for her, she was against her.

Suzie learned what that meant one evening soon after she arrived when they went to receive their goodnight kiss from Madame Veyrines, Madame de Cazalle and Madame Ariane, who were sitting together on the terrace. Madame Ariane had kissed her cheek and then, impulsively, put both arms around her, whispering in her ear, 'Don't worry. It'll be all right one day.'

In their bedroom Sabine had exploded with fury. 'You mustn't let her do that. She's trying to take you away from me, to turn you into a traitor.'

Suzie had protested feebly, denying her pleasure in the moment, insisting that she had only received, not given anything in the exchange. Sabine's emotional tirade had been kept up late into the night until, sobbing, beaten, Suzie had promised to have no conversations with Madame Ariane. She would hate her, for Sabine's sake, she swore. From then on she had to ignore all overtures of intimacy from Madame Ariane and to ally herself with Sabine. She had no choice but to submit to Sabine's regime of terror.

17

FLORENCE REAPPEARED IN the forest after a couple of hours to summon them home, where they found the Germans installing themselves in the house, and Micheline and Madame Ariane busy moving their belongings and those of the aunts into the tower. The officer in charge had demanded a roll-call of the household and seven o'clock found them, all of them, in the hall waiting for the hour to strike, to knock on the door of the library.

'There is something profoundly humiliating about queuing at the door in one's own house,' Madame Ariane remarked to Henri, 'which is presumably why we have to do it. They've already made me take them round and recount the history of Bonnemort, as if they were guests being given a house tour.'

'More likely so that they learn what is valuable, in order to carry it off to Germany,' Henri replied cynically.

One officer was seated at the desk with another, wearing an eyepatch, standing behind him. The residents of Bonnemort lined up in front of him, as if for a family photograph. Madame Ariane and Henri encompassed the group at either end; in the middle stood the aunts, radiating a haughty indignation, refusing to look at the Germans. Micheline and Florence also lowered their eyes, each of them clutching a child. Suzie shrank into the comforting softness of Micheline's belly, her shoulders wedged just below her bosom. Sabine, Suzie observed, like Madame Ariane, stared boldly ahead. The lieutenant took the bundle of their papers and placed it before the major, who examined each one.

'De Cazalle, Ariane? De Cazalle, Marguerite?' He looked up after each name, while Madame Ariane indicated its bearer. 'De Cazalle, Sabine? Ollivier, Suzanne? Menesplier, Henri? Menesplier, Micheline? Menesplier, Florence? Veyrines, Odette?' He spent some time examining the documents, then slapped the last one down.

'Who is the owner of this property?'

'My stepdaughter, Sabine de Cazalle.'

The major spoke in German. Madame Ariane replied in the same language. Suzie realised that she was the only other person, apart from the lieutenant, who understood what was being said.

'And your husband?'

'He is dead.'

'Who is the other child?'

'She's the daughter of a friend of mine who became ill with tuberculosis; she's been living with us for several years now.'

He picked up Suzie's card again. 'And where was she born?'

Suzie held her breath. This was the first time her story had ever really been tested.

'In St Sever, Pas-de-Calais, in 1931.'

'And this is your farm manager?'

'It is.'

'Are there any other family members?'

Without hesitation Madame Ariane replied, 'The sons of Mr Menesplier are conscripted workers in Germany.'

The major folded his hands on the pile of documents. He was wearing black leather gloves, even indoors. 'We found some interesting things in our search of your property,' he remarked.

Suzie felt Madame Ariane beside her stiffen.

'Do you not want to know what we noticed in particular? A car, a fine car, Hispano-Suiza 1937.'

Still no reply from Madame Ariane.

'What do you say?'

'There's nothing to say. It's my car and it rests on blocks because I have no petrol to run it. It hasn't been on the road since 1940.'

'From now on the house is ours. Neither you nor your family will enter. The garden, the park, the lake are ours also. Please instruct your people they are to keep strictly to their own areas. There will be a curfew from eight p.m. to eight a.m.'

'The cows are milked at six every morning,' Madame Ariane said.

'They must be milked at eight.'

'Cows are milked every twelve hours. A twelve-hour curfew does not allow time for the milking,' she insisted.

'Very well,' he said indifferently. 'Eight p.m. to six a.m. for the sake of the cows.' He obviously could not care less for the cows. Nevertheless, Suzie felt a small surge of triumph at the two hours won. 'The car also we shall use,' he finished.

The lieutenant was handing back their papers.

'May we go?'

'You may.'

Suzie began to turn before Madame Ariane indicated to them they could leave. She told herself she must be careful not to show that she understood what they said. No one noticed this time because, as the rest of them turned, the major spoke again, addressing Madame Ariane directly. 'You will return at eight for dinner.'

Madame Ariane stopped and looked back at the major. Suzie, too, halted with her and for the first time examined the German closely. He had risen and was standing by the desk, not wearing his cap, which rested on the table beside him. He looked very fine in his black uniform, she had to admit, tall and frightening. He was not an old man, for his hair was thick and smooth and dark. He had a long thin tapir's nose, golden-brown eyes, placed too close together. He did not smile. There was nothing, absolutely nothing, about him that was...Suzie sought what she meant... Friendly. Men usually appear polite to women, kindly to children, even if they do not care about them. This man did not bother with even a pretence of good will. He did not like Frenchwomen or children.

What would happen, she wondered, if these men, her countrymen, who spoke her language, discovered who she was? She had no doubt that it would be something terrible. She would certainly be removed from Bonnemort and from Madame Ariane, who was her only link with Maman and Papa. If she were taken away to one of the camps that they used to speak about with horror in Clermont Ferrand, how would her parents find her when the war was over, as Madame Ariane promised it soon would be? The threat lay in Sabine, whose power over her, absolute since her arrival, was now made immediately dangerous. Even the most trivial act, interpreted as disloyalty, could arouse Sabine's bullying, a subtle combination of sulking, denial of friendship, taunts, threats and sly physical persecution. Now these trials, which she had lived with daily, seemed nothing in comparison with denunciation to the Germans.

When Sabine understood that Madame Ariane was to dine with the officers, she exploded with rage. Suzie could not work out whether she was infuriated because her step-mother was being awarded a privilege which should somehow have gone to her, or whether, by sitting at table with the German officers, Madame Ariane was collaborating.

'We'll watch them, to see what's going on,' Sabine decided.

'We can't,' Suzie objected, in alarm. 'We're not allowed to go into the house. We have to stay in the tower.'

'She just says that, so we shan't see what she's doing.'

'No, no, the officer said...'

'You understood what he said?'

'Yes,' Suzie admitted reluctantly.

'That's good. We shall understand what they say as well as see what they do.' As always, Sabine's will overpowered Suzie's.

It was not difficult for them to enter the house from the upper storey of the tower, to creep down the stairs and to hide. It was made easier when they discovered that the batman had prepared the dinner table in the blue salon, which had a gallery. Sabine led Suzie up the spiral staircase while the servant was out of the room. At eight o'clock they were lying flat on the floor of the gallery, with a God's-eye view directly onto a round table laid for three.

They heard footsteps and the major and lieutenant entered, preceded by Madame Ariane. The major took Madame Ariane's usual place at the head of the table. She sat on his right and the lieutenant sat opposite her, with a view out of the window. There was silence while the batman placed in front of each of them a bowl of thin vegetable soup. Sabine nudged Suzie as he stood back and wiped his thumb, sticky from the soup plate, on the seat of his trousers. Suzie resolutely refused to look at her, keeping her eyes fixed on the three figures below them. In that way she might prevent Sabine from starting an irresistible burst of giggling that would risk everything. Sabine did not understand that these were not people who would punish a childish prank with a reprimand.

Below them there was no conversation. The major and the lieutenant unfurled their napkins and began their meal. Madame Ariane did not move. It was only after taking several mouthfuls of soup that the lieutenant observed this. With his head bent and his spoon arrested in front of his mouth, his single eye looked at her and then at the major, whose attention was thus caught. Suzie felt the menace as he slowly turned his head to look at Madame Ariane. The lieutenant was smiling. He was awaiting, and welcoming, an outburst. The major put down his spoon with exaggerated care, so that it did not chime on his bowl.

'You're not eating?' he remarked.

'Thank you, I prefer not.'

The tense silence that followed produced a spurt of adrenalin in Suzie. Madame Ariane appeared submissive; she kept her eyes lowered and said nothing.

The major smiled and lifted his spoon once again. 'We won't let your abstinence spoil our enjoyment. I believe,' he went on, 'that rigorous dieting is a way of life for fashionable Frenchwomen. A sign of their decadence. Nazi womanhood prizes strong healthy bodies to fulfil its duties of childbearing and homemaking.'

The lieutenant burst out laughing, and Suzie saw Madame Ariane relax slightly. The joke was on her, her action of defiance rebounding on her by the major's acceptance of it. Suzie thought of the loose folds of Madame Ariane's dresses, signs that she had once been rounded and filled them out. The agony of not eating the food twisted her own stomach.

The batman removed the soup dishes and placed plates in front of them, returning with a platter containing pieces of fowl and some vegetables, carrots and leeks.

'What is this?' the major asked, as the man went to serve him.

'Guinea fowl, sir.'

One of Micheline's, Suzie thought. Soon there would be nothing left for them.

'Serve Madame first.'

The smell of the guinea fowl made Suzie's saliva run. She clenched her belly to forbid its rumbling and betraying her hunger, hoping that Micheline had something good for them when they escaped from this torture. From the major's expression, she guessed that he was enjoying Madame Ariane's suffering.

'This looks excellent,' he remarked. 'Cut it up for me.' The batman approached and was waved away. 'No, her not you, I want her to do it.' He stared straight at her. 'Cut it up for me.'

Madame Ariane did not move immediately. Suzie wondered if she had understood.

He repeated, 'Cut it up for me.'

She rose tentatively and stood beside him. With one hand he pushed his plate in front of her. Taking her knife and fork she cut the meat into pieces, manoeuvring it off the breastbone, slicing the thigh meat from the leg. When she had finished, watched by all eyes around the table, she returned the plate to its position in front of the major and sat down again.

Then Suzie understood. She saw him pick up his fork in his right hand, while his left hand, still in its black leather glove, lay inert on the table. She wondered how far it was dead. To the wrist? To the elbow? To the shoulder?

The lieutenant had begun eating the minute that the major took up his fork, bending low over his plate and shovelling the food fast into his mouth. He stared at Madame Ariane who seemed to find his one-eyed glare disconcerting. She raised her eyes to a portrait on the wall.

'She didn't understand what you wanted her to do or why,' he commented to the major. 'She didn't realise that this is a company of the wounded, the lame and the blind and the limbless. She didn't know that they,' he jerked his head at the world outside the window, 'call themselves the Hospital Company. And it doesn't mean they're invalids; it means we're all survivors of wounding on the eastern front. To survive there, wounded, meant you were harder than the men who were still fit. The Russians take no prisoners, you know, and in that climate... It was twenty-five degrees below zero for weeks on end in the winter of forty-two. So if you were left wounded on the battlefield, there were only two alternatives. You froze to death or you were bayoneted where you lay.'

Suzie found the lieutenant easy to understand. He was just the boastful warrior, trying to impress Madame Ariane how tough he was. The major was another matter. He wanted humiliation. He took pleasure in making Madame Ariane knock on the door in her own house, in commanding her to cut up his food. These were cruelties that Suzie understood: petty in themselves, they mounted up to make life unbearable.

'The major lost his arm last autumn,' the lieutenant was saying. 'His hand was smashed up in an attack and he retreated for five days with a tourniquet round his elbow and gangrene creeping into his fingers, before he reached a field hospital where they amputated his hand at once without anaesthetic, to kill him or save his life. And he survived.'

The lieutenant's face was mobile; he saw no need to maintain the dignified impassivity of the major's expression. He chewed his food as he talked and swilled the red wine to cleanse his mouth before he swallowed. He pursed his lips, trying to extract a shred of poultry meat from between his back teeth.

'Now, I lost my eye two years ago, at Stalingrad. A piece of shrapnel, the luckiest hit I ever received. It got me out of that hell-hole before the lid of the coffin came down on us. I was walking wounded and I managed to get on a plane and stay on it. When they found it was too heavily loaded for take-off they started to kick people out. The unconscious can't protest. They're the easiest to dispose of and they're probably going to die anyway. But I still lost my toes to frostbite while I waited for the plane at the landing ground at Pitomnik. Five days and five nights I was there, without medical treatment. Beside me was a comrade who had been shot up. He was on a stretcher and lay in agony, crying and calling for his mother for two days. Finally, he understood he wasn't going to make it and he begged us to put a bullet through him to end his misery.'

He pushed his plate away, scraped clean. Suzie understood that he had answered his comrade's pleas and that this action on his part and that of the wounded man was meant to illustrate their common heroism.

The major had taken no part in the recital, but he listened approvingly, nodding at the last anecdote. Then he rose to his feet.

'We shall expect you whenever we dine here. Not tomorrow, as we shall be engaged, but the day after, perhaps.'

18

SUZIE WAS ALONE, crouched in her favourite refuge, Lou Moussou's sty, in a rare respite from Sabine, who had been given some extra homework by Madame Ariane, to be supervised by the aunts; Suzie had been allowed to leave. The punishment lay not just in the task of the extra work, but Suzie's freedom from it. She had made a deprecating face behind the back of Madame de Cazalle and run thankfully away. She would receive the full force of Sabine's bad temper when the work was over, but she could not be blamed for her release.

She had gone immediately to Lou Moussou's house, slipping through the farmyard as quietly as possible in the hope that Micheline would not see her and find her a chore to occupy her solitary hour. She crawled into the musty straw that pleasantly irritated her nose with the beginnings of a sneeze, and curled up, facing the door so that she would be immediately alerted if anyone approached. This place had been her retreat since Sabine had shown it to her on the day of her arrival. Here, she was enclosed in a dark space that seemed to fit around her protectively. At first Lou Moussou was there, as a friend and comforter. Mostly he took no notice of her, after nosing at her on her arrival to see whether she had brought him something edible, taking it gently from her fingers. He then just got on with his piggy life, which seemed to consist of eating, rootling around in his bedding to see if he had dropped something to eat, and lying contentedly waiting to eat. He let her scratch his back companionably. It seemed an ideal existence.

It was still her hiding place. She had often thought in recent weeks, now that the Germans were living at Bonnemort, that when the worst came to the worst and they decided to shoot them all, or burn down the house, she would run in here where they would never find her. She would sit here in the darkness and wait until the war ended, not moving, not speaking, in suspended animation, just watching, until one day the door would open wide and Papa would be standing there with Maman and Lou Moussou himself, saying, 'You can come out now. It's all over.'

After the first few days the German presence had become normality. The terrifying clamour of their arrival had subsided to a background hum of dull fear and Suzie could now distinguish personalities and routines in the newcomers. The two officers, SS Sturmbannführer Knecht and SS Obersturmführer Hartenstein—she knew their names now—occupied the house. The rest of the men camped in the field, using the caves as living quarters and, according to Henri, had made themselves very snug there. A faint smell of woodsmoke and frying floated appetisingly up from their field kitchen, which was evidently kept well supplied. This German zone—house, courtyard, field, stables—was meticulously ordered. Suzie could see from her window the precise rows of motorcycles and the staff car, drawn up near the front door. Then a new car was added: Madame Ariane's Hispano-Suiza. The major liked to be driven in it, and often took it in preference to his own. In the field armoured trucks were parked in a neat row beside two half-tracks with guns mounted on them. Guards always patrolled the house and camp, even when the men and their vehicles were out.

Suzie would listen to the adults' conversations to learn what she could of the Germans' activities. When they first arrived Henri had hoped that they would be recalled immediately, because of the Allied landings in Normandy. All the other units of the SS tank division stationed in the region were being moved north to repel the invading Americans and British. Reports reached them of the tanks lumbering through the countryside and the clashes that followed, but their Germans made no preparations to move and the hope died. They realised that this unit, of the young, the old, the wounded, had been left behind; were with them indefinitely.

Which was worse, she asked herself. Living under Sabine's power, or the Germans'? Once Sabine's moral domination over her was assured and Madame Ariane's influence defeated, Sabine had developed new lines in tyranny. The possibilities of physical terror were opened up by Suzie herself.

The summer of her arrival at Bonnemort was hot. Days of relentless sunshine were broken intermittently by nights of storm. Every evening the children would take the cliff path to the lake to swim. For Suzie this was one of the first and worst ordeals of living at Bonnemort. She did not know how to swim and was terrified of the water, of the way it seemed to rise up to envelop her, however hard she tried to keep her head above the surface, of the way it seeped, stinging and choking her, into her eyes, ears, nostrils, mouth. She was squeamish, too, and although the water was kept pure by the ceaseless, invisible flow that filled the lake from the spring and drained it to the river, she disliked the idea of sharing it with fish and waterfowl.

Madame Ariane was a formidable sportswoman. Suzie had turned the pages of her photograph albums, which portrayed her before the war, swimming, sailing, skiing. For her it was natural that the girls should ride and swim, even if other sports were denied them. She familiarised Suzie with the water and the strokes she must make to master it. Then she suggested that Sabine should help her practise. Sabine herself had only learned to swim the previous summer, also taught by Madame Ariane. She had been an apt pupil and now spent hours swimming up and down, or perfecting her diving. She was delighted to take over as teacher.

Immediately she discovered the difference between her own boldness in the water and Suzie's timidity. She would manipulate Suzie's fear, using it to punish or threaten, whenever she wished. If she wanted to please Suzie, she would help her, or even better, leave her alone. When they pulled themselves out of the lake, their woollen costumes drooping with the weight of water, Suzie would be filled with relief that she had survived the afternoon without drowning. However, when Suzie was in disgrace for some imaginary act of disloyalty, Sabine would use her power to terrify her, jumping into the pool, diving beneath her, seizing her legs to pull her under. She enjoyed the exercise of power and extended her rule, bit by bit, creatively, to demand all kinds of acts of physical daring. Her cruelty was not applied every day. Suzie came to recognise threatening situations and did what she could to evade or postpone them. Sometimes they could not be avoided.

One afternoon that first autumn they had been sent out by Micheline to gather chestnuts. Suzie enjoyed such activities. The woods were always beautiful. The golden light filtered between the trunks of the trees of the chestnut wood, illuminating their blotched, silvery bark. She was a good observer and, squatting under the trees, she hunkered round, picking the fattest bulbs out of their prickly shells. It was an undemanding activity, one in which her sharp attention had no reference to herself.

When their baskets were full, they walked home, climbing the cliff path from the valley. Suzie was trailing behind Sabine, searching for late field mushrooms in the field in front of the house. She heard Sabine calling to her and, looking up, could not see her.

Awakening to danger, she realised that Sabine had disappeared into a covert of rough undergrowth and young trees.

'Suzie, come down here. I need you. I want you to give me a hand.'

Abandoning her basket, she crept forward, stooping under the gothic architecture of dead bramble canes, until she reached the edge of a rocky pit hidden from view by the tangle of vegetation. Sabine was squatting below ground level, like a frog beside a dry pond, at the edge of a hole in the ground fringed with dead grasses.

'I can't see where...'

It was no good; excuses never worked. Sabine's peremptory voice, ordering, then threatening, compelled her to ease herself down on her stomach, legs dangling until she found a foothold. She knew that she had reached Sabine when her ankles were seized and she was pulled abruptly onto the ledge to join her.

'Sabine, how are we going to get up again?'

'We're going on down.'

Suzie clung miserably to the rock while Sabine looked for the next stage of their route, peering down into the narrowing bowl. Suzie could envisage the next stage: a descent into the abyss. She dared not even look at the hole which should have contained something—earth, grass, water—but was filled instead with nothing but darkness. She tried to convince herself that there was no danger. Even if they were stuck, glued to the rock like lizards on the house wall, if they shouted and shouted, surely someone, Henri in the fields, Micheline in the farmyard, would hear them and come to their rescue. Sabine, however, was not interested in relying on others to extract her from danger.

She had seen a foothold and was lowering herself further into the pit. Suzie was obliged to follow. Soon the sky above them was reduced to a disc, shaded with branches. It was harder to see where they were placing their feet and hands. The circumference of the bowl was narrowing. Suzie could see no way out and no way back.

'There's fresh air coming out of there.' Sabine licked her finger and held it over the darkness. 'We must be able to get out down there.' She contemplated the hole, tipping a pebble into the void. They listened to the silence that swallowed up the stone. 'You go first.'

'No, Sabine, please, no. Let's just shout. Henri will come.'

'And then what? We've still got to get out and we'll do it by ourselves.'

'You go down. If there's a problem I'm here to help you up again.'

Sabine's command over her was such that, crying and begging, Suzie was forced further into the hole. She was entering a rock tomb and would never come out alive. She braced her back against the wall of the chimney and lowered herself away from Sabine, crouching above her.

'What's happening?' Sabine called out. 'Tell me what you find.'

Suzie refused to speak. She was so far down now that there was no more vegetation for her hands. She was held in place by the narrow bore of the hole and descended by pushing her body down, scraping her back on the rock, until her knees were bent and then, extending one leg after the other, she found a new foothold. The pressure on the muscles of her thighs increased. Her descent was for ever and for good; she would never, never be able to climb up again.

The pipe opened out. As she put out one foot to find somewhere to wedge it, the rock wall below her vanished. She kicked wildly and lost her purchase. Her fall was a matter of feet. She landed, miraculously, on a soft bed. She lay on her back and her hands discovered hay. It was not wholly dark; rolling over, she could see cracks of light below her and could make out shapes in the darkness, masses, which resolved themselves into structures. She was in a loft in one of the cave storerooms on the path down to the lake. She could distinguish a ladder leading down to the rocky floor and she quickly scrambled down. Wooden doors closed the entrance. Nowhere on the farm was ever locked and the double doors swung open to the push of her shoulder. She found herself on the cliff path, the water shining darkly in the late afternoon light. Returning to the cave, she shouted up to Sabine in the rock chimney, 'It's all right, you can come down.'

She stood outside in the sunshine, gratefully breathing in the fresh air.

Sabine wants to kill me, she thought. She'll go on and on until she does.

Walking back into the barn, her eyes full of the radiance of the sun, she was forced to duck in terror. A powerful projectile had swung just over her head and back again.

'Watch out,' she cried in alarm.

Sabine was standing in the loft, watching the swing of the free end of a rope, weighted with an iron hook, suspended from a pulley. She caught it on its return, and once more sent it in a sweeping arc across the empty space of the barn. When its diminishing swing brought it at last to a swivelling halt, Suzie saw that it hung well above her head. It could not have hit her.

Sabine reached the ground, euphoric at their adventure. 'We must do it again,' she said. 'It was brilliant. We can use it as our hiding place from *her*, instead of the chapel.'

In the light that flooded in through the open doors Suzie examined what they had discovered. The space was empty. Around the walls were wide wooden racks and the rock floor was carved with an enormous circle.

'What is this place?' she asked.

'It's the winepress,' Sabine explained. 'That's where the vat used to be. They put the grapes in it in the olden days and then everyone trod on them to mash them and get the juice out.'

'They didn't,' Suzie said sceptically.

'They did once. But they took the press away when they abandoned the vineyards here.'

Lying in the hay, Suzie asked herself why she had done it. Why? If she had found the courage to make that descent, why could she not refuse to do what Sabine demanded? She had often asked herself this during the first terrible six months at Bonnemort. It seemed as if she was more afraid of Sabine's taunts than of the physical tests she was put to. And perhaps it was true: isolation was worse than danger; friendship at any price. Sabine had a command which sabotaged her will, converting it to her, Sabine's, ends, not her own. But, however much she puzzled over this power, she knew that she had surrendered her freedom herself, in an act of folly and betrayal. She had yielded to Sabine from the start, not knowing how to resist her, but she did not blame herself for that, for what else could she have done? What she regretted was the madness of voluntarily giving up the information that had made Sabine's control complete.

Madame Ariane had made her promise never to tell anyone she was Jewish. Maman had commanded it, too. She could not understand why this element in her identity should be shameful, criminal, yet she could see that it was. And the shame was infectious; other people fled from them. Madame Ariane had welcomed her, but on the condition that her Jewishness was hidden. She understood that she had a duty not to allow the harm she carried to affect others. Was this why she had told Sabine, as a revenge for the suffering she had inflicted, to pass the danger on to her? Or had she hoped that this willing surrender of her greatest secret would somehow show Sabine that her demands had reached the end? There was nothing more she could give.

As soon as the confession was made, one afternoon when they were sitting in the chapel, she had regretted it. She regretted her broken promise to Madame Ariane, for now she was irrevocably committed to Sabine, who recognised her new power at once. 'I'll tell who you are,' or 'I'll tell her what you told me,' were weapons which destroyed all resistance. She could never appeal to Madame Ariane for help, for she would have to admit that she had broken her promise. She was in Sabine's hands until the war ended and her parents came back to claim her.

19

SABINE WAS FASCINATED by the occupiers. She
and Suzie had no direct contact with them, confined by the
Germans' rules to the tower, the farmyard and Micheline's
cottage, but there were opportunities to observe them nonetheless. Madame Ariane's field glasses had lain unused for
months after her failure to interest them in bird-watching.
Now Sabine picked them up every day and trained them on
the Germans' camp. She liked to watch the soldiers in the late
afternoon when, hot and thirsty from their day's patrol, they
would stand around the pipe which flowed into the drinking
trough standing in their underwear to throw water over one
another. Or, they would go, a group of ten of them, to bathe,
naked, in the lake, jumping into the water with shouts of
pleasure. For long minutes Sabine would prop her elbows on
the windowsill to support the weight of the binoculars, and
stare, without moving and without commentary. Suzie would
lean beside her. To her unaided vision, they were indistinct,
forked, tasselled creatures, running and shouting, splintering
the water into iridescent shards of spray.

One evening when Sabine lost interest in the spectacle,
Suzie picked up the abandoned glasses and refocused them

on the field. The young men were just leaving the drinking trough. The head and shoulders of two of them jumped forward under the magnification. She saw the collar of brick-red skin on their necks between their cropped hair and the silky whiteness of their shoulders. She found it hard to believe that these boys, playful and unarmed, speaking her parents' language, wished her ill. It seemed so strange to hate someone for being what she was, Jewish. It was like Sabine's hatred of Madame Ariane, without a reason, just for being what she was, a stepmother.

She swung the glasses from the departing boys to the cobbles in the yard to pick out one of Micheline's decorative hens. The head and shoulders of Madame Ariane swam out of the haze. She was frowning. Her hair was tied back which emphasised her large nose and dark eyebrows; normally pale, her face was coloured with sun and exertion. She was in motion and disappeared at once, to be replaced in Suzie's view by the major, bareheaded.

Suzie abruptly lifted the binoculars away from her eyes to understand what she had seen. The figures shrank back into their context: Madame Ariane, carrying her saddle and bridle, was walking rapidly towards the barn, followed by the major. Suzie quickly replaced the glasses before her eyes. She could see that the major's expression was purposeful. It was harder to decide whether Madame Ariane knew he was behind her, was leading him or fleeing from him.

Stealthily, Suzie laid the binoculars down, saying nothing. There was nothing wrong in the two of them being in the farmyard at the same time. Yet she did not want Sabine to see Madame Ariane and the major together, whatever chance, or purpose, had brought them there.

Two days later it happened again. Micheline had sent the girls to pick peas for dinner. They had brought back the basket and Suzie had been set to pod them. She was much more apt than Sabine for such tasks. Willing, patient and dextrous, she had learned many kitchen skills from Micheline and Florence in her two years at Bonnemort. She could fillet a fish, or bone a chicken, deftly manipulating Micheline's fiercely sharp knives, skilfully separating flesh and bone. Sabine, on the other hand, was impatient and clumsy, usually cutting her own finger and mingling her blood with the meat. Suzie loved to be with Micheline, sitting at the table in front of the open fire in winter or squatting on the doorstep in the summer, tranquilly peeling vegetables.

That day she had placed a colander on the step and was stripping the tiny peas into it, dropping the pods into a basket to feed later to the rabbits. One of Micheline's young turkeys was parading up and down the farmyard, his regular course to and fro mimicking that of the guards in front of the house. Every so often he puffed out his chest and gobbled, his black wattles shaking with self-importance.

Henri walked through the yard, crossing the turkey's path, causing the bird to swell with indignation and rivalry. Henri caressed Suzie's head in passing and went inside, closing behind him the glass-paned door with its red and white check curtains. A little later Micheline opened it again.

'Run to the tower, Suzie, and tell Madame that Henri's here. He wants a word with her.'

Suzie dropped her pea pod and set off. Halfway up the stairs she saw from the tower window Madame Ariane approaching through the garden. She turned back and they met on the stairs. Madame Ariane descended with her to see Henri. In the dimness of the hall Suzie was startled to find a black figure standing at the foot of the stairs waiting for them: the major. Madame Ariane showed no sign of having seen him, passing straight out into the sunlight of the farmyard. Suzie followed more slowly and sat down again on Micheline's step. He had not been there when she went up. Had he been following Madame Ariane, was he stalking her, laying traps for her? Madame Ariane had not noticed, or did not want to notice. Should she warn her?

She finished her job, not drawing it out as she usually did, and put the containers of peas and pods quietly inside the kitchen door, without asking Micheline for another task. She crept into Lou Moussou's little house. The dust danced in the sun shafts that broke through the cracks in the door, and in the womb-like dark of her straw nest, she tried to work out what Madame Ariane was doing. She had dinner every day with the two officers; they all knew that. They all knew that she hated doing it, was obliged to do it. It was not her fault if the major followed her around.

She chewed her fingertips, gnawing at the nails already bitten to the quick, her tongue finding a tiny flap of loose skin to work on. She imagined Madame Ariane living under the major's persecution, as she did under Sabine's. It would be a different sort of tyranny, using different methods, but the result would be the same. You lived in occupied country. At any time, in any place, the attack could strike. You lived perpetually, wearingly, on the alert for the accusation and the penalty. She, Suzie, had never been able to break free of Sabine's power, but perhaps Madame Ariane would be able to outwit the major. Madame Ariane, powerful, independent, must be able to throw off his domination. Suzie willed it with all her strength, with the double identification of a fellow victim, of Sabine and of the Nazis.

But Sabine must not know. Whatever the state of war between the major and Madame Ariane, Suzie wanted to protect her from Sabine. She knew that Sabine had a profound sensitivity to atmosphere. The very act of formulating the thought of hiding something from her was enough to rouse Sabine's awareness. Even though she could not discover the particular incident that Suzie wished to hide, she was able, subliminally, to identify the subject.

That night the heat broke with a thunderstorm, one of the clashing, rainless storms of the region, during which the thunder rolled around the hills and sheets of lightning hung for seconds at a time from the sky. In Madame Ariane's dressing room where she and Sabine had slept since the Germans' arrival, Suzie woke at the first growl and lay watching the white flashes at the window. She could hear the wind in the trees behind the tower. A loud clapping sound came from the room next door. She waited to hear Madame Ariane's quiet movements in her bedroom, getting up to close the window, or refit the shutter. The noise came again and again.

The bed in the dressing room was boat-shaped, the most beautiful bed she had ever slept in. It was meant for one large person, but she and Sabine were obliged to share it. She slept lightly, without movement, lying along the very edge of the mattress to allow Sabine the maximum space. Her companion was a wild sleeper, thrashing her legs and crying out in her dreams. The worst was when she ground her teeth together, making Suzie shudder. Now Sabine was lying quietly, face down, sprawled over three-quarters of the bed.

Suzie lifted the sheet with infinite precaution and slipped out of the bed, tiptoeing across the wooden floor. The communicating door was unlocked and she pushed it open gently, to see if Madame Ariane was sleeping through the storm. The bed was empty, had not been slept in that night, the linen lying as flat as when Micheline had smoothed it into place that morning. One wing of the casement window had broken loose and was swinging in the wind. She anchored it again to its hook and leaned on the sill to look out at the view, which

on this side of the tower overlooked the house and the courtyard. In the quiet and darkness between the rolls of thunder
and the flashes of lightning, she saw a red pulse throbbing
in the courtyard, then another. She thought they were the
glow-worms that she had seen in the garden last summer. She
leaned out further and then jumped back as Sabine's hands
fastened on her waist from behind.

'What are you doing?' she spoke in a whisper, as if
Madame Ariane were asleep in the room.

'I came to fasten the window. It was banging in the wind.'

'Where is she? Why isn't she in bed?'

'I don't know. She wasn't here when I got up. Perhaps
she's gone to see that the house or the animals are all right
in the storm.'

'Move up.' Sabine pushed in beside Suzie and looked out.

'There's someone smoking down there,' she remarked.

'The guard?'

Sabine did not hear her suggestion under a new fusillade
of thunder, much closer. A sheet of lightning ripped through
the sky, illuminating the courtyard for two or three seconds
with a piercing white light that bleached away all colour,
arresting movement, so that the scene resembled a black and
white photograph. The smoker in the courtyard was revealed
as Madame Ariane, seated on the low stone balustrade that
divided the terrace from the cobbles. She was looking out at
the storm; behind her, in the open doorway, stood the major.
A second later, darkness had returned.

Sabine gripped Suzie's shoulder. 'Did you see that? Did
you see who it was?'

Suzie was overcome with guilt. If she hadn't thought
it, two days ago, perhaps it wouldn't have happened. If she
hadn't come to see what the noise was, Sabine would not have
awoken. She had revealed Madame Ariane to Sabine.

She padded back to the dressing room. Sabine remained leaning on the sill, waiting for the next lightning flash. Suzie got back into bed and pulled the sheet over her head. With deliberation she stepped back into Before. She was walking down the wide, dingy stairs of their apartment house in the Marais, holding Maman's hand in one of hers and in the other clutching Rahel. They were going for a walk to the children's playground where there was a see-saw that she loved...

The sheet was dragged back and Sabine sat on the pillow beside her, her knees drawn up, her nightgown pulled over them. Her body was rigid with excitement.

'What were they doing there together in the dark? It was a secret meeting. She's a collaborator, a traitor.'

20

THE GIRLS WERE perched in their new vantage point in
an unused bedroom on the first floor of the house, in the
German zone.

'What you have to know about the Russians as fighters is that they are inhuman,' the major was saying. 'I don't
say subhuman, the term that is so often used. It may be tech-
nically correct according to ethnological principles, but it
is not the right word in a military context. *Subhuman* implies
a lack of intelligence, as well as a lack of other human qualities,
and this mis-understanding may lead military commanders
into unwise moves, in the belief that their opponents are
stupid.'

At the sight of Madame Ariane and the major sitting
together in the dark, Sabine's interest had switched abruptly
from the young soldiers to the major. She now trained her
binoculars on him, noting where he was during the time he
spent at Bonnemort. As Suzie had done several days earlier,
she rapidly became aware that the major stalked Madame
Ariane, although her interpretation, expounded to Suzie in
long sessions in the loft of the winepress, was that *she* was
leading him, not that he was following *her*.

They had discovered that the officers now often sat outside on the terrace at the back of the house after dinner to finish a bottle of champagne that they had requisitioned from the cellar. Madame Ariane's nightly duties now extended beyond the cutting up of the major's food and being present through dinner. She was obliged to accompany them onto the terrace and sit in the long pale evenings while the major drank and talked.

'He likes an audience,' she told the aunts, 'for his lectures.'

In pursuit of their prey, Sabine and Suzie were watching an after-dinner meeting. Suzie had protested that they couldn't expect anything to happen under the eyes of the batman and the lieutenant, and Sabine couldn't understand anything that was said, if they talked at all, which they hadn't much last time. However, Sabine's hunting instinct was aroused.

'They are inhuman because they can endure extremes of cold, hunger and pain beyond the limits even of trained and hardened SS troops...' The major droned on. He was a theoretician; he liked to generalise his personal experiences so that they fitted his ideology. Madame Ariane sat so still, showing no reaction to what was being said, that she appeared to have drifted into a trance, lulled by the interminable stories of the eastern front.

The steward came out to pour more champagne for the officers. It was at least the third time that he had done so, Suzie noticed. Madame Ariane's glass remained untouched. The major sipped his wine and the lieutenant began to talk. He had no time for philosophising. He only recalled reality, mostly descriptions of battle. Today, he was talking about hunting. Suzie only gradually understood that the 'special operation' in which his panzer company had been involved had been the hunting of humans. He was indignant that his troops had been used for such work, not because he objected to it, but because it was not what tanks were built for. In the open, on the streets of a town, no one could outrun his machine. He would give chase, knock down his victims, trample over them, grinding them into the earth; an enjoyable game. But the hunted would try to hide where the tanks could not operate. He was describing how the rats were beaten out of the cellars and granaries, vermin killed. Tough work, which only the strongest and most dedicated could undertake.

Madame Ariane sat, stony-faced, making no comment. The major cut him short by unexpectedly pouring him more champagne.

'The barbarism of the Russians is simply underlined by their refusal to sign the Hague Conventions,' he remarked repressively.

The interruption only made the lieutenant's need to talk more insistent. He described his revulsion from the pests he had seen killed, the boys' corkscrew curls, the men's bushy black beards, the women's shaven heads. Suzie had a flash of recognition. She had never met a Hassid, but she had seen pictures in a book, and could hear Maman explaining that the little boys were forbidden to cut the hair in front of their ears, so that it grew long and curly, longer than Suzie's own hair. And the men wore beards and the women wigs. But he could not mean these people. They were, Maman had said, very pious, good people.

The bottle was finished and the lieutenant called for another. Both Madame Ariane and the major seemed offended by the lieutenant's incoherent rambling about the human slaughter on the eastern front, for different reasons. Madame Ariane had turned her head away and was looking fixedly at the shaggy bushes of box that marched in pairs up the slope of the garden. The major once again broke in on the lieutenant's discourse.

'But these were easy to recognise. Much worse is the Jewish virus that lives in Germany and France in disguise, sapping the strength and morale of the people like a parasite. I never participated in one of the special treatment operations, as the lieutenant has. My own very modest contribution to the effort of making the Reich Jew-free took place before the war, when I was in Berlin and had to call at the Ministry of Foreign Affairs. I was passing through an office on my way to an appointment when I saw a man whom I had known in my youth in Bavaria. I knew that his mother had been Jewish, or at least half-Jewish. This foolish man, who was Aryan by half his heritage, compounded his situation by marriage to a Jewess. I had lost touch with him for some years, but I recognised him at once. He had clearly succeeded in hiding his true identity and, at a time when Jews had been removed from the Civil Service, was working at the heart of government. When he saw me, he recognised me also, and he knew that justice would overtake him. Naturally, I informed his superiors and when I enquired later, I heard he had been removed to Dachau.

'True power,' he continued, reverting to his preferred generalisations, 'is a moral force, not a physical one. It is one to which the people submit willingly, recognising its inevitability. When I was fifteen I was taken to a rally at Nürnberg and I saw there the joyful surrender of a people to its leader, the subordinate submitting to the power of the superior, as his nature obliges him to do. Just as when a woman surrenders to a man: it is what nature intends. The role of the German people in Europe and in the world is that of the superior. We are natural leaders and this war will impose that understanding on others. Like a horse that struggles, or a woman who resists, people have to be forced to do what their own nature requires.'

Suzie closed her eyes for a moment. She could feel Sabine stirring beside her, bored by the monologues in a foreign language and the evident disengagement of her stepmother from the Germans. The officers were rising from their seats. Madame Ariane stood up too, and holding onto the back of her chair she said, 'I shall wish you goodnight.'

'Wait,' the major said, abruptly. 'Lieutenant, I shall join you for coffee in the *petit salon* in a moment. Please tell the steward to serve it at once.'

The lieutenant left. Madame Ariane remained where she was, as if she needed the chair to support her after what she had heard that evening. Sabine's interest was quickened by the long silence. They could not see the major, who was standing almost directly below them. Then his heels sounded on the flagstones as he moved slowly forward. When he was a step from Madame Ariane, he put out his real hand and placed it on the back of her neck. Suzie could see that he was gripping the column of flesh, pressing his thumb and forefinger on either side, below her ears. He moved even closer so that he stood at right angles to her and spoke into her ear. Suzie could barely make out the words.

'So, what have you to tell me today?'

Madame Ariane spoke loudly. 'Nothing, there's nothing…'

'I've been watching you.'

Madame Ariane tried to move away, but like a metal bar his false arm closed in front of her.

'Let me go,' she begged.

'Tell me what you know.'

He had forced her to face him. His hand was now around the front of her neck, caressing it under her ears. Suzie saw the fingers tighten and Madame Ariane's head tip back. Suddenly he let go and she stepped away, unsteadily, stumbling.

Her voice was clear. 'Longas,' she said. 'I've heard there will be a demonstration…'

'Good, good. When?'

'I don't know...'

'When?'

'The day after tomorrow. The fourteenth.'

'Good. Don't move.'

Madame Ariane ignored him and, breaking free, walked round him to the garden door. Just before she reached it, she stopped and said rapidly, 'Be careful. It could be an ambush.'

Sabine could hardly contain her impatience until they reached the safety of their own territory.

'You see, I was right. He put his arms around her. That only means one thing.'

She stripped off her cardigan, then her dress, leaving both of them draped inside out over the end of the bed. Suzie reached behind her back to undo the buttons of her dress.

'He was bullying her,' she said, almost in a whisper. As you do me, she might have added.

Sabine's anger shifted from Madame Ariane. 'Why are you always on her side? Why don't you agree with me? You always contradict me.'

She emerged from the enveloping folds of her nightdress, thrusting her arms into the sleeves, her head poking out last. Suzie had unthreaded one arm from her dress. Sabine grasped it with both hands. Suzie was not going to make matters worse by contradicting this statement, however false it was. She allowed her wrist to lie limply in Sabine's grip, which tightened painfully, grinding the bones together.

'You're a traitor too. And if you like her and them so much, I'll tell them who you are.'

Suzie emitted no protests. Sabine had not asked what had been said after dinner, and Suzie herself had had no time to reflect on what she had learned. Once they were in bed, Sabine fell asleep immediately, while Suzie lay with her back to her, gazing at the luminous rectangle of the unshuttered window. Her thoughts scurried to and fro between the terrible messages that had been conveyed to her that evening.

Her mind went back to harvest time, a year ago when Henri and Micheline had been cutting hay in the orchard. Georges had already been taken off to Germany and Roger had disappeared into the forest, so they all had to do more work on the farm. She and Sabine had carried some water down to them at the end of the afternoon, the terriers accompanying them. Only a small rectangle of standing grass remained in the middle of the field, which they would finish before long, then drink the water thirstily and climb back towards the house with the children carrying their scythes.

As Henri and Micheline turned and moved back towards them, three rabbits burst out of their last refuge, running haphazardly in different directions. The terriers, yelping ecstatically, pursued them, Sabine shouting encouragement and praise. Suzie had watched one rabbit racing along a stubble track between two long swathes of drying grass. At the edge of the field it doubled back, straight into the dogs. Boys with their ringlets flying, pursued by the lieutenant in his tank, his hunting cries mingling with Sabine's; the major watching Madame Ariane, recognising a hidden Jew by his special power. She had shrieked in horror as the terrier in the lead seized the rabbit in its jaws and broke its neck.

Henri, who had stopped to watch the chase, looked at her kindly. 'Don't fret,' he said. 'It's their nature.'

Would Henri, in his generosity, forgive the lieutenant, who was savage by nature? She turned onto her stomach and put her forehead onto her hands to think more of the problem of Madame Ariane and the major. Had Madame Ariane gone over to the Germans? This was not credible, but in a world in which the impossible happened all the time, in which parents disappeared and men in tanks hunted children, people betrayed their natures. Perhaps she was giving information as a trick, to trap the major in some way. Suzie liked this idea, but could not think how it could work, nor what purpose it would serve. Another worry presented itself: Madame Ariane could be attacked by her own side as a collaborator. Suzie had heard of such killings, of bodies found on lonely roads with notes pinned to their chests. *Here lies X, collabo.* Until now, she had felt a sense of justice fulfilled when she had heard Micheline tell of such executions. But how did the executioners know who was a collaborator? Perhaps they made mistakes.

She thought again of Madame Ariane stopping before she opened the door to the house and saying, 'Be careful...'

She had betrayed the Maquis to the major, but she had been forced, she had been afraid.

Yet there had been no need for her to tell him to be careful.

Suzie screwed her eyelids tight to cancel out the memory. She knew what had happened to Madame Ariane. Madame Ariane had done what she herself had done in revealing her secret to Sabine; she had voluntarily surrendered to the enemy, admitting its power. Suzie vowed that she would remain loyal to Madame Ariane, whatever happened. She was Maman's friend; her father was a friend of Omi and Opa, a long time ago; she was her last refuge.

21

TWO DAYS LATER the girls were woken at dawn by the German trucks departing. Sabine flung open the window to watch them go, disappearing into the trees, swallowed up by the mist that hung in the valley.

'They're out on a big rampage,' she said. 'They're taking Madame Ariane's car; the major is getting into it now.'

At breakfast Madame Ariane announced that there would be no lessons today; they were going on an expedition. She would not say where.

'We might be stopped on the road, so it would be better if you were able to say honestly that we were going for a picnic,' she explained. 'When—if—we get to where we're going, I'll tell you what's happening.'

'How far will we ride?'

'About thirty kilometres, so we'll set off as soon as possible.'

Their food was wrapped in napkins and stowed in the paniers of their bicycles with their water bottles. It was only eight o'clock when they cycled out of the farmyard and into the lane. Any diversion from routine excited Sabine and she was in high spirits, resentment and plotting put aside for the day. Suzie was in a fever of anxiety. Were they going to Longas, to be led into a trap? Where was Longas? Madame Ariane had not spoken willingly to the major. But it was not possible to tell whether she had spoken the truth, or whether she had lied to trick him. Suzie's mind spun with the wheels of her bike. She had no doubts any longer about what would happen to her if she was caught by the major or the lieutenant. They would chase her and hunt her down, like the rabbit in the hayfield.

After two hours they reached their destination.

'Where are we?' Sabine called, as they cycled into the village.

'It's Lavallade.'

'What's happening? Why are we here?'

Suzie was gripping her handlebars, looking at the ever-changing patch of road in front of her. It wasn't Longas. Madame Ariane wouldn't enter the trap herself, that was obvious. Or would she? Would she be there when the Germans arrived, to make it look as if she had nothing to do with it? Then they would quietly let her go later, when they had taken everyone else they wanted.

Madame Ariane looked at her watch. 'We're going to be in time,' she said.

'What are we here for?' Sabine demanded. 'What's going on?'

Her tone was marginally less abrupt than usual, because she really wanted to know the answer. People were gathering in the street as if it were market day, mothers holding children by the hand, women walking together, old men shuffling along on sticks. The doors of the houses were open and the occupants stood on their steps, watching the passers-by, as if uncertain whether to join them or not.

'Do you know what day it is today?'

'Friday,' said Sabine.

'The fourteenth,' said Suzie.

'Yes, the Fourteenth of July, our national day.'

Suzie could remember the Fourteenth of July, long ago, Before, in Paris, with parades and dancing in the street at night.

'We haven't celebrated the Fourteenth of July for five years,' Madame Ariane was saying. 'You probably don't remember much about it. They're going to hold a ceremony here.'

'Lunch,' said Sabine longingly. 'Will there be lunch with soup and pâté and *confit* and salad and cheese and a tart?'

'No, I'm afraid not this year. It'll have to be quick, in case the Germans or the Milice hear of it and come to break it up and arrest us all.'

'But we'll be all right, won't we? Your major will take care of us.'

Sabine spoke with the naivety which, although the insolence of her intention was clear, normally made it impossible for Madame Ariane to take issue with her. For two years Suzie had watched her submit to Sabine's rudeness without losing her temper. This time Sabine had struck a nerve.

'I don't know why you should think I can protect you from the major, Sabine,' she said furiously, 'but, believe me, you're wrong. The major is beyond anyone's control.'

Sabine turned away with a little smile on her lips, as if well pleased with the response she had aroused. Madame Ariane walked on, looking dissatisfied with her attempt at self-defence.

The church clock struck eleven and for a moment the crowd in the square hesitated. They all had an air of wariness and of false innocence, Suzie thought, as though they half-expected to be challenged and would be ready to provide elaborate excuses for why they happened to be there.

'*Français, françaises...*'

A small voice floated over the company. People ceased talking, turning to the balcony of the Mairie, where a rotund figure, wrapped in a sash of office, had appeared. The crowd seemed to draw together, moving inwards, concentrating on the figure half-obscured by the tricolour which flew above his head.

Suzie could not hear the mayor very well. He turned his head to address different sectors of the square and as he did so his voice faded and was lost. She could only catch phrases.

'This is a time of pride... Liberation from the oppressor... France is freeing herself, with the help of the heroic efforts of the Red Army and the Allies... This is a time of hope... The return of the prisoners and the deported from the camps in Germany to their families...'

Suddenly he was speaking directly to her. She understood that Madame Ariane had not led her here into a trap. She had brought her to hear this news. Maman and Papa would soon return to France and come to Bonnemort to find her. The terrible image of the lieutenant hunting men with his panzers slid away. She saw others moved by the same words. A woman nearby had taken out a handkerchief and was blotting her eyes with it. She was not alone, Suzie told herself. Many people, Micheline and Henri included, had relatives who had been taken away by the Germans and they would all come home soon. She found comfort in the idea of there being lots of them. Two individuals, Papa and Maman, each alone, might disappear, but it was impossible for so many people to be lost. They would all come back together.

The mayor had finished speaking and there was movement at the end of the square. Suzie squirmed forward through the crowd to see what was happening. When she reached the front, she saw that a company of men had marched in and were now forming up in front of the war memorial beside the Mairie. An accordionist began to play the Marseillaise and at once all noise ceased. Everyone stood to attention.

When the anthem ended, three men detached themselves from the front rank of the *maquisards* and marched to the memorial. One of the three came forward and laid a wreath, saluted, turned. Suzie saw that it was Henri. Around her the emotion that had been generated by the reference to the deported reached a new level. To her astonishment she saw men weeping, tears unashamedly falling down their cheeks. The woman who had put her handkerchief to her eyes at the mayor's speech was now crying openly, her face red and contorted. Another woman, also weeping, put her arms around her. The last post was played. The *maquisards* presented arms and marched out of the square, leaving an atmosphere of festival. This would have been the moment for the lunch that Sabine had longed for.

Suzie turned to look for Madame Ariane and spotted her talking to Henri and Monsieur Vernhes, the schoolmaster from Lepech Perdrissou. You could see that she was full of happiness, for she was smiling and put out her arm to Suzie, pulling her towards her in a sideways hug. Suzie allowed herself to respond. After all, Maman and Papa would soon be home and she would be safe for ever, and Sabine was not there to witness her defection.

Sabine joined them a few minutes later, pushing her bicycle, her face sparkling. Suzie saw the enthusiasm die out of her expression as she approached them. She knew that this was not due to Madame Ariane, who would have normally been entitled to an afternoon's grace after a morning of such excitement. Monsieur Vernhes, the only person who made Sabine afraid, was responsible for the look of gloom. Suzie did not know what had happened during Sabine's two years at the village school, but she had observed that Sabine always encountered her former teacher with wariness.

She and Sabine stood by while the adults talked. Sabine's eyes were cast down and she tapped the edge of one foot against the other. Suzie was thinking how easy it was to tell someone's mood from their actions. Henri and Monsieur Vernhes did not like one another; that too was very plain. They faced Madame Ariane and spoke to one another through her.

'Are you satisfied with the demonstration?' Monsieur Vernhes asked.

When Henri hesitated, Madame Ariane replied, 'It was wonderful. Everyone was so moved.'

'I'll be pleased as long as there are no reprisals,' Henri said at last.

'That will be the moment to attack them.'

'It would be an act of folly. If we ever faced them in a fire-fight we would be wiped out. Our duty is to protect the young people and wait until the Germans go, not to waste lives.'

'Very heroic.' Monsieur Vernhes had a very flat, unem-phatic voice, Suzie noticed, yet his tone was sneering. 'We should drive them out ourselves, not sit here waiting for de Gaulle and the Allies to arrive and do it for us. If we wait for them, it could be winter before the Germans are gone. Can you hold out that long?'

'We'll hold out as long as we have to, provided there's no killing.'

'So there'll have to be a massacre before you'll act?'

'Don't spoil the day,' Madame Ariane begged. 'We've been round this track before. Let's see if there is any reaction to today's demonstration. Let's see what happened at Longas.'

The schoolmaster was not placated. 'Look at this place,' he said. 'We've taken it over; it's in the hands of the Party and the people now. The mayor, the gendarmes, the local author-ity, they're running it now and neither Vichy nor the Germans can do anything about it. That's what we want at Lepech.'

'No we don't,' said Henri. 'What we want is the Germans out. We don't want the Party in. And if we're allowed to choose, we won't choose them.'

'We're the party of the martyred, the shot, the deported. We've done everything to rid this country of the fascists and we'll run it when they've gone.'

'Others resisted too, from the very first.'

Madame Ariane was looking from one man to the other anxiously. Suzie thought, she is caught between the two of them, like me between her and Sabine. One is powerful and has to be soothed; the other she agrees with, but can't show it. So she speaks with a calm voice to try to prevent a quarrel. She doesn't want to be forced to choose. She would choose Henri, of course, anyone can see that. And would I choose her or Sabine?

'If we were questioned,' Madame Ariane said to the girls when they were ready to set off for home, 'it's most unlikely to happen, but if there was a denunciation…' She seemed to be talking more to herself than to them, convincing herself that she had taken no risks. 'But if you were questioned, you would say that we went for a picnic.'

'You're telling us to lie,' Sabine said.

'I want you to omit part of the truth. But, yes, if you were obliged to reply directly to the question, did you attend the Fourteenth of July celebrations at Lavallade, I think you should lie.'

'The sisters said we must always tell the truth, whatever it cost us.'

Madame Ariane gave a small smile, not looking at her stepdaughter. 'Sabine, let's have no more of this. If you decide to sacrifice yourself because of your fidelity to absolute truthfulness, I can't stop you. I just ask you to remember that you have no right to implicate others. I think that even you, with your religious scruples, might hesitate when truthfulness demands a list of names. Some people die under torture rather than do that.'

Sabine looked sulky at the way her provocation had been turned against her. Suzie had no problem about lying. She would lie and lie and lie again, spin any tale, if it would be believed and save her. Her fear was that her interrogators would step immediately beyond lie and truth, and that violence would descend impartially, on liar and truth-teller, guilty and innocent alike.

22

SUZIE AND SABINE were cycling back from mass in Lepech Perdrissou. The aunts, who made the expedition in the donkey cart, their one outing of the week, always remained behind to lunch with the curé, leaving the girls to ride home by themselves.

Mass had been an occasion of fear for Suzie when she arrived at Bonnemort, heightened by the physical as well as spiritual preparations that Micheline insisted upon. She would wash the girls' hair on Saturday evening, and lay out their best dresses, newly ironed. Suzie had been terrified of exposure through ignorance, and had no one to ask what she should do, for Madame Ariane did not attend mass. Suzie would therefore cultivate her blankest expression, practised in Clermont Ferrand when she was looking after Maman, which usually made adults think she was a little stupid, or even deaf. In this way she did not have to reply to such questions as, 'When is your saint's day, dear?' or 'When did you make your first communion, my child?' The method had worked with the curé who, soon after her first appearance in church with the Cazalle family, ceased to make enquiries about her knowledge and origins. The first time that she attended mass she had been astonished at what they were doing, a Shabbat dinner performed for a Christian audience every Sunday. Now she was used to it, sitting, standing and kneeling automatically, moving her lips in time to Sabine's responses.

The sun was almost at its peak and the road shimmered in front of them in the heat. Ahead, in the centre of the road, lay a tangle of rope which, when they reached it, suddenly thrashed itself into a paroxysm, coiling and recoiling, twisting and writhing in their path. Suzie yelped in disgust, swerving widely and riding on. Sabine braked and put her foot to the ground to look back.

'It's two snakes,' she shouted. 'Stop, stop, Suzie. Come and see.'

Suzie drew up, but would not go back.

'They're fighting, wrestling, killing one another,' Sabine reported, walking closer, springing back as the live skein leaped like a single creature. 'No, they're fucking.'

'It's probably shedding its skin,' Suzie suggested, when Sabine came alongside her.

'No, there were too many, a whole knot of them. They were vipers, too. I saw the V mark on their heads: V for viper, V for victory.' She began to chant, faster, as she put on a spurt and overtook Suzie. 'V for viper, V for victory,' she sang.

Suzie made no effort to catch her up, pedalling despondently behind. Sabine's spirits had been manically cheerful since the parade at Lavallade two days earlier. She refused to admit this expedition as evidence of Madame Ariane's innocence or good faith. They had been sitting in the winepress the previous evening to discuss the question of Madame Ariane and the major. 'It's nothing to do with the Resistance,' she had explained to Suzie. 'It's sex, sex, sex.'

'But you keep saying she's a traitor; she's not. She must be helping Henri...'

'Of course she's a traitor. She's a sexual traitor.'

When they had first met, Sabine had immediately discovered the extent of Suzie's ignorance and took it upon herself to inform her about sex and reproduction. Suzie had been secretly offended by her new companion's teaching about a subject which Maman had already discussed with her, in horticultural terms. Seeds, Maman had explained, were planted by fathers and kept warm by mothers until they germinated and babies were ready to be born. Sabine had poured scorn on this metaphorical knowledge and had ruthlessly demonstrated its defects and limitations.

Suzie now understood the hydraulics of reproduction. Sabine's information, startling and implausible as it had first appeared, had been confirmed by her observation of the life of the farm: the cocks' pursuing and mounting their hens in the orchard, the dogs' restless howling when one of the bitches was on heat, the litter of kittens, born, naked and bloody, before her eyes on the chair in front of the fire in Micheline's kitchen. Micheline and Florence dealt with all these alarming aspects of procreation in an entirely matter-of-fact manner which Suzie found reassuring. However, this reassurance was undercut by Sabine's excited interest, her self-caressing, which Suzie avoided seeing, but could not avoid knowing of. Up till now Sabine had never linked her detestation of Madame Ariane with her interest in the sexual life of the farm. As there were simply no men, apart from Henri who was a father to them all, there was nothing to suggest it. Now the uniting of these two subjects was ominous in Suzie's eyes.

She had never understood why Sabine hated Madame Ariane so much. When, early on, she had timidly questioned her on the subject, Sabine's replies had been incoherent.

She had taken her away from the convent.

But Sabine had hated the convent.

She had taken her away from the village school.

But Sabine had been bullied at the village school.

Incomprehensible.

Once before, in the autumn of the previous year, Sabine's resentment against Madame Ariane had reached an acute phase. Suzie was not sure what had brought on the murderous fury that had consumed Sabine for a period of about two weeks; she only recalled that it had begun on one of the few occasions when Madame Ariane left Bonnemort, at the time that Dr Maniotte and Henri were arrested.

They had got up early to go mushrooming. It was early autumn and the weather was ideal, warm and damp after a heavy downpour the previous day. They had left the house soon after six in the morning and had discovered Madame Ariane, dressed in the smart suit that she had worn to collect Suzie, her foot poised on the pedal of her bicycle, her handbag and a large parcel in the basket.

'Where are you going?' Sabine asked abruptly, without even saying good morning.

'Just to Racinès. I'll be back for dinner, so I hope you find plenty of ceps. Goodbye.' She pushed off and rode out of the gate.

Sabine looked after her in fury. 'She's not going to Racinès. She never wears that suit to go to Racinès. Where's she going?' She led the way into the forest in a brooding silence.

Suzie was soon absorbed in her task. Although she had never got over the foreignness of the countryside, and disliked the violence of animal existence, she liked the vegetable side of country life. She was a willing gardener, patiently watering the rows of salads, carrots, leeks and onions, carrying her watering can from the sink or the water-butt to the kitchen garden. She patrolled the orchard throughout the summer watching the fruit ripen until the moment came to gather it, the cherries in July, the peaches in August, the apples in September, the quinces in October. She looked forward to the grape harvest in September and the walnuts in November.

She was particularly good at mushrooming, which she had learned with Papa, walking in the woods near Paris when she was a little girl, reciting the Latin name for each variety they found. He had taught her the landscape and season for each variety: open grassland for field mushrooms with their tender pinky-brown gills; pine woods for morels with their reticulated, bulbous heads; mixed woodland for the sinister, black horns of plenty, and open woodland for prized ceps, with their velvety surface and spongy underside. She had a quick eye and could single out the fungi under the leaves, needles and ivy of the forest floor.

That morning her basket was soon covered with the fat brown caps of ceps. She could hear Sabine moving behind her some distance away, following their customary route. When they turned for home, Sabine's basket was almost empty. Suzie made no protest as Sabine put her hand into her full basket and transferred some to her own.

'I've been thinking,' Sabine said. 'We could poison her.'

'What do you mean?' She knew quite well what Sabine meant.

'With mushrooms. Listen, it's a wonderful idea. No one would ever know.'

'But why?'

'We go mushrooming and gather all the worst ones especially for her. We make a ragout, two ragouts, one for her, one for the rest of us. We all eat the mushrooms. She's ill; we're well.'

'But she might die. Some of them are very powerful.'

'Of course she'll die. That's the point. It's the best way of killing her.'

Sabine became a person obsessed. She talked about her plan whenever she and Suzie were alone, to the exclusion of all other topics, repeating herself single-mindedly. She spent unaccustomed hours in the library, studying the engravings in an old book on fungi, noting the most lethal types.

'The problem,' she complained, 'is that it gives the shape but not the colour. You'll have to help me, because you're much better at recognising them than me.'

Suzie, too, was busy, planning her counter-coup. She could not believe that Sabine would carry out her idea, but she could not be sure. If Sabine really made a lethal stew of mushrooms, she, Suzie, would have to tell Micheline that she was afraid she had made a mistake with one of her ceps and then the whole lot would be thrown away. Or she would take Madame Ariane's dish and drop it on the floor.

Sabine slipped her hand loosely through Suzie's arm and pinched the flesh on the inside of her elbow between her nails. Suzie felt no pain at the time, although afterwards matching crescents of deep blue bruises marked Sabine's threat: her life or Madame Ariane's.

'And you won't tell anyone. You won't betray me. No one will believe you anyway. And if you do, I'll tell them who you are. I'll write to the police in Racinès, a denunciation, written in green ink. All the best ones are in green ink, apparently.'

Suzie felt the teeth of her trap. She had promised Maman and Madame Ariane not to tell anyone that she was Jewish; she could not go to Madame Ariane for help, out of shame for having betrayed her trust.

Sabine reached for her chin and pulled her round to face her. 'Say you'll help me.'

'All right,' Suzie conceded reluctantly, not looking her enemy in the eye.

'Promise not to tell.'

'I promise not to tell.'

Dropping a plate was not covered by such a promise, but she was still not sure if she would have the courage to do it. Sabine let go of her chin and as Suzie turned her face away, she lunged towards her and bit her ear. Suzie cried out at the sudden, sharp pain, putting her hand up to feel the blood on her fingers.

'That's so you don't forget.'

Woken early by Florence, the girls were sent mushrooming again the next day. Sabine was exceptionally diligent, gathering a large basketful of mushrooms. As they walked home, she said. 'You'd better look at them to make sure they're the kind we need.'

Suzie took the container and examined its contents. Sabine appeared to have picked everything she had seen, without discrimination, for several genuine *Boletus edulis* lay in the basket. Yet she had not done badly for her purpose. She had found an enormous *Boletus satanas*, which Suzie knew you must not pick, and a greeny-white mushroom, which she thought must be a highly poisonous *Amanita phalloides*. She boldly picked these two out and threw them away.

'They're no good to you.'

'I thought they looked really wicked.'

'The problem is that some of the poisonous ones look really like the edible ones. It's a problem even for me. You'd got the wrong ones. Those are edible, and these too.' She chucked out four more. 'Those aren't very good to eat, that's why we don't pick them normally, but they don't do any harm.'

'There'll be none left soon,' Sabine said angrily.

'I can't help it if you don't pick the right ones.'

Sabine sulked, but not badly; she knew that she would get nowhere if she had to consult the book.

'I've got some here for you.' Suzie transferred several from her own basket. Sabine looked suspicious, but made no comment.

They took the spoils of their walk into the kitchen. Sabine shouted to Micheline, 'We're going to make a ragout for lunch.'

Suzie was not sure that she had really stripped Sabine's basket of all its deadly contents. She had no opportunity to sort through them again, as she was set to wiping clean her own fungi and to cutting them up with the garlic. When Sabine left the scullery for a moment, she seized a handful of Sabine's mushrooms, now sliced and prepared, and substituted a heap of her own before she heard Sabine returning.

Her final effort to save Madame Ariane came at lunch. They were to eat the mushrooms as a first course, and the girls served them to Madame Ariane and the aunts. In the kitchen Sabine handed Suzie the Judas plate.

'You can give it to her.'

Suzie nodded and took it in her left hand. She let Sabine walk ahead of her to the dining room with the plates for Madame Veyrines and Madame de Cazalle. Sabine put down a plate in front of each of her aunts and returned to the kitchen to fetch her own. Suzie carefully placed the dish in her right hand in front of Madame Ariane who smiled and said, 'Thank you, Suzie.' The other she put in her own place.

'Bon appetit,' said Sabine, in her sprightliest tone, patently false to Suzie's ears. She continued to prattle, about the beauty of the forest that morning, eating with relish and darting a glance at Madame Ariane who had speared one piece of mushroom on her fork and was about to eat it.

Suzie pushed her food around her plate.

'What's the matter, Suzie?' Madame de Cazalle asked. Suzie saw Sabine frowning at her.

'Nothing, thank you,' she replied.

'Then eat properly.'

She took a mushroom into her mouth, bit into the springily resistant flesh and forced herself to swallow it. Did it taste odd? Was she going to die? Then another, and another. She put down her fork. 'I'm afraid I don't think I can finish all of them,' she said.

Madame Ariane did not die. Nor did Suzie. Sabine did not appear to realise a trick had been played on her, insisting that it was a sign of Madame Ariane's links with the devil that she was able to eat a whole plate of poisoned mushrooms and remain none the worse for it. She made no suggestion of repeating the attempt, as if her fury had been consumed in her plan which though unsuccessful, had been sufficient to staunch her rage.

23

WITH A SINGLE-MINDED frenzy Sabine now dedicated herself, and Suzie, to the pursuit of the major and Madame Ariane. Suzie, whilst preferring reconnaissance to action, took part reluctantly. Sometimes she thought of what they were doing as the observation of wild animals. Sometimes she thought of it as spying on the enemy. Yet Madame Ariane was not the enemy and her identification with her was so great that she felt as if she was watching herself. She knew, although she did not tell Sabine, that Madame Ariane gave information to the major. It was obvious to Suzie that she was in the major's power and did not do it willingly. The question that concerned her was whether Madame Ariane was being forced to give away real secrets, or whether what she told him was false and useless.

Sabine's interpretation of what was going on was entirely different.

One afternoon they were playing on the shady side of the farmyard, when they had heard German voices at the gates. The soldiers on duty, two of the elderly ones, were confronted by a small girl and a large cow.

'It's Marie-Jeanne come for the bull,' Sabine reported.

The Bonnemort bull had a high reputation locally. Without fail his efforts impregnated the cows offered to him; the calves were invariably healthy, the bulls tender and white-fleshed, the heifers good milkers. For years Henri had allowed the smallholders of the neighbourhood, those who existed with no more than one or two cows to feed their families, to make use of the services of the bull without payment.

Marie-Jeanne was younger than Suzie and Sabine, about nine years old. Her mother and her aunt worked the family farm, with Marie-Jeanne's help, while her father had been held since the defeat as a prisoner of war, in a camp in Germany. She was standing in front of the sentries, barefoot, a stick in her hand to tap the cow's bony rump when it lingered too long grazing on the verge. Even though she spoke French, she was explaining her errand to the soldiers in the local patois, as an act of defiance, although even if she had used French, they would have understood her no better. Her voice was becoming increasingly shrill as she repeated her explanation which she reinforced with descriptive gestures that astonished the guards. Finally, she thwacked her cow and the two of them walked in, ignoring attempts to stop them, through the courtyard and into the farmyard.

'The idiots,' she commented to Sabine and Suzie, before yelling, 'Micheline,' at the top of her lungs.

Micheline emerged from her kitchen and kissed Marie-Jeanne four times, alternating from cheek to cheek. 'Is it time for that cow of yours again, the most troublesome we ever have?'

'It's true,' Marie-Jeanne agreed with complacency, as if her cow's reluctance to accept insemination was a confirmation of her refinement and excellence.

'Henri brought the bull in, but he's away. He must have forgotten you were coming. Girls, you'll have to lend us a hand.'

Sabine and Suzie joined Micheline and Marie-Jeanne in driving the cow before them towards the pen in which Henri had put the bull the night before.

He was a fine beast and Suzie, with her anthropomorphic sympathy for the animals of the farm, had always admired him. His hair was a rich caramel colour, as soft as cashmere, like the coat Opa used to wear long ago in Düsseldorf in the wintertime. He had heavy shoulders and short sturdy legs. His head was broad, with creamy curls on his forehead between his widely separated dark eyes, which gave him, for Suzie, an air of wisdom. He looked commanding, paternal, as he stood in the field among his cows and calves, who gave him precedence at the feeding trough.

Now he had lost some of his habitual calm, moving about the pen and bellowing at the sight of the cow. She had become increasingly skittish and at first refused to enter the pen, so that Micheline, Suzie and Sabine had to make a cordon to drive her in to meet the bull. Marie-Jeanne, who had been holding open the wire, promptly closed the picket on her, shutting herself and the cow inside for their encounter. Micheline climbed into the enclosure to join them.

The bull was in a hurry, already clambering on the back of the cow, his hooves scoring her hide. Suzie hung back, wanting to leave, but Sabine had clambered onto the fence, hanging over the top rail, and she returned reluctantly to join her. She saw with amazement that the bull's penis had emerged; its long creamy oval testicles jerked. The cow swung round, so that the bull slid off his target. Micheline and Marie-Jeanne were calling to one another in patois, trying to back the cow onto the bull. She was turning her head seductively to look over her shoulder, while sidling away from him around the pen, swishing her tail from side to side. The bull made a second attempt, which she sidestepped neatly, and again his front hooves came crashing to the ground.

Suzie's ears were full of the roar of breathing: the snorting of the bull, the nervous huffing of the cow, Micheline's exasperated intake of air as the cow evaded her outspread arms once again, and the excited, rapid breathing of Sabine beside her, leaning eagerly forward to watch.

Micheline and Marie-Jeanne exchanged instructions and set about forcing the cow back, holding her still to allow the bull to mount her. This time they were successful in synchronising their actions. The cow retreated in front of Micheline's advance. Marie-Jeanne seized the cow's tail and pulled it over her back. At the same time, when the bull reared up, its pizzle extending to an astonishing length and rigidity, the child took hold of the penis and guided it to its goal. Then she ducked out from beneath the momentarily united bodies and, seconds later, the bull had disconnected. The cow, as if nothing had happened, moved away, lowering her head to tug at the grass.

In the few seconds that the conjunction lasted, Suzie heard Sabine speak. 'That's what *they're* doing. I know it.'

Later they sat on the low chairs in the chapel, out of range of Micheline and Florence who might require them for chores.

'You can't believe that she's working for the Germans,' Suzie protested. 'It doesn't make sense.'

'She could work for both sides,' Sabine argued. 'Just because she goes to a Fourteenth of July parade doesn't mean she isn't also betraying them to the major.'

'She might tell him things to mislead him,' Suzie suggested.

'She might,' Sabine conceded. 'But it hasn't anything to do with that. It's just sex, like the cow and the bull.'

'It's obvious she's afraid. How can you think it is sex?'

Sabine crossed her arms and drew her hands down her torso. 'I just know. You can't yet.'

It was true, Suzie thought; two fleshy cones, small but distinct and separate, were visible under Sabine's dress. Suzie's own chest was a flat as a child's, the nipples the palest lilac blemishes on her white skin. She frowned. She could not understand how developing a bust would help you to see something that wasn't there.

Sabine was frowning too. The trouble with Suzie was that she was almost simple about some matters. She was a good companion. Life had improved enormously since her arrival. Sabine now liked Bonnemort better than either the convent or the village school. But Suzie refused to comprehend certain things, even when they were explained to her. Sabine knew what was happening, not because of anything they had seen, although they had seen enough: they had seen him take *her* hair, tugging it to pull her round to kiss her, for example. Suzie was right, he was violent and threatening, but Sabine couldn't make Suzie understand that that was sex. Nor did Suzie have any sense of atmosphere. Sabine remembered at the convent that one of the nuns, Sister Cécile, who had wide blue eyes and a mole on her upper lip from which a single black hair grew, had a crush on Antoinette. Sabine had never known what, if anything, had ever taken place, for she had been too little and too despised to have been informed. Yet she remembered the tension that radiated from each of them. It had been so palpable that Sabine could smell it in the air. And it was the same now at Bonnemort. Suzie couldn't see or smell or understand anything.

She dropped her hands into her lap and said, 'I long to be grown up. I can't wait. Eighteen is old enough. In five years' time I shall be grown up.'

Suzie could not imagine five years. Would the war still be going on? Or would it all be over and Maman and Papa back from wherever they had been taken? When she thought about her family it was always in the past, so that when she visualised the future, normal development reversed itself and she felt herself shrinking. She hoped that in five years' time she would be a little girl again, living with Maman and Papa and Rahel in Paris.

'Why?' she asked, with real curiosity. 'What's so good about being grown up?'

'You never understand anything,' Sabine spoke venomously. 'I want to be grown up so I can have power over other people. That's what being adult means. When you are a child, people can do things to you, things you don't want, things that hurt. When I grow up, it'll be my turn.'

Suzie made no comment, although she pondered what Sabine had said. It was true that people did things to you that you didn't want, but they did them to Maman and Papa, too, and Madame Ariane, so having things done to you wasn't a question of being a child. And Sabine had quite enough power already. How much more could she want?

Late one afternoon Sabine was at the sitting-room window watching Madame Ariane leave on horseback, leaning down and lifting the saddle flap to check the girth as she rode out of the farmyard. No sooner had she seen her go than she heard the motor of the major's car start up in the courtyard. She ran over to the window on the other side of the room.

'She's going and now he's going.'

Suzie, who was reading *The Misfortunes of Sophie* with the book propped up against her raised knees, did not respond.

'They're going to meet somewhere.'

'We can't follow them if they're on horseback and in a car,' Suzie said thankfully.

'If we were somewhere like the ridge above La Peyre, we could see the road from there almost all the way to the village.'

'Suppose they don't go that way.'

'It's worth going, just in case.'

'Sabine, let me stay and read.'

'No, you're coming too.'

Suzie was forced out and marched off into the forest. When after thirty minutes' climb they reached their vantage point on the bare ridge they could see nobody in the whole expanse spread out in front of them. The road, intermittently visible through the trees on the other side of the valley, was empty. The woods and the folds of the hills hid all life and all movement.

They sat while Sabine raked the road with the binoculars. Eventually abandoning their fruitless wait, they made their way back down the hill into the forest. Suddenly, as they reached an open clearing cut through by a cart track, they saw the Hispano-Suiza. Suzie's reactions were quicker than Sabine's. She ducked into the bracken, dragging Sabine down to join her. No shout or movement. They had not been seen. Suzie thought at first that it was because there was no one to see them. Then a voice came to her ear.

Standing on the track well clear of the car was the major, unmistakable in his black uniform and peaked cap, and beside him a smaller figure, a man. Not Madame Ariane. Suzie felt a wave of relief wash over her. The likelihood of coming across Madame Ariane and the major together had been remote, but she had feared it nonetheless, a scene so culpable that even she would not be able to defend her any longer.

She listened to the voices floating faintly in incomprehensible snatches across the pasture. She could only just make out what they were saying, but it seemed to her that they were speaking German. Then, she thought, of course it would have to be: the major doesn't speak French. So the other, a Frenchman, must speak German. The men had their backs to them, facing the view. They began to walk towards the car and Sabine grasped Suzie's arm.

'It's Mr Vernhes,' she said.

Suzie in the same instant saw that the major's pistol was in his hand, not aimed but pointing at the ground. He held it easily, as if it were a natural growth from his fist, a replacement for his lost hand. The stories she had overheard in Micheline's kitchen came back to her. The major must have caught Mr Vernhes and any moment now he would lift his arm, place the gun at the schoolmaster's head and fire.

Vernhes' voice reached them. He had a strange accent in German; his tone was defiant rather than pleading. The two men went round to the far side of the car. The major climbed in and slowly the Hispano-Suiza moved off down the track. When it had gone there was no sign of Vernhes.

They emerged cautiously from their cover.

'Where's *she* gone?' Sabine said irritably.

'He didn't come to meet her,' Suzie replied. Then she added, 'He speaks very funny German, Mr Vernhes, with French all mixed up in it. Do you think the major captured him and he managed to talk his way out of it?'

Sabine was uninterested. All she wanted now was to go home. They resumed their path through the chestnut woods. They had reached a point where the route divided when abruptly someone moved to block their way: Vernhes.

'Sabine,' he said, 'and her little friend...'

'Suzie,' said Sabine. She took Suzie's arm in self protection as if to form a single defensive unit.

'What are you doing here?'

'We're walking.'

'Of course, we're quite close to Bonnemort here.' Vernhes was looking round him as if establishing his position for the first time. He turned onto the small path away from the house, signalling them to follow him. 'Come.'

Sabine seemed about to run; then as the impulse left her she dropped Suzie's arm and followed. They walked until they reached a ruined farm. It was situated off the path and the track up to it had almost disappeared. Its roof was intact, but on one side the window openings were empty, on the other boarded up and covered with creeper, giving the place the same crooked, lopsided look as the lieutenant with his eyepatch. Looking abandoned from the outside, inside it showed signs of occupation: wine bottles and saucepans littered a table; the fireplace was full of dead ash. Vernhes led them into a smaller room where a door laid over some trestles made a table around which were gathered a few chairs.

He seated himself, while Sabine and Suzie remained standing.

'So, Sabine,' he said. 'It's a long time since I saw you. Sit down.' The invitation appeared more like an order. With exaggerated slowness, Sabine pulled out a chair and obeyed.

'What are you two doing wandering around the woods?'

'We were out for a walk, just walking.'

Sabine was uneasy, glancing at Suzie for support. Vernhes concentrated the fire of his questioning on her, taking no notice of Suzie. How had he escaped with his life from his encounter with the major, she wondered. He must be very cunning. She could not understand why he wanted to question Sabine whose replies, at first minimal, became longer and more circumstantial. There was something odd about the tone of Sabine's voice, Suzie thought. It must have something to do with Vernhes' being a teacher, for she sounded anxious, as if she was unsure whether her answer was correct and feared she might be punished. He wanted to know about Bonnemort, as much about Henri and Madame Ariane as about the major and the German occupiers. He knew Sabine well, for he was aware of her hatred of her stepmother and played upon it, encouraging her to tell him about her.

Suzie felt her fear grow, rippling out from her stomach into her limbs, in case Sabine should blurt out her suspicions of Madame Ariane and the major. She could do as much harm to Madame Ariane by betraying her to the Resistance, as she could do to Suzie by betraying her to the Germans, and to harm her stepmother was what Sabine wanted. Would she realise that this was her opportunity to kill her, far more effective than fantasies of poisoning? Suzie stilled her own movements, drawing in her breath and releasing it slowly to make the time pass.

However, Sabine said nothing of the subject that dominated their waking hours, the relationship between Madame Ariane and the major. As they left the ruined farm, Suzie wondered why Sabine had kept silent. Had she not understood the opportunity, or was she still secretly uncertain of the facts? Or did she see that it was all really a game, beyond the boundaries of real life?

24

SABINE LED THE way back to Bonnemort at a run. When Suzie called to her to wait and Sabine shouted her refusal over her shoulder, Suzie saw that she was crying. The path, steep and stony, still covered with the fallen leaves of last autumn, was dangerous taken at Sabine's pace. Suzie kept her eyes fixed on the track, a narrow channel between tumbledown walls, afraid of falling, afraid of falling behind. She had no wristwatch, yet she could tell, by the texture of the depleted light, lying almost horizontal, shining through the trunks of the trees into their eyes, that it was late. When Bonnemort came into view on the other side of the valley, Suzie noticed at once that Madame Ariane's horse was grazing in the field with Madame de Cazalle's donkeys. They must have been away for a long time. Ahead of her, as they approached the clutter of farm buildings, Sabine had swerved off the track and was making for the thicket that concealed the secret entrance to the winepress.

'Sabine,' she wailed. 'Let's go home now.' Sabine halted, but did not turn back.

'I've got to think.' She ducked under the branches and Suzie followed her to the rim of the funnel, which was a bowl of darkness in the weakening light under the trees. Sabine squatted down and lowered herself over the edge. They knew their way down by now, clambering from foothold to foothold with the ease of custom. Sabine had almost reached the bottom, with Suzie above her, wedged in the narrowest part, when the first sounds from inside the winepress reached them.

Suzie immediately thought that an animal was trapped there. Its heaving, angry breath rose up to them, amplified by the funnel, the air grating its way out of its body. Her heart began to beat faster in sympathetic anguish. The creature was suffering; it moaned in pain. She lifted her lower foot to climb out, but Sabine reached up to grasp her ankle, pulling her back again. She herself was moving down, as slowly and quietly as she could. The animal was trying to escape, for it was knocking, knocking, rhythmically, repetitively.

Suzie lowered herself alongside Sabine. They were now crouching side by side on the narrow ledge where the funnel emptied into the loft. Sabine had twisted round so that she no longer faced the rock wall. As Suzie dropped into place beside her, Sabine's hand gripped her arm, not letting go, tightening and loosening in time to the ramming below them.

Now Suzie could hear not one animal, but two. Below the gasping breath of the furious beast was a counterpoint, the sobbing murmur of another. She could feel their frantic distress and growing fury. The beating went on through it all, at a faster tempo now and with gasps of agony. It was like listening to torture that nothing could relieve. The nail of Sabine's index finger, driving into the muscle of her upper arm, pierced the skin, leaving a rim of blood. Suzie covered her ears, but it was impossible to blot out the cries of agony which echoed from the rocky walls, swelling to fill the space where Lou Moussou had died.

Suzie still felt sick with horror when she thought about it. From the time of her arrival she had found the animal side of country life terrifying. Even the poultry disturbed her; she recoiled from their chattering rush and beating feathers. She never became accustomed to the dogs and since she lacked authority, they were all the more boisterous in her company. Whilst Sabine would unleash the big ones and throw sticks for them, Suzie flinched even from the terriers' emphatic rage, barking at anything they considered unusual.

Only Lou Moussou, visited every day, talked to, fed, eventually became familiar enough not to horrify her. He moved slowly, predictably, within the confines of his sty. His pink skin with its sparse stiff bristles gave him a human appearance, which was only increased by the knowingness of his tiny eyes. She and Sabine would carry his swill from the boiler by the bread oven, sharing the weight of the bucket between them, to tip it into his trough and watch him eat it. She could interpret his approving grunts and was sure she could tell which ingredients he most appreciated.

Her feelings for him were complex, for although he was admired and revered by Sabine and the Menesplier family, and was more domesticated, more of a personality, than any other of the farm animals, she was well aware of the taboos associated with him by her own people. Maman and Papa were secular. They had rarely attended synagogue and did not keep kosher at home, even in the days when it was possible to regulate food in such a way. Yet they never voluntarily ate charcuterie, did not touch *choucroute* with sausages, avoided *porc aux pruneaux* on the menu. She had never been told not to eat pork; they just didn't do it. And in the ancient rejection of this human-like, intelligent, amiable beast she saw, oddly, a parallel to her own hidden, rejected Jewishness. Maman and Papa regarded the pig as unclean because they had never had a chance to know and understand her beloved Lou Moussou.

One January day, as Micheline poured out their hot milk at breakfast, she had said, 'You won't have any schoolwork today because the Mr Jouanels are coming.'

'Oh, wonderful.' Sabine was pounding some stale bread into her milk, into which mixture they were allowed a teaspoonful of honey. It was as if it had unexpectedly been announced that it was Christmas or the Americans had arrived.

'Who are the Jouanels?'

'It's the end of Lou Moussou. Crrk.' Sabine swept her spoon across her throat.

'Everyone has to help,' Micheline explained. 'That's why you're not studying today, so don't run away.'

'We don't want to run away. We want to be here. There'll be a special lunch, Micheline?'

'There'll be *boudin*, as usual, and you'll have to help with it. I'll be busy. Suzie, what's the matter, child? Why's she crying?'

The idea of the death of Lou Moussou was bad enough. She thought of his sharp, trusting eyes, his delighted grunts of anticipation when he heard the clanking of the bucket. The betrayal was so terrible, she could not imagine how they could bring themselves to do it. Sabine's excitement was of a piece with her nature. She knew her well enough now to expect her to delight in the suffering of her pet. But how could Micheline so carefully nourish someone only to lead him to his death?

Everyone prepared for the event; even the aunts came down from their room. Madame de Cazalle became nostalgic as Florence helped her on with her apron.

'I remember when Odette and I did the pig-killing. There were no men left at Bonnemort by 1917.'

Micheline made a doubtful face. Twenty-five or thirty years ago the old ladies might have had more strength than today, when sitting at the table to cut up the meat was all that could be expected of them. The killing was to take place in the winepress, chosen because there was a pump there with fresh water from the spring. Lou Moussou was an illicit pig, his presence hidden from the Requisition, so the butchery had to take place out of sight, for fear of a visit by the authorities, or even a casual caller who might make a denunciation. In the farmyard Sabine and Suzie were set to stoke the fire under the boiler that had been filled with water early in the morning. Florence set out large numbers of metal receptacles for different purposes: bowls and basins, cauldrons and pans were piled up inside the winepress. Micheline unrolled her clothful of special knives, testing each one, and sharpening them all with her steel. Finally, Henri and Micheline placed a low wooden trough upside down in the middle of the winepress.

In the valley the sun was just beginning to melt the frosting of ice on the grass of the orchard, as they made their preparations.

'It couldn't be better,' Florence said. 'A fine day in the waning moon. It's perfect. I remember the first winter of the war, we had four pigs to kill and it rained for a week, by which time the cycle of the moon was wrong. It was hard to know what to do.' Perhaps because her mother was so rigorous a pessimist, Florence was always cheerful.

'We'll say it was perfect when we've got through today without the requisitioning folk turning up unexpectedly,' Micheline warned.

The official pig-killing was set for next week and for that occasion Florence did not care about the phase of the moon. The bureaucrats would carry off the pigs for slaughter and nothing would be left for the household.

'Too cold for me to wait out here,' said Madame Vey-rines, turning on her cane towards Micheline's door. As they all followed her, Madame Ariane observed Suzie's dejection and was suddenly smitten with the significance of the occasion.

'Oh God,' she said. 'Oh Suzie, I'm sorry.'

No one paid any attention to her exclamation, for at that moment the Jouanels came into view on their bicycles, rounding the corner of the drive. Madame Ariane drew Suzie to one side.

'Perhaps you don't feel well,' she suggested. 'If you had a headache, you could spend the day resting in your room.'

Suzie could not take the escape route offered to her. She had too much fear of what Sabine would do if she disappeared from the ceremony. And she could not leave Lou Moussou to suffer on his own.

'No,' she said. 'I'll stay and help like everyone else.'

The Jouanels, the pig-killers, were twins, in their sixties, from Lepech Perdrissou. They were both tiny men of immense strength, with leathery skins criss-crossed by hundreds of lines and smiling dark brown eyes. They laughed and joked all the time, sometimes adding comments in the patois to Micheline and Henri on the performance of the gentry. The whole household made its way down to the winepress, where the Mr Jouanels took off their coats and wrapped themselves in their white aprons.

Suzie did not witness the moment of betrayal when Henri, Micheline, Florence and Little Mr Jouanel went into the sty to bind the victim, but she heard the roar of outrage, the squeals of fury, the breathless commands of Mr Jouanel and Henri as they struggled with Lou Moussou. She suffered with him, his terror and bewilderment, and felt the rough stones of the path scoring his skin as he was hauled down to the winepress.

She only saw him at last when he was dragged in on his back, his trotters tied together across his belly.

The next stage was the most difficult moment of the day, for he had to be lifted onto the killing block and it took everyone, both Mr Jouanels, Henri, Micheline, Florence and Madame Ariane, to achieve it. Even Sabine, dancing round the group, pulled on one bound leg to bring him into position. Suzie shivered by the door, unable to bring herself to assist, unable to stop herself from looking.

The screaming of the prey and the shouts of his torturers died away. The extra assistants backed away, leaving the four guards on the four quarters. To Suzie the victim looked hideously human, a grotesquely fat baby, lying on his back, his trotters joined like beseeching hands, his ears flapped back and his snout in the air.

Big Mr Jouanel picked up one of the knives, testing its sharpness by laying the side of the blade against the ball of his thumb. Sabine picked up a large enamel basin and stood behind him. In their white aprons, moving in unison, the two of them looked like the priest and the altar boy who officiated at the services in the village church.

With a single, swift gesture, Mr Jouanel slit the side of Lou Moussou's upturned throat. He stepped aside and Sabine moved forward with the basin, holding it so that it caught the fountain of blood that pulsed out of the wound. She was spattered by drops that showered upwards as the force of the blood hit the pool that had already run into the pan. Lou Moussou shrieked, his harsh scream ululating in time to the spurting of the blood. Everyone watched in silence for the long minutes until the flow reduced to a trickle and the cry to a sob, then to silence.

Suzie, who watched throughout the drawn-out agony and death of Lou Moussou, ran out of the winepress, up the path, into his sty. Here she crouched in the straw, still warm and redolent of his presence, putting her head on her bent knees.

'Suzie, Suzie,' Micheline was calling her. 'We need you and Sabine to carry the water.'

By the time she returned, Lou Moussou had been lowered to the ground, the trough righted, hollow-side up, and he had been placed within it, like a baby in its bath. The water was simmering in the boiler and Sabine and Suzie were employed carrying the buckets to douse him. When he was submerged, the Jouanels, Henri and Florence scrubbed furiously to lift off the bristles, which were gathered up by Micheline and put aside for use as brushes. While this was going on, Madame Ariane slowly, cautiously, carried the great basin of blood up to Micheline's kitchen. The girls pumped up more water.

The aunts were seated in the kitchen in front of the fire ready to prepare the lunch. Suzie gratefully undertook the task of setting the table, and stirring the soup, while Madame de Cazalle fried the *boudin* and the apples. Then the men, and Sabine who had remained outside with them, were called in to eat. They did not linger over the meal, although the Jouanels ate and praised heartily. Micheline smiled a little. The worst was over and she liked knowledgeable appreciation of her cooking better than anything.

Lunch finished, the working party returned to the wine-press. Madame Ariane climbed the ladder into the loft and released the rope of the pulley from its anchorage. Lou Moussou, white, naked and hairless, more human than ever, was tipped out of his bath by Henri and Little Mr Jouanel and dragged by his back legs to the pulley. The metal hook on the end of the rope was inserted under the ligatures around his hind legs, and Big Mr Jouanel and Florence hauled him to the vertical until his snout just touched the ground.

Sabine and Madame Ariane spread out a cloth in front of him and Big Mr Jouanel took up another knife from the battery, a long one this time. They all stood back, respectfully, while he made a cut, not swift and slashing as before but with deliberation, down the whole length of Lou Moussou's belly, so that his entrails tumbled out, steaming, writhing, onto the cloth, which Micheline gathered up by its corners. With Florence's help, she carried it to a trestle table set up in one corner, where she distributed yards of viscera to the children. She instructed Suzie how to take her pail of intestines and rinse them carefully, turning them inside out without piercing them, so that the chitterlings would form perfectly clean, unbroken containers for the sausages she would make.

Suzie had settled into a routine of horror. Lou Moussou's shrieks of agony and the sound of the pulsing of his blood still echoed in her ears as she worked, her fingers blue with cold and corrugated by the water, as she rolled and turned, rolled and turned.

The Jouanels were butchering as rapidly as they could, with Henri their assistant. Micheline and Florence supervised their amateur workers and took on the skilled tasks themselves. The pluck was handled by Micheline, who, with her tiny knife, cut the heart from the lungs, put the liver aside for pâtés and piled up the web-like membrane from the lungs that she used to wrap her stuffings and faggots. By five o'clock when darkness fell, Lou Moussou had been divided into his component parts. The Jouanels departed, each with a sizeable joint of pork rolled up in his apron. They joked about an identity check on the way home.

'Go through the woods,' Micheline urged.

'No, we can't ride; the road is too rough. It's not far, we won't be caught.' With the shouts and waves that mark the end of a happy and successful day they left.

The girls were now given the job of cleaning the wine-press. Sabine pumped the water into the bucket, which Suzie

threw onto the rocky bloodstained floor, swabbing the pinkish flood out of the door and over the edge of the cliff.

Normally the processing of a pig would take several days,
but the need to remove all sign of Lou Moussou's existence
demanded that they work until late that night. In the kitchen
Suzie helped with the mincer, feeding in the raw meat and
back fat and tamping it down while Madame de Cazalle
turned the handle. At last Micheline cleared the table and
served dinner. Suzie, pleading tiredness, rejected her pork
chop and crept away to bed.

Sabine had understood first the meaning of what they heard.
As the terrible sound of the climax died away, she slid forward on her belly towards the edge of the loft. Suzie, imitat-
ing her silence and precaution, advanced to join her. Below
them the winepress was in darkness, save for lances of faint
light that penetrated the cracks in the door, and in the layers
of blackness she could not interpret what she saw: two forms
like trees leaning away from one another, yet joined at the
trunk, grafted and entwined. Then the sound began again.
Not caring whether she was heard or not, Suzie turned back
to the funnel, to climb back to the open air and the light.

Part Four

BONNEMORT
10–15 March 1945

25

'I DON'T WANT to alarm you, Theo.' His aunt's voice, disembodied, was faint and crackling, a call from another world. He was already alarmed. The aunts used letters to communicate at a distance. They normally reserved the telephone for mundane local matters or dire emergency. For Aunt Odette to have put through a call to Paris already indicated that it was serious.

'I think you should come to Bonnemort for a few days, if you could spare the time. Or Ariane. We really need Ariane. Could she not come to us for a while?'

'Of course I'll come if necessary. What's the problem?'

'Sabine has been…has had an accident.'

'What's happened to her?'

'Her life isn't in danger, but she is rather ill. I think you should come, Theo.'

'What happened?'

There was a pause so long that he thought the line had been cut.

'Hello, hello…'

'… attack…' Aunt Odette's voice swelled to audibility and faded again.

'Can you hear me, Aunt Odette? I'll try to get a line this evening to tell you when I'm coming.' He slowly replaced the receiver. Although it was deeply inconvenient, he suddenly saw an opportunity. He must persuade Ariane to come back with him.

It took considerable determination to fulfil Aunt Odette's demand. To leave the Big Man for several days on the plea of a family emergency, to persuade Ariane to come with him, was not easy. He expected Suzie to be left behind in Paris to attend school, cared for by Pascal Wolff's housekeeper. However, Ariane had insisted on her coming, in spite of what she had said earlier about separating the two girls. They went by rail, a journey of twelve hours with three changes. Suzie, installed in a window seat, read her book or gazed out of the window at the wintry landscapes of central France. Ariane spent long periods with her eyes closed. They arrived at Bonnemort late at night, to be welcomed by Micheline, Florence and the aunts who were waiting for them in their old sitting room, which they now reoccupied, on the first floor.

'How's Sabine?' Ariane asked, embracing each member of the household warmly. Her question was answered by a Greek chorus of women's voices.

'She's alive.'

'Thank God.'

'She's asleep.'

'We've taken a nurse, for the nights…'

'So someone is with her all the time.'

Theo interrupted the cycle of commentary and explanation. 'What happened?' he asked again. There was a pause from the four women, as if each was waiting for one of the others to answer. Then they began to reply together.

'It must have been an accident…'

'She was found unconscious…'

'The Baillet boys came to tell us…'

'Old Franco had to bring her home in the cart…'

'We called the doctor…'

'We have to call Dr Arnoux now in St Saud…'

'It was he who told us to call the police…'

'But what happened?' Again Theo's voice cut through the recitative. Silence fell.

'Sabine is too ill to tell us.' It was Florence who replied.

Ariane rose. 'I think Suzie should go to bed now. It's been a very long day.'

'I've put her in the little white room,' said Florence, 'so she won't disturb Sabine.'

'Suzie, come with me. Florence will show us what she has arranged.' She put her hand out to Theo. 'And I think we should go to bed, too. We'll understand everything much better by daylight.'

Theo went to Sabine's room and opened the door. A nurse was sitting at a table, reading. At the far end of the room the bed was in darkness, so he could barely distinguish his daughter's form.

'How is she?' he enquired, awkwardly.

'Asleep,' came the reply.

In his own room the fire was lit and one lamp shone beside the bed. A moment later Ariane entered and began at once to unpack her suitcase. This immediate acceptance of a joint life at Bonnemort, which she had resisted in Paris, alone made the journey seem worthwhile.

'Ariane, what is going on? What happened to Sabine? Why will none of them answer a direct question?'

When the straight answer came he understood why no one else would reply: because it was impossible to believe.

'Sabine was very badly beaten.' She came over to him and took his hand. 'I know. It's incredible. Florence told me and she was making no mistake. I am not sure whether the aunts have really taken it in.'

'But why? Who did it?'

'No one knows. No one has the least idea. The police know less than anyone, according to Florence, until Sabine is able and willing to speak. Tomorrow you can see the doctor, the nurse, Sabine, the police, and find out what you can.'

'How can I?'

He lay awake for a long time savouring the comfort of the room in the light of the dying fire. Ariane was soon asleep beside him. The primrose silk curtains, at least fifty years old, so worn at the inner edges that they were as fragile as cloth from a tomb, were reflected in the mirror above the fireplace. The clock on the chimneypiece, doubled by the mirror, was a golden globe held up by an ebony figure. He remembered all of it from morning visits to his mother forty years ago. Yet amid the familiar he was confronted again with the inexplicable. Each time he returned, where Bonnemort should have offered the reassurance of continuity, there was instead a shock of violence. Until Ariane had spoken, he had assumed his daughter's illness was an accident, or even a disease: he had interpreted Aunt Odette's reference on the telephone to an 'attack' as meaning pneumonia. Why?

There was no answer. In all his enquiries at Bonnemort, he felt, he had sought facts and been given feelings. He would approach this with logic. The first hypothesis was that the attack was a chance encounter, having no relation to what had happened last year. This seemed unlikely, unless the police could show him that there was a history of violent attacks in the area. His heart and thoughts seemed to stop simultaneously at this point. Had she been raped? Ariane had not said so. Florence would surely have given her that cardinal information and Ariane would not have held it back from him.

If the attack was not random, why would anyone bear a grudge against Sabine? For who she was? For whom she was connected to? Himself? Ariane? Henri? For what she knew? His ideas grew wilder, but none of them so wild as to be rejected. He recalled that just over six months ago the house had still been occupied by the SS. Frenchmen had been living rough as guerrillas in the woods roundabout. Ariane herself had been stripped and shaved. He realised now that there was something here that, obsessed with his wife's supposed guilt, he had failed entirely to grapple with last time.

Henri. It must come back to Henri. But how could Sabine be connected with this? He knew from Ariane that the children had never been involved in her Resistance work, had been given no idea of Henri's role until she had ridden with them to Lavallade for the Fourteenth of July celebrations. Even that risk, so late on, she had regretted.

The questions revolved, unresolved, until he fell into a heavy dreamless sleep, from which he was woken before it was light by the crowing of the cockerels in the farmyard. As soon as they were dressed, he accompanied Ariane to see Sabine again. The nurse had already left and the patient was awake, lying supine on her pillows. Her arms were extended at her sides on top of the bedcover, one of them in plaster. The bandage that wrapped her head served as a frame to emphasise the condition of her face. One eye was so severely bruised that she could barely open it.

Ariane gave a little moan of horror and put her hands to her own face in empathy. She sat down on the edge of the bed and took the ends of her stepdaughter's fingers, where they emerged from the cast, into her own. Theo stood at the end of the bed. She was changed as well as injured. Her round face had been hollowed out in some way. Her shoulders were visible, like a metal coathanger holding up her nightdress.

'Sabine, how are you, little one?' Theo asked.

Sabine made no response. He knew that she had heard him, but she made no effort to reply.

'Have you had breakfast yet? I hope you ate well. It's very important for you to get strong, so that you feel well enough to tell us what happened to you.'

Theo walked to the window to conceal his rage that any-one should do this to a child. He stood looking at the view of the garden that rose steeply behind the house. The box trees, unkempt, marching up the hill in pairs, were rimed with frost so that they looked like balls of stone. He glanced back at his daughter and felt a stirring of guilt for having abandoned her for five years, for longer, ever since her mother died. Her brown eyes met his gaze crookedly through her swollen lids, fully comprehending. He saw something accusingly resentful and despairing in their expression.

What he required was facts, precise accounts of actions and deeds. For that he would go this morning to the doctor, the police, to men who would be able to answer his questions.

When he returned from his morning's enquiries and joined his family for lunch, no one asked what he had discovered. The aunts could only deal with the inexplicable by treating it as if it were normal. Sabine was ill, had had an accident, must be encouraged and helped to get better. The conversation was about the farm, about food supplies, the urgent subjects of the day.

The morning had been overcast, cold seeping rain falling relentlessly. Now it had stopped and he and Ariane went into the garden together. The clouds had lifted so that the view over the ranges of hills had re-emerged in layers of grey, paler in the distance, darker nearby, like a Chinese painting. The garden dripped. In answer to her queries, he admitted that he had learned nothing that she had not encapsulated for him in one sentence last night. The doctor had given him an account of Sabine's injuries: a broken humerus, multiple lacerations, concussion, inflicted by a club.

'We used to see such wounds on victims of the Milice, or the Gestapo. They used a special cosh, but you could get the same result with a heavy stick of some kind,' the doctor had told him.

'Does she speak?' Theo asked before he left. 'Can she understand? She hasn't said a word to me yet.'

'That's something separate from the physical injuries. There is no reason why she should not speak, although she has not spoken to me or to the police, I understand. She is traumatised, or afraid. You may find that the psychological recovery needs more time than the physical one.'

Ariane walked with him along the terrace. He took her hand and held it on his arm. She stopped to examine the clumps of grape hyacinths under the bay tree. Facts had got him nowhere.

'And you? Did you learn anything?'

'A lot,' she said, 'but not much in answer to your questions. Micheline, Florence, the aunts, all told me things separately, things they can't bear to talk about openly. Sabine has lost an enormous amount of weight since I last saw her in September. Florence admits that she eats almost nothing. I can't understand it. She always had a very healthy appetite before, much more than Suzie. And she used to long for sweet things.'

'Did you see her again? Did she speak to you?' For Theo the refusal to talk was almost the worst thing. The answers to all his questions were there in his daughter's head, if he could only spin the thread out of her brain.

Ariane's voice was suddenly sharp. 'She won't talk to me, Theo. It's no good thinking it. She hates me,' she said flatly.

'What do you mean, she hates you?'

'Exactly what I say. From the moment I took her from the convent, after you left, she hated and resented me. I can't tell you what I endured: rudeness, insolence, mockery...'

'Ariane, you are the adult and she is the child. You had all the power. How could she...'

'Oh, Theo, that's easy to say.' She took her hand from his arm and strode up the steps towards the higher terrace. 'You've never tried to look after someone else's child, who holds you responsible for her parent's death.'

'But you weren't responsible...'

'Of course I wasn't. That has nothing to do with anything. It was a nightmare, living with her. And the worst time was when the SS were here. Sabine infected Suzie. The two of them were like mad creatures and in the end...' She stopped abruptly, turned round and began to walk slowly back to the house. 'Anyway, there's no hope that Sabine will speak to me. I would suggest that Suzie might talk to her, if I didn't feel that their relationship had been strange, unhealthy. You're her father. You'll have to wait until she's prepared to talk to you.'

He did not follow her inside. From the woods he could hear the creaking double call of a hen pheasant, reminding him of chill grey afternoons like this, out shooting with Henri. He missed him badly. The old grey wall, demarcation line between forest and garden, had collapsed at one point, the stones tumbling down the hill, the inner ones, newly exposed, shining gold, like the brilliance of flesh gaping through a wound. Neglect and decay; the absence of Henri showed everywhere. He could not for the moment think of what more to do about Sabine, yet he needed action. He had not come here from Paris to sit beside the library fire and read a paper. He decided to make another attempt to meet the Russian Nikola who had perhaps been with Henri when he was captured and could tell him how it happened.

26

FROM SOMEWHERE UP the slope beyond the cottage at Pechagrier Theo heard the rhythmic blows of an axe. He walked round the house, disturbing a couple of red-necked hens, which ran from him squawking, hopping with surprising agility into the branches of a bare fig tree. He passed a wired-off vegetable garden, where leek fronds, onion shoots and yellowing cabbages were scattered without pattern in an expressionistic muddle. A dog bounded down the hill, barking fiercely, followed by his master, carrying an axe, which he looked ready to wield at an intruder who displeased him. Like the dog, he halted at a distance to view his visitor.

'Mr Nikola?'

'Yes?'

'Could I have a word with you, if you're not too busy?'

'What about?'

'Henri Menesplier.'

'Oh, very well. Come on up.'

Looking at Henri's lieutenant, he saw someone who was defined immediately as Russian. He was a big man, tall and solidly built, with a round, bald head that made up for its lack of hair on the skull by its profusion on the jaw; a thickly curling brown beard tinged with grey. Below the massive forehead was a face like a hunk of uncooked bread, doughy and pliable.

'I've about finished,' he said. 'You can take the tools.'

He handed them to Theo and he himself dragged a sack of logs behind him.

'So, you're a friend of Henri's?'

'Yes. He was like my older brother. I'm Théophile de Cazalle from Bonnemort.'

'You're the one who was supposed to be dead? Rose again with the liberation?'

It took some time to reach the point of conversation. First the wood had to be tipped onto the wood pile, tools chucked into the tangle of instruments on the shelf in the porch, boots and coats removed and hung on a hook so overburdened that they simply slid off onto the floor, before they could enter the house, in stockinged feet, through the back door. The Russian closed the door of the living room behind them with care.

'Sit down,' he said, indicating a rush-seated armchair, sagging and frayed, that looked like a natural growth projecting out of the flagstones of the floor. A sudden chirruping and Theo ducked instinctively as a missile of Cretan blue swooped past him. Canaries and budgerigars, yellow, blue and green, filled the air. In one corner the red glow of a lamp in front of an icon was almost obscured behind a half-drawn curtain.

'Will you have tea?' Nikola spoke fluent French with a pronounced accent.

'Tea, ah, yes, please.'

He detested tea, the drink of his London years, yet this was not that sickly, fatty, opaque brew which the English drank ad nauseam. When it came, in glasses encased in filigree holders, it was black, translucent and fragrant, accompanied by a teaspoon and a saucer full of a thick dark brown substance.

'Jam?' His host held out the saucer.

'No, thanks.'

'No lemons for five years, but I still have jam.' He ate it appreciatively. 'What do you want to know about Henri? I'd have thought they could tell you anything you wanted to know over there at Bonnemort.'

'You don't always hear...' Theo began.

'Women, eh?' Nikola commented shrewdly. He looked at him out of small pale blue eyes set deep in their sockets. 'Well, what is it you want to know?'

'I want to know what happened to Henri. I've been given hints and rumours: he was betrayed; he was incompetent; even that he was a coward.'

The Russian laughed. 'All that? What can I say? Henri was a good man. He wasn't a fool; he wasn't reckless; he wasn't a coward. You know that anyway. Perhaps it helps if someone else says it to you, eh? Now, what happened here? You mean with the Resistance?'

'Yes.'

'Ah, that takes longer. Up at Bonnemort, that's where it began, early on. You know the mayor here?' he asked, leaning forward to pour more tea.

Theo had by now realised that he had found a raconteur. This was probably going to take a long time, but he would get a full story.

'Not this one now, Vernhes; the old one, Gargaud,' Nikola continued. 'He was Pétainist through and through. Me, I'm French now. I got my citizenship in thirty-four. But these French quarrels, they mean nothing to me. I'm waiting for Russia to be put right. Gargaud was all for the Marshal and so your family were already against him. I knew what was going on sooner than the others down there in the village. Me, I can tell a Russian Jew when I see one. And I can tell a Polish Jew, too. You know how I can tell? He looks Russian. And the Pole, he looks Polish. Round here they think everyone is foreign. You could come from anywhere, Paris, Marseilles, even Toulouse and you're still foreign. So when I see a Polish woman and two kids walking up the track to Bonnemort in April 1941, I knew what I was seeing. So that's when it began.'

He sucked the last of the plum jam off his spoon, turning the bowl face downwards on his tongue like a child, relishing his story.

'But I wasn't involved then. It wasn't until June forty-one that I went along to Henri and said, I know you're up to something and I want to be in it. That was when Hitler invaded Russia,' he added helpfully, in case Theo had missed what was happening in Europe as well as at Bonnemort. 'Now, I don't like that bastard who's in charge in Russia. If you ask me, there's nothing to choose between Stalin and Hitler. But I fought the Germans in the first war, and I wasn't going to put up with the buggers invading my country without doing something about it. You don't want to hear this stuff about me,' he said, now that he had finished talking about himself, 'but I'm just telling you how I joined the Resistance. June forty-one it was, when Henri put me on to Dr Maniotte. So this is the first Resistance group in Lepech. We're all legal, quiet, steady. We look after communists and Jews. We make false papers. We keep in contact with others.

'Now the second group begins. I don't know when exactly, but by the end of forty-two there was a communist group here. They weren't locals, mostly town people, boys from far away: Toulouse, Bordeaux, Racinès. Group Noix, they called themselves, hard nuts. Communists.'

Suddenly, with terrible noise and violence, he snorted, hawked, chewed his phlegm for a moment and spat with vicious accuracy into the flames, which hissed at him in reply, like a disturbed viper.

'Did the two groups co-operate at all?' Theo asked.

Nikola leaned back in his chair and laughed, so that Theo could see his tongue and throat, glistening red against his dark beard. 'Co-operate? You're a Frenchman and an army man and you ask if they co-operated? I don't know how you professional soldiers make an army out of the French. You do, but God knows how. Russians are sheep: they are driven to do everything together. The English are geese: their instincts tell them all to do the same thing at the same time. The Germans are dogs: they obey their master. But the French! Every one of them is an individualist who decides for himself whether to get up in the morning. No, they didn't co-operate. Don't tell me you in London thought they would co-operate?'

Theo was laughing by now. 'No, we didn't.'

'Trying to make fighters out of those French boys was no holiday. They were keen, I'll give them that. And a lot of the country boys could shoot already; they made very nice snipers. But discipline? Drill? Impossible. But it wasn't just that. There was hostility, jealousy, rivalry, all the local quarrels you can think of. If the man that you had a dispute with about the price of hay or a sliver of land supported Group Noix, then you would help Group Rainbow. Henri spent days on end, riding round, getting the farmers to agree to help us. And then these buggers in Noix would turn up and take without asking. So then, naturally, the peasants wouldn't give anything to us. Noix stole one of our arms caches. When that happened, in forty-three, we almost had a local war here. It was just after Dr Maniotte was arrested and then Henri. That's when the FTP began to say that it was Henri's fault; that he was no good. Things were very bad. You know what I think was the real trouble? It was Henri being socialist. Communists hate socialists worse than fascists, you know that?

'At the beginning of forty-four we began to get organised, at last, and they set up the National Council of the Resistance, with regional committees and local committees and liaison officers to try to make the communist and the free Resistance work together. By then the FTP were more royalist than the king. You wouldn't think they'd spent two years sitting on their arses, doing nothing from thirty-nine to forty-one.'

Nikola got up to throw more logs onto the fire. 'You know all this,' he said, half-question, half-statement. 'Madame Ariane was our area liaison officer with the FTP. She and Henri took over here when Dr Maniotte was arrested and they split the work between them. She went to the regional committee as the representative of the Secret Army.'

Theo, gazing at the new flames flaring round the logs, did not reveal that he had not known. 'You tell it anyway,' he said. 'Tell it as you saw it.'

'Two months, three maybe, she worked with them on our plans for D-Day. German Army Group G covered this area of France. We knew that whenever D-Day came, wherever the landings were, in the Mediterranean, Normandy, Pas-de-Calais, wherever, some of those troops, particularly the armoured divisions, would be ordered immediately to the front. We had to delay them. We made plans to blow up the river bridges, to cut the rail lines, east-west and north-south. And not just once, you understand. The Germans could repair a blown track in forty-eight hours, maximum. So over and over again we had to be able to do it, until we ran out of plastic. I'm not exaggerating when I say that the Germans hardly dared step out of the towns around here.'

He stretched out his long legs and arms until his chair creaked. 'D-Day. I tell you, the night before, 5 June, I'll never forget the excitement. Someone came for me at about eleven at night to say, it's for tomorrow. We thought it meant a general uprising. We were all going to meet the following morning at our appointed rendezvous and then each group to its task. That was the theory.'

One of the canaries, which had been flying about the darkening room from time to time, suddenly landed on Nikola's head. He reached up and clasped it in his huge hand, absently stroking its exotic feathers while it grasped his fingers as if they were twigs on a tree.

'God knows if it would have worked. I doubt it. And if it had, we might have been carved up like the guys on the Vercors plateau in July. So we, or some of us, were saved by what happened. Next morning, the SS rolled into Bonnemort.'

27

NIKOLA TOSSED THE bird into the air. 'We need food. We need drink. We need wood. We still have a long way to go. That is, if you want to hear the whole story?'

'Of course,' said Theo.

As Nikola had talked the light had gone and the fire had fallen in. The Russian disappeared, still talking, shouting from different points around the house.

'I come from Orel, a small town between Moscow and Kharkov, you know it? My parents were small shopkeepers, but we had a dacha, two hours' cart ride out of town. I was born Nikolai Nikolaievich Dekanozovochenko. When I came to France, they don't use patronymics and they couldn't pronounce Dekanozovochenko, so they call me Mr Nikola.'

He was outside now, clapping the shutters closed the length of the house, re-entering by the front door, his beard pearled with moisture. 'A bugger of a night.'

Theo had given up hope of letting Ariane know where he had gone. 'How did a boy from Orel arrive in Lepech Perdrissou?' he asked.

'I was called up into the Tsarist army in the last war. When the Revolution came, I was all for it, but the Bolsheviks didn't approve of shopkeepers' sons: class enemy, I was. So then I joined the Whites, and fought against the Reds instead. We damn near won, for a time. But it wasn't to be and I had to leave my homeland, like you did. You're back after four years and I'm still waiting.'

He threw logs on the fire and stacked more beside the hearth. From the cupboard he took out two small glasses and a stoppered wine bottle. The liquid, like oily water, undoubtedly home-brewed, slid silkily into the glasses. With an air of formality that contrasted with their tousled surroundings, Nikola handed Theo his glass, and held up his own, looking him directly in the eye.

'*Nasdrovie,*' he said. '*Santé,*' and threw the spirit down his throat, refilling his glass at once. 'Now where were we?'

Not until much later, when he had recovered from that night of drinking, a night such as he had never before experienced, even in a Scottish mess on Scapa Flow, did Theo ask himself what the Russian did not tell him that evening. In the inundating flow of words, Nikola appeared so overwhelmingly open, with the solitary man's eagerness to talk, that it did not occur to Theo that he might be holding details back, from discretion or cunning or embarrassment. Each event recounted seemed to burst out of him under pressure, without a filter. But when he replayed his memory of the evening, Theo recalled, drink after drink, the clear shrewdness of the childlike pale blue eyes.

'So,' Theo prompted him. 'The SS arrived. What did you do?'

He groaned. The memory demanded another drink. 'A terrible anticlimax. Everything countermanded; everyone home. There was a lot of grumbling about it at the beginning. They, the others, wanted action. Even some of our guys argued that it was time to face them, that if everyone, all over

France, rose at once, the Germans could not hold on. They wanted to reverse forty, you see. But I told them, look, the Nazis aren't defeated. And look, they're not defeated yet; it's March and we've only just crossed the Rhine. Henri always said, if we can't protect our people, we can't take risks with them. And he meant the villagers, not the fighters.'

'What was the SS unit actually doing here?' Theo asked.

'They were supposed to clear the countryside of the Maquis, but they didn't have the manpower. All they could do was to try to cut off our support, to threaten the local people with such terror that they were too afraid to give us any help. And they had to keep the main roads open. That took up a lot of their time. That's really where we did good work. We held them down here for two and a half months. But they were dangerous, believe me. Bit by bit we won certain areas. At Lavallade the FTP took over running the commune, with a new communist mayor. They loved it, the communists; committees for food supply, sanitation, refuse collection, national festivals, committees for everything.'

'So what happened to Henri? Was he betrayed? Or was it just chance?'

'Ah, there's the question that I've asked myself every night since that day in August. But first, food. I can't tell about that day without food in my belly.'

He drained his glass of the teardrop of liquid in its base and, staggering slightly, led Theo into the kitchen. Eventually, emerging from the indescribable filth, they sat down again beside the fire each with a plate piled high with fried onions and chicken, a wedge of bread. A new bottle of vodka nestled on the floor against Nikola's calf.

'By August last year,' Nikola spoke through a mouthful of onion, several strands hanging from his lip, mingling with his beard, 'the frustration was building up. We knew that there must be an invasion from the Mediterranean coming soon. So there was a big debate in the Resistance here about what to do with our Germans, still dangerous, more dangerous than ever because they could see as well as us how their position was deteriorating. Perhaps they would be left like the Sixth Army at Stalingrad, abandoned to the enemy, swallowed up by the Maquis, who didn't always take prisoners.

'I didn't take part in this debate, you understand. I didn't attend these meetings. I just heard what Henri told me. What he said was, we've got the countryside, more or less. Let them keep the towns; when they retreat, we take over without bloodshed. But the others, the FTP, wanted to drive them out. They were action men. The FTP was dominant on the regional committee where Vernhes was the boss and he made this plan to capture the SS officer commanding the unit at Bonnemort. They were going to lie in wait for him at Longas. Henri was against it, but the plan was agreed and given the go-ahead. We had superb intelligence, from Madame Ariane. She was a sort of double agent, you see. She passed on to us anything she could learn about the Germans' movements. And she fed them false information, too. She was part of this kidnap scheme, I remember. The hours we spent planning it. And what for? Did anyone mention, apart from Henri, what would happen afterwards? What they would do, the Nazis, when we'd taken their officer hostage?'

He put his empty plate on the floor and picked up a chicken bone, gnawing on it, reflectively.

'You know what I think? I've never said this to anyone, because it never came off, this plan. I think that was the point of it. It wasn't for the glory of taking a high-ranking SS officer, it was in order to provoke reprisals. And where would they have fallen, do you think?'

He paused. The question was real rather than rhetorical.

'Bonnemort?' Theo suggested.

'You're dead right.'

Theo pondered what he had learned. In any alliance in which the allies hate one another only marginally less than they hate the enemy there comes a moment, at victory, or when victory is within sight, when the alliance cracks.

'So you think that the FTP wanted to use the Germans to wipe out their rivals, so when the SS had gone they would have a clear field in the region.'

Nikola stroked his beard, pleased to find that Theo understood. 'That's it.'

'Vernhes wanted to eliminate Henri.'

'That's it.'

'What went wrong?'

'Oh, nothing. It aborted. The major didn't turn up where he was expected. Perhaps he got suspicious. Then we were into a new plan, and that one was forgotten.'

Nikola threw his chicken bone into the fire, and leaned back, picking his teeth with a black thumbnail. 'The old mayor of Lepech Perdrissou was still there, Gargaud. Like I said, many of the mayors had gone, resigned. The gendarmes had gone over to the Resistance. But in Lepech, Gargaud hung on. He's a stubborn old bugger, now up on a charge of collaboration. But although he was always keen on the Marshal, he was never pro-Nazi; he never denounced anyone, as far as I know.

'The plan was for the Resistance to take over the town and drive Gargaud out. It was the FTP leader who was especially keen on this, and you won't be surprised to hear that he is now our new mayor. But it had to be both groups who entered the town, the Secret Army as well, not just the FTP. Why? Because it would have looked like a communist take-over and he knew that the people wouldn't stand for it.'

As Nikola, whose rate of consumption was at least twice that of Theo, poured himself more vodka, Theo asked, 'When was this, exactly?'

'Oh, this was right at the end, in August. This was the culmination of our three years of heroic struggle against the Germans.'

Although Theo did not find that the Russian's heavy accent and odd way of expressing himself impeded his understanding of what he said, it did make it more difficult to understand what he meant. Or was it the vodka? Was this last remark satirical, mocking the petty battles of a handful of amateurs who had, in truth, done little to fight against the Germans during the Occupation? Or was he trying to put Henri's death into context, glamorising war to justify his death, to say that it was worthwhile, that he didn't die in vain?

'The Allied landing in Provence, 15 August,' Nikola went on. 'That was what decided us. Two days later we assembled. We entered the town, the United Resistance of the Secret Army and the FTP. This was our liberation at last.'

28

AT THE TIME he hadn't been so cynical. When he'd marched into Lepech Perdrissou with his guys behind him, he'd been proud of them and proud to be a Frenchman by adoption. They'd raided a youth work camp up in the mountains and taken a big haul of clothes, so they weren't dressed like Rag, Tag and Bobtail, as they normally were. They'd sewed flashes onto their tricolour armbands: FFI, Forces Françaises de l'Intérieur. They looked like an army, waiting to meet their returning brothers in the Free French. And they'd show them that they hadn't just sat there passively under German rule for four years. They marched down the rue de Paris and formed up in the Place de la République, and it was a great moment. They arrived at the same time as Group Noix. In order to avoid quarrels about who should head the parade, it had been agreed that the FTP would approach from the other side, marching up the rue de Toulouse, and that they would arrive in the Place simultaneously. The gendarmes had made themselves scarce. They knew what was going to happen and didn't want to stop it. Gargaud didn't appear.

Vernhes made a speech, flanked by members of the Committee of the United Resistance, announcing the deposition of the mayor and the establishment of the Fourth Republic, to ecstatic cheers.

Afterwards Nikola had thought a lot about what had happened and he'd remembered the surge of annoyance that he'd felt when the FTP had placed themselves too far over in the square. Even at the time he'd thought, contemptuously, that they looked as if they were ready to make a quick getaway. The noise of engines at the end of the speech was like a dream of thunder; you wondered if you'd really heard it. Then you knew you had. The townspeople had evaporated. One minute they were standing there applauding, the next there was not one of them to be seen, except an old girl desperately trying to reach a shutter on an upstairs window that kept evading her reach.

Nothing for it, they couldn't just run away after marching in so proudly. The Germans were up on them fast and in force. They received fire at the entrance to the village and responded at once. The shoe mender's house, opposite Dr Maniotte's, was targeted and a fire started. Very rapidly he recognised that the situation was hopeless. They were being pushed back towards the centre, rounded up.

Where, he asked himself, then shouted the question aloud, Where are the fighters of the bloody Group Noix? None of them were to be seen. He rallied his men, the ones close enough to him to hear and obey. He wouldn't let them be herded into the square, like a troop of cattle to the slaughter. He saw that Henri was still going strong as they ran down one of the narrow alleys where no vehicle could follow them, over a wall into a back garden. Through the cabbages, into the next. They could run more freely here, with houses between them and the German armour. Finally, over the last wall and into a green orchard where two sheep huddled together in one corner under arthritic apple trees, laden with ripening fruit. They were out of the town now. Their trucks had been left on the road to Racinès and they couldn't go back for them. The Germans would certainly have taken them, so there was no alternative but footing it into the forest to count their losses.

Nikola blew his nose loudly. 'You want me to tell you that we fought a famous battle, retreating from house to house; that we caught them in the rear and captured the lot? We didn't. We ran away. What could we do? Who wants to die the day before peace breaks out?'

Theo, who had offered no word of professional criticism, had no difficulty in understanding that the Russian's military pride was bitterly offended by this episode, from its opening braggadocio to its ignominious end.

'But the question!' Nikola was shouting now, leaning forward, forearms on his knees, his face flushed with vodka and flames. 'The *real* question you're asking yourself is...'

He poured some more vodka. They were well into the second bottle by now.

'The *difficult* question is, how did the Germans know? How did the Germans know so damn quick?'

'Perhaps they didn't know. Perhaps it was just bad luck that they turned up there and then.'

'Yes, perhaps.' His voice dropped. 'Yes, perhaps. The whole unit, turned out to visit Lepech Perdrissou one Thursday afternoon. Perhaps they just happened to have a field gun, flame throwers, mortars with them? Perhaps it was just bad luck. The other question is, where did the FTP get to? I didn't see them fighting alongside me, hiding behind garden walls, lobbing grenades at the bastards. Was anyone from the FTP captured? Perhaps we were just unlucky, like you say.' He brooded over ill luck and the vagaries of chance.

In the forest they had regrouped. He found Henri in a clearing with some more of their men. The boys flung themselves on the ground panting, some laughing aloud with relief at their escape and the exhilaration of the chase. Henri was breathing hard, wiping sweat from his neck.

'Jeannot was shot outside the *boulangerie*,' he said. 'I'm afraid he may have copped it.'

There were no recriminations. Henri wasn't one to start asking why did we do it; he just got on with what he had to do, but he must have thought, what a bloody waste.

Nikola grunted and said, 'What next?'

'We'd better move ourselves as fast as we can over towards La Peyre,' Henri said. 'The Germans will be around here like a disturbed wasps' nest for the next day or so. We want to be as far from them as possible.' He began to count how many men they'd managed to assemble. 'I'm going back to Bonnemort, but I'll join you tonight or tomorrow morning.'

'Henri, don't go home. It's asking for trouble. Leave Madame Ariane to deal with them. She's got them wrapped round her finger.'

'No, I must go back. After this, they might do anything.'

Just then they heard the sound of a truck bumping up the track. They all picked up their weapons and scattered, but only half-heartedly. They could tell from the sound that it was a wood burner, so it must be French and, sure enough, the two lorries that drew up were full of men from Group Noix, Vernhes sitting up front with the driver of the first vehicle.

Nikola had no thought then to ask them what the hell they had been doing back there in Lepech; he simply wanted news of his own guys. From what Vernhes told them it was bad, worse than he had imagined. At least five of Group Rainbow had been killed and two had been taken prisoner, Pierre Rouget from Cavialle and Philippe Boysse, both of them local boys. The Germans had put them into one of their trucks and it was moving out; back to Bonnemort, they supposed.

'We ought to try to get them back,' Henri said. Vernhes nodded. He strolled away from his truck, signalling with a movement of his head for Henri to follow him where they could not be overheard. Nikola went too.

'Look, we could get them before they even reach Bonnemort and have a chance to work our guys over,' Vernhes urged.

Henri said, 'I'd rather wait till dark and gather a few more men.'

'No, no. You'll have fewer rather than more. They'll be patrolling the roads, picking up anyone they see, not to mention putting the screws on Pierre and Philippe. We must act at once. This is what I suggest: you hold up the lorry and we'll come up behind.'

Henri was looking thoughtful. He wasn't sold on it. Vernhes grew impatient. 'It's only one truck. What are you of afraid of? You must have twenty guys here, and we've got the same.'

When Henri still did not reply, Vernhes said, 'I don't want to keep my men hanging around here. If you don't like the plan, say so and we'll move out at once and no more time wasted. But don't count on us tonight. We'll be a long way from here by then.'

Nikola could see that Henri didn't like it, but he wanted the back-up that Vernhes could give, so he agreed. Vernhes had it all worked out.

'This is what we'll do,' he explained. 'You lot'll take our Renault truck and drive as fast as you can through the woods to the Bonnemort track. You'll make it in time because they'll come the long way round by the main road. They haven't dared take the short cut for weeks. We'll drive the other truck to the junction and wait till we see the Germans turn up the Bonnemort track and then we'll come up behind them.'

It was all planned and agreed so fast that within minutes Vernhes was walking back to the men, shouting for his lads. Henri climbed into the cab, and Vernhes slapped him on the back.

'Don't worry, Henri. We'll get them back for you.'

The top of Nikola's bald head gleamed in the firelight. He put down his vodka glass on the floor between his feet and heaved himself upright, almost tipping into the fire. He opened the front door, fumbling with the shutters.

'Got to pee,' he mumbled.

Theo, whose bladder had been begging for relief for at least half an hour, followed him gratefully. The solace of sending the jet of urine steaming into the earth just beyond the rectangle of light thrown from the house was so great that he felt he had reached the understanding that he sought. He had it, he understood what had been going on. But, by the time he had rebuttoned his flies and stepped indoors once more, it had disappeared.

The cold air outside, only a degree or so above freezing, had sobered the Russian a little. The flow of his story was arrested and Theo could not at first coax him back into his rhythm, the piston of memory driving the engine of speech.

'Why am I telling you this?' Nikola grumbled. 'No one knows this. We made this plan on the spot, Henri, Vernhes and I, standing on the edge of the track. No one was listening to what we said. So I know what we agreed, but if what I say is different from what he says, then I must be wrong. I'm not French; I don't speak French good. I'm not a communist. He'll have two witnesses to support him, to say they heard what was said and he's right. So I decided to say nothing. What's the point when Henri's dead?'

'Wait, slow down a bit. Who's *he* here? Who are we talking about?

Nikola looked at him witheringly. 'Him, Vernhes, the mayor, who else?'

'He denies that you made a plan to rescue the prisoners?'

'He doesn't deny it. He doesn't even acknowledge that we saw one another. After the liberation, at Henri's funeral, he made the oration. *Henri was a hero*, he says. *He died for France, trying to save his compatriots from the hands of the invader.* He spoke to me afterwards. *Henri wasn't a soldier*, he says. *Pity he had to rush off to Bonnemort to get the guys back without waiting for reinforcements. If we had all attacked together that night, we might have done something.* I may not speak French good, but I can tell when someone is warning me off in any language.'

He picked up the third vodka bottle and waved it at Theo, who shook his head.

'You're Henri's friend. You're high up in the Free French. You've got power...'

Here Theo expected a plea for help to reveal the truth and let justice prevail. Nothing of the kind.

'You'll want to make enquiries, demand justice. Don't do it.' He slapped his thigh for emphasis. 'Don't do it. Go back to Paris and forget about it. I've seen what these people, the communists, can do. I saw it in Russia, more than twenty years ago...'

'But that was in Russia at the time of the Revolution...'

'You mean, Russians are barbarians and it couldn't happen here among civilised Frenchmen, who don't denounce or torture or betray one another for the sake of politics?' Nikola said combatively. 'Where have you been living for the last four years? Not in France, that's for sure. And now the communists will have their turn.'

The vodka had made him aggressive.

'In August and September last year they were shooting prisoners, executing men from the Milice on the spot. It was only necessary for one of the comrades to accuse you and that was it.'

'What happened to Henri?' he asked quietly. 'Just tell me what happened.'

Nikola looked mulish. 'You've got to promise me you won't stir things up with demands for justice.'

'I can't do that. I can't tell what I'll do until I know.'

'I want to live here quietly. I'm not going to take part in the French civil war. I'm not going to be used by you.'

They had reached a stand-off. Theo could think of no way of persuading the obstinate man beside him to speak. There was nothing Nikola wanted, except to live in his French dacha without interference.

Nikola was moving round the room, picking things up and replacing them amid the chaos. He trimmed the lamp on the table, opened the cupboard and took out another bottle, two more glasses.

Theo held up his hand. 'I couldn't, thank you.' He lifted himself out of his chair, his brain turning in his skull, stabilising itself in its new position moments later, like the point of a compass coming, with some wavering, to rest.

'Sit down, sit down. These are my cherries in marc, from the last year before the war. You'll have some before you go.'

Theo sat down again and took the proffered glass, sensing a change of heart. The Russian sucked sulkily on his cherry, like a child with a sweet. He was obviously disappointed not to have been cajoled into continuing his story.

'You can work it out anyway,' he said. His tone was still argumentative, carrying on the debate that Theo had refused. 'You know what happened.'

'Nobody else was there. I've not heard the story from someone who was there with Henri.'

Nikola spat out his cherry stone, took another fruit.

'How many were you?' Theo asked, as if he were debriefing him.

'On our side? Nineteen with Henri and me. All Secret Army, note that.'

'How many survived?'

'Five plus me, two of us wounded. Henri and five others were captured and executed in the square, along with one of the guys we'd been trying to rescue, Pierrot Rouget, who'd been caught that afternoon in Lepech. Seven were killed there on the track and so was Philippe Boysse, who'd also been taken prisoner in Lepech. The Germans had made him drive the lead car. That tells you something, doesn't it, putting him in the line of fire.'

They had scrambled down the escarpment above the Bonnemort track, so that they would be facing the arriving German vehicles as they climbed up the road. It wasn't an ideal spot for an ambush because the slope was too steep, but there was plenty of cover in the rough undergrowth and they were above the sight line of the driver. Henri took up a position low down. Beside him was Richard, one of the best shots in the group. Nikola placed half a dozen of the others on the slope and the rest on the top of the hillock, ready to attack when the lorry was brought to a halt.

'We heard them coming, two of them, a car first, a truck following. I thought that our guys would be in the second vehicle, and I hoped that even if they were handcuffed, they would be able to save themselves once we'd engaged. I saw the German staff car. I'd hoped it would be the Hispano-Suiza, then we would have been sure it was the major. The car was notorious in the whole area: Madame Ariane's car. The evil tongues said that she gave it to him, as a bribe or a gift…' He suddenly recalled to whom he was speaking.

Theo did not react. 'Go on,' he urged. He wouldn't let him stop now.

'Everything was perfect. These boys sometimes are so excited that they can't stop themselves loosing off before time. But Henri held them back until they were just below us. First round, the windscreen of the car shatters, the driver is hit. The car swerves, hits a tree trunk. Truck can't pass. The Germans jump out and take cover. We hit two more then, killed them. That cheered us, I can tell you, seeing them lying there. I tell five of our boys what to do: leave us to hold their attention while they take off, up the hill and round to outflank them. We're exchanging fire now. They're trapped, but we can't winkle them out until our guys get down there, or Vernhes comes. He should arrive any minute. I hear an engine, more than one. Is this the first sign that things aren't right? I think I start backing off already then, changing my position. Now I can see the staff car, the glass all smashed away. The driver is lying face down, tipped a little away from the door. Then I see who it is: our guy, Philippe Boysse. He isn't going anywhere, for he is dead and his wrist is handcuffed to the steering wheel. Then I'm sure there's something wrong and the trucks come round the corner. It isn't Vernhes and his boys; it's the rest of the Germans, the whole bloody lot of them. They're out of the trucks in seconds, firing all the time. The next thing I know, I hear shots in the forest behind us. They aren't just coming up the road, they're already outflanking us. At that moment I know it's time to leave. I get together the guys nearest me and we quit. We could hear the firing going on and on, as we made our getaway. I got five of them out of there, one with a wound in his head, another a scratch. You know what happened to the rest of them.'

In the silence that followed the wood on the fire crumbled, folding inwards onto the glowing ash.

'And the SS major?' Theo asked. He thought Nikola was going to finish the story for him. 'Was it you who killed him?'

For the first time Nikola hesitated, breath indrawn, as if reflecting on the consequences of saying yes, saying no.

At last he said, regretfully, 'No, I didn't kill the bastard. I wish I had. I'd have done more than slit his throat. But, no, it wasn't me. I walked thirty kilometres that night, so I didn't hear what happened to Henri and the others until two days later. And by that time the Germans had gone. We were liberated.'

29

THE NEXT MORNING Theo's head was pulsing like a lighthouse. Moving it was, he had discovered while tilting his jaw to shave, a painful manoeuvre. His eyelids were lined with sandpaper, abrading his eyeballs with each flicker in defence against the assailing daylight. His mouth, even after cautious toothbrushing, was a silage pit, sweet and fermenting.

The walk home, about four kilometres through the dark woods with a torch borrowed from Nikola to guide him along the track, had not cleared his head enough to draw any conclusions from the massive Russian epic to which he had just been subjected. The problem lay in separating the significant from the trivial, which returned to his mind with distracting vividness. He had entered their bedroom as quietly as he could. The fire was a crumble of ash. Ariane was asleep with a lamp still burning. She woke up, instantly alert.

'Theo, where have you been?'

'I couldn't let you know. No telephone. With Nikola.'

'Have you been drinking? Theo, you're drunk.'

He had fallen into bed in a haze of spirits, having succeeded in removing his clothes, but without any thought of washing.

'I hope I am not so drunk that I forget everything in the morning.'

'Forget what?'

But he was already on the edge of a heavy alcoholic slumber and did not reply.

When he woke, the strength of the light penetrating his crusted eyelids told him that it was already mid-morning. The gilded clock in front of the mirror confirmed this by striking eleven. He lifted his head from the pillow and with a groan allowed it to fall back. He closed his eyes again. He had a vision of Nikola out in the wind, chopping his wood, shrugging off the effects of vodka as if it had been no more than water.

The Russian was such an odd mixture of prejudice, shrewdness and emotion that it was hard to interpret his evidence with proper Gallic reason and balance. He must ask Ariane what she made of him.

He went to the kitchen for a bowl of ersatz coffee. Micheline glanced at him and went to her cupboard of preserves.

'I'll make my special receipt for what's wrong with you.'

'No, thank you, Micheline. I'm not strong enough for it yet. Chicory will be enough.'

'This will do you much more good.'

She made him drink several glasses of water while she concocted a mixture of raw eggs, beaten with walnut spirits and a ladleful of chicken stock. To his surprise, twenty minutes later he began to feel a little better. He remained seated peacefully in the ladder-backed chair by the fire, watching Micheline moving round the kitchen preparing lunch. She did not talk and neither did he. As his head eased, he thought about the problem of Sabine.

The story that he had heard last night from Nikola appeared to have nothing to do with what had happened to his daughter. Yet he wondered whether a link between the two events, the death of Henri and the attack on the child, might not emerge. When you scraped the surface, you exposed a tissue of conflicts far more complex than you expected.

The kitchen door opened and Florence entered. 'The schoolmaster's here. I've just lit the fire in the library, so I put him in there. Shall I tell Madame Ariane, or will you see him?'

'You mean Monsieur Vernhes?'

She looked at him compassionately, in the way that all the women of the household regarded him that day, with a kind of reproachful sympathy. 'Yes,' she said patiently, 'Monsieur Vernhes.'

Theo rose. 'I'll see him. I need to speak to him.'

In the library the thin flames of the new fire leaped at the logs without sending out much heat. The two men shook hands and took their seats with the formality and caution of a diplomatic encounter between Metternich and Talleyrand. This was their third meeting, Theo calculated, and he was, at last, properly informed about whom he faced. He might not have exposed his need for knowledge in quite such a blatant way last time if he had known what he knew now. This time they were both on their guard, armed to probe for information or weakness.

'I came to ask how Sabine was,' Vernhes began. He saw Theo's look of surprise and went on, 'I heard she had been badly hurt in some accident. I taught her for two years, you know,' he added, as if some explanation for his concern was needed.

Theo had dismissed the enquiry as an excuse for the meeting, nothing more. Vernhes must have some other, less easily declarable, reason for his appearance at Bonnemort.

'Very well, thank you,' he replied automatically and saw Vernhes look surprised in his turn. 'That is, she was very severely injured, and not by an accident, but she's progressing well.' He did not believe in long recitals of accident and illness. Everyone in his family was always well or getting better until they actually died

'I am pleased to hear it.' Vernhes persisted in the subject of Sabine. 'I understood she could neither speak nor move and it had been decided it was too dangerous to try to take her to hospital in Racinès.'

'She's doing very well,' Theo repeated.

Vernhes hesitated and Theo decided that, rather than wait for him to produce the real reason for coming, he would ask his own questions.

'Last time we met,' he said, 'you gave me the details of the attack on my wife in August. I wonder if you can help me with more information about the events of those days, which are rather more complicated than I realised when I arrived back from exile. This time I'm interested in the death of the SS officer who was billeted here during the period June to August. Major Udo Knecht, he was called, I believe.'

'What do you want to know about him?' Vernhes' grey eyes behind their steel-framed spectacles were wary.

'I wanted to know if you killed him.'

Vernhes replied smoothly, 'You're asking me to confess to murder?'

'I wouldn't call it a confession. There are no witnesses; no statement would have any legal force.'

'In the heat of last summer, many actions were taken by the United Resistance, fully justified by the cruelty and illegality of the enemy, which are now being called into question by the military courts. In some cases, the forces of fascism have already regained the upper hand, and some Resistance fighters have been accused and even condemned for their actions during the liberation. And de Gaulle now commutes the sentences of traitors and criminals like Béraud, who spent the war denouncing communists, Jews and Anglo-Saxons in the newspapers.'

Theo was familiar with the technique, employed by communists of every nation, of evading a specific point by enlarging the field to include other people's failures.

'My question wasn't a trick,' he said calmly. 'I've always assumed it was a revenge killing for the hangings in Lepech Perdrissou, or for other atrocities that he had committed in his time in the region. I wondered, since the Secret Army was decimated by his action that day, whether the FTP had decided to dispense justice before the Germans fled.'

Like Nikola when he was asked this question, Vernhes hesitated, probably for the same reason. Would he claim the killing, for the glory of the action? Had he done it, in truth? It would have been a form of justice, but if he had really colluded with the major to destroy Henri, as Nikola had suggested, it would have been very useful for Vernhes to have the major dead, never able to bear witness against him. Vernhes had excellent reasons for killing the SS man.

'No,' Vernhes said. 'I didn't kill him, nor did I order his execution by the FTP. Although I knew the Germans couldn't remain here indefinitely, I didn't know that they were on the point of departure. I was reluctant to attack them, and I have to say it, I thought Henri Menesplier's action that day was unwise, because of the danger of reprisals. Look what happened: Henri shot, six others hanged, not to mention the numbers of those killed earlier that day at Lepech and Bonnemort. We were lucky that the major didn't decide to shoot the men who dug the graves, or to set fire to the church, which he seemed to be planning to do at one stage.'

Theo found that he believed him. Vernhes might have liked to have organised the killing of the man who had tyrannised the neighbourhood for more than two months, but he had not done so. His statement was credible, but not for the reasons he gave, which were Henri's own arguments turned against him. Now that Henri was dead, Vernhes could be the protector of the people as well as the scourge of the Germans. The schoolmaster was a much harder character to read than Nikola. The latter's prejudices were declared; they ran right through his personality like the rings through a tree trunk. Vernhes was protean; he would change any opinion or action from one moment to the next to achieve his advantage.

They paused, each assessing how the points should be distributed before the next round.

'Have a glass of wine?' Theo offered. He poured two glasses of Saussignac and handed one to his adversary. His own he put beside him without drinking.

'You're evidently not satisfied with what you have discovered so far,' Vernhes commented. 'Are your enquiries official, or personal?'

'Oh, personal,' Theo replied. 'I have no official mandate, I assure you. Although if I discovered something out of the ordinary, beyond the usual rough and tumble of the liberation days, I would have no hesitation in directing the attention of the authorities to it. The executions of the *maquisards* may well make up part of the dossier of war crimes that I have no doubt is already being drawn up to the account of Major Knecht and his men, but that's not my concern.'

'Insofar as your investigations may have official repercussions,' Vernhes said, 'I suggest you concentrate on the Vichy fascists and other notorious collaborators. These people persecuted patriots of the Party for four years and are still lying low, a fifth column waiting for its moment to regain power. All the hounding of the Resistance for the rough and tumble of the liberation, as you call it, shows that the fascists still have power in the organs of the administration. If, on the other hand, you're following a purely personal trail, I have some information for you which you may not care to hear, but you should certainly put into the total balance of your discoveries.'

Theo's head, which for a while under the influence of Micheline's receipt, had cleared, was aching again. He considered whether wine would help, and decided that it would not. 'And that information is?' he said politely, his tone suggesting that he would listen, but would not guarantee to believe what he heard.

'Last time we spoke, I told you of what happened to your wife after the liberation. It was a factual account. I made no comment about the justice of what was done; indeed, I believed it to be unjust, but unpreventable...'

'Such actions are unlawful, whether the victims are guilty or not of their supposed crimes,' Theo interrupted sharply.

'Ah, there I can't agree. The people's anger sometimes has to be expressed in revolutionary justice. However, that was my opinion at the time. I have since had cause to change it.'

'And what does that mean?' Theo stood up. The contents of his skull rose with him, but more slowly, belatedly catching up and colliding with the roof of his head.

Vernhes also rose. 'It means that I've since learned that the suspicions of the people were correct, that your wife was guilty of a specific sort of collaboration. To put it bluntly, the commander of the SS unit here at Bonnemort was her lover.'

To hear what he had feared, known and rejected, now put into words hit Theo like a blow, winding him, leaving him without words. Before he could speak, to contradict, to vindicate Ariane's Resistance record, pre-dating that of this self-righteous prick, Vernhes spoke again.

'If you think very carefully about this information I've just given you, you may reach some conclusion about the death of Henri Menesplier and where responsibility for it lies.'

Only with difficulty did Theo control the upsurge of rage, the physical impulse to strike. He said, very drily, 'This is a very neat trap. She was ordered to act as a double agent, and now you denounce her for it. It's the perfect crime, and she's the perfect victim.'

Vernhes was as cold as Theo, colder, for he saw himself in the winning position. 'That's not how things were, whatever she may have told you. Let me reassure you, however, that I've no intention of destroying her reputation. I don't wish to make any of this public. I pass the information on to you for your researches. The accommodation that you make between you is none of my business. I just want you to bear this in mind in any plans you may have to take your enquiries to the authorities, as one of the elements of the situation.' He stopped short, as if he could say more but had decided against doing so.

'Where did this calumny come from, that changed your opinion?' Theo demanded scathingly, indicating that he thought Vernhes had fabricated it on the instant.

'From an excellent source, within your own family: your daughter. I'll leave you now.'

30

THEO MADE NO attempt to see Vernhes out of the house. He sank back into his chair and closed his eyes. On his return from exile he had immediately accepted his wife's guilt on the sole evidence of her shaven head. It had taken him months to convince himself of her innocence, and now, confronted once again with an assertion of her crime, he found that he could not stop himself from believing it. Vernhes' words, on his daughter's authority, carried total conviction. He could not persuade himself that the man had made up the story for his own purposes. Yet this time Theo regarded the charge in a different light. He no longer saw in it, as he had the first time, the seduction of the conqueror. He had come to understand something of the complexity of the Occupation, of Ariane's role in passing information backwards and forwards between the Germans and the Resistance. He could imagine that she had been trapped, blackmailed, threatened, even ordered. Or had she simply consented? He did not know how he would ever find out. He was never going to achieve certainty unless she told him what happened. This she seemed unlikely to do; she had shown a marked reluctance to talk about the period when the Germans were at Bonnemort.

In dealing with Vernhes it hardly mattered what was true or false, for the story of Ariane and the major, with the shaving of her head to lend it veracity, whispered in the right places inside the Party hierarchy, circulated among the political class in Paris, would ruin him as surely as it would ruin Ariane. Vernhes meant it to be a double threat, against her and against him. What he could not understand was why Vernhes felt it necessary to threaten him. Why had he decided to make his accusation against Ariane now? There was a missing piece to this jigsaw. Perhaps the general was right. What had he said? *It would be a disaster to rummage through the injustices of four years to try to put right every wrong. We must put the past behind us.* Theo had not wanted to accept it then; now he saw things differently. The truth was indecipherable. Neither France nor his family could stand too much of it.

If he sat motionless, the thumping in his head was stilled. This was to condemn his wife without a hearing, to accept a calumny because it was impossible to counter it. And Henri: the stupidity and wastefulness of his death was tragic. Had it been Henri's own fault, the result of his rashness or of his inexperience as a soldier? He hoped that it was not just his loyalty that rejected this idea. At the very least Henri and his men had been let down; perhaps they had even been betrayed, driven, like Ariane, into a trap from which there was no escape. He doubted if he would ever have evidence sufficient to accuse anyone, but he would not give up his search.

The door opened and Ariane came in. She said, with an anxious note in her voice, 'What's the matter, Theo?'

'Vodka.'

'Apart from your hangover, I mean.'

'I'm fine.' It didn't answer her question, and he could see that she wasn't reassured.

'Florence told me that Vernhes came this morning. What did he want?'

'To ask after Sabine.'

'Is that all?'

'Does it surprise you?'

'That won't have been his real reason for coming.'

'No.'

She sat down beside him.

'Is it very bad?' she asked.

'Terrible.'

'You were away about twelve hours; were you drinking vodka all that time?'

'Not all the time. Tea to start with.'

'And what were you talking about in this marathon drinking session?'

'The exploits of the Resistance. Its hatreds and rivalries. Nikola told me about the bad relations between Group Rainbow and the FTP Group Noix. Is it true?'

'Yes, it is. You didn't have to drink a bottle of vodka to learn that; I could have told you. Nikola doesn't know even half the story, because he never tried to work with them.'

'Whereas you were the liaison officer between the Secret Army and the FTP.'

'Giving me a title like that makes it sound much more... real than it was. I tried to persuade the FTP not to do things, or not to do them in a certain way. And to convince Henri that certain things had to be done, for the sake of good relations, if nothing else. I don't think I ever succeeded. Each group did what it intended to do anyway. This wasn't an army in any sense that you would recognise, Theo.'

'My problem is that I don't know whether Nikola is a man with persecution mania and a strong gift for fantasy, or whether he has got something. He says that Henri was betrayed, that someone alerted the Germans to the plan to liberate Lepech. His theory is that it was the communists.'

'The communists?' Her astonishment was unmistakable.

'Yes, he meant Vernhes.'

'*Vernhes* betrayed him? How?'

'You thought it was someone else?'

'No, no. Go on.'

'Nikola thinks that on the day that the Resistance took over Lepech Perdrissou, which was the day before liberation, you remember, the arrival of the Germans was too pat.'

'This is paranoia,' Ariane objected. 'The FTP were there as well. It was my supreme triumph of co-operation. He can't use that as evidence of an attempt to get rid of Henri.'

'It's more complicated than that. According to Nikola the FTP disappeared from the scene as soon as the Germans began shooting; they suffered no injuries, no casualties, no captives. Then he claims that he was present when Vernhes proposed to support Henri in an attempt to rescue the two prisoners, Pierre Rouget and Philippe Boysse. Henri went ahead with the plan that they made, but Vernhes and his men failed to turn up and do their share. Instead, the rest of the German unit caught them in the rear. As a result, Henri and five others were captured and seven of his men were killed. Only six got away. Those are heavy losses for an afternoon's parade. He says that Vernhes now denies ever suggesting a rescue attempt.'

'Do you believe this?'

'Wait. There's more. So far the story is that Henri was let down by an ally. But Nikola's paranoia goes deeper than that. It is not just that Vernhes did not assist Henri; Nikola claims that he invited the Germans to do the job of wiping him out, if I picked up all his dark hints and suspicions. So after agreeing the rescue plan with Henri, Vernhes tipped off the Germans and retired quietly home with his men, leaving Henri and his men to be massacred.'

'Can it be true?'

'It's hard to say. It's a well-established tactic to let the enemy destroy your rival. Look what Stalin did outside Warsaw last year. The free Polish underground was wiped out by the Germans, while the Red Army held back on the other bank of the Vistula. It then marched into Poland with its own Polish exiles in tow.'

'But what for?' Ariane cried. 'Why would it be worth doing such a terrible thing?'

'I wanted to ask you that.' She spun round, as if he had accused her; then, seeing that he was continuing to speak, she relaxed. 'You know the characters better than I do.'

'Vernhes likes power. I would say that is his defining characteristic. Nikola is a far shrewder man than his wild appearance would let you think.'

Theo put his aching head in his hands.

'What are you going to do about it?' Ariane asked.

'Nothing. In such a case, Vernhes' people would hold a revolutionary court, condemn the victim, execute him out of hand. Look what happened to you. But I can't do that, and I don't have the evidence to do it properly. Nikola would never speak.'

The general had been right after all. True justice required more than a jumble of suspicions and guesses, however acute and lucky they might be. He knew, or thought he knew, what had happened to Henri, and that would have to be enough.

'Nikola also told me that you were used to spy on the Germans while they were based here and to feed them false information. A nasty, dangerous little job. Did they ever suspect you?'

Ariane stood up and walked over to the window. She remained with her back to him, looking out.

'It was the worst thing I have ever had to do,' she said passionately. 'Yes, they suspected me all the time, both the

Germans and the Resistance. I got information, I gave information, but neither side trusted it. I didn't want to do it. From the first, I hated it. I begged not to have to do it. The United Committee of the Resistance, that is, Vernhes, ordered me.'

'The trouble with feeding the enemy false information,' Theo said, 'is that when it is revealed as false they suspect the source. That never happened to you? Then they try to turn it round, create a double agent.' In contrast to the emotion in her voice, he spoke as if he were discussing an abstract question of an intelligence technique with his students at the Ecole Militaire.

'No, the Germans were always suspicious, but I was never actually caught out. In a horrible way the information was self-fulfilling. Wherever they went, the Germans would always find somebody to arrest.' She moistened her lips. 'There was another reason, too, for them to trust what I said. It was always given under duress: that validated it for him.' Theo noted the unconscious change in the pronoun.

'The other thing I asked Nikola about,' he said, 'was the death of the German officer. I assumed it was a Resistance revenge killing and I thought someone like him might not have had too many scruples about the rules of war. So I asked him if he had done it.'

'And what did he say?' She turned back to face him now, leaning against the windowsill, her arms folded in front of her.

'With evident regret, he said he didn't do it. He would obviously have loved to have come back to avenge his fallen comrade. But he knew nothing of what had happened to Henri and the others, nor of what was happening in Lepech that evening. He just made off with five of his men, trying to put as much distance as possible between himself and Bonnemort.'

'Yes,' she said. 'There were a lot of people who would have liked to kill him, and might have done it, if they had thought there would have been no reprisals.'

'Like Vernhes?'

'Possibly.'

'I asked him, too, the same question.'

'If he had killed him? And what did he say? Do you really think a direct question is the best way to reach the truth?'

'Not necessarily. It's not the only tactic I employ, but it has the merit of surprise, which is always an advantage, militarily speaking. You have to choose at once whether or not to lie.'

'And you think you can tell which it is, lie or truth?'

He looked at her without answering for several seconds, and she held his gaze.

'Vernhes said he didn't do it. I don't think he was lying.'

He had never asked her the direct question, so she had never yet had to lie to him. He wondered if she would take the opportunity to tell him what she knew. They were both aware that the time would come when he would ask her. He was giving her notice, denying himself the advantage that he had taken with the other two. She dropped her eyes; it was clear that this was not the time.

'Theo, I don't see how any of this helps us with Sabine. You must concentrate on that now.' She was moving towards the door, refusing his challenge.

Leaving the library she made for the tower. Her old room, that had been the communal sitting room during the summer, used by the aunts and the children, was now abandoned. No fire had been lit and the frost pattern on the windows had barely begun to melt. She sat down at her desk, letting the cold creep into her, as if it could turn her to stone and petrify all emotion.

Up till now she had let him answer his questions for himself and in Paris that might have been enough for him. Here she had the sense that at any minute someone would stand up and bear witness against her. She was naturally open and the idea of lying was repugnant, especially to Theo. But she had learned many things in the last year and one was that there are some things it is better not to know, even about yourself.

Nikola's story, recounted by Theo, was a consolation. It might not be true, but if it were, it cancelled her greatest fear: that she had been, unwittingly, implicated in Henri's death. She had asked herself constantly if she had somehow alerted the major to what was planned for the liberation of Lepech; if her false information had rebounded at last and aroused his suspicion. Living through the weeks of the Germans' presence, the turmoil of the liberation, Theo's lightning return, her flight to Paris with Suzie, she had never thought of anything beyond the moment. Once the horror was over, the memories were inextinguishable. There had been moments when it seemed that the only way to escape from the compulsive recall of events that she did not want to remember was to kill herself, and only some dim sense that she must wait to do it until she had handed Suzie back to her family kept her from acting on it.

When the Germans had arrived she had been afraid, but afraid of the wrong things. She had feared injury and death and fire and looting. She had imagined the aunts shot on the stairs and Suzie taken away to Germany, Florence raped and Micheline tortured. She had not visualised the insidious effect of proximity, the wearing down of living side by side with the SS.

It had begun in such a small way, at the meeting of the United Resistance on the evening of 6 June. The Allies had just landed. The Germans had just occupied Bonnemort. She had crept out of the house, evaded the guard and, with Henri, reached the appointed house on the other side of Lepech Perdrissou. Vernhes had been there with about five others. She had reported the major's parting remark that they would be away the following night. Vernhes, noting that she spoke German as if it were a moral fault, asked that any information, however trivial, that she could pick up be relayed at once to him. The following morning on her ride she had watched the German convoy snaking down the track and onto the road, turning east. She rode fast to the village and passed on the message. At the junction with the *route nationale* a few miles further on, a child with some geese was posted to gawp at the trucks and report which way they were heading. This early warning system was simple and effective. It was the kind of thing she enjoyed. If only the spying had gone no further than that.

Looking back, she saw that the major had chosen his victim from the start, from the moment that he forced her to dine with him, to cut up his food. She had felt him watching her when he was at Bonnemort. Although the family and the troops were forbidden to enter one another's zones of the house and grounds, the major did not apply the prohibition to himself. He did not actually penetrate the family's rooms upstairs in the tower, but he roamed freely in other parts of the house. She came across him in the entrance hall, in the farmyard, in the stables. She felt besieged; she hesitated to leave the sitting room; she scanned the garden from the window before going outside.

He finally caught her in the stables early one evening. She could still feel the pleasant chill on her skin, damp from the heat of her ride, as she stepped into the dimness of the barn out of the evening sun. She had walked through the storeroom to the tack room beyond when she heard the sound of a boot on the rock floor. The rivulet of sweat on her back turned to a runnel of ice. She was trapped. She gave no sign of having heard him, hanging up the bridle and humping the saddle onto its pole.

The footsteps rang loudly, on their deliberate approach. She retreated to the furthest end of the room and remained there, frozen like a rabbit in the grass waiting to leap out in a desperate, hopeless run for life. She never made that leap. She didn't even try. Over and over again, afterwards, she asked herself why she had done nothing, why she had not dodged, run, scuffled, swung her fist. What good was all her resistance if she had not resisted then? She sometimes told herself it was fear: for herself, for the aunts, for the children, above all for Suzie. It was true that she had been afraid; she was always afraid. But during those seconds when action was demanded, it was not calculation of fear and consequences that held her back. It was a recognition of, a submission to, overwhelming power. Every time the memory of that first encounter forced itself upon her, she tried to replay it as it should have been played.

He walked inexorably towards her, blocking her against the wall. Took her neck in his good hand. Kissed her. His face, roughly bearded, luminously pale, with a light sheen of sweat and a strange, sharp smell, like a tainted apple.

She could perhaps tell Theo about that. It was bad enough, but such things happen in war. Occupiers have powers to which the defeated have to submit. What she would never admit to him was the effect that those powers had had on her. She wished she could forget it herself.

She remembered the night of the thunderstorm. She hadn't been able to sleep. She hadn't even gone to bed and finally, to escape from the oppressive stuffiness of the house, she had walked outside, sat down on the terrace to smoke a cigarette that she had made of Micheline's dried herbs. She had inhaled the odd fragrance, listening to the dry boom of the thunder, like distant artillery, watching the curtains of lightning in the sky over the hills to the south. She knew why she had chosen to sit in the German zone of the garden. She could explain it as defiance: by sitting there at night she was recovering her own property, challenging the major's right to take it from her. In truth the defiance was of another order: defiance of common sense, of caution and of right behaviour. To be there was an invitation, which he accepted.

When Vernhes decided to extend her role from gathering information to passing false information in the other direction, she had objected that her relationship with the German officers was not such that she was likely to tell them anything. They would be suspicious from the start. She begged not to have to do it. Vernhes had insisted. It was an order and he had the authority to give it. He was now the commander of the battalion of the United Resistance in the region.

The major made it easy for her. He liked to use force or the threat of force, so each occasion that she had something to tell him had the appearance of compulsion. Yet she knew that although he put his hand on the pulse of her neck, or struck her with his false hand, it was for show. She was in a cage made of her own submission and could not escape. The violence was unnecessary.

She had slept little and badly all the time that the Germans were in occupation of the house. Sometimes, sitting up in her bed at night watching the stars through the open window, she would tell herself that it was part of the skill of the bully to make the victim feel as if she were to blame, as if she had willed her own subjection. She did not convince herself. She should never have allowed herself to become his creature. She thought of Lucien Maniotte dying, silent, under torture; Henri beaten and starved in prison in Racinès, and was filled with shame.

Yet the next time he used coercion, she submitted once again.

He would summon her late to the library, where he had made his office. When the summons came, her palms began to sweat lightly and she held them to her sides, pressing them into her cotton skirt to calm herself. He would be seated when she entered and kept her standing while he talked, a monologue, which required only a listener.

She saw his pistol lying on the blotter on the desk in front of him. She fixed her eyes on it as soon as she entered, its implicit threat stoking her terror of what he would require this time.

When he ordered her to approach, she did so. Would he have shot her if she had turned and run out of the room? She did not try to escape, so she never knew. Unbuttoning himself, he pushed her to her knees. When she turned her head aside, her eyes closed, his false hand rammed her face round; the gun in his right hand clattered against her teeth. He used it as a lever in a lock to force her mouth open, tearing her lip. Her head was held as if in a vice, that moved it like a machine, his false hand on one side, his live one, still holding the gun, its butt pressed against her skull. Her ears were full of the crackling of her hair.

She found she was holding her head now. The memory would spring on her without warning as she sat at her desk. Or it would wake her in the night, making her retch, as she had then, tears of rage and shame starting from her eyes.

31

SUZIE OPENED THE door of Sabine's room and entered quietly. The bedroom she had shared for two years seemed puzzlingly strange. Then she realised that although nothing in the room itself had changed, the smell, the familiar animal scent of her own lair, was different. A sharp medicinal odour mingled oddly with that of woodsmoke, the background scent of Bonnemort in winter. Sabine's head was all but hidden in her pillows and, as she made no movement, Suzie assumed she was asleep. She sat down on the chair by the bed.

She noticed that her side of the dressing table still carried her collection of objects: an ammonite, a thrush's nest with, inside it, a wren's egg that she had found in a deserted nest, a cluster of acorn cups, an ox's slipper and a tiny blue glass bottle. Their existence as a collection, each one still correctly positioned, surprised her. She had had no intention of coming back to Bonnemort when she left, because she was going to live with Papa and Maman when they came home; she had not cared what happened to her *objets trouvés*. Yet she was touched that Sabine had not swept the whole lot into the bin, as if she thought Suzie might come back to claim them.

She looked at the segment of Sabine's head that was visible, a slice of bruised cheek, a tuft of hair, and felt the power of the conscious in the presence of the sleeping. She had been liberated from her; she was no longer afraid. In Paris she had not allowed herself to think of Bonnemort at all. Sometimes the soft snorting of Lou Moussou, or the velvety warmth of Florence's goodnight embrace recurred involuntarily, not as memory but as sensation, and she had rejected them immediately. Now she saw that she was free. Sabine's occupation was over; she could not threaten her or tyrannise her, even if the two of them were living together once more. She let out a shuddering breath and glanced at Sabine, to find that her eyes were open and she was watching her.

'How are you?'

Sabine's expression was fill of anger and resentment. 'Alive.'

She could tell at once that Suzie had changed in the months she had been away. The placatory undertone that had always coloured her voice had gone. Sabine had felt Suzie's absence bitterly when she had first been taken away by Madame Ariane: another debit to her stepmother's account. She had been furious, jealous, that Suzie had gone and she was left, so she had heaped on the absent one's head all the terrible things that had happened at Bonnemort since she had last been there, and since she had gone. Suzie was to blame; she had made her, Sabine, do things she would never have done if she hadn't had Suzie to do them with, or to. Her father had been angry with her when she had said it was because Suzie was Jewish. But if she hadn't been Jewish, she wouldn't have had to hide at Bonnemort in the first place.

Suzie leaned forward and pulled down the covers a little so that she could see more of Sabine's face. The swelling round her eyes had subsided a little and the bandage on her head had been removed, showing where her hair had been cut short to dress her scalp. She was unrecognisable as the Sabine with the moon face and the cloud of hair, who had rushed Suzie from the pigsty to the chapel when she arrived at Bonnemort.

'It was *him*, wasn't it?'

Sabine nodded. Suzie stroked the hand that was curled on the edge of the covers, as if she was petting Lou Moussou. She didn't know what else to do or to say. She saw that tears were slipping down Sabine's cheeks. They sat silently for a while, then Suzie said, 'How did it happen? You didn't have to go back to school, did you?'

Sabine shook her head. She had stopped crying. Suzie thought that she was not going to reply, but at last she said, 'After Christmas, he came to find me and asked about my lessons, who was teaching me.'

'Who was?'

'The aunts.'

'And?'

'He offered me some books for my classes. The aunts, of course, didn't know about the proper courses or anything. They just taught what they liked. When I told him he made fun of what they were teaching me. But even more about *her*, what she taught us when you were here.'

Suzie said nothing. My enemy's enemy is my friend. What had they been studying when Madame Ariane had produced that saying? Anyone who scorned her stepmother was Sabine's friend. She would not stop to ask herself why.

'He hated her, too.'

'Why?' Suzie asked, herself rather than Sabine. 'Why does he hate Madame Ariane? Why do people hate me because I'm Jewish?'

Sabine ignored these questions as irrelevant, so Suzie asked, 'What happened then?'

'We went for walks. He wanted to know about Bonnemort.'

'What about Bonnemort?'

'All about when the Germans were here. He wanted to know about you, for example. He was surprised that you were Jewish. He thought you couldn't be, because you stayed so long.'

'What else?'

'Oh, Henri. Henri was in the Resistance, but he wasn't any good, so that's why he got killed.'

'Sabine,' Suzie's voice was shocked. 'You hate Madame Ariane, so I can see why you let him talk like that about her. But you loved Henri. How could you let him say such things?'

'I only listened,' Sabine said defensively.

'But you talked as well. That's why he wanted to see you. He was finding things out from you. What did you tell him?'

'I only told the truth.'

'Sabine, it's not whether it's true or false, it's who you tell it to. Don't you remember...'

She was about to recall Madame Ariane's words after their visit to Lavallade on the Fourteenth of July, but it was pointless to quote her to Sabine. How dangerous life with Sabine had been. Even more than she had realised at the time. Sabine might, on impulse, have told someone, anyone, about her being Jewish, at any time. But she hadn't done so. She had held the gun, which Suzie had given her, to her head, but she had never pulled the trigger. In the instant of gratitude for that concealment, Suzie knew what Sabine had betrayed.

'You didn't tell him about...what we saw in the winepress?'

'You mean *her* and the major?'

'Yes.'

'Yes.'

'Sabine, how could you?'

'It's *true*.'

'You shouldn't have done.'

Suzie had been so deeply revolted by the sounds they had heard that she had difficulty in recalling the memory now. What they saw must have meant what Sabine said it meant. She could only remember the dust in her nostrils and under her eyelids, the mist of cobwebs between the beams, the terrible sounds, the hoarse gasping of Lou Moussou struggling to die.

'But it's the *truth*.'

They had been walking along the path of the walls of Lepech Perdrissou. It was six in the evening. Above them in the falling darkness the plane trees held out their gnarled lopped branches like lepers' hands, amputated and twisted. She had been laughing, dancing along sideways, relishing the memory of that scene, grotesque and anguished, which proved what she knew instinctively: that love was pain. He had often asked her before, 'Did you ever see them alone together?' She had understood exactly what he wanted to know and had evaded his questions with vague and irrelevant answers. She did not know why she told him then, when she had kept silent before.

She began to sing a playground song, one she had heard in the mouths of the big boys.

'It's only natural, after all,
To take a girl...'

She left the quatrain unfinished, but he had heard those words too, filtering through the open windows of the classroom while he marked books during the recess. Without making any effort to pursue her, he waited until she was within reach to catch her wrist.

'So you did. You saw them together?'

She pulled away, but his grasp did not relax, and she continued to sing, turning her head away from him.

'It's only natural, after all...'

They had already reached the grassy mounds that marked the old gates and they walked between them, taking the road past the walled orchards that surrounded the town. His glance swept the dark and empty road before he struck her, hard. She swerved just in time and the blow caught her, not on the side of the head, which had been his target, but on the neck. She shrieked and swung to the ground, still held at the wrist. Scrambling up, like a dog on a leash, she received the next blow of his closed fist square on the cheek. Involuntary tears sprang to her eyes.

'Why do you want to know?' she cried, defiantly. 'What's it to you what I saw or what they did?'

At this stage his actions were still familiar, the punishment of an impertinent student. It was she who broke the pattern, who did not submit as she was supposed to do. It was long past that point when she was on the ground with him crouched over her that she said, at last, 'Yes, I saw them together, walking together, talking together. That's what you want me to say, isn't it? So now I've said it,' devaluing her confession as she made it. He had not let go of the stick that he had picked up earlier, but his voice was calm, gentle.

'And what did you see?'

She was only whispering, her strength to shout gone, yet her words were full of venom. 'They were fucking, fucking.'

As she said it she sobbed. She knew that she had given away a source of power. She endlessly had lived the memory, rehearsed that curious amalgam of agonised sounds in which pain was wrung out with an obsessive pleasure. She had thought that he of all people would understand the significance of what she had heard, but all he wanted to know was when, where, how.

'Did you see them together often?' he demanded. 'Did you hear what they said?'

She lay exhausted on the sodden ground, resigned to telling him. 'I heard them speaking, but they used German so I didn't understand. Madame Ariane spoke good German. That's why he liked her. It wasn't like yours, with lots of French words in it.'

In part, she had meant to placate him, by complimenting him on his bad German. In part, she wanted to threaten him, by hinting at how much more she had seen. The next blow came without warning. He did not bother to check whether he was unobserved, for they were well away from the village now, the forest closing around the road, arching above it to shut out even the sky.

'How do you know how well I speak German?'

She wanted to retract then, all of it, for she saw that the patterns of the past were broken and she could not guess what he would do next. His fury was beyond reason. 'I don't, really…'

'Yes, you do. You just said I spoke bad German. There's only one way you could know that. You spied on me too, didn't you?'

'I don't know…'

'You do know.'

The punishment for knowing would be more severe than it ever was in class for not knowing. She had been tricked. She should have kept it to herself, as one of her own treasures. And it did her no good; she gained nothing from having pleased him with the story; it had not mitigated his fury. She put up her arm to protect her face, and heard it crack under the blow from his stick.

'Do you remember,' she said to Suzie, 'the time when *he* was there with the major? The major had his gun out and we thought he had captured him. But he hadn't. They were talking together in German. You remember that? It was *true*, wasn't it?'

32

UNABLE TO FACE lunch, Theo asked for a bowl of soup on a tray in the library. As he ate, his eye fell on Sabine's jigsaw on its board, still uncompleted. It was difficult to imagine in what circumstances Sabine had told Vernhes about Ariane and the major. The fact that, according to his wife, Sabine hated her, added another layer of unreliability to the web of stories. Had Vernhes accepted in good faith a malicious tale fabricated by Sabine?

He needed to talk to his daughter, but he could not imagine how to engage her in conversation. Children were another race whose language he did not speak. Even if he had little hope of learning anything from them, he could at least tell them the truth about Ariane. He picked up the board and carried it carefully up the stairs.

When he entered Sabine's room he found the two girls there and a silence that suggested they had stopped speaking as he opened the door. Sabine was almost submerged in her bed. Suzie was sitting beside her.

'How are you?' he asked his daughter.

'Very well, thank you.' Her reply, although patently untrue, confirmed that Suzie had got her to speak again.

He organised the puzzle on a small table in front of the fire, persuading Sabine to get out of bed and to join him and Suzie. She did so with reluctance, but once seated in front of the jigsaw, her interest was roused and she began to turn over the pieces, testing them against the finished part.

'I still don't know what the picture is,' he complained.

'Don't tell.'

'It's a picture of…'

Sabine and Suzie had spoken simultaneously.

Suzie addressed Sabine, 'It's only fair that he should understand what it's meant to be. We know what it is, why shouldn't he?' She turned to Theo. 'It's a picture from an old manuscript. There's a knight riding a horse and he has killed someone who is lying underneath him. It's decorated round the edge with leaves and branches. And there's a big letter Q. It's very complicated.'

'I can imagine.'

They worked on the puzzle for a while in silence. Theo, who was looking at it upside down, soon abandoned any effort.

'I'm not going to be able to stay much longer at Bonnemort,' he said eventually. 'I shall have to go back to Paris, in a day or so. Ariane will stay here with you two until Sabine is well enough to travel and then you will all come back to Paris together. We shall live in our flat, all of us together as a little family.' He had no authority from Ariane for saying this. He simply willed it.

Suzie turned towards the window, as if detaching herself from this plan, and Theo, suddenly understanding, corrected his view of the future. 'That is, until the war ends and Suzie's mother and father return and she can go back to live with them.'

He paused, holding his temples between his thumb and middle finger, wondering how to begin. The girls looked up curiously, taking the gesture for a sign of emotion, as he supposed it was.

'Sabine, you are going to live with me and Ariane from now on, and I want to tell you something about her. All through the war, while she was living here and looking after you, she was working, with Henri and Micheline and Dr Maniotte, whom you may remember, for the Resistance. Not, like some people, just at the last minute, in the few months before liberation, but right from the beginning. She took very great risks and was incredibly brave. At the time you didn't know what she was doing, because she wanted to protect you and make sure that you were not involved. One day you will learn about what she did. The most dangerous and difficult time for her was last year when the Germans came. Just when it seemed that the worst was over and the Allied army had landed to liberate France, here at Bonnemort you had to face the SS. Not least of her worries was the danger to you, Suzie. If the Germans had realised who you were, you, and she, would have been deported immediately.'

Suzie nodded, holding up a piece of the puzzle, turning it one way and then the other, trying to see what it might represent. She was wondering whether, if Sabine had understood that, she would have denounced her, in order to get rid of Madame Ariane.

'But the hardest thing she had to do,' Theo went on, 'was to act as a spy for the Resistance, to tell them anything she could learn about what the SS was doing here. So she had to pretend, sometimes, to be friendly with the Germans in order to carry out her mission.'

Suzie was now watching him fixedly. Sabine appeared absorbed in the puzzle.

'You may have seen, or heard, some things that you thought were odd, or wrong, but I want you to understand their true meaning. Things are not always what they seem. Ariane will never tell you what really happened, nor explain what she did. But I want you to know about it.'

Now that his speech was ended, Theo was at a loss. His audience was silent, without reaction. They both picked up pieces of the jigsaw and studied them carefully. He could not tell whether his words had been received as a revelation of truth, with relief, with scepticism, or with bewilderment.

'We were spies, too,' Suzie remarked eventually. She did not look at him, concentrating on a small red piece of jigsaw, trying to insert it in different ways, then rejecting it.

'Suzie.' Sabine's voice was minatory.

'Well, we were.'

Theo had revised his impressions of the infantile Suzie of their first meeting. She now seemed more mature than Sabine.

'We watched everything that was going on at Bonnemort when the Germans were here.'

'Did you realise what Henri and Madame Ariane were doing?' Theo asked. He did not want to end these confidences prematurely by broaching the story of the major at once.

'Henri, no,' Suzie said. 'I suppose we should have guessed because he was never here. But Madame Ariane, yes.' The small red piece was at last set in its proper position. 'We watched her with the major, but because no one explained things to us, we thought she might be a traitor.'

'Why did you think that?'

Sabine broke in. 'Because she let the major kiss her.' Her tone was one of accusation and self-justification.

'I could see,' Suzie went on, 'that when the major put his arm around her, she did not like it. He did it in a threatening way. I could see she was afraid, because I was afraid, too. I knew what it was like to be afraid. Sabine didn't agree.'

'You understand now, I hope, Sabine,' her father said. She did not reply, moving the pieces around, in search of one particular shape.

'But I could understand what they said, because they were speaking in German,' Suzie went on, 'and Sabine couldn't. And although I didn't always tell her...' here she darted a glance at Sabine to see how she reacted, 'I knew that Madame Ariane sometimes told the major things, when he asked her questions. So I was worried. I didn't think that she would really work for the Germans. But I thought that if she was too afraid, she might give something away by mistake.'

'How did you hear this?' Theo asked. 'Did you listen at the keyhole?'

Suzie looked at him witheringly, to make him realise that he had misjudged their level of skill as spies. 'Several times we hid in the gallery when they had dinner in the *salon bleu*. Madame Ariane never ate, but the major used to make her cut up his food. He had a false hand, you know. I think he could have probably cut up his own food; he just pretended he couldn't, to make Madame Ariane do it for him. He was like that. He liked to feel he had power over people. We once heard him tell how he denounced a Jew whom he recognised. That was in Germany, not France.'

'We saw them...'

Suzie thought Sabine was going to say, 'We saw them... fuck', but at the last moment awe of her father prevented her.

'...together.' She was twisting a piece of the jigsaw to force it into position. 'In the winepress.' She wrenched it out and tried a new place for it.

'We discovered a way into the winepress by accident,' Suzie explained. 'It's a hole in the ground all covered by trees and brambles. We climbed down it and found ourselves in the loft in the winepress. From there you could see everything and no one knew you were there.'

The children concentrated on their jigsaw in silence, as if there was nothing more to be said on the subject.

Theo watched them. This was the moment he had searched and waited for. He was being offered proof, the evidence of eyewitnesses, of what had happened between his wife and the German. He had only to ask and he would be given it. Even as he recognised the opportunity, he knew he was going to turn away from it. He imagined what Sabine meant when she said 'together', and rejected the evidence.

'Were you watching the night the major was killed?' he asked.

Both children were scrabbling among the pieces, searching, not finding.

'Suzie, have you seen a piece with a cross-bar going like this?'

'No.'

They continued to seek for the elusive piece. 'But we're building it up quite well on that side,' Suzie added encouragingly.

They were not going to answer any more questions, Theo realised. They looked so vulnerable, Sabine with her jaggedly cropped hair and bruised face, Suzie with her evasively hesitant expression, locked in a world of childish play. They probably knew more than anyone else about what had happened, but did not know that they knew. The information was coiled into their games and fantasies in a form unusable and unrecognisable to him.

'Henri should have asked us to help him,' Suzie remarked a few minutes later. 'We would have been able to tell him a lot of things.'

'He wanted to protect you. Too much knowledge was dangerous.' The children did not respond. It was as if he had not spoken.

'If Madame Ariane saw the major and she was working for the Resistance...' Although she did not lift her head, Suzie seemed to address Sabine. Long pauses separated each of their utterances. Theo listened.

'Try this.'

'There must have been other people doing the same thing...'

'We saw Monsieur Vernhes when he met the major too...'

'That was in the forest...'

'Perhaps he was also working for the Resistance then, if he went to see the major.'

'We tracked the major. We thought he was going to meet Madame Ariane...'

'But when we found the car, there were two men talking...'

'We didn't hear what they were saying...'

'Except he spoke very bad German...'

'The major didn't speak French at all...'

'This is what you want.' Suzie handed a piece to Sabine, who took it, tried it, rejected it.

Theo at last asked, 'What did he want with the major, Mr Vernhes?'

To that there was no reply. An absorbed silence lengthened until Theo realised that they were going to say nothing more. He rose and went out and the children did not stir as he shut the door. They had unexpectedly given him confirmation of Nikola's story. This was why Vernhes had come this morning, why he had felt it necessary to threaten him. He feared that Theo had gleaned information about him, or would soon do so. He had asked carefully whether his enquiry was official or personal, had reacted angrily to the idea that Theo might report anything to the authorities. What Nikola had said must be true.

He descended the tower stairs and glanced out of the window that looked down on the farmyard. Ariane, wearing an old coat, was at work with Florence. She was holding a pitchfork in one hand and was pushing back a strand of hair from her eyes with her forearm. Theo noticed that her bare wrists, protruding between her sleeves and gloves, looked so fragile that they might snap if she applied the slightest force to any action. He paused to watch the silent co-operation of the two women. Florence had taken hold of a sack leaning against the barn wall by its two top corners and was dragging it across the cobbles. Ariane laid down her tool and joined her, taking the other end. The two of them swung it up and into the barrow, which Florence then began to push towards the animal pens. Ariane picked up the pitchfork once again and speared a bundle of hay with it.

As he stood there and observed the fluid movements of the two women hefting the sack into the barrow, Theo experienced a leap of understanding. He felt that he was witnessing, fleetingly, life at Bonnemort during the Occupation, when he was not there, when the men were absent and the women were in charge. Suddenly the idea that the SS major had been Ariane's lover, which had so maddened him, became almost insignificant, reduced to triviality by his flare of insight.

Ariane had killed the major.

33

ARIANE WAS WAITING for Theo's interrogation; she wondered what she would say. He had given her warning and she knew it must come. The wariness of her expectation filled their bedroom like smoke from a blocked chimney. That night she sat on a stool in front of the fire in their bedroom, still dressed, stretching out her hands to the warmth. She heard him approaching the door and thought that the sound of the months of the Occupation had been that of footsteps: leather on wood, steel on stone, heels on rock.

The eleventh week of the Occupation. She had not counted the time at the beginning because she had not understood how long she would have to endure. They had borne it now for ten weeks and two days. She had begun counting when the major had grasped the hair at the nape of her neck and forced his tongue into her mouth. She counted back to the day they came, and forward to infinity, for it seemed as if they would never go.

The first thing that she thought of every morning was of *his* presence or absence. The last day, the day that Henri died, *he* had left early in the morning with the lieutenant and most of the unit. When the sun rose through the mist that hung in the walnut trees in the valley, she watched it with a mixture of relief at his absence and dread of his return. The morning was routine. She rode before breakfast and then spent two hours in the tower teaching the children. August should have been the holidays, as Sabine continually reminded her, but Ariane had remained firm on the need for study every morning, because it was a refuge for her as well as a discipline for them. After lunch, as the Germans were still absent, she had succumbed to the girls' pleading and the heat, and they had slipped down the cliff path, past the tents and storerooms occupied by the troops, to the dark earthy waters of the lake, to swim.

Henri had not been at Bonnemort for the last two days. She knew that there had been fierce debates between him and Vernhes about plans for a demonstration at Lepech. Each day the desire for local action grew as the Allies inched towards Paris. When they had heard two days earlier of the landings in Provence, frustration in the Maquis camps in the forests reached an almost unbearable pitch. Henri remained convinced that they should be patient. The occupiers were contained within a narrow compass. Soon the Germans would withdraw of their own accord. All they had to do was wait patiently. But patience was intolerable for Vernhes, who wanted a victory and a public triumph. Whatever they decided to do, Ariane had told Henri, she could not be there. She would remain at Bonnemort with the girls and hear about it afterwards. Her sympathies were all with Henri on this subject. She longed for the country truly to be free, the Occupation to be at an end, to regain her own freedom. Yet a demonstration while the major's back was turned, leading to reprisals later, seemed pointless.

In the early evening as they climbed up towards the house, refreshed by their bathe, she thought that she heard a shot, a single crack, as if a solitary farmer were out after vermin. She listened attentively, hearing nothing but the restless cawing of the rooks in the elms. Nevertheless, she hurried the girls up the path. Soon the sound of gunfire was unmistakable. They had never heard shooting before. Suzie sat huddled in a chair with a cat on her knee, stroking it rhythmically, less for its comfort than her own. Micheline plodded round the kitchen, refusing to acknowledge what she heard or what it might mean.

Ariane went to her room, resolving that when things had quietened down she would venture out with Florence to see what had happened, if any help was needed. After an hour or so the shooting ceased and the sound of engines filled the courtyard. Looking out of the window, she saw the Hispano-Suiza drawn up in front of the door. The sight of her own car always produced a lurch of fear. This was not the return of the unit in strength, just of the major himself. Later she worked out that he had fitted in this visit to Bonnemort, to destroy papers and to speak to her, after the fight on the road and before returning to Lepech Perdrissou to execute Henri and his companions. Between one job and another. She stood tapping her nails on the sill. She was afraid to leave the house now, in case she was called for. Time slipped by while she hesitated, until Florence appeared at her door.

'*He* wants you,' she said. 'He's in a hurry, slamming around downstairs. And watch out; he's in a mood.'

Ariane walked reluctantly down the tower stairs. Since its occupation by the Germans the house smelled alien. Before, it had smelled of lavender and damp, a mild, elderly, feminine scent. They had taken over everything, she thought, even the air, and it now smelled rankly masculine, of cigarettes and sweat, of leather and fear.

In the library the major was alone. She recognised all the danger signs and her palms began to sweat with fear. He saw her, ignored her, moving around the room, piling up documents into open boxes that were stacked on others, already filled, by the door. The meaning of what he was doing leaped at her instantly: he was packing. The emotion that flooded through her was so violent that she found she had to hold onto the jamb to support herself.

'Shut the door,' he ordered abruptly.

He was bending down by the hearth, a match flaring in his hand, a flame that seemed to gush from the ends of his fingers, as if he had literally a firearm, with no need of any other weapon. The papers that he had piled there refused to obey him. The fire was too densely packed; the flames died at the edges, spluttering into a glowing fringe, smoking evilly.

'Come and do this for me.'

She took the matches from him and loosely crumpled a few papers, so that they would catch fire. He was standing beside her, looking down.

'We're leaving. Do you hear? Tomorrow we'll be gone.'

She remained crouching, pretending that the fire needed her attention, his boots just within her range of vision.

'But you'll hear from me. When things have settled down again, I'll let you know. I'll send for you.'

Is he mad, she wondered and leaned forward to push more paper into the flame.

'I'll be back with my men later; there are a few things to settle in Lepech. So I'll see you once more before I leave for good. Get up.'

She rose, stumbling, and he put his hand round her neck, his thumb painfully caressing her windpipe.

'I'll meet you down there, say two o'clock tonight. I should be through by then. If I'm not there, wait for me.'

He was gone. She heard a car manoeuvring in the court-yard, then driving off. By the noise of the engine she knew that he had driven away in her car. He would take it later for good, she was sure. Nothing would induce him to abandon that particular piece of booty.

Florence was in the farmyard, watching him depart.

They went out together, cautiously, not knowing what to expect. Under the trees the evening light lay almost horizontal, the shadows striping the track like corduroy. With a superstitious fear that it might not come to pass, she said nothing to Florence of the news she had just received, even when they passed the entrance to the field where the Germans parked their vehicles. She could see that the guards were busy piling boxes outside the storerooms that they had used as their quarters.

Florence remarked, 'They're up to something. I can tell.'

The road climbed steeply and on the crest Ariane saw a line of light from the setting sun touching a low branch, its end leaf already tinged with gold, flaring like the match in the major's fingers. The next instant they saw below them one of the German cars half off the road, its door open, its windscreen shattered. For a sudden, bewildered moment she thought that it had just happened. *He*'d just been killed; they would find his body slouched beside his driver's. Then she realised that this was the wrong car and it was facing the wrong way, up the hill, towards Bonnemort. This was the result of the firefight that they had heard earlier.

She began to run down the hill, but before she reached the car Florence's cry halted her. The man she had found was dead. He wasn't a local. They didn't know his name, didn't even recognise him, but they knew at once that he was French. Not until they reached the car and discovered Philippe Boysse handcuffed to the wheel did the dread turn into reality: it was Group Rainbow that had been involved.

In the failing light they ran, bowed, through the bracken, frantically searching for the living. The next body they found was that of the garage mechanic from Montféfoul, a stout man in his fifties who had been picked up by the police at the same time as Henri a year earlier, and released soon afterwards. He had been shot through the head and the blood that had soaked from his eye socket had already darkened, the flies settling on his face. Florence was crying, quietly. Ariane could hear her saying over and over again, 'Mother Mary, not Claude; Mother Mary, not Claude.' A string of mucus swung from her nostrils, which she wiped away with the back of her hand. When they came upon their fourth corpse, the extent of the tragedy struck home to them. They assembled the dead, carrying the bodies between them, laying them in a line on the verge. At one point Florence said, 'We need help. We'll have to get help.'

Ariane would not let her go. 'Someone might still be alive. We've got to go on until we find them all.'

Even when they left, in the dark, when they could no longer see, when they had hauled seven bodies through the undergrowth to the side of the road, closing their eyes, arranging their limbs, they could not be sure that there were not more *maquisards*, alive or dead, lying in the forest.

At the gates Florence stopped Ariane. 'Don't tell Mum yet. She'll only worry about Dad and Roger. It looks as if they got away. So let's not tell her until we know he's all right.'

They all went to bed early and Ariane waited in the dark, making no attempt to read. She heard the return of the Germans late at night, and listened to their voices and engines as they worked in the field, loading their lorries. She stood at the window of the tower room watching the headlights of the trucks riding up the track, away from Bonnemort. The Occupation was over.

The silence lengthened, stretched thinner and thinner. Theo broke it.

'It's very curious,' he said. 'They left without their commanding officer.' He paused, to see if Ariane had anything to contribute. 'The only way to account for such an action is that he had ordered them to leave without him, saying he would rejoin them, or that he had gone ahead and they were to join him. But we know he was not ahead of them. When they left, he was still here, possibly already dead.'

Ariane made no comment.

'How was he going to leave?' Theo went on, thinking aloud. 'Ah, the Hispano-Suiza. He was going to take that, wasn't he?'

'Yes.'

Theo waited, letting the silence run. Finally, he asked his question. 'Did you kill him?'

'No.'

Her voice was sharp in its denial, but it came too quickly. She had expected the question and had rehearsed her monosyllabic answer.

Then she added, 'But I wish I had.'

34

FLORENCE WAS CROSSING the courtyard when Suzie came out, wrapped in coat, hat and gloves.

'Where're you off to?' she called.

'I'm going...out on my bike,' Suzie replied, as if she had only just decided.

Florence was already striding away from her. 'Don't be late,' she said.

Her own bicycle had flat tyres, Suzie discovered, but Sabine's was serviceable. She wiped the seat and wheeled it into the yard. She had no plan, although she had a purpose.

The colonel's words to them the previous day had been an enormous relief. He had confirmed that her instincts had been right: Madame Ariane was not a traitor. He had put things right. He was also going to find her parents for her. There were limits, however, to what he could or would do. She had tried to explain the story of Vernhes and the major to him, but he had not understood its significance. He did not see that it explained what had happened to Sabine. She had said sadly to Sabine when he had left them to their jigsaw, 'He didn't understand, did he?' She had done her best. It was like holding the piece you needed and simply not seeing which way to turn it to make it fit.

'I didn't expect him to,' Sabine said.

'So what shall we do?'

'Nothing. There's nothing to be done.' Her voice was resigned. The defiance of the old Sabine had disappeared.

'What will you do? *He* might…'

'You heard what my father said. I'll go back to Paris with you. When the war's over you'll go off to live with your parents and I'll have to stay with them.'

They had worked on the puzzle for some time in silence.

'Is that so bad?' Suzie asked eventually. 'I mean Madame Ariane… You were wrong about her. Isn't that all over now?'

'I don't have any choice. I'd rather stay here with the aunts, but they don't want me.' Self-pity crept into Sabine's voice.

Suzie said nothing more, but the problem remained with her. Could you just leave what had happened to Sabine like that? Walk away from it? The major had met a just end, terrible but satisfying. She had stood with the aunts and Micheline and Florence in the courtyard looking at his naked corpse and had been filled with awe. He had terrorised them all and now had come to this.

She lay awake that night, watching the moonlight on the wall, wondering whether Madame Ariane would be the person to confide in, and then put the idea aside. She had not been able to save herself or them last summer. And the problem was how to tell. She and Sabine understood one another. When the subject did not have to be expressed, it was possible to talk. But to begin at the beginning, to describe and explain, was out of the question.

She had hardly used a bicycle since she left Bonnemort in September and her legs ached from the effort of pedalling. It seemed much longer than six months since she had last ridden along this road to Lepech to go to mass. She didn't go to mass any more in Paris and she missed it, in some odd way. Madame Ariane had found a religious study class at the synagogue and insisted that she attend, even though she had protested that Maman and Papa had never made her go. She reached the climb to the village and halfway up she was forced to dismount. She did not know what she was going to do or say. She simply knew that if she confronted him, something would happen, or an idea would come to her.

As she had hoped, she had timed her arrival so that the school was emptying as she arrived in the square. She propped her bicycle against the outer wall of the playground and waited until the last pair of children had dawdled out into the street. She did not know her way around the building, nor whether the schoolmaster would still be there, so she wandered from the entrance hall along the corridor and peered into the classroom. The board on its easel was wiped clean, the chalks lined up in their tray. All the seats were raised, the desk tops closed and bare. Walking down the aisle between the double desks, she looked out of the windows set so high that only the tops of the trees and the sky, darkening now, were visible. She heard footsteps and stood waiting for the door to open.

In the dusk he did not recognise her.

'What are you doing here so late?' he said sharply, then, realising who she was, repeated with a new emphasis, 'What are you doing here?' When she did not reply he went on, 'It's the little Jewish girl from Bonnemort, isn't it? What's your name?'

'Rahel Kahn, monsieur,' she said politely, 'but here they call me Suzie.'

He was holding a large key in one hand, tapping its end in the palm of the other, as if uncertain of what to do.

'I understood you had left Bonnemort,' he said.

'I had, but I've come back.'

'For good?'

'No, just to visit Sabine.'

'And she sent you to speak to me?'

'Not exactly. She'd like to see you.'

She watched the key. He was no longer tapping, but sliding it to and fro across his palm.

'I called at Bonnemort yesterday to ask after her.'

Suzie did not hurry to fill the long silences that were stitched together with hasty phrases.

'She'd like to see me?' he repeated.

'Yes.' She waited and then spoke fast. 'But it's difficult at Bonnemort. The winepress, do you know it? On the path down to the lake. She could meet you there.'

She cycled home in the dusk. It had been so easy. It was going to be easy. She knew now what she was going to do.

35

THEO AND ARIANE were walking round the walnut plantations in the late afternoon. They moved in silence under the cage of branches that ribbed the seductively mild blue of the sky.

Theo was thinking that he knew what had happened to Henri, could guess what had happened to Ariane, but he still didn't know what had happened to the major. Nikola, Vernhes, Ariane; each had denied killing him. He glanced sideways at his wife, who was absorbed in thought oblivious of where she was. He wondered why he believed them and not her. They had all denied it, yet each wished to have done it. One of them must be lying and have fulfilled the wish.

Nikola could have left the survivors of his group in safety to return alone. Bonnemort would have been the obvious place for him to have come for news of Henri. But Theo had no difficulty in believing that if he enquired further, among other members of Group Rainbow, he would find Nikola's story confirmed: that he was miles away on the night of the major's death, camped beside a fire in the middle of the forest, or tending his wounded comrades in the barn of a friendly farmer.

Vernhes had good reason to kill, to eradicate a witness to his treachery. He had the ruthlessness and the will. He could have made his way to Bonnemort during the evening, and waited there for the major's return to complete his plan. The case against him was plausible. But Theo could not convince himself that Vernhes had been the killer. For all his military airs during the liberation, he was a politician, not a soldier; a man who worked from behind the scenes; a puppet master, not a man of action.

Ariane, in every way the least probable killer, was the most likely suspect. She had been present at Bonnemort; she had motive and ability. Petignat had assumed that the major had been kidnapped somewhere on the road and his body returned to Bonnemort. It was more likely that he had been killed at Bonnemort and his body dragged to its final position in the courtyard. The actual killing place would have been obvious, but Petignat had made no effort to search the area to discover the scene of the murder. She had been given all the time she needed to clean it up. There was no doubt that a woman, or women, could have done the killing, once they had stunned their victim.

The image of Ariane and Florence in the farmyard, their concerted power in hoisting the sack into the barrow, came back to him. Of course, he thought, they were all in it, all the women, Micheline as well as Florence. He could even imagine the aunts covering up, perjuring themselves if necessary, to save Ariane. His conviction that she had killed the major had revolutionised his understanding of what had happened here. Vernhes had locked her into a relationship with the major; she had been trapped in a situation with no escape.

He stopped for a moment, and she halted too. The trees stretched in every direction, their lines and rows perfectly accurate, adapting themselves to the folds of the land. The symmetry of the plantations, the wide avenues between the trees, had always pleased him as a child, the imposition of human control on the wildness of the landscape. The spring ploughing beneath the trees had started and ahead he could see where Franco, the Spanish labourer, was turning the oxen at the end of a furrow.

'What sort of person was he, the major?' he asked.

'In what way?'

'What did he look like, what was he like, as a man?'

'He was like… He was a Nazi. Physically, he was not a little runt like Hitler; he was one of the Aryans. Tall, well-built, athletic.'

Theo heard Petignat echoing and confirming her, '… a fine man.'

'…but damaged. He'd lost a hand fighting in Russia and been wounded there as well. As for his psychology, it's hard to know whether it was his war experiences that affected him, or whether he was always like that.'

'Like what?'

'Cruel. He had a passion for power. When he arrived, Aunt Odette wanted to believe that he was like the German officers of the First World War. She thought that the French and German officer corps had the same ideals, came from the same backgrounds. She wanted to think that the major was just like you, only German. But he wasn't. His family lost their estates in Poland in 1918, so he said. His father, who had been wounded in the trenches and was not fit, became a minor bureaucrat in the police service in Bavaria. The son fell for Hitler at school, joined the SS, went to the SS officer school at Bad Tölz and fought in every campaign since 1939: Poland, France, Russia.'

'You know a great deal about him.'

'I know even more, if you'd care to hear it. I know about his mother and sisters, his school friends, about his neighbours, the Jewish family whom he denounced, and about his war in the East. I sat night after night watching him and the lieutenant eat and drink and talk. You learn a lot that way.'

'Was he happy to be in France, sitting at your table, eating your food?'

'No. The lieutenant was. He was glad of the respite. He judged that the time would come again for fighting and he was happy to wait for it. The major was humiliated to be left with the job of rounding up terrorists when his regiment was at the front in Normandy. He was an arrogant, angry, impatient man.' Her tone was detached, without hatred or affection. 'I sat with them every evening but I didn't eat. Did they tell you that? It was a stupid idea. Someone, one of the refugees from Paris, left me a copy of Vercors' novel *The Silence of the Sea*. I only remembered it after they had arrived, and I realised that not only had I spoken to them, I had used their language. I had failed to meet the standard of resistance from the first moment. So although I spoke to them, I wouldn't eat with them. It wasn't a very good idea, but it was all I could think of.'

'How did they take it?'

'Oh, the major used it to draw a little lesson on French decadence. He was a perverse idealist. I never saw his ideals in action, but I heard enough about duty, faith and honour. He functioned in an abstract universe, because in reality he was entirely without awareness of others. Most people were outside the circle in which his idealism operated, so nothing was due to them. He spoke of Jews and Slavs as if they were diseases to be wiped out to cleanse the world. We French did not quite come into that category, although our persistence in not understanding what was good for us exasperated him. When I think about what he did at Lepech, shooting Henri, hanging the other *maquisards*, I realise that he was applying a Russian solution to a French problem. It's what they did all the time over there.'

'Did you see him again, after he told you they were leaving?'

She sighed, a resigned release of air that at last they had reached the point when she had to tell.

'Yes, but—you must believe me—not alive.'

'Tell me what happened, exactly what happened,' he repeated. 'How did you find him? Was he lying in the court-yard where Petignat found him?' They were walking again, blindly, simply patrolling up and down the avenues of walnut trees.

'No, no he wasn't.' She spoke slowly, forcing herself to explain. 'We put him there.'

'Why did you move him? What was the point?'

'The point was to make it look as if he had been dumped there. We were afraid that they would come back, the Germans, I mean, looking for him, when he failed to meet them. If it were clear that he had been killed here at Bonnemort, there would have been no hope for us. If it appeared that he had been killed somewhere else and brought back here, we might have stood a chance. It wasn't a very good idea. I don't suppose it would have fooled them, or that they would have even tried to work out the significance of where he was found. In the end, no one paid any attention to what had happened to him. The Germans had gone for good and Petignat just carted him off and that was that. And we were overwhelmed by Henri's death.'

'Don't rush.' Theo patiently brought her back to the facts. 'When Micheline and Florence called you, where was he?'

'He was lying on the cliff path. His feet were uphill, as if he had been dragged that far and then abandoned. We took him up to the courtyard and then cleared up. He had been killed in the winepress, which was like a slaughterhouse. We sluiced it with water. We burned his uniform and the girls' dresses and my blouse in the fire under the linen boiler.'

'The girls' dresses? Were the girls there?'

'Yes, they discovered the body in the winepress... They were covered... Look, Theo, I can't talk any more about this, it was hideous, hideous, I've not spoken about it before now, never, we don't mention it...'

She was gabbling, out of control. She stopped and turned her face away from him. Theo put his arm around her shoulders.

'Ariane, I have to know. You must see that. Now that I've got this far, I must know the rest.' He could feel her listening to him. They began to pace again. 'Let me get this right. The Germans came back for the last time after carrying out the executions in Lepech, loaded up their trucks and left in the middle of the night. I suppose they did so because they had actually been ordered to leave that day, 17 August, and had delayed their departure in order to hang the *maquisards*, so they had to reach wherever they had to go by first light next day. You say that you heard them leave, but after that you heard nothing and saw nothing else until you were woken by Micheline in the morning.'

He paused so that the significance of his summary was felt by them both. Finally, he said, 'Ariane, I don't believe you. I can't conceive of anyone settling down to sleep in those circumstances.'

She made no attempt to convince him.

'What you haven't told me is whether you went to see him. Did you keep the appointment that he made?'

Reluctantly, she said, 'I did.'

'Tell me what happened.'

Involuntarily she saw the false hand that they had found in the corner of the winepress, the cobbles running with blood, the dogs licking the water in the runnels of the drain. 'Don't ask, Theo. What I've told you is the truth. It's really too much to describe it. Skip it if you can. It would take me from now to eternity to explain it to you and still you wouldn't understand.'

'If the bit you want to leave out is the story of how you came to be the major's lover, that's fine, we'll skip it. We'll take it as read that he forced you. Go on from there. What happened when you went to meet him?'

As she waited for the appointed time, she had told herself that she would not go. This was the end and there would be no consequences to fear from now on. She was about to be free. But, although she struggled to persuade herself to stay where she was, she knew that she would go for the last time. She went out of the tower, across the courtyard and down to the winepress, like a bead on a string. The moon was a quarter full, low in the cloudless sky, the stars clear and brilliant, lighting her way with the curious dark brilliance of summer nights. Hating herself, doing what she could not prevent herself from doing, she ran down the path. The doors of the winepress were half-open, so she knew he must be there already, waiting for her. Although she paused for a moment, her hand on the worn wood of the door, sensing his presence, she had no premonition of what she was to find as she pulled open the doors. Her eyes were already accustomed to the dark, and she saw him immediately, stretched out at her feet. It was as if her wishes had been full of power and she had felled him by her thoughts alone.

Her heart began to race with grief and terror. She had had moments of fear before. When she had hidden in the ditch watching a German patrol pass; when she had been stopped by the Milice and had had to explain her reasons for being out on her bicycle forty kilometres from home; but never had she experienced the terror she felt now. Sweat broke out on her body, turning instantly cold. She crouched down beside him. His eyes were wide open and there was a mark in the centre of his forehead. She passed her hand in front of his eyes; his glassy stare remained fixed on the rock roof of the winepress. She remained beside him for no more than a minute before she closed the doors and raced up the path, back into the house, into her room.

The question for her was never who killed him, but why hadn't she done it herself. She should have done. She had every reason to kill him. Why had she gone down to the winepress? He was leaving. What could he do to her? But she had gone. And it had never even occurred to her to kill him.

'Was he dead?' Theo asked.

'Of course he was dead.'

'His throat had been cut. There must have been blood everywhere.'

'No, there was no blood.'

'So he was simply stunned at that stage. Did you listen to his heart, or find a pulse, or put a finger in front of his nostrils?'

'No, I didn't. Do you think he was still alive, and was finished off later?'

'How do you account for the cut throat?'

'I can't, I don't. I don't account for anything.'

'You could tell if he was still alive when you saw him by how much blood he had lost. If he had lost a lot of blood by the time you found him in the morning, he was still alive and the blood was pumped out of the severed artery. If he had not lost much blood, then his heart had already stopped and he had been killed by the blow on the head. Think about how you kill a pig. It has to stay alive for as long as possible, so that the blood pumps out of the body. It's the difference between Islamic and Jewish butchery and Christian slaughtering practices...'

'Theo, what does it matter whether the blow or the cut killed him? He was dead. If he wasn't dead then, as I thought, he was certainly dead in the morning.'

'You didn't think of doing anything for him that night? Helping him, removing him?'

No.' She was speaking more slowly now as the pressure of memory slackened. She sounded exhausted. 'No, I thought he was dead, so there was nothing to be done for him. The one thing I knew was that I couldn't be the one to find him there. I had to get out of there and let someone else discover his body. So I ran away.'

36

THEY WALKED TOWARDS the house, poised above them on its grassy ledge, between the cliff and the forest. Theo took the path that led along the edge of the lake and Ariane guessed his intention at once.

'Theo, no, please.'

He made no reply, continuing on his route. Soon he heard her footsteps hurrying after him and stopped to let her come abreast of him.

'I've talked to the children,' he said, 'and told them that you were working for the Resistance. I explained to them that you were trying to learn what you could from the SS.'

'Oh, Theo,' she protested, 'what's the point?'

'It was the right thing to do. They know far more than you think, or would like. They used to spy on you and the major. I'll show you how. Do you see that?' He pointed to the clump of elm saplings and wild clematis in the field in front of the house. 'In there is a rock chimney which drops into the winepress. They used to climb down there and hide in the loft.'

They climbed the path, single file, until they reached the double doors of the winepress. Theo pulled them open and stepped inside. It was years since he had been in here. When he was young, the great vat had still been in place, in the circle that marked the centre of the floor. The funnel used by the children had had a purpose then: the grapes had been loaded onto a cart in the vineyards and then brought to the cliff top where they had been tipped directly into the vat in the cave below. The wine had never been very good, sharp and dark, only fit for drinking on the estate. After the last war the vines had been pulled up and the equipment dismantled. Against one wall were the slaughter bench and all the utensils for pig-killing. Micheline had told him that the secret pig, Lou Moussou, was always slaughtered in the winepress, to hide it from the Requisition.

Something had struck the major so powerfully that he had immediately fallen to the ground, thrown backwards by the force of the blow. Had she been waiting here in the dark, ready to strike? It seemed an unnatural, difficult method of attack. From Petignat's description the blow had landed in the centre of the forehead, and it was hard to imagine how she would have achieved such an angle, or such force. She would have had to be above him.

He climbed the ladder to the loft, crawling on hands and knees, as the rock roof sloped inwards towards the darkness of the rear of the cave. Ariane was inscrutable, a silhouette in the doorway. Looking down at her, he saw what had been invisible from ground level: a pulley wheel fixed into the rock in the centre of the roof. The rope threaded through it was secured to a beam of the loft and the free end was looped back and caught in the same place. It must originally have had some use in lifting baskets of grapes, or barrels of wine during the processing of the grapes. Later it would have hauled hay into the loft, and hoisted the dead pigs vertical to be butchered.

He suddenly saw what its most recent purpose had been. It must have been that hook that had hit the major in the forehead, as Petignat had described. No wonder he hadn't seen it coming. It would have swooped at him from above eye level. Theo loosened the rope and called to Ariane to stand clear. He let go of the hook; it swung straight at the door. The pendulum swung his thoughts on a new arc.

Could it have been an accident? A man hated by a whole community, killed by a random blow? If the hook-end of the rope was loose, lying on the edge of the loft, could the opening of the door by chance have caused it to fall free the whole of its length, just sufficient to catch the major on the top of his head? It did not seem very likely, but it had to be considered as a possibility if Ariane was speaking the truth: that he was already lying concussed or dead when she found him. But whatever had happened at that moment, nothing so far explained the cut throat. That could not have been an accident.

He wondered if he would succeed in peeling back any more layers of Ariane's confession, or whether it was even wise to try. He was now more doubtful that she had killed the major. The story that she told rang true for the very reason that it explained nothing. If you were going to fabricate a story, it would at least be one that fitted the facts. This tale of finding him dead but uninjured was too implausible to be anything except the truth. But not the whole truth. The gaps in her story, the killing itself, the slashing of the throat, the fountain of blood that must have pulsed out of his neck, his dying cry must be too horrible for her to recall. She had probably told him as much as she could bear and he could not expect any more.

He climbed down again. The hook now hung vertical, still swivelling a little under its own impetus. Theo stood beneath it. The hook was on a level with his eyebrows; he noted that the major must have been about his own height. Even though he knew it was there, and it was not propelled towards him at speed, his eye did not pick it up immediately. He put his hand up to hold it and tap it against his forehead.

'The children,' he said. 'You said the children's clothes were covered in blood.'

Ariane stepped forward tentatively. 'The children?'

'You found him here at two in the morning and you ran back to the house. How did the children come into it?'

'About the children. I didn't tell you because... I don't know why...' She halted, began again. 'Everything else I can account for. I may not like what happened, what I did myself or what others did, but I understood what was going on. Yet this I can't explain.'

'What is it?'

'I told you, I found him lying here. When I realised what had happened I just ran. I didn't stop until I was in the house. But when I reached my room, I began to consider what I should do.'

It was some time after she had reached her room that her heart ceased to pound sufficiently for her to think straight and take decisions. She was sure that her first impulse was correct. She must not find him, that must be for someone else. For a while she thought of trying to move his body away from Bonnemort, but only a little reflection showed that it could not be done before the morning, even with Florence's help. And the lieutenant and his men might return at any time, searching for him. It must look, rather, as if he had been killed somewhere else and then brought back here, as if the killing was nothing to do with Bonnemort. It was only then that the question came to her of who really had killed him, but she dismissed it as irrelevant to the immediate problem.

No one would find him in the winepress. No one normally went there for days on end; that was why he had chosen it for their meetings in the first place. She wished that she could just leave him there, and forget about him, but she knew that if the soldiers came back and instituted a proper search, they would discover his body in half an hour. So he had to be put somewhere more obvious, where Florence or Micheline would find him at first light.

After an hour, when she had calmed down and steeled herself, she made up her mind to go back to the winepress. She intended to pull the body out onto the path perhaps, or, if she could manage it, to haul it up towards the courtyard and leave it there where she knew that Florence would see it as soon as she emerged to feed the animals. She changed into trousers and went out again into the starlit darkness.

She reached the head of the path and for the second time that evening her heart almost stopped with fright. Below her on the path she saw two troll-like figures bent double over what appeared to be a sack on the ground. They jumped up when they heard her and she and the children faced each other in horror and astonishment, the body of the major lying between them. He was naked, his ankles tied together. They had been dragging him up the path by his feet.

None of them spoke; words were unnecessary. It was as if they all knew what had happened and what had to be done. She ran down to join them, taking hold of his ankles. They stepped back and took his shoulders, one of them at each side. They dragged him up the path together. At the top of the slope she stopped as it dawned on her that she had no idea where they were going with the corpse. The children dropped their burden and she lowered the feet to the ground.

As she raised her eyes, she realised that his head was hanging in a strange, lopsided manner. There was a slash in his throat and the children, dressed in the summer frocks they had been wearing the previous day, were drenched in blood. Suzie's dress was soaking, clinging to her body; Sabine's was spattered to the hem which was bordered with blood and coated with dust. Ariane was by then beyond feeling horror, beyond exclamations and questions. Still without words, the children abandoned the body where they had dropped it and pointed down the path. She followed them to the winepress and gasped when she saw the blood. She started to draw water, jerking the lever of the pump with a desperate urgency. The children, without being told, set to swilling the floor, pushing the bloody water out of the door, just as they had done at the end of the pig-killing. It was as if it had been rehearsed.

They found his clothes, sodden with blood, piled in a corner near the door. His false hand, wooden with a leather socket, had become detached from his arm and they swept it up, bouncing in front of the broom, as they cleaned the floor.

Ariane's only desire was to cleanse and purify. She had no plan to deal with returning, vengeful Germans beyond her initial idea when they had roared into the yard two months earlier: to get the children out of the way with Micheline and Florence, and to remain herself with the aunts. When the winepress was sluiced and scoured, she called the girls and they climbed back to the house, walking past the body of the major, ignoring it.

Ariane carried his clothes and false hand to the boiler in the farmyard. Crouching down she struck a match and fed the flame with the kindling that was kept nearby. The children stood in front of her in the greyish light of the pre-dawn, in their blood-drenched dresses. Their limbs and hair and faces were spattered with red. Frantically, she seized Suzie, turning her round, unbuttoning her dress, dragging it off her. She pulled her over to the farmyard pump and forced her to bend down so that the cold water ran over the back of her head and neck.

'Wash, wash,' she said. They were, she realised, the first words she had spoken. 'Sabine, come here. You must wash yourselves clean.'

The door of Micheline's cottage opened and Florence and her mother came out. Ariane made no attempt at explanation.

'Micheline,' she said. 'Will you take the girls and wash them and their hair. Florence, I'll need you to give me a hand.' She kneeled down and stuffed the dresses, one after the other, into the fire under the boiler, pulling off her own blouse to join them.

She led Florence to the path where the body lay and heard her catch her breath.

'So they got him in the end,' she said. 'Serves the bugger right. What are we going to do with him?'

Ariane explained that she wanted to give the impression, in case the Germans returned, that he had not been killed at Bonnemort.

'Surely,' said Florence, 'we could take him in the pony cart to the forest and dump him somewhere. It could take them weeks to find him.'

'But we haven't time.' The sun was already rising. The eastern sky was turning from grey to pink, streaked with the clearest sea-green. 'They could be back at any minute. We must make it look as if he was brought here from somewhere else.'

'We'll need the barrow,' said Florence. Between them they hoisted him like a sack of grain in the wheelbarrow and carried him as far as the centre of the courtyard, which seemed as good a place as any to put him. They looked at him for a moment or two and Florence said, 'We'll turn him over. It's more decent. The ladies'll be awake very soon.'

They left him face down and untied his ankles. Ariane had lost any capacity to deal with the future, but Florence had now taken charge.

'If he'd been left here,' she said, 'we'd just have found him. So I would phone the village and speak to the Gendarmerie. That's what I'll do.'

They were sitting on a ledge of rock on the path outside the winepress. 'We, that is Micheline and Florence and I and the children, have never spoken about it since.'

'You all knew what had happened, so there was no need to speak?'

'Yes.'

'And what did you all assume?'

'Micheline and Florence probably believe that I killed him, but they'll never say anything.'

'And what do you think?'

'I think the children did it.'

37

SUZIE OPENED THE doors of the winepress and watched a narrow blade of light slice across the darkness of the floor in front of her. She left the doors ajar and slipped inside, standing for a moment to allow her eyes to adjust to the chiaroscuro. So much had happened here that she expected to sense her own lingering fear or hear an echo of Lou Moussou's screams, but she felt nothing. It was just a rocky space, empty of the past. She crouched on the edge of the loft gazing down at the ridged floor. The pulley rope was for some reason hanging free, dangling from the centre of the roof. She loosened it so that it was long enough for her to reach, then descended to retrieve the end, holding onto it as she climbed back to her hiding place. Without pausing to take aim, she threw it with all her strength at the open doorway.

After she and Sabine had seen the major and Madame Ariane rooted in one another there, the momentum of Sabine's fury against her stepmother had become unstoppable. They established, over a week's observation, that the winepress was the fixed rendezvous, although the day and the time varied. Sabine's imagination quickly adapted their own experiences to the needs of her plan. The hook that had skimmed Suzie's head was to be the weapon. They would adjust its length to the precise height necessary to hit Madame Ariane. As at the time of the mushroom episode, the details occupied Sabine obsessively. Calculations filled her school notebooks. If Madame Ariane were one metre seventy-five tall and if twelve centimetres were allowed for her hair and the top of her head, that meant that the hook of the pulley had to hang one metre sixty-three above the ground. Further calculations were made in an effort to establish at what point in its upward swing the hook would be at a point two metres inside the door. The variables became too complex and Sabine returned to simplicity: Madame Ariane's height and the length of the rope. She stood on a box with a tape measure, while Suzie played out the rope so that the drop was exactly what was required. When the rope was securely wound round its pegs and anchored at that length, Sabine climbed up to the loft and practised throwing the hook with all her force, hearing the satisfying smack of the metal against the wooden doors opposite them. Suzie was commanded to walk into the winepress in order to estimate the timing of the launch of the rope. Finally, Sabine investigated the slaughtering equipment that was stacked against the wall waiting for the next pig-killing. She unrolled a sleeve of fabric that lay on top of the slaughter bench.

'What's that?' Suzie asked fearfully, knowing the answer.

'Knives.'

'Knives?'

'Yes. Just hitting her with the hook may not be enough. We shall have to stab her too.'

'Sabine, no, no, no.'

'Suzie, yes, yes, yes.' Sabine advanced on her, laughing, waving a knife in each hand.

Suzie submitted to the planning and practising with a fatalistic acquiescence. She had thwarted Sabine's intention last time; something would happen this time too. She would see a way to protect Madame Ariane and herself. For several days after the plan was ready, it seemed that there would simply be no opportunity to put it into action. They twice waited in the winepress, but no one came.

They might have missed that last night, too. The major and the Germans were not at Bonnemort in the evening, had not been there for two days, and the girls had gone to bed at the normal time, in spite of the excitement of the shooting that they had heard in the early evening. Sabine had detected Madame Ariane's absence from her bedroom.

'She's not coming to bed,' she reported. 'She's in her sitting room, walking up and down in the dark. She's going to meet him tonight.'

She made Suzie get up and dress. They arranged pillows in their bed to give the appearance, at a cursory glance in the dark, that they were asleep, and slipped down the stairs and into the farmyard. They climbed down into the winepress through the funnel and waited.

As they crouched together in the darkness, Sabine holding the looped-back rope, nursing the heavy hook in her hand, Suzie suddenly knew what she had to do. If she shortened the rope, it would hang too high. When Sabine launched her lethal pendulum, it would pass harmlessly over Madame Ariane's head, just as it had missed hers. She inched herself over to where the rope was secured, and with infinite care began to pull in the slack sufficiently to twist it one more time around the pegs.

'She always comes first,' Sabine whispered, 'so the instant the door opens, I'll do it. You must take the knife,' she instructed Suzie. 'You must hide down there behind the bench.'

Without protest, Suzie slithered down the ladder. She was feeling sick and her hands trembled as she unrolled the cloth with its pockets full of knives and chose one of medium length, with a slender blade. She crouched down behind the slaughter bench and silence settled around her. She was suddenly at peace. While she held the knife Sabine would not have it and Madame Ariane would come to no harm. She felt comforted in the way that, at the last moment, these ideas had come to her. It made her feel that God, some God, the Jewish one that Opa used to visit in the synagogue with his prayer shawl on, or Madame Ariane's invisible Protestant God, or Sabine's Catholic infant, with his mother and his dove and his admiring saints, was watching over them, saving them all, Madame Ariane and Sabine and her.

She had the odd sensation that she had left her body and she, Rahel, was above the physical Suzie, watching over her. She felt no surge of fear when she heard the tug at the door and when the tall figure stepped inside, she recognised it at once, almost as if she had been expecting him.

He had made three strides into the winepress when Sabine, in the gods, launched her missile, and the hook, too high to have touched Madame Ariane, hit him squarely in the middle of his forehead and toppled him like a toy soldier.

Rahel maintained her watch. Neither she nor Sabine stirred, frozen by the shock of their success. The doors opened again. Rahel realised that in all their planning they had entirely discounted the other half of the couple. If they had hit Madame Ariane, the major would have been there immediately afterwards. They had in fact struck the major and Madame Ariane had arrived. She heard a movement in the loft, as though Sabine was startled by Madame Ariane's appearance, as if she had not understood whom she had hit. The noise was abruptly stilled.

Madame Ariane fell on her knees by the major's head and a long ululating sob came out of her, like wind in trees. She passed one hand over his face, her fingertips pulling down his eyelids. She remained there, her head bowed, for several minutes. The all-seeing, hovering Rahel saw her reach out and pick up one of his hands and kiss it, without wondering why. Then Madame Ariane ran away.

Sabine scrambled down the ladder.

'It's the major. We've killed the major.' There was no doubt in their minds that he was dead. Madame Ariane had confirmed it for them.

Suzie crawled out from her hiding place. The light from the stars was bright enough to see him clearly. The hook had hit him in the centre of his forehead and he had fallen straight back, his jaw sticking up, exposing his neck to the full. It was a warm night and he wore no shirt. His skin gleamed faintly in the moonlight, as if he had been sweating. Sabine walked around the major, her fist in her mouth. It was hard for Rahel to determine whether she was disappointed because it wasn't Madame Ariane lying there, or worried at the thought of reprisals.

Then Rahel saw Suzie standing opposite Sabine, with the body lying between them. The knife was in her hand, the knife with which she would not have struck the unconscious Madame Ariane. She was not making a mistake; she knew who lay there; and with one neat backhand stroke, like Monsieur Jouanel, she drew the blade down the side of the major's neck. Sabine's shriek coincided with the spray of blood that leaped from the slashed throat. Suzie stepped neatly aside, allowing the fountain to gush onto the rocky floor. Her dress was splashed nonetheless, as was Sabine's, for, with some memory of her task at the pig-killing, Sabine ran over to the shelves, seized one of the enamel pans from the wall and shoved it below the major's neck as his life gushed away.

Suzie slithered down from the loft and stood under the hook, waiting for its swinging to slow to a halt. She could not make all the calculations that they had made last time, but she could tell by eye that it hung too low now. He was a smaller man than the major, about the same height as Madame Ariane. She would have to go and take in the rope by at least one turn. She climbed up the ladder again, like a dog, hands and feet pattering on the steps. She shortened the rope, descended once again to collect the hook and carried it back up to the loft with her. She installed herself in Sabine's position, in line with the door, and made two practice throws. It was, she discovered, harder than it seemed. It was more a question of letting it drop, so that the weight did the work. After two more journeys up and down the ladder to retrieve the hook, she decided against any further trials. Fate would decide it, as it had before.

She had said nothing to Sabine of what she planned. They had never mentioned the major's death, even to one another, a silence reinforced by that of Micheline, Florence and Madame Ariane. She wondered whether Sabine would approve of what she was going to do, or whether she would resist, as she herself had tried to resist Sabine's attack on Madame Ariane. But this was different, she told herself. Madame Ariane had been innocent, she had known it instinctively, but Monsieur Vernhes was guilty and the guilty should be punished.

Epilogue

1999

38

Two ELDERLY WOMEN were sitting side by side in the large seats of the Concorde lounge at JFK airport. Apart from their proximity they showed no other sign of connexion. Among the finely shaded categories of old age, both could be placed within the range of the young elderly: their faces were marked by the events of years, but their movements were still energetic and decisive.

The air crackled with the announcement of a half-hour delay in boarding. One of them, wearing a trouser suit, rose irritably when the speaker had finished and walked away, leaving her silk raincoat in her place. As she stood up, her passport and boarding card fell to the ground and lay unheeded under her seat.

Her neighbour watched her placidly, without stirring. Half an hour here or there made no difference to her. She made a quick social assessment of the impatient one: a French-woman by her appearance. The plane, when it eventually took off, was bound for Paris, and this woman with her elegant suit and thick, crinkly dark hair, badger-striped at the temples, was unmistakably European. The seated woman's eye caught sight of the passport, its pages fanned out, the boarding pass slotted within. She leaned down to retrieve them, and read the name on the boarding pass: *de Cazalle, S.*

She felt a blow in her chest as if someone had punched her, not hard, just enough to stop her breath and leave her gasping. She concentrated on steadying her breathing, telling herself that she had had a check-up only two weeks ago and her doctor had given her a clean bill of health. Apart from her blood pressure, she was fine, fine. She kept her eyes closed for a minute, counting the seconds, until the world settled down. When she opened them again, she saw that her neighbour was at the far end of the lounge, idly choosing a magazine from a rack. Rapidly and furtively she rifled through the passport, seeking the personal details. *Sabine de Cazalle.*

She would never have guessed. Nothing in the woman's appearance would have recalled the past, as her name had just done so violently. Why should it? It was now more than fifty years since they had seen one another. The cells of their bodies had grown and renewed and died; they had lost vitality and elasticity; they had thickened and hardened and changed. They were no longer the people who had last seen one another as children in 1946.

She studied the approaching figure of Sabine. She might be wrong, her memories and emotion roused at a false alarm. There must be more than one Sabine de Cazalle in the world and this one could be a Sabine married to a Cazalle. That was much more likely. She felt a loosening in her chest, as if her not being *the* Sabine de Cazalle somehow changed things.

The woman sat down beside her and she held out the passport and boarding card.

'You dropped these,' she said.

Sabine de Cazalle took them with a quick word of thanks. Her English was heavily accented, but automatic, her reply formal. She was clearly not someone who fell into conversation with fellow travellers. As she began to study her magazine, her attention firmly focused, her companion said, 'I'm sorry, I have to ask you this. I saw your name and I wondered if you were Sabine de Cazalle of Bonnemort.'

The look of astonishment was confirmation enough. 'Yes, I am, or at least I was.'

'My name is Rachel Oppenheim. It won't mean anything to you, but if I say I was known as Suzie as a girl, you will know who I am.'

Sabine de Cazalle's expression was distant, her magazine remained half-open. 'No,' she said, 'I don't think the name means anything to me.'

Rachel Oppenheim was not going to be put off by European reserve. 'I lived with you during the war at Bonnemort. I was called Suzie Ollivier then.'

'You lived with us?' Sabine was genuinely puzzled. 'I think there must be some mistake. I don't recall...'

Rachel turned towards her, speaking feverishly. 'I'm Jewish, of course, and I was taken in by your stepmother, Madame Ariane. I lived with you there for two years and then another two years in Paris.'

Sabine now understood that she could not brush away this encounter. She looked at the well-preserved American face under its smooth cap of white hair knotted in a chignon. She saw a stranger gazing at her with an almost hysterical intensity, someone she had never met before in her life.

'My stepmother was made a Companion of the Resistance for what she did during the war. I know we sheltered a number of people at Bonnemort during those years, but I wasn't involved. I was only a child. I had the impression that the fugitives stayed for a matter of days, not more than a week or so.'

'Your stepmother should be named a Righteous Gentile. She saved my life,' Rachel said passionately. 'Both my parents died in the Shoah. My grandparents, great-uncles and great-aunts, cousins, every member of my family in Europe, except me, was murdered by the Nazis.' She opened her large Hermès bag, fumbled for a handkerchief and blew her nose. 'I'm sorry. I never talk about these things normally. I never think of the past; it's necessary to forget. It was the sight of your name that brought it all back to me.'

Sabine de Cazalle was gathering up her raincoat and bag. 'We're being called,' she said, glad to escape from this outburst of inexplicable emotion.

Rachel Oppenheim said, 'May I ask if we can make an exchange of seats and sit together for the journey. I have so much I want to ask you.' She was shocked by Sabine's refusal to recognise her. Not to acknowledge her in the present was understandable; she herself would not have known Sabine. But to deny the past was another matter.

Sabine hid her reluctance and said with a show of interest, 'Yes, why not. You can tell me what you recall about Bonnemort in the old days. I have to say, I have an awful memory.'

When they were seated in the narrow, uncomfortable cabin of the Concorde, a glass of champagne in front of each of them, Sabine said, 'I do now dimly remember that for a while I used to share my lessons with another girl. Suzie, it must have been Suzie. So that was you. I had a very erratic education. I went to a convent before the war, to the village school at Bonnemort, and then a *lycée* in Paris. There was a short time when I was taught by my stepmother and my aunts.'

'I remember your aunts very well, Madame de Cazalle and Madame Veyrines, one fat, one thin. And Micheline and Florence. I learned to cook from Micheline.'

'You *did* know Bonnemort.'

'Did you think I was making it up?'

'No, no, I was simply marvelling at your powers of recall. My own memories of my childhood are very hazy. For me the war was so uneventful that I hardly knew it was happening. I can't remember a single dramatic incident connected with it. Well, in the depths of the French countryside I suppose it's not surprising.'

'I remember everything.'

'I suppose for you the whole thing was so traumatic.'

'Yes and no. I lived in fear the whole time, but the real trauma came afterwards, when I understood what had happened to my parents. But even in the depths of the French countryside, the house was occupied by the SS for a time. You don't remember that? You don't remember the German major?'

She stopped speaking and took a large mouthful of champagne. She had never before mentioned the major to anyone, not even during her long analysis. The memory of the death of Lou Moussou had lived with her for years, half-suppressed, reviving in her nightmares, making her sweat and cry out until she woke. She had practised forgetting with the rigour of a religious fanatic and for months at a time the past had been submerged by the present and the real. Then without warning it would rise through the waters, to surface in the cry of her own child waking her in the night, or in a dream of drowning in a fountain of blood. Her approach elicited no response.

'No, not at all,' Sabine said. 'Were we really occupied? I don't remember Ariane speaking of it either. Of course, my experience was the opposite of yours. All through the war I thought my father was dead, then he turned up when it was over, alive again. I never had a good relationship with my father. Correction, I never really had any relationship with my father, so his absence didn't really affect me much. My stepmother on the other hand was very important to me.'

'You hated her.'

'I did not.' The denial was immediate, indignant. For the first time Sabine de Cazalle showed emotion.

They both awkwardly sipped their champagne to dissipate the sharpness of the contradiction. Had Sabine really forgotten, Rachel asked herself. Had she been successful in erasing the memory, inscribing over the palimpsest the story of an innocent war in a remote house in the depths of the countryside? Afterwards, when she and Sabine were still together, before she had left for America, they had never spoken of what had happened, but each was aware, of the other and of their complicity. When the memory became overwhelming, Rachel had cried, and everyone thought she wept for the loss of her parents. Sometimes, when Madame Ariane comforted her, she thought that she knew and understood.

'What happened to you after you left us?' Sabine asked.

'I came to America to be adopted by some New York cousins. I went to college in America, Vassar. I married and I've lived in New York all my life since. My husband died two years ago. I have two sons and two daughters, all married, and twelve grandchildren. So I became American. Yet...' She broke into French. 'French is my language. I spoke French to all my children. My youngest daughter is married to a Frenchman. I'm on my way to visit them now. In some way, France is my refuge and ideal country. I never forget that I was saved in France, by the French. We were German by origin, you see. I never was really French myself, I just feel I should have been.' She paused, thinking over the recital of her life with some satisfaction. The children and the grandchildren, their existence vindicated something. 'And you?' she asked.

Sabine put down her empty glass carefully. 'I wish I could encapsulate my life so well. I've been married twice and divorced twice, once to—and from—an American, which is why I speak English. But that was a long time ago. I'm a photographer, still working to keep myself and to keep myself busy. No children. I adopted a Vietnamese child in the sixties and she now owns Bonnemort.'

'And you really don't remember those years, forty-two to forty-six, when I lived with you?'

'What was there to remember? Life was so unexciting.'

The steward was laying cloths in front of them, arranging cutlery, handing out menus. Rachel fussed with the place setting. Her fingers were encircled with several diamond eternity rings, set with extravagantly large stones.

'I spent a long time in analysis,' Rachel said. 'When I was about forty, I suddenly felt I had a lot to straighten out in my head, a lot of guilt and grief. I remembered everything then. My analyst told me to write it all down and I did. I wrote it all by hand in an exercise book. Those were the days before personal computers. Then I locked it up in a bank safe. One day my sons will open it up and learn about the past. The odd thing is that once I'd done it, the nightmares went away and I now only remember what I wrote down, in the words that I used in that exercise book.'

Her analyst had said, 'You will have to acknowledge what happened before it will go away.' But she had not told him; she had written it down and it had been fixed in the word. She began to feel desperate at Sabine's refusal to recognise the past. Remembering had caused her much suffering, but it was better than pretending. She paused. 'Henri,' she said. 'You must remember Henri.'

'I remember the name, but I can't picture him. He was Micheline's husband who was shot by the Germans, I know that. I just don't remember him as a person.'

Rachel sighed and picked up her glass of white wine. 'What became of you all? Micheline, Florence?'

'Micheline lived at Bonnemort until her death. One of her sons, Georges, died in deportation, but the other, Roger, came back from the war and took over the land. It's his son who farms it now. Florence married. My stepmother kept in touch with her to the end of her life. The aunts died soon after the war.'

'And your parents?'

'My father went into politics, for which he was not well suited. He was a minister several times in the fifties, when governments came and went all the time. As I said, I never got on with him very well and relations between us broke down completely when I married my first husband, the American. I was very left-wing in those days and my father, who was a Gaullist and very anti-American, used to regard my activities as having no purpose but to embarrass him. My stepmother was always angelic and supported me against him.'

'Strange,' said Rachel meditatively, more to herself than to Sabine. Was she lying, refusing to admit a memory which hammered at the doors of her mind? Or could you forget a killing? 'You don't remember the communist schoolmaster who used to beat you?' she asked.

'No, did he really? I do remember I was bullied at my convent when I was very little. I must have been so feeble. A terrible child called Antoinette used to play doctors and stick pins in me, but my stepmother rescued me from that hell when she married my father.'

'Well, he did beat you. Once I wanted to kill him for what he did to you. Do you remember how he broke your arm?'

'How sweet of you. I know my arm was broken when I was a child. Was it then?'

'Yes. I made an elaborate plan to kill him, inside that cave, the winepress.'

'And did you succeed?' Sabine was laughing.

'No, I didn't. I relented and didn't carry it out. I had every intention of doing it and, at the last moment, my will failed and I reprieved him.'

'Would it have worked if you had done it?'

'Oh yes, it would have worked. I knew that already. But he was punished in a way. I lured him there to see you. He had the disappointment and humiliation of finding no one there. I watched him from my hiding place.'

'It sounds like a big commutation: community service rather than the death penalty.'

'Yes, it was. But community service was probably more appropriate. I had already rejected the death penalty in principle.'

When she wrote her account of the war years, in her attempt to exorcise the past, she had ended with the sound of Vernhes' footsteps on the rocky floor of the winepress. She remembered crouching in the loft with the hook of the pulley pulled against her chest, poised to act and to kill. She had listened to him moving in the darkness, calling Sabine's name; then she heard him opening the door, leaving. Each moment she had told herself that she could do it now, release the pendulum to strike him down, while all the time she knew she would not.

Sabine put down her coffee cup. 'I'm hopeless,' she said. 'We haven't found a single memory in common. I'm beginning to feel that I'm an impostor who wasn't living at Bonnemort and you were the genuine resident. There must be something we can both remember.'

Rachel was recalling the pages of the exercise book. She could visualise her own large European handwriting, the French in which she had written. There must be something that she could use to make Sabine acknowledge what they had done.

'Lou Moussou,' she said abruptly. 'Surely you remember Lou Moussou.'

'Of course I remember Lou Moussou. There was always a Lou Moussou at Bonnemort. He lived in a sty out of sight, beyond the farmyard.'

'Because he was hidden from the authorities.'

'I used to go and sit with him and talk to him.'

'He was the first person you took me to meet when I arrived at Bonnemort.'

'He was one of those pink pigs, who looked like a huge naked baby...'

'And he had such an intelligent face...'

'And every day we used to take his bucket of pigswill down to him, carrying it between us...'

'And the pig-killers came...'

'He was stunned with a blow to his head. We used the pulley in the winepress...'

'His throat was cut with a knife...'

'Yes, I remember that.'